I parked in the underg the elevators.

I have to admit, my mind was
Dagny, food, and my bed, and not on my surroundings. I was tired, too, and wasn't as alert as I should have been. That's probably why I didn't notice the two big guys in suits coming up behind me until it was too late.

They shoved a shock baton into my neck before I could pull my gun or even turn around. Every muscle in my body locked up and I fell to the pavement. They stopped zapping me long enough for one of them to give me a good, hard kick in the guts. Even with my body armor resisting the blunt force trauma, it hurt like hell and knocked the wind out of me. The guy kicked me again, flipping me onto my back, and his partner shocked me with the baton one more time.

Lying on the pavement, twitching, gasping for air, I finally got a quick look at my two assailants. One was built like a freight truck. He grabbed me by the collar and hoisted me to my feet. He clamped a huge titanium hand around my throat while his partner restrained my arms behind my back. They patted me down, quickly and efficiently, and stripped me of all my weapons and possessions. They then roughly pulled a black bag over my head and forced me into a car.

The whole thing only took a minute. They injected something into my neck and, as I started to lose consciousness, I hoped to God that Dagny and Lily were alright.

ANNE BISHOP

"The Queen of Fantasy...Bishop's literary skills continue to astound and enchant."

—Heroes and Heartbreakers

TROUBLE WALKED IN

MIKE KUPARI

TROUBLE WALKED IN

Copyright © 2022 by Mike Kupari

A Baen Books Original

Baen Publishing Enterprises
P.O. Box 1403
Riverdale, NY 10471
www.baen.com

ISBN: 978-1-9821-9281-5

Cover art by Dominic Harman

First printing, August 2022
First mass market printing, July 2023

Distributed by Simon & Schuster
1230 Avenue of the Americas
New York, NY 10020

Library of Congress Control Number: 2022018477

Printed in the United States of America

10 9 8 7 6 5 4 3 2

"I keep two magnums in my desk.
One's a gun, and I keep it loaded.
The other's a bottle, and it keeps me loaded."
—Tracer Bullet

CHAPTER 1

My office was lit with a red-orange glow from the setting sun as I gave my report to my client, a man named Dwight Cullender. He was a lawyer, a partner in an uptown firm called Frankfurt, Cullender, and Rowe. He seemed like a decent enough guy, his profession notwithstanding, and he hired me for a simple job: he thought his wife was cheating on him and wanted me to find out one way or another. It's unglamorous but this is the meat and potatoes of detective work. The job is rarely like it's portrayed in the media, where the brilliant investigator helps baffled law enforcement solve a murder or something. Most of the time it's telling some poor bastard that the woman he loves is screwing around with other men, or that his business partner is cheating him, or even telling bereaved parents that their missing kid is dead. Sometimes you're a bodyguard, sometimes you're a bounty hunter, but you rarely get to be the hero. You do this job long enough and you start to grow numb to it. You have to, otherwise it'll drive you crazy.

"Are you sure?" he asked, his eyes almost pleading with me. "Could this somehow be a misunderstanding?"

I sighed. I hate this part. "I'm sure, Mr. Cullender. Look for yourself." I slid an envelope across the table to him. It was full of high-resolution printouts of the pictures I had taken. "I can give you electronic copies of these if you want," I said. His hands trembled a little as he looked through the photos, and I could tell he was fighting to not tear up. It had to be tough for him. He was an average-looking guy, middle-aged, balding, with the pasty complexion of someone who spent all of his time indoors. As near as I could tell he was a faithful husband, the workaholic type who maybe didn't pay enough attention to what was going on at home. His wife was another matter—she was a fitness nut with the figure to match. While he was putting in long hours at work to pay for her lavish lifestyle, she was having trysts with both her yoga instructor and her personal trainer. I had pictures of her with both of them, and they left little doubt as to what was going on.

"I can't believe this," Cullender said. He set the pictures down and held his head in his hands. "We haven't had sex in months. She said it was a hormonal thing, that it was her, not me, that she was talking to her doctor about it. It was all lies."

"I took these pictures over the course of a week. I'm afraid your wife gets around."

"Oh, God," Cullender said.

I could see the shock and humiliation on his face. Like I said, I hate this part of the job. "Let me get you a drink," I suggested. One of the nice things about being your own boss is that you can drink on the job. Cullender looked like he needed a drink and after the day I'd had, I needed one, too. I pushed away from my desk, stood up, and walked across my office. I have a liquor cabinet in one corner with a supply of booze for every occasion. My client was having what was probably the worst day of his life and he'd paid me handsomely for the trouble. This seemed like as good a time as any to break out the good stuff. I poured two glasses of Darwin Ducote Single Barrel, on the rocks with ice from the cooler, and brought them back to my desk. "Here you go," I said, setting a glass in front of him.

"What is this?" he asked, looking at the glass.

"Bourbon, aged ten years in a real wooden barrel."

"Sounds good to me," he said. He picked up the glass and took a long drink. "Oh. Wow."

"Pace yourself, Mr. Cullender," I said, sitting back down. "That's one hundred proof."

"One hundred proof? Damn." He took another sip, a smaller one this time. "It's a good thing I'm not driving."

"I'll call you an auto-taxi if you need it."

"I just can't believe it," he said, looking at the pictures on the desk in front of him. "I do everything for her. I work my ass off so she can have everything she wants. I . . ." He fell silent, then looked back up at me. "I suppose you don't really care about my marriage problems."

"You see this stuff a lot in my line of work," I said.

"Of course. You're a professional. What now?"

"There's only the matter of the remaining bill. Like I said, I can send you electronic copies of these pictures if you want. I'll also be sending you a notarized, sworn statement of my findings for your records. As per our contract, I'll make myself available for a court deposition if you need it, but in my experience the signed statement is usually enough."

Cullender finished off his bourbon and put the photographs back into the envelope. "Why do you bother with printouts in the first place?"

"To protect my clients' privacy. None of my files or records are stored on a computer that's connected to the planetary network, so they can't be hacked or accessed remotely. If anyone wants to steal my files, they'll have to come in here and physically take the drives, and even then, it's all encrypted. I take protection of your personal information very seriously, Mr. Cullender."

"I see. It's appreciated." He stood up, envelope in hand. "Thank you for all of your help."

I stood up, too. "It's a tough break. I'm sorry it worked out this way."

"I suppose I'm not that surprised. I suspected, but I didn't want to believe it, you know?"

"You going to be alright? You're not thinking about, you know, shooting your wife and jumping out a window, are you?"

"What? No, nothing like that! I'm going to show her these and tell her to get out of my house. I'll have her served with a divorce notice by the end of the week. I'm glad I listened to my mother and signed a prenuptial agreement!"

"Well, then." I offered my hand to my client, who shook it firmly. "See Lily out front to get your bill taken care of and to get a portable drive with the photos if you want. I hope things get better for you."

Dwight Cullender turned to leave, but paused by the door. "Are you married, Mr. Novak?"

"Me? Not anymore, not for a long time."

"Huh. I suppose, seeing what you see, that you might be hesitant. Listen, if you ever need a lawyer, call me first. My firm specializes in criminal defense and civil litigation. If I can't help you myself I can direct you to someone who can."

"I appreciate that, Mr. Cullender, but I know the kind of work your firm does and I'm afraid you might be a little bit outside of my budget." Frankfurt, Cullender, and Rowe was one of the top law firms on Nova Columbia. They didn't even have to advertise because their potential clients already knew who they were.

He shook his head. "You saved me a lot of pain and humiliation, and you did it for a very reasonable price. If you find yourself in trouble, please, give me a call and don't worry about the price. I'll work with you."

"That's mighty decent of you. I hope I never have to take you up on that, but in this line of work you can never be too sure. If you ever find yourself in need of my services again, or know anyone who might, don't hesitate to give me a call."

"I will. You do good work, Mr. Novak." We shook hands again and he left without another word, closing my office door behind him.

Alone again, I turned around to look out the window. My office is on the sixtieth floor of a commercial tower in East Downtown. I had a pretty good view from where I stood. Delta City sprawled out before me, a congested metropolis of thirty million people. Built in and around the forty-mile-wide crater left behind by an ancient meteorite impact, the Big D is the second-biggest city on Nova Columbia. The Economic Engine of the Northern Hemisphere, they call it. The hundred-foot video screen on the building across from mine, which at that moment was showing me an advertisement for aesthetic body-sculpting surgery, attested to that.

The sun had sunk below the artificial horizon created by the city's towering skyline. As darkness fell, the man-made lights of the city increased their output, enveloping much of the Crater in their amber-white glow. You can never see the stars in the city, what with all the light pollution, but it never really gets dark so long as you're on a major street.

Most locals call it *the sun*, by the way. Our system primary, 18 Scorpii, I mean. Some of us still call it *Scorpii* from time to time, but that's gotten less common with all the off-world immigration coming in these days. I did my share of interstellar travel during the war and I learned that most people, regardless of which planet they live on, refer to their star as *the sun*. I guess it's just easier that way.

If you're not familiar with Nova Columbia, it's one of four planets orbiting 18 Scorpii and is the closest one to the star. It's a cool, rocky world, with gravity close enough to Earth's to make no difference, and an atmosphere you can breathe without assistance. The days are longer than on Earth, but not so long that you can't adjust naturally. It's not like Harvest, with its long, thirty-four-hour day, or Styx, with its ridiculously short fourteen-hour rotational period. Most people don't need their circadian rhythms chemically altered to live here comfortably.

The official name of our colony is the Commonwealth of Nova Columbia. We're not the richest colony, or the oldest, and we're kind of out on the edge of inhabited space. We're known primarily for still using the old Imperial measurement system for nonscientific purposes and for having the highest-per-capita manpower contribution during the Terran-Ceph War. Not too bad for a planet with only ninety million people.

Before you book your visit, though, remember that we're a pretty young colony. Planetary engineering is still a work in progress, and a lot of the terrain can be charitably described as *bleak*. There's a reason most of us live in one of a handful of huge cities, and it's not because we love the congestion. The continental interior beyond the terraformed zones is an arid, lifeless wasteland, most of it only accessible by air.

I looked over my shoulder as my office door slid open again. It was Lily, my assistant. Her friends call her Lilith but that always seemed too formal to me. Like usual she was dressed in black: short skirt, tall boots, patterned hosiery, and some kind of corset over her blouse. Her hair was as black as her clothes but had purple streaks in it. She also wore a transparent display eyepiece over her right eye. I didn't get the whole techno-goth-punk style, but she was young, and we didn't have much of a dress code at the office.

She had her jacket on. "Headed home?" I asked her.

"Yeah. Mr. Cullender settled his bill so that's all taken care of. That's too bad, what happened to him."

8 *Mike Kupari*

"It really is," I agreed, sipping my drink again. Lily is a sweet girl despite her grim fashion sense. She's pretty, too, real easy on the eyes. Were I a younger man I'd probably chase after her, but as is I'm old enough to be her father. Besides, she's my employee. Never trust a man who goes sniffing around the women who work for him; at best it's unprofessional and at worst he's a creep. "Moral of the story is, be careful who you tie the knot with."

"What about you?" she asked. "Putting in another late night?"

"Not tonight. I'll be on my way home shortly."

She looked at the glass in my hand. "I don't think you should drive, Boss, and you still haven't fixed the auto-navigation on your car."

I hadn't had nearly enough booze to feel buzzed, much less drunk, but I knew there was no point in arguing with her. She was a good kid like that, always worrying about me. "Tell you what, I'll take the train. I can take it back in the morning. Would you mind getting me a two-day pass?"

Lily smiled. "Will do. Just give me a minute." She stepped out of my office, sliding the door shut behind her as if she was afraid I was going to try and sneak past her when she wasn't looking. I chuckled. I pay Lily as well as I can for what she does, and that goes above and beyond just being an office assistant. She keeps records, she does the billing, she looks after me, and she remembers things like how I need to get the auto-nav in my car fixed.

On top of that she's the best net-diver I know. She'd been some kind of child prodigy, writing code when other girls were having tea parties with dolls. She graduated with a degree in computer science as a teenager. She'd probably be making big money with some tech company if not for a couple of felony convictions for illegal hacking. The way she told it she got careless, a dumb kid who got in over her head. Her lawyer got her off on probation on account of her technically being a minor at the time. Like I said, I pay her as well as I can, but sometimes I feel like she's wasting her potential working for me. She seems to like it, though, and running the agency would be a hell of a lot harder without her.

She came back in a couple of minutes later. "You're all set. I got you a fifty-two-hour city-wide transit pass and sent it to your handheld."

"Thanks, kid. I couldn't run this place without you."

"I hope you remember that when it's time for my annual bonus," she said, smiling at me. "I'm headed out. Walk me down to the monorail station?"

"Sure," I said, grabbing my coat. "You take the train home every day. Since when do you need a chaperone?"

"I don't," Lily said, "but this way you won't be tempted to wait until I leave and drive home."

"You don't need a chaperone, but apparently *I* do." I chuckled and shook my head. "Fine. Let's go." I grabbed my hat off the coatrack and followed her out of the office.

The corridors of the building were usually quiet in the evenings and that night was no exception. We usually kept the office open until 20:00, which was a couple hours later than most of the corporate outfits I shared the floor with did. We didn't see another soul as we made our way to the elevator. The only other things moving were the cleaning robots.

The monorail station was on the tenth floor of the building. That, too, was deserted, but the whole thing was automated so it didn't matter. The trains kept their schedule, twenty-six hours a day, four hundred and one days a year. There were urban legends about people dying on the monorail, right in their seats, leaving their dead bodies to ride around on the train for days before anyone noticed they weren't just sleeping.

My handheld automatically transmitted my train pass to the gate as I approached. It let me through the turnstile and the security robot on the other side kept patrolling without giving me a second look. If you jumped the turnstile, the robots would follow you around, loudly telling you that you were trespassing while sending video of you to the Delta City Transit Authority. I don't know how often they bothered to follow up, but Lily told me that it was usually an effective deterrent against gate-jumpers.

I said my goodbyes to Lily. We were headed in different directions and wouldn't be taking the same train. Hers arrived at the station a few minutes before mine was scheduled to. No one got off the monorail as it was stopped at the station, even though there were plenty of passengers on board. I saw Lily off and then was alone in the station. Well, not entirely alone; the security robot told me to have a nice night in its tinny, synthesized voice as it rolled by.

The ride home was quiet, which I appreciated. When I was a kid, groups of punks would ride the trains all night, being obnoxious, harassing passengers, and committing petty crimes. The city had worked hard to clean up the transit system in the past decade and it showed. The monorail cars were cleaner than they used to be and the passengers on board all seemed to mind their own business. It's a rare treat to see taxpayer money actually being put to good use, especially in this town.

I had a good view of the city on the ride home. The monorail track runs about a hundred and twenty feet above street level for most of the city, enough to give you a sensation that you're flying down a canyon as the train snakes between skyscrapers. Every so often the track goes through a building, sometimes to stop at a station, sometimes just passing through. It's impressive if you haven't seen it a thousand times already, but I suppose anything can get tedious if you do it often enough. Hell, I fought on two different planets during the war and the whole time I just wanted to go home.

It took me more than an hour to get home on the monorail, between regular stops and having to change trains once. I lived in Residential Tower 77 on the West Side, and there was a monorail station right in the building, one that took up a good chunk of the twelfth floor. Seventy-seven was one of the newer buildings, two hundred stories tall and home to tens of thousands. Rent was a little high but it was nicer than most places I've lived. On-site security (real security, not just robots) patrolled the building and kept the gangs, the pushers, and the pimps from setting up shop. I was doing alright for myself, all things considered.

My place was on the 109th floor and, unlike a lot of my neighbors, I had exterior windows. The lights turned on automatically as the door slid shut behind me. "Welcome home, Easy," said Penny, my virtual domestic assistant, using her sweet, synthesized soprano voice. "Would you like me to prepare a meal for you?"

"Sure, darlin'," I said, hanging my coat and hat by the door. "Heat me up some corned beef hash and eggs." I slid my shoes off and left them by the door.

"It should be ready in ten minutes," Penny said. Her speakers beeped and the appliances in the kitchen got to work on heating my dinner. She could only prepare prepackaged meals, but it was still nice to not have to cook after a long day. The next thing to come off was my gun. It was tucked away in a shoulder holster under my right arm, and I was so used to it that I wore it all day. You get what you pay for in a holster—buy cheap junk and it'll be uncomfortable, unsecure, conspicuous, or all of the above. Buy a quality holster and you'll be able to carry even a large-frame handgun, comfortably concealed, all day.

I had to remove the holster to take my body armor off, though, so that's what I did, hanging it over the back of my recliner armchair. Next I undid the fasteners on my armor vest and took it off, laying it out so that the inside would air out. Made of flexible ballistic material, the vest won't stop armor-piercing or explosive rounds, but it does protect against common street weapons like pistols, carbines, shotguns, and knives. I was trying to get into the habit of wearing it every day—body armor doesn't do you any good if you leave it at home.

"Penny, play the Relaxation Mix," I said. Her speakers beeped again and my apartment was filled with light instrumental jazz. I removed my tie and unbuttoned my shirt collar before sitting down on the couch. I kicked my feet up while dinner was being prepared.

The music volume lowered for a moment and a tone sounded, telling me I'd just received a message on my handheld. "Penny," I said, looking up, "put that message up on the big screen." I didn't answer work calls after hours unless it was from an active client or an emergency, but people could leave me messages if they wanted. My call screening usually did a good job of filtering out the junk.

"The message is audio only," Penny said.

"Play it."

The system beeped and the message began. "This message is for Ezekiel Novak. You were recommended to me by a friend." It was a woman's voice but it sounded a little off. Probably scrambled to avoid voice-matching. "You have a reputation for discretion," she continued. "That's important to me. I know this is short notice but I plan on coming by your office tomorrow morning. I hope you can help me. Someone I care about has gone missing. She . . . it's complicated. I will explain everything in person tomorrow."

That was all there was to it. I checked my handheld and, sure enough, the message had been sent from a randomized number. There was no way for me to know who had sent it. *Very interesting.* I rubbed my chin.

"Easy," Penny said, interrupting my thought, "your food is ready."

Ah, well, I thought. *No sense trying to figure it out tonight.* It was either a crank call or I'd find out the next day. Sometimes people just like to be dramatic, and you'd be amazed at just how eccentric some of my clients are. Based on previous experience, there was a very good chance the whole thing would end up being a lot less interesting than it sounded.

As it would turn out, I was dead wrong about that.

CHAPTER 2

I got into the office a little later than I'd planned the next morning. The monorail system is a lot busier in the mornings and sometimes the trains run behind. It was a quarter past nine when I walked in the door.

Lily was already at her desk, scrolling through the Net on three big computer screens. "Good morning, Boss," she said, flatly. She was not a morning person. She held a big cup of coffee in her hand and still had her coat on. "It's cold in here."

"Yeah, it is a little chilly. Anything on the schedule for today?"

Her right eye looked away from her computer screens and at whatever was on her transparent eyepiece. "No meetings scheduled. I don't think we have any active cases right now."

"We might. Someone left me a message last night, said she'd be coming in today."

"Who was it?"

I shrugged. "She scrubbed all identifying information, even disguised her voice. I guess we'll find out."

"Assuming she shows," Lily added.

I shrugged again and headed for my office door. "I guess we'll find that out, too. Let me know when she arrives. In the meantime, check the corporate listings and see if you can't scare us up some work." I didn't have to look back to know that Lily was making a disapproving face. The girl has no love for the big, powerful corporations that operate on Nova Columbia. That's understandable, given how much pull they have and how many politicians they've bought off. "Not my first choice either, kid, but we got bills to pay."

"I know," Lily said. "Just be careful, okay?"

I looked back at her and grinned as my office door slid open. "When have I ever not been careful?" I stepped inside and closed the door behind me before she could rattle off a list of examples.

It was a slow morning. The business gets like this when you're between clients. I made a fresh pot of coffee and tried to keep myself busy. I scanned the job listings for potential customers, checked on the finances, made sure that month's bills were paid. I had enough money saved up that I could get by for a while without work, but I made it a point to not get complacent. Being your own boss requires a little discipline and a lot of work ethic. There's no one breathing down your neck, but likewise there's no one to cover for you if you slack off.

I was reading a news article when a video chat window appeared on one of my screens. It was Lily. "Find something interesting?" I asked, accepting the call.

"There's someone here to see you. She said she called you last night."

Well, I'll be damned, I thought. "Is that right? Send her in."

"Will do, Boss." Lily ended the call before I could even thank her. I turned in my chair so that I was facing the door. I had an L-shaped desk and kept the computer off to the side so that when a client sat across from me, he wasn't trying to talk to me over a wall of screens. My door hissed as it slid open on its pneumatics and there she was.

I knew she was trouble the moment she walked in. Maybe it was the way she carried herself, striding in like she owned the place. Maybe it was the way she held eye contact as she approached. Hell, maybe it was the tight violet dress she wore under her coat. She was tall, maybe five foot ten, made taller by knee-high boots with four-inch heels. There was an elaborate tattoo on her left thigh, partially visible below the hemline of her dress. It was a dragon, I thought, or some kind of serpent, coiled around her leg. Her fingernails were painted bloodred and matched her lipstick. She had long hair, black with dark blue highlights, which hung over her shoulders in loose waves. A scar ran down her right cheek, out of place on such a pretty face.

More than anything else, though, it was her eyes. They were pretty, blue like the girl next door, but they were hard. This woman, whoever she was, had seen some things. I stood as she approached my desk, leaned forward, and offered her my hand. "Ezekiel Novak."

She grasped my hand and shook it firmly. "Dagny Blake. Thank you for seeing me on such short notice." Her voice was smoky and troubled, noticeably different from the one in the voice message.

"It's my pleasure," I said. "Please, have a seat." She sat

down in one of the two chairs that face my desk and crossed her legs. I sat down as well, folding my hands together on my desk. "Now, Ms. Blake, what is it that I can do for you? You said someone is missing?"

She paused, looking down at her lap, and took a deep breath before responding. "Yes," she said, looking me in the eye again. "My sister, Cassandra Carmichael. I haven't heard from her in two months."

I made a mental note that my client and her sister had different last names. It might be relevant later but wasn't worth bringing up at the moment. "I see. I'm sorry to hear that. First thing's first, what does your sister do? Was she in some kind of trouble?"

Ms. Blake sighed and shifted in her seat. She uncrossed her legs and put both feet on the floor, keeping her knees close together, her hands folded in her lap. I could tell she was worried. "I think so. Cassie works for Ascension Planetary Holdings Group."

"Ascension? Oh, boy."

"I take it you're familiar with them?"

Just about everybody on the planet is familiar with the Ascension Planetary Holdings Group. They're the biggest corporation on the planet. Their primary focus is planetary engineering, something most people call terraforming. They were one of the original sponsors of the Nova Columbia Colony Project a hundred and fifty years ago The company's original owner, Rafael Taranis, was one of the colony's Founding Fathers. Hell, there's a statue of him in the Capitol Building.

"Tell me, what does she do at Ascension? How high up on the company ladder is she?"

"Her official title is *Resource Coordinator*. She works in logistics management. It's nothing exciting so far as I know. She's not even an executive."

"I see. Then what makes you think she might be having trouble with Ascension? Mind you, I'm not doubting anything you've told me. I'm just trying to follow your line of reasoning so I can assess the situation for myself."

Ms. Blake was quiet for a few moments. "It's . . . complicated. You mind if I smoke, Mr. Novak? It helps me concentrate."

"Not at all," I said, digging an ashtray out from a desk drawer. I tapped the office environmental controls to get the air filtration system going so the smell wouldn't linger.

She reached into her jacket and produced a black-and-gold cigarette case. Popping it open, she withdrew one long, skinny cigarette and placed it in between her lips. I held out a plasma lighter, the one that I always carry with me, and lit it for her.

"Thank you," she said, inhaling. She tilted her head back and exhaled, sending a puff of smoke upward toward the air vent. "Our stepfather *is* an executive at Ascension. He helped Cassie get a position at the company straight out of university."

"That's not uncommon. A lot of families end up working for the company for multiple generations."

"I know, and it's been fine, from what she told me, at least up until recently."

"I take it something changed."

"A few months back she had me over for dinner at her place. We split a bottle of wine and talked about the old days. That's always a touchy subject but Cassie is such a lightweight that a little wine really loosens up her tongue. We bonded like we haven't for years. We actually talked about everything that happened between us. It felt good to clear the air."

"What I'm hearing is that you and your sister weren't especially close, at least not in the past."

She looked down at her lap. "Not especially. We had a . . . falling out . . . a long time ago. We didn't speak for years after that. That didn't really change until Mom died two years ago. We were, you know, patching things up. It wasn't always easy."

"I see. I don't mean to pry into your personal business. I'm just trying to get a feel for the situation. What else did you talk about at dinner?"

"Cassie wouldn't get into it, but I got the feeling that there was something weird going on at the company. She said she'd had almost no contact with Arthur, our stepfather, in weeks. Some big project that was real hush-hush. She was concerned."

"Tell me, what is your relationship with your stepfather like? He's working for Ascension just like your sister. Did you contact him after she went missing?"

"I don't have a relationship with Arthur," she said, bitterly. "But that was the first thing I did. At first, he just ignored me, but I was persistent. About a month ago he left me a brief message. All it said was that Cassie is fine and that there's nothing to worry about."

It was clear that there was some bad blood between Dagny Blake and her stepfather, but it wasn't yet clear if it was directly relevant to the case. It was obviously a touchy subject for her so I decided not to press her on the issue for the time being. "I see. Since we're having this conversation, I presume you didn't believe him?"

"I didn't. This whole thing stinks."

"Did you try contacting the authorities?"

"I reported her missing to SecFor. All they did was contact Ascension, and the company told them that she's accounted for. They didn't want to look into it any further."

You didn't need to be a detective to tell how frustrated she was—it was in her voice and all over her face, and with good reason. Delta City alone is huge, and the Colonial Security Forces Corps has system-wide jurisdiction. Even at the best of times they can't keep up with their caseload, and a missing person whose employer says she's accounted for is pretty far down on their list of priorities. "I'm sorry to hear that," I said. "When was the last time you saw your sister?"

"It was two months ago. We met for lunch at a sidewalk café uptown. She looked like hell."

"Really? How so?"

"Wired and tired. You know, like you get when you're not sleeping enough so you make up for it with coffee or maybe stims?"

"What did you two talk about?"

"It was strange. Cassie acted like she couldn't speak freely, like she was worried somebody was watching her or listening in. I've never seen her act so paranoid. She wasn't herself."

"Who arranged this lunch date?"

"She did. Called me up that morning and asked me to meet her for lunch. She seemed, I don't know, kind of desperate, like there was something she really wanted to talk about. I figured it was something to do with Arthur or her work but neither subject came up. She barely spoke and when she did, it was just small talk about the weather, or asking me how I was doing. She looked exhausted but kept insisting that she was fine when I asked her about it."

"That *is* concerning behavior," I said. "Is this why you didn't believe your stepfather when he said that she's fine?"

"Yes. Also, she hasn't been home in two months now. She hasn't answered any calls or replied to any messages."

"That *is* unusual," I agreed. I thought about it for a moment. "Are you sure she didn't just run away, maybe off-world? That happens sometimes, people just up and leave without telling anyone. They get an idea in their head to walk away from everything and start over someplace else."

Dagny shook her head. "No, not Cassie. That's not her style. She was always careful. She had her whole life planned out from when we were just kids. I was the impulsive one, always getting her into trouble. Besides that, I went to her apartment. I don't have access to her place, and the superintendent wouldn't let me in, but he did tell me that she hadn't broken her lease or moved out. If somehow she was going to up and leave without telling anyone, she wouldn't go without settling her accounts, would she?"

"People can do surprising things when they decide to run." I held up a hand before my client got angry with me. "I'm not saying she *did* run, mind you, only that I can't rule it out yet. It's not like your credit history follows you from colony to colony. Lots of people will book a last-minute flight off-world if they're running from something, whether it be debt, personal problems, or something worse. It's half the reason the down payments for everything are so big in this town. It begs the question, though—if she just up and left, why would Ascension and your stepfather lie about it?"

"Exactly!" Dagny said. "It doesn't make any sense!"

"It doesn't, at least not from what we know right now. Is there anything else you can think of that might be relevant?"

"The last time I saw her, she gave me this." Ms. Blake reached across the desk and handed me a small plastic object.

"This is an electronic key," I said, holding it up to the light so I could see it better. It was dull gray in color and just over an inch long. On one end was a knurled knob, on the other was a series of tiny electrical contacts. "What does it go to?"

The client shook her head again. "I don't know. It definitely doesn't go to her apartment door. I tried."

I handed it back to her. "Keys like this usually aren't used for residential doors. You see them used in safe deposit boxes, secure storage containers, things like that. It contains an encryption code that only works a specific lock, or set of locks. What did she say when she gave it to you?"

"She didn't say anything at about it. We were leaving the café. She stuck this in my pocket as she was hugging me and saying goodbye. She didn't tell me what the key was for. She just said that she'd message me that night, but she never did. She hurried off before I could ask her about it."

I sat back in my chair and rubbed my chin. "What about before? Were you in regular contact with your sister?"

"I guess you could call it regular. We'd text back and forth once in a while. Every so often we'd have a video call. She likes to cook, sometimes she'd invite me over for dinner."

"So you said. Maybe giving you that key was her way of explaining everything."

"But I don't know what it goes to! Why wouldn't she have told me?"

"That's a good question. Maybe it was as you said, she thought that she was being watched."

"Oh, God. Do you think something happened to her?"

"I don't have enough information to have a theory yet," I said, trying to sound reassuring. "I'm just entertaining possibilities right now. What you've told me so far indicates that she believed that she was in some kind of trouble, if not in actual danger."

The look on my client's face told me she was more worried than she'd previously let on. I guess having it all laid out before her like that cracked the façade a little. "I'm afraid she's dead. I'm afraid that they did something to her and I'll never know what or why. Can you help me?"

I leaned forward, resting my elbows on my desk and lacing my fingers together. "Ms. Blake, I want you to know first of all that you're not crazy. Your sister is missing and I think it's obvious that something is wrong. You did the right thing by seeking help."

"But?" she asked. "I feel like there's a *but* coming."

"But," I continued, "a case that involves Ascension is a tall order. I'm just one man who runs a small business. They're a trillion-dollar multi-planetary corporation with an army of lawyers and God-knows-how-many judges and politicians in their pocket."

"Are you saying you won't take my case because you're scared of them?"

I furled my brow involuntarily. "What I'm trying to say is that a job like this might involve a lot of effort on my part, a lot of personal and professional risk, and that the chances of success might not be great. A larger investigative firm might be a better fit for this sort of job."

"I went to Kensington already," she said. Kensington Specialty Services is the biggest and best-funded independent investigations and personal protection company on Nova Columbia. They're the ones who the wealthy and connected hire to protect them and smooth over their messes. "I couldn't possibly afford their asking price. That's why I came to you."

"If you don't mind me asking, how did you come to hear about my little business?"

"You have a good reputation, Mr. Novak," she said, looking me in the eye again. "Your verified customer reviews are all positive. More importantly, an acquaintance of mine vouched for you, said you helped him out a couple years ago. He said you help normal people, not just the superrich."

That is a personal point of pride for me, as a matter of fact. I grew up in Delta City. My dad was a robotics technician and my mom was a schoolteacher. We weren't rich. Hell, rich people didn't even pass through my old block; at most they glanced down at it as they flew over in their private VTOLs. I've tried my best over the years to not forget where I come from.

"I try to help everyone who comes to me," I said, "and I'm willing to try in your case, but you need to understand . . . this kind of job is likely to be significantly more expensive than my usual fees. I want to be up front about that before we proceed. My assistant, Lily, can break down the specifics for you if you want. I run a pay-as-you-go business and I will always be straight with you about the costs as the case goes on."

"I understand. That's fair. I have been able to get the money for this, just not enough to hire Kensington. To be honest, I think they quoted me an outrageous price as a polite way of telling me they weren't interested. I expect I'll be able to manage your fees if you're willing to take the case."

"Okay then, it sounds like I'm your man. If you don't mind, I'm going to bring my assistant in here and we'll go over the contract and fees." I tapped one of my screens and Lily's face appeared in a video chat box. "We've got ourselves a client."

"Got it," Lily said. "I'll be right in." The chat box closed and, a few moments later, she entered the office with a data pad in her hands. Dagny Blake put out her cigarette.

"Ms. Blake, you met my assistant already."

"Lilith," she said, reaching down to shake Dagny's hand. "Also, forgive me if this is unprofessional but I wanted to tell you that I love your look."

Lily didn't give empty compliments. If she told you she liked your clothes it meant she really liked them. Being perfectly honest, I liked my client's *look*, too.

CHAPTER 3

The first order of business was figuring out what Cassandra Carmichael was doing before she disappeared. I couldn't yet rule out the possibility that she had been intimidated into fleeing off-world, kidnapped, or even murdered. Things like that do happen in Delta City, no matter how much the media and the Chamber of Commerce try to deny it. I was tactful in how I relayed all this to my client, of course. The poor woman was under enough stress without me giving her the idea that it was hopeless. Besides, I wasn't convinced that it was hopeless, at least not yet. I didn't have enough information to even take a guess.

It seemed to me that the best place to start was Cassandra's apartment. Dagny Blake had tried and failed to get the building super to let her in, but in my business you develop a talent for getting where you aren't necessarily supposed to be. I don't usually involve my clients in my work, but in this case, I figured that having her along might be useful, especially in going through her sister's things. She was eager to help. For a lot of people, just having something to do can help them work through a difficult situation. It gives them something to focus on so they don't wallow in their own anxiety.

Dagny lived in a huge residential building on the South Side called Starlight Tower. The 150-story apartment complex was over a hundred years old and had definitely seen better days. The South Side used to be the nice part of town, years back. These days it's the sort of place where it's best if you go armed. Hell, even SecFor patrol in pairs there, and usually heavily armed.

The parking garage below the building was a cavernous hole bored into the ground, six levels deep, with enough space for thousands of cars. Finding a place to park was easy; the garage was barely half full. A lot of the people who lived in places like Starlight Tower couldn't necessarily afford a vehicle of their own and, truth be told, you didn't really need one to get around most parts of the city.

The apartments in Starlight Tower were arranged in a box shape around a huge open space in the middle. At street level there was a big indoor plaza, with a bustling market full of cheap places to eat and discount retail merchants. Above that, for another 149 floors, there was nothing except the occasional walkway bridging the gap across the center of the structure. At the very top there was a big square of gray daylight, visible through a dirty skylight half the size of a football field. Spend too much time staring up and the view might give you vertigo.

I found a working elevator, made my way up to the forty-fourth floor, and walked around to Dagny's apartment. The door slid open immediately after I hit the ringer.

"You have any trouble finding the place?" Dagny asked, stepping out of her apartment. Her clothes weren't nearly as eye-catching as they had been the day before. Instead of a slinky little dress she wore tight black pants, what looked like combat boots with wedge heels, a blue blouse with a stand-up collar, and a black leather jacket. Her hair was tied back and if she was wearing makeup it wasn't much. She had a small sling bag hanging over her right shoulder.

"The building or your apartment?"

"Either, I guess."

"No trouble at all," I said.

"You didn't have to come all the way up here," she said as we made our way to the elevator. "It would have been enough to send me a message. I could have met you down in the parking garage."

"I guess I'm old-fashioned," I said as the elevator doors opened. I paused for a moment and let Dagny go in first. "The way I was raised, if you're picking someone up you meet them at the door."

Dagny smiled slyly. "This is not a date, Mr. Novak."

I grinned back at her. "Of course not, Ms. Blake, I would never be so unprofessional. I'm just a creature of habit." The elevator we were in didn't go directly to the garage, for security purposes. We had to get out, cross the ground-floor plaza, and use an entirely different set of elevators to take us down to the underground parking garage.

The doors opened to the first sublevel of the garage

where I had left my car. "I hate this place," Dagny said as we stepped out of the elevator. "Building security doesn't come down here very often. There are supposed to be cameras but they get destroyed as fast as they can replace them."

"You don't park down here?" On heightened alert, I scanned my surroundings as we walked to my car. I really needed to get the auto-navigation fixed.

"Oh, I don't have a car," she confessed. "I walk down the street to the monorail station when I need to get across town. It's only a couple blocks. Sometimes I take an auto-taxi."

It seemed like Dagny was struggling financially. That was none of my business, but it did make me ask myself once again how she'd come up with the money to hire me. My first instinct was to pry a little bit, see if I could get her to tell me, but I wondered if maybe it would be better if I didn't know.

Turning a corner in the massive garage, I spotted a group of young men coming toward us. There were five of them and they looked like a bunch of hoods. As a matter of fact, with their shabby clothes, luminescent tattoos, and wild hairstyles, they didn't look too different from the street rats that used to try and push us around on my old block, when I was a kid. Some things never change.

They were all wearing respirator masks, too. They're not uncommon in Delta City. Most immigrants from off-world wear them until they can be fully inoculated against Kellerman's Syndrome, and inoculation is only about ninety percent effective at the best of times. It doesn't take much exposure to the spores from the native slime molds to get sick, and despite the best efforts of the city sanitation department, the purple goop can be found all over the city. Many people take precautions, especially if they live or work near or below street level. You can wear a mask and nobody will look twice at you. As a bonus, it can help conceal your identity from facial recognition software.

They approached, wolf-whistling and cat-calling at Dagny, and my muscles tensed. Maybe they were just a bunch of all-talk punks, maybe they'd pull a gun, you could never tell. The one who seemed like the leader of the group circled around us, looking my client up and down like a piece of meat. "Daaamn, girl, you fine," he said, his voice distorted by the mask. He was tall and wiry. His skin was so pale he looked sickly, made all the more noticeable by the glowing tattoos on his arms and neck. "What are you doing with this fucking pile?" he asked, gesturing at me. "You should come party with us."

The punk and his friends had spread out a little to where they were between us and my car. I kept my cool but my heart was pounding. They were positioning themselves to jump us at close range. The posturing and shit-talking was just a distraction technique. Experience told me things were about to go sideways. One of the thugs, a heavyset fellow with a bald head and a thick neck, took a step toward me. His right hand was in the pocket of the bright red jacket he wore.

"That's close enough, friend," I said levelly, pulling my own piece out from under my jacket. The mook froze in place, his eyes wide, as he looked down the barrel of my

.44-caliber revolver. Out of the corner of my eye I saw that Dagny had pulled a gun herself and had it pointed at the mouthy punk who had been sizing her up. "I suggest you boys step aside so we can be on our way."

The thugs, hands raised, slowly backed off. "We were just fucking with you," the mouthy one said, but he kept backing up. I kept my weapon leveled at them as Dagny and I backed away. I lowered it, but kept it in my hand, as we turned and headed for my car. The punks watched us for a bit but soon wandered off.

Once we were safely in my car, behind locked doors and armored glass, I carefully re-holstered my gun. Dagny did the same, sticking the small pistol she had pulled back into her jacket pocket. "That was intense," she said, staring straight ahead. Her hands were shaking a little bit, probably from the adrenaline dump.

"This is why I wear this every day," I said, tapping the armor vest under my jacket. "You did good back there. Kept your head in what could have been a life-and-death situation."

She looked over at me and forced herself to smile. "I'm no shrinking violet. I'm not one of your uptown clients, some jealous housewife wondering if her executive husband is seeing another woman on the side." She gestured at the poorly lit parking garage beyond the window. "This is the world I live in."

"Fair enough," I said with a nod. "I'm not surprised you can handle yourself. I'm not too surprised that you're carrying that piece, either."

"Oh? Why is that, Mr. Novak?"

"Easy."

"What?"

"Please, call me Easy. *Mr. Novak* is my father. My mother was the only one who ever called me Ezekiel. Everyone else called me E-Z, hence the nickname."

"Okay then, Easy it is. You can call me Dagny, by the way. I'm no stranger to this sort of stuff, unfortunately. It comes with the territory if you live around here. Also, you didn't answer my question."

"What question?"

"I asked you why you weren't surprised that I'm carrying a gun."

"Oh, right. I could tell from the moment you walked into my office that you weren't one of my 'uptown clients,' as you put it, or some jealous housewife. The fancy clothes were a good distraction but I could tell from the way you carried yourself, and from that scar on your face, that you've lived a more interesting life than all that."

"'Interesting' is certainly one way to put it," Dagny said. "Speaking of guns, what's the deal with that cannon you're packing?"

"Oh this?" I asked, tapping the butt of the gun under my right arm. "It's a cannon, alright, a Sam Houston Mark-Four-pattern Combat Dragoon, .44LRM caliber." The design came from the Republic of Texas back on Earth. It's a seven-shot revolver with a quick-change cylinder for fast reloads. Push the lever with your thumb and the old cylinder is ejected upward. Slap a new one in and you're ready to go. It has a bright flashlight and laser sight in the housing under the barrel and, on top, a small holographic sight for quick and precise aiming. It doesn't hold a lot of rounds but it sure packs a wallop. Even the clankers take notice when you pull one of these out—a couple .44 armor-piercing, high-explosive slugs will put down even the most amped-up cyborg. "Me and this gun go way back. It was given to me when I got home from the war."

She raised an eyebrow at that. "You served?"

"I did. Third Mechanized Infantry Brigade, Commonwealth Defense Force, Combined Joint Task Force 19, Terran Confederate Expeditionary Forces. I fought on Harvest and was there for the invasion of 220 Colfax-B." I paused for a moment. "This gun belonged to my squad leader, Staff Sergeant Victor Redgrave. He, ah, bequeathed it to me years ago. I've carried it everywhere since."

"Oh. Oh, I see," Dagny said. "I'm sorry, I didn't mean to bring up anything like that."

"Ah, it's alright," I said with a smile. "It's been a long time since I've told anyone about it, is all."

"We should get out of here," she said after a moment. "Those goons might get some friends and come back."

"Sounds good to me." I started my car's quiet electric motor and pulled out of the parking space.

The drive across town was uneventful and mostly quiet. Dagny scrolled on her handheld and didn't say much for most of the drive. Her sister Cassandra's apartment was closer to my place than hers, over on the East Side. Apparently the missing sibling was doing alright for herself, which no surprise given where she worked. She had an apartment in Residential Tower 61, which was only a few miles from where I lived.

RT61 was nearly identical in layout to my building, from the subterranean parking garage to the street-level marketplace to the twelfth-floor monorail station. The main difference was that this building was much nicer than mine, the apartments were bigger, and it cost more to live there. Where RT77 was a bland monolith of tan ceramicrete with some brown accents, RT61 was painted bright red and white. The interior color scheme was similarly colorful but the building superintendent's office was in the same place on the ground floor.

"What are you going to do?" Dagny asked. "I already tried talking to them and they wouldn't let me into her apartment."

"I know, but sometimes flashing my credentials opens doors for me. If this doesn't work we'll come up with a different plan. That's what the bag is for," I said, indicating the small pack I had slung over my shoulder. "Just follow my lead when we get in there. What was her apartment number?"

"Eighty-eight-dash-oh-ninety-one. Apartment ninety-one on the eighty-eighth floor."

"Got it."

The superintendent's office was somewhere behind a heavy security door. Just like in my building, there was a small, sparsely decorated waiting room with bland music playing softly over a speaker. Set in one wall was the service counter. Behind a thick pane of armored glass, a bored-looking attendant sat in a chair and played with his handheld. He set it down when we approached but didn't stand up.

"Can I help you?" he asked, pushing a button that

activated a two-way speaker so we could hear him through the glass.

I leaned down so that my mouth was closer to the speaker embedded in the glass. "We need access to apartment eighty-eight-oh-ninety-one. I'm a detective conducting a missing person investigation."

"You SecFor? I need to see your warrant."

"No," I said, pulling out my credentials. "Private investigator. That apartment belongs to one Cassandra Carmichael, correct?"

The attendant looked at his computer screen for a moment and tapped a few keys. "I, uh, I'm not supposed to disclose that. I can't let you in, either."

"Listen, friend, this is serious. Cassandra Carmichael has gone missing. This woman here is her sister. We just need to see if we can figure out what happened to her. You can escort us if you want, we're not going to ransack the place or steal anything. Can't you help us?" I held up my credentials. Below the identification plate, partially tucked into a pocket, was $250 in crisp blue-and-silver bills.

"I . . . uh . . . can I get you to put your ID into the tray, please? I need to verify that it's legit."

"Sure thing." Doing as he asked, I closed my credential wallet and placed it in the tray. It slid through to the attendant, who picked it up and looked up at me. "I just need to check this real quick. I'll be right back." He stepped away from the counter and was out of sight.

"What did you do?" Dagny asked in a loud whisper.

"I'll explain outside."

Before she could press the issue the attendant

returned. He placed my credential wallet and a plastic key into the tray and slid them through. "Everything checks out," he said, sitting back down in his chair. "This key will get you into apartment eighty-eight-oh-ninety-one. It's only coded for the next hour so this is a onetime thing. There are security cameras monitoring the hallway."

I nodded at the young man. "You know who I am. I assure you, this is all on the up and up. Thank you for your help." I paused. "Say, has anyone else been in there recently?"

"Not that I know of," the kid said. "I'm only here a couple days a week." He looked at his computer screen, his right hand on the scroller. "Nothing's been logged. We don't keep track of when residents enter or leave their apartments—privacy laws and all that. But none of our people have entered the apartment in months. We haven't even had a maintenance robot go in. Huh. That's weird."

"What's weird?"

"The security camera covering that section of the corridor isn't working. What the hell? How come nobody logged this? The diagnostics should have caught it and sent out a service request automatically."

"You didn't notice that a camera wasn't working until just now?"

"Mister, there are a thousand cameras in this building and I've only got two eyes. If the system doesn't catch it, it might take us a while to realize there's a fault. Besides, we have armed security on the premises at all times. The cameras are just there for evidence purposes."

"Are the rent and utilities for the apartment still current? Has anything been shut off for nonpayment?"

The kid looked at his screen for a moment. "Uh . . . no. Her lease payment for the next quarter just cleared two days ago. Everything has been paid on time."

"Interesting. Thanks for your help. We won't be too long." I looked at Dagny. "Come on, let's go see what we can find out."

To my satisfaction, the key worked as the superintendent said it would. When you try to bribe your way into places there's always the chance that they'll take your money and not uphold their end of the bargain. You've got to learn to read people, to get a good feel for who will be good to his word and who will screw you over. Being too trusting means you'll end up paying the Stupid Tax and have nothing to show for it.

The apartment was dark when we walked in. The lights in the front room automatically came on and two things became obvious: First, it was clear that Cassandra hadn't been home in some time. There was a domestic cleaning robot parked at a power station in one corner, but nothing in the apartment looked like it had been recently used.

Second, the place had been searched already. Every cabinet, drawer, and closet had been opened, their contents spilled onto the floor.

"Oh my God," Dagny said.

"Looks like someone beat us to it," I said.

"But the door was still locked."

"Electronic residential door locks aren't hard to beat if you have the right tools and know-how. The disabled camera, the clean entry . . . this wasn't some street thug like those boys back in your parking garage."

She shook her head slowly. "Oh, Cassie, what did you get yourself into?"

"I know this is tough. Normally I wouldn't have a client along on an investigation like this, but you know her best. Besides, I'm pretty sure that fellow downstairs wouldn't have let me in without you here, even with the two-fifty I slipped him."

She nodded her head. "I know. I guess I'm just afraid that I'll get my hopes up only to have them dashed later. I've been telling myself all along she's probably dead. I know what the statistics say about someone who's been missing for as long as she has. Now we find this?"

"Well . . . look, Dagny, I can't promise you that your sister is okay. What I *can* promise is that I'll be straight with you during this investigation. I won't get your hopes up if I don't think there's any reason to. This?" I motioned toward the ransacked apartment before us. "This doesn't mean your sister is dead. This doesn't even mean that they have your sister. If you have somebody you can make them talk. You can get them to tell you where to find whatever it is you're looking for. This mess tells me that whoever was here was trying to find something and he was in a hurry. If they'd done a really clean job we'd never even be able to tell that they were here."

"The attendant downstairs said that her lease was paid up a couple days ago. Do you think that means anything? Who do you think did this?"

"Not necessarily. It could just be automatically debiting her account. As for who, I don't know. Maybe someone looked here before they got to your sister. Maybe they came here because they couldn't find her. For all we know, this could be the work of a third party. Right now, let's just focus on why we came here. Do you know if she had a safe installed?"

"I never saw one, but, you know, I didn't ask."

"What about a virtual domestic assistant?"

"Yeah, a pretty nice one called Bosley. It usually activates when someone comes in."

"Whoever broke in probably disabled it. What about her computer? Did she have a desktop system or a portable? Do you know her login?"

"She used a retinal scanner. Her computer was a portable, one of those ruggedized ones like the military uses. She was always careful with it."

"Well, odds are, if it was left here at all it was probably taken in the break-in, but have a look around anyway. Check for hidden safes. Look under carpets, behind mirrors, anything like that. I'm going to take a look at that cleaning robot and the VDA system. Maybe there will be some information left on them that we can use."

We split up then, with Dagny heading to her sister's bedroom as I walked over to the cleaning robot. It was a *Mrs. Tidy* model with an elongated, trapezoidal body, done up in their trademark pink-and-powder-blue color scheme. Its two tentacle-like arms, with vacuuming and dusting attachments, hung limply at its sides. The front screen, on which it projected its "face" when operational, was dark. I pulled the robot out of its charging dock so that I could see the back side. Sure enough, the back panel had been pried open. The drives were gone. I was willing to bet that the apartment VDA would be in the same condition.

"Easy! I found her safe!" Dagny said, coming back out of the bedroom. "It's been opened." She led me into the bedroom and pointed to the wall. "Right here."

"Yeah, this is it," I said, moving in to get a good look at the safe. "Damn it." It had been hidden behind an ornate mirror mounted on the wall. The mirror, an old-fashioned glass model with a frame made of what appeared to be real wood, had been taken off the wall and set on the floor. The safe was embedded in the wall, set into it a few inches so as to make getting a pry bar in there difficult. It wasn't very big, a foot wide by six inches tall, just large enough for a few valuables or documents. The door was open. Whatever had been in there was long gone.

I rapped on the door with my knuckles. "Titanium composite. This is a good safe." I examined the door. It had been drilled out in several places, allowing direct access to the internal electronics. "This is the work of a professional. They knew just how to attack the safe."

"Is it really that easy to break into a safe like this?"

"Yes and no. A residential security locker like this will keep out junkies with pry bars or even power tools. A professional thief with the knowledge and the proper tools, though? He's mainly limited by how much time he has and how much noise he can make."

"Do you think Ascension is behind this?"

I shook my head. "There's no way to know for sure. I could guess, but it would only be a guess."

"Well, that's that, I guess," Dagny said, dejectedly.

"We're not at a dead end yet," I said, trying to sound reassuring. "Can I see that key she gave you?"

Dagny handed it to me. "The safe is already open."

"It is," I said, taking out a small flashlight so I could get a better look at the safe, "but right now we're only assuming that this is what the key goes to."

"What? What else would it be for?"

"That I don't know," I said. I peeled back the manufacturer's sticker on the safe door, the one that covered and sealed the keyhole. "Safes like this use biometrics to unlock them. It looks like this one has a retinal scanner. The physical key is just a backup." The key that Cassandra gave Dagny was not the right size or shape. I stepped back and handed the key over to my client. "This key doesn't go to this safe. It won't even fit in the keyhole."

"What do we do now? We still have no idea what this goes to."

"Think back to the last time you saw your sister, when she slipped the key into your pocket. Did she say anything, anything at all, that might be a clue as to what the key is for?"

"I already told you, no. She just told me she'd message me later, but she didn't."

"You didn't receive any messages that night?"

"Not from her, no."

"From anybody."

"From anybody . . ." She trailed off as she realized what I was getting at. "You think she may have contacted me from a different number?"

"It seems reasonable if she was paranoid that she was being watched or followed. Check your old messages, see if there's anything that might be from her."

"I auto-block calls from unknown numbers, and I filter

out messages from unknown senders," Dagny said, scrolling through her handheld. "There are a lot of people I'd rather not hear from. I don't think I ever told Cassie that. Let me see."

She read old messages on her handheld for a few moments. "Anything?" I asked.

"Oh my God," she said, looking up at me. "I'm such an idiot. It was right here the whole time! It's from a hidden number."

"What does it say?"

"Not much. It just says, *Dagny this is Cassie* and has an address and a number."

"Mind if I take a look?" She handed me her handheld. "Thank you." I brought my handheld up in my other hand. Tapping the screen with my thumb, I typed in the address from the vague message into my handheld's map program. "This address is for a local branch of the First Colonial Bank and Trust."

"She wants me to go to a bank? You think the key is for a safe deposit box?"

"I'd put money on it. I'd also bet that this number, two-four-nine-five, is the box number."

"I'm sorry to have wasted your time coming here. I should have checked."

"Hey, don't sweat it," I said. "You didn't know. Come on, let's take one last look around this place then head out."

About an hour later, my client and I were at the First Colonial Bank. A disinterested bank manager scanned the key to verify that it was to one of his branch's safe deposit boxes, then let us into the secure vault that contained them. He stood by the entrance and stayed quiet as we used the key in box 2495.

"It worked!" Dagny said in an excited whisper.

"Sure did," I said, pulling the sliding drawer out of the box. There was nothing in the safe deposit box but a portable data stick, one of the plastic ones a couple inches long.

"That's it?" she asked.

"Seems that way," I said, pocketing the drive. "Let's head out. When we get back to the office, I'll give it to Lily to look at."

"Can't you just use your handheld?"

I lowered my voice. "Not in front of prying eyes," I said, nodding toward the bank manager. "Besides, there's no telling what's on this. Maybe it's got malware or a tracking program on it. Safest thing is to let Lily run it on our off-line computer."

"Wow. I never would have even thought of that."

I shrugged. "I've been doing this a few years. Come on, we should get out of here."

"Yeah," Dagny said, looking around the bank vault one last time. "Let's go."

CHAPTER 4

Lily was waiting for us back at the office. I called ahead, telling her what we found, and she was excited to see what we would bring her. She loved this kind of stuff.

"Here's what we found," I said, handing her the drive. "Like I said, I thought it would be best if you did your thing with it instead of just plugging it into my handheld."

Lily's workstation was made up of two computer consoles, two large, translucent screens, one smaller screen, and several different peripheral attachments. The second console was what she called her quarantine machine, the one not connected to the planetary network. It's where we kept our case files. "I'm glad to see my wisdom is finally rubbing off on you, Boss," she said, flashing me a smile as she plugged the drive into an access port on the portable computer. "Now, let's see what's on this bad boy." She tapped the touchpad a few times, staring at the screen as if it were a particularly interesting book.

"Well?" I asked.

"It's encrypted," she said. "It says it needs facial recognition and voice-match data from an authorized user." She looked up at me. "Who's the authorized user? Do you know?"

I looked at my client. "It's got to be you. She gave you the key."

"I guess. What do I do?"

Lily flipped the smaller screen around so that it was facing Dagny. There was a window open on the screen, displaying a feed from its internal camera. "Center your face on the screen. Then say something."

Dagny did as she was told, leaning forward so the camera could see her face clearly. "What do I say?" Before Lily could answer, a message popped up saying that the drive was granting access to an authorized user.

"Perfect!" Lily said, turning the screen back around. "Now, just give me a moment." She was quiet for a bit. "Okay, so far so good. Initial malware scan is negative. I'll have to do a deep analysis of every file before I'm willing to say it's all clean, but I think it's safe to start opening files."

"Where do we start?"

Lily squinted at the screen for a second. "There's a video file named 'For Dagny.'"

Dagny perked up at that. "What? She left me a note?"

"Seems that way," Lily said with a half shrug. "Here." She stood up, came around the desk, and turned the screen around again so that we could all see it. "You ready?" Dagny nodded. Lily played the video.

A woman's face appeared on the screen. She bore a striking resemblance to Dagny but was maybe a couple years younger. Her dark brown hair was short, not even shoulder length. She looked exhausted, too, like she hadn't slept in days. "My name is Cassandra Carmichael," she said. "This message is for my sister, Dagny."

Dagny's face was a mask. She didn't say anything.

The video continued. "I'm leaving this message on an encrypted drive in my safe deposit box. I've moved everything I have onto this drive and have a fail-safe in place to wipe everything else."

Cassandra paused for a moment. "I know we haven't always gotten along. I regret that. I regret wasting so many years of my life not speaking to my sister. It's not what Mom or Dad would have wanted. This past year, when we've gotten to know each other again? It's been wonderful. I didn't even realize how much I missed you."

I glanced over at Dagny. Her expression had softened, but only a little. She was the type who was used to controlling her emotions.

"I wish I would have told you about this sooner," the video continued. "I could have used your help, but I was afraid I'd drag you into something that wasn't your mess to clean up. You've had enough trouble without me bringing you more."

The woman in the video paused again, briefly looking down. She looked like she was having trouble deciding what to say. It seemed to me she'd recorded this in one take and didn't have a script she was going off of. "But . . . I think this is big. The company found something at a dig site in southwestern Hyperborea. I don't know what they discovered, exactly, but they believe it's of alien origin, and it's old. They've codenamed it the *Seraph*."

"Well, I'll be damned," I said quietly. The case had just gotten much more interesting.

The recording continued. "There are protocols in place for the discovery of alien technology. An immediate stop-work is supposed to be put into effect. Both the Colonial government and the Terran Confederation are supposed to be notified, their teams brought in to inspect the find and determine a course of action. That didn't happen, at least not as far as I know. Instead, the whole thing got moved into the Advanced Research Division's black budget. Everything about the find is being kept secret. That's illegal. There are rumors that Xavier Taranis himself is overseeing the whole thing."

"Xavier Taranis?" I asked aloud. "You don't say." I rubbed my chin. "Lily, pause the video."

She stopped the playback and looked up at me. "He's been retired for decades now."

"Wait," Dagny said. "Xavier Taranis? *That* Xavier Taranis, the son of Rafael Taranis?"

"That's the only one I know of," I said. The younger Taranis took over the Ascension Planetary Holdings Group decades ago, after his father died unexpectedly. "The man's got to be old as dirt by now."

Lily did a quick search on her computer. "He was born on Earth not long after the founding of Nova Columbia. He's a hundred and thirty-one local years old now."

"Practically one foot in the grave. Interesting." Even with the miracles of modern medicine and all the money in the world, time catches up with everyone eventually. "What could be so damned important that the richest man on the planet, in the final years of his life, would come out of retirement to manage it?"

"He wasn't exactly sedentary, even after he retired," Lily said, looking at her screen again. "He made a big splash seventy-five years ago when he joined the Cosmic Ontological Foundation. It was a big scandal at the time. His father practically disowned him. Since retiring from Ascension, he spent a lot of time off-world. He financed a couple survey expeditions, looking for aliens. Never found any, so far as anyone knows."

"Interesting. Resume the video, please."

Lily tapped PLAY and the video continued. "The excavation at Site 471 has continued under designation *Project Isaiah*. They're using top-of-the-line excavation and construction robotics to minimize the number of personnel who have access to the site. It's all under high security, too. They're trying to keep it quiet."

I pondered that for a moment. The problem with grand conspiracies is that it's almost impossible to keep people from blabbing about things. The bigger the secret and the more people are involved, the more likely it is information will leak. The larger the project, the larger its logistical requirements will be, and that makes it all the more difficult to hide.

"Everyone who's been up there has been made to sign a nondisclosure agreement," Cassandra continued, "but I think it's more than the fear of being sued that's keeping everyone quiet. Xavier Taranis handpicked a lot of people for the project and a lot of them are members of the Cosmic Ontological Foundation. When I started looking into this myself, things got strange. I never said a single word about it to anyone at work, but I think they know. People are . . . people are following me, I think. Listening to me. *Stalking* me. Th-there are at least three or four of them. Everywhere I go, there they are, watching me. I disabled my neural implant but I worry that they've got my apartment bugged. I'm recording this while locked in a restroom at a public library because it's the only place I can be sure isn't monitored. They're . . . um . . ."

The recording of Cassandra trailed off and she paused to rub her eyes. "I'm sorry. I should have made notes or something. I've gotten maybe four hours of sleep in the past few days. People keep banging on my apartment door at night. I think they're trying to scare me." She looked into the camera with a determined face. "It's working. I'm scared . . . but I'm not going to quit."

Dagny's eyes narrowed and she folded arms across her chest.

"I've learned that Arthur is involved in this. He's been tapped to be the assistant security manager for Project Isaiah. I know you and he never got along, but he's a good man, and he's not a member of the COF. I don't believe he would sanction anything that was unethical or unsafe. He wouldn't. I'm going to bring this up with him. Maybe he's doing the same thing I'm doing, trying to figure out what's going on up there.

"But . . ." Cassandra trailed off again and looked down, like she was trying to figure out what to say next. "If you're watching this, it probably means that my plan didn't work. Maybe they really did get to Arthur, or maybe something happened to the both of us. I'm not as naïve as you think, though—I have a backup plan. I've been talking to

Arcanum. They've agreed to help me. So, I guess if you're seeing this, and you haven't heard from me, that's where you should start." She looked up and over her shoulder suddenly, as if something startled her, before turning back toward the camera. "I have to go now. Dagny, I'm sorry. You might have to finish this for me. I love you."

The video ended. I didn't say anything for a few moments. My client looked like she needed a minute to process everything she'd just heard. It was a lot to take in. She shook her head, slowly, then looked at me.

"You look like you could use a drink," I said.

She nodded. "A cigarette, too, if you don't mind."

"It's no trouble. Come on into my office. We'll have a sit-down, a drink, and talk about what our next steps will be."

Lily piped up. "Ms. Blake, with your permission, I'd like to start going through the files on this drive. There's a lot here, and it looks like she copied it in a hurry. It's not very well organized. It'll take some time to figure out what's relevant and what isn't."

"Lily is very good at this sort of thing. If you have any privacy concerns, don't worry. She's a professional and she takes data security very seriously."

"No, no, it's fine," Dagny said to Lily. "Please. I wouldn't even know where to begin." She looked up at me. "Mind if we head into your office now? I really need to sit down."

It had begun to rain outside as Dagny seated herself in front of my desk and lit up a cigarette. "I should really quit these things." The way she said it told me she had no intention of giving up the habit just yet.

"It's not a world for smokers anymore," I said, turning on the ventilation fan. I walked over to my liquor cabinet and opened it.

"That's quite a selection you've got there. Do you invite a lot of women up for drinks?"

I looked back at her, grinning. "Sure. They love the ambiance of a soulless corporate office tower. What's your poison?"

"What are you having?"

I grabbed the bottle of Darwin Ducote, the same one I'd shared with Dwight Cullender a couple days earlier. "How's bourbon sound?"

Dagny exhaled a puff of smoke. "That sounds good. Do you have ice?"

"Bourbon on the rocks, coming right up." I retrieved two glasses, dropped an ice cube in each, and poured a stiff shot in each. I placed one in front of my client before sitting down opposite her, behind my desk.

Placing her cigarette in an ashtray, Dagny lifted the glass to her lips and took a sip. "Wow," she said, setting the glass back down. "That's stiff."

"One hundred proof," I said, pausing to take a sip myself.

"What's our next move?" she asked.

I took another sip then set my glass down. I had some concerns that I needed to address. "How would you judge your sister's mental state, overall? Not just the last time you saw her, but before that. Did she seem okay?"

"She did. What are you getting at, Mr. Novak?"

"I'm just trying to assess the situation as best I can.

Before that last meeting with her, did your sister seem nervous at all? Paranoid?"

"Not that I noticed. Are you trying to say that she's just crazy? Even if that were true, she's still missing!"

"I understand that. It's just, what she described, being followed and harassed by multiple people? That's called gang-stalking. Now, sometimes you do run across an organized effort to intimidate someone like that, but nine times out of ten gang-stalking is a symptom of mental illness. You also told me that your stepfather said your sister is fine. One possibility that we have to consider is that she had some kind of mental breakdown, and he checked her into a mental health clinic."

"You really think she'd make up a story so elaborate? Invent project names, places, all that?"

"Ms. Blake, I once had a prospective client try to hire me to find her missing son, a boy named Stanley. She told me all about him, even showed me pictures. It turned out that not only was her son not missing, but she never had a son at all. I contacted her family and they told me she was having an episode. It was cyber-psychosis."

"Really? I've never heard of a case that bad."

"Neither had I, until then. Her family told me she was quite the tech-head when she was younger, had to have all the latest cybernetic implants and upgrades, but couldn't always afford the best quality doctors for the procedure. She suffered neural burnout, which resulted in severe chemical imbalances in her brain. The pictures she showed me, the boy? He was a character in an augmented reality game. They couldn't remove all of her wetware. She was having false memories triggered by residual code from a corrupted neural implant."

"Holy shit," Dagny said. "If that were the case with Cassie, why wouldn't Arthur just tell me?"

"That's a good question. I can think of some reasons, but I'd only be speculating. It may be that Lily finds evidence on that drive that corroborates your sister's story. We also need to keep in mind that even if the story your sister told you, about Ascension uncovering buried alien technology, isn't true, she might have *believed* it was true, and acted accordingly. She said she'd been working with Arcanum. Are you familiar with that organization?"

"Only by reputation. The circles I used to run in didn't exactly get along with the likes of Arcanum."

"I've read up on them," I said. "They're a tough organization to pin down. Some people think they're just a hacker group, and while they have hackers and net-divers that isn't their whole deal. They have a network of informants and whistleblowers, too. They engage in corporate espionage and data theft. They routinely leak damaging or embarrassing information about public officials, corporations, the government, the Security Forces, banks, anyone in a position of power, but they never target regular people. In the past few years, every exposé they've done has been proven to be true. Every document they've leaked turned out to be genuine."

"Are you a fan?"

I shrugged. "Some of what they do is illegal. Politicians like to say they spread disinformation, but nothing they've published has been debunked as far as I know. They seem to have their own code and I can respect that. What they do isn't that different from what we're doing now. In any case, that's our best lead, so that's where I'll start."

"Do you have a way of contacting Arcanum?"

"Not directly. If I were them, I'd make it a point to avoid private investigators, too. I'll get Lily to do some digging. She comes from that world. If she doesn't know somebody, maybe she knows somebody who knows somebody, if you follow me."

"I hope she does."

"If I can't contact Arcanum, or if they won't talk to me, that doesn't mean I'm giving up. It just means I have to pursue other angles." I paused and took another sip of bourbon. I had questions for my client and some of them were going to be personal. "Dagny, I need to ask you about some things, but before I do, I want you to understand that I'm not trying to be nosy. I know that sounds funny coming from a guy who makes a living off of being nosy, but it's true. Snooping on people professionally gives me a pretty good appreciation for their privacy. Of course, you don't have to tell me anything, and anything you do tell me will be kept confidential."

She knocked back the remainder of her bourbon in one swig, grimacing as she set the glass down. "I think I know what you're going to ask. It was bound to come up sooner or later."

"You and your sister both have alluded to your past. Your stepfather is apparently involved in this. I think it's time we talked about it."

"I'm surprised that you haven't looked into me already."

"Like I said, I appreciate the value of a person's privacy."

"Okay, then. My past. Where to start?"

"You said that you and your sister had some kind of falling out. Let's start with that. Can you tell me what happened?"

"I guess it all started when we were little. We grew up in Epsilon City. Our father died of Kellerman's Syndrome. Cassie was just a toddler at the time."

"I'm sorry to hear that. My grandparents died from Kellerman's when I was a kid. It's bad business."

"Our mother remarried five years later."

"To Arthur?"

"Yes."

"I see. How would you describe your childhood, your home life?"

"It was good, for the most part. Arthur and Mom tried their best. He had a good job with Ascension, so we never had to do without. We weren't rich, but we were well-off, and our situation only got better as the years went by and he got promoted. We got along fine until I was a teenager. I would, I don't know, act out just to try and shock Arthur. He was so straightlaced, such an uptight company man. He was sending us to an in-person, private primary school, so naturally I started skipping class just to spite him. Before long smoking, going to parties, joyriding with my friends, you know, all the usual trouble kids can get into."

I raised my eyebrows. "Rebellious youth, I see."

"Cassie looked up to me and all I did was set a bad example. Some big sister I was. I didn't mean to push her away, too, but I did anyway. Maybe it was for the best. She was getting straight-As in school while I was a juvenile delinquent. If she'd have been hanging out with me, she might've done all the stupid things I did and screwed up her life, too."

"I get that you were a wild child when you were a teenager, but how did that screw up your life?"

"It didn't, not until we got older. Cassie got a scholarship to the Nova Columbia Colonial University, Epsilon City North School of Business. Arthur, despite all the trouble I'd caused, wanted me to go to university, too."

"You were still living at home after high school?"

"Technically. I spent a lot of time staying with friends. I went through a few different entry-level jobs, just enough to keep me from going hungry, but I didn't have a plan for my life, or, really, any goals. Cassie was two years behind me. When it was time for her to go off to university, Arthur and Mom talked me into going with her. Don't get me wrong, he didn't have to twist my arm. I thought it would be fun. You know, go to a real school, not remote learning. I was going to get to live on campus, make friends, go to parties, all that."

NCCU-ECN is an expensive school, but with the exception of the Colleges of Business, Astronautics, and Planetary Engineering, isn't exactly prestigious. A lot of Epsilon City's upper crust use it as a daycare for their spoiled kids and it has a reputation as a party school. "Did you have fun?"

Dagny grinned. "I'm not going to lie, I did. I don't know how many classes I showed up to hungover. Cassie made the dean's list every year and I was a C-student, but I stuck with it for a couple of years."

"You didn't graduate?"

"No. I, you know, dropped out."

"What made you do that?"

She was quiet for a few seconds. She picked up her cigarette and took a drag off it. "I was in the political science program. I never had much of an interest in politics or anything, but the curriculum didn't require any math and there were a lot of interesting people there, even the professors. In my first year I met a boy named Reza."

"Oh, boy."

She chuckled, but there was a bitterness to her laugh. "He was handsome, and sweet, and funny. He was confident, too, a smooth talker."

"Sounds like a real dreamboat."

"I thought so at the time. So did a bunch of other girls he knew. But we went out a few times and the next thing you know we were a couple. He was ... exciting. Smart without being pedantic. Clever without being mean. He knew so many interesting people, too—artists, activists, musicians, counterculture types. You know how it is."

I didn't, actually, at least not from personal experience. I never went to university. I'm a proud graduate of the Delta City College of Technology and Trades. All of one semester in person for hands-on training, the rest virtual. My Autonomous Systems Technician certificate is framed and hanging on my office wall. Like most schools, the course of study is built around remote learning. There wasn't much time for partying, especially since I also had a day job at the time. I nodded along anyway, to keep Dagny talking.

"Toward the end of that year, Reza and I got pretty serious as an item, and he started to get pretty serious with his activism. He would always talk about the injustices of society. He was so passionate about it, when he'd talk about the inequity built into the system of Nova Columbia, how the people are ruled over by corporations and the system. His academic advisor, Dr. Ruthenberg, was a hard-core Neo-Corbynite. He invited us to attend a meeting of the local chapter of GLF—the Global Liberation Front," she said, pronouncing the abbreviation as *Gliff*.

It now made sense what Dagny had said previously, about the people she used to run with not getting along with Arcanum. I wasn't well-versed on the GLF or their radical Corbynite ideology, but I knew that it clashed with Arcanum's philosophy of nonviolence. The GLF didn't want to reform the system, they wanted to tear it down and replace it with their own regime. "The professor talked you into that, huh? Doesn't sound like he had the best interests of his students at heart."

"The revolution needs soldiers," Dagny said, darkly. "Young, idealistic idiots to go do the dirty work while the academics and scholars wax poetic about political theory and social inequity. Anyway, that's how it started. I got more and more involved with the GLF during my second year. They were my friends. I thought of them as my family after a while. I stopped associating with my nonmember friends and grew distant from my real family. The tenets of the traditional family were a tool of the oppressor, used for indoctrination, violence, and abuse." She made a noise somewhere between a laugh and a scoff. "They were the ones doing the indoctrinating."

"Sure sounds that way to me."

"I dropped out of university before my third year began. Reza and I had been convinced to go off-grid and join the GLF as full-time members. Arthur was furious with me. Mom was heartbroken. They tried to convince me to come back but I wouldn't listen. I came home one last time to get some stuff and we had a huge fight. I called Arthur a greedy, corporate pig. I accused Mom of replacing Dad with a rich man. I . . . Jesus, I called my mother a gold-digging whore. I screamed at Cassie." She looked up at me, the pain obvious in her eyes. "I screamed at my baby sister and told her that people like her would go up against the wall during the revolution."

"Ouch."

"Yeah. Mom and Arthur kicked me out of the house and banned me from having any contact with Cassie. It was . . . well, I suppose it was better that way. It protected her from my mistakes."

"What kind of mistakes are we talking about here? Aside from turning on your family, I mean." She visibly winced at that, so I softened my tone. "Dagny, it's not my place to judge. It would be some serious hypocrisy for me for me to sit here and look down on other people for being stupid when they were young. I'm just trying to understand what happened."

She took another long drag off her cigarette. "They don't trust new members with serious stuff. You have to prove yourself and your loyalty. We were usually tasked with doing minor things that they claimed would benefit the cause. It started off with attending protests and vandalism. Then they'd have you commit petty crimes, like knocking over bank kiosks for the cash or stealing from warehouses. You had to prove you were willing to fight the system by being a criminal."

"Makes sense. Gangs operate the same way. Makes them harder to infiltrate. They start you off with small, easy stuff, then up the stakes and the risk as you prove yourself. After a certain point, you've amassed such a criminal record that you couldn't back out if you wanted to."

"That's what it felt like. They also handed out drugs like candy at a kids' party. Not just the lightweight stuff, either. Illegal stuff. Dangerous stuff. Before long I was addicted to Crush because we'd huff it before every operation."

"Crush?" I said. "That's not good." If you're not from Nova Columbia you might not have heard of Crush. It's been making its way through the entire Confederation for the past few years but it originated here. It's a chemical concoction that boosts adrenaline, dulls sensations of pain, and increases physical strength to the body's maximum biological capability.

The biggest effect it has, though, is the suppression of fear. A person hopped up on enough Crush literally isn't afraid of anything, not even death. The drug gets its name because it comes in an aerosolized form, in little pressurized ampules. You load these capsules into an inhaler, crush the ampule, and inhale the fumes. Chronic users become addicts who, without the drug, often find themselves struggling with crippling anxiety.

"It was another way of keeping us under control," she explained. "Crush is expensive. None of us had jobs, or money of our own. You had to keep working for the GLF to get your fix." She took another puff off her cigarette. "Do you remember the Summer of Rage?"

"I do. Made quite a mess down in Epsilon City, if I recall." The city was rocked by riots, arson, and bombings after a series of law enforcement crackdowns. "I assume you were involved in that?"

"That's how I got this," she said, pointing to the scar on her face. "We made small explosive devices that we would throw at the riot troops. One blew up before it was supposed to and I caught a piece of it with my face. I'm lucky it didn't hit me in the eye."

"I'll say. I caught some frag myself, back in the war. Got some mean scars on my legs."

"It didn't stop there. Reza had big plans. He wanted to make a name for himself." She paused for a second. "You know, I don't even know if he really believed the GLF dogma. I think he wanted to be respected and feared more than anything else. He wanted to feel powerful. He came up with this plan to bomb a SecFor barracks downtown."

I let out a low whistle. "There were quite a few bombings that year, if I remember right, but I don't recall a Security Forces post being hit."

Dagny took another drag and exhaled smoke upward toward the vent, then looked me in the eye again. "It didn't happen, but it almost did. SecFor did a few big raids and arrested a bunch of GLF members, and Reza came up with his plan for revenge. I didn't know all the details. I don't think he even wanted to bring me in on it, but between the arrests and people getting scared and quitting, we were short on people. I don't even know if it would have worked, but . . ." She trailed off.

"Go on."

"Reza had gotten ahold of a bomb. An industrial mining charge, I think, something like two thousand pounds of high explosive."

"Wow," I said. "That could do some damage."

"He was still really worried that the bomb wouldn't destroy the SecFor post unless it was detonated on the inside. He was adamant that he wanted to kill as many troopers as he possibly could. I'd never seen him so . . . so vicious, so driven. He didn't want to make a statement, he wanted a bloodbath. He was even talking about getting a second bomb and placing it to blow up the firefighters and ambulances when they arrived. It scared me. I was even more scared because we'd run out of Crush, so I was going through withdrawal anxiety and could barely hold it together."

"What did you do?"

"Reza wanted to get the bomb into the underground parking garage. He sent me to do reconnaissance on the place, see what security was like. I walked in the public entrance, turned off the hidden camera he'd put on me, and turned myself in."

I nodded. "That took guts. What happened after that?"

"I told them everything. Reza was killed in a shoot-out with SecFor when they tried to arrest him. I went to prison for two years for the crimes I'd confessed to, but got a reduced sentence for my cooperation. I was on the drug rehab program while in prison. I've been clean since I got out."

"I suppose your ex-comrades in the GLF weren't too happy with you."

"I'm a traitor. If I ever set foot in Epsilon City again

they'll probably try to kill me. They just don't have much of a presence here in Delta, and I've kept a low profile ever since. I even changed my name."

That explained why she had a different family name from her missing sister's. There were a few more things I needed to know about the situation, though, so I had to keep prying. "Seems to me you made some mistakes, but you did the right thing when it counted. Did your family ever come back around? Did you try to get back in touch with them?"

"Arthur wouldn't talk to me. Mom did, though. She stayed in touch with me when I was in prison and helped me move out of Epsilon City when I got out. Cassie was a different story. I put the family through hell. I didn't have to see the results of it but she did. She wanted nothing to do with me, despite Mom's best efforts. I thought it was a lost cause, and it was, until a few years ago when Mom got sick."

"First your father and then your mother. That's a tough break. Did she contract Kellerman's, too?"

"No. She developed an aggressive brain cancer. They did everything they could, but, you know, it's not as if they can replace the brain like they can a heart or liver. Her dying wish was that Cassie and I reconcile, and as angry as she was at me, she loved Mom more, so she was willing to try. It took years, but we got through it. We became a family again."

"I assume that Arthur was less receptive to your attempts to make peace."

"He wanted nothing to do with me. I found out later that my actions cost him a big promotion at work. The

GLF targeted Ascension a lot, you know. He works in corporate security, and my behavior made them think he was less trustworthy, even though he disowned me and kicked me out. Cassie told me that he's angry that I wasn't there for the final years of Mom's life."

"That's a tough break."

"That's why we have to find her. I let my sister down before. She's counting on me now."

"I will do everything I can to find her, I promise you that. For right now, though, I think the best thing you can do is go home. We've had a hell of a day and you look exhausted. Get some rest. Lily and I will be going through the files your sister left us. We will keep you updated on the situation."

"Just like that? Just sit at home and wait?"

"I'm afraid so. There isn't much you can do. I'll work as quickly as I can."

She sighed. "I suppose you're right. Would you mind calling me a taxi?"

"Sure, no problem."

I forwarded Lily the automatically generated transcript of my conversation with Dagny and asked her to call the client a taxi. I then walked Dagny down to street level. The car was waiting for her when we got there.

"You'll let me know as soon as you know something?" she asked as she climbed in.

"I will. If you think of anything or hear anything that might be useful, don't hesitate to give me a call. Try to get some rest."

"Thank you, Easy, for everything." She flashed me a sad smile before closing the car door. I watched the taxi for a moment as it drove off, merging into afternoon traffic.

Lily was waiting for me back in the office. "So Cassandra Carmichael was working with Arcanum," she said.

"So she claims."

"You don't believe what she said in the video?"

"I haven't decided yet. Is there anything you've found in her files that corroborates anything she said?"

"Not really. It's mostly financial and logistical reports and I haven't had time to get into them. There is a big Ascension project in southwestern Hyperborea, though, at the base of Mount Gilead."

"Mount Gilead," I repeated. "The volcano?"

"The same. It's going to be the biggest terraforming plant in the northern hemisphere. The estimated completion date isn't for another two years, though."

"You think that's the location of Site 471?"

"Could be. The location is pretty remote. That whole region is sparsely populated. The closest settlement is a town of twelve thousand called Freedom's Prospect, but that's still almost a hundred miles from Mount Gilead. The closest actual city is New Fargo, but that's even farther away. They still have a claim on a huge tract of land up there, millions of acres."

"Our best bet right now is to see if she actually was in contact with Arcanum." I looked down at my assistant. "Lily, you used to run in those circles. Do you know anybody who would be willing to talk to us?"

Lily rubbed the side of her head. "I knew you were going to ask me that. I do know somebody, but I don't know if he'll be willing to tell us anything."

"I can tell you're not thrilled with this. Is there something I need to be concerned with?"

"It's not like that," Lily said, shaking her head. "It's just . . . he's my ex. We, uh, haven't spoken in a while."

"Oh. Oh, I see. I'm perfectly willing to go through someone else if you have another contact. There's no reason to drag your personal life into this."

"No. If we're going to do this, we need to talk to him. I don't know anybody else who would be willing to vouch for me, and that's the only way we're going to get any useful information out of them. It's just going to be awkward as hell."

"Thank you for being willing to do this, even if it's awkward. Say, did you look over the transcript of my conversation with the client?"

"I did. I looked up a couple articles about the Global Liberation Front and Corbynite ideology while you walked her down to the taxi. The GLF was basically gutted after the Summer of Rage and never recovered. They're still around, but they're not as open or brazen as they used to be. That college professor she mentioned, the one who recruited her? His name is Dr. Emil Ruthenberg. He's now the Chair of the Political Science Department at the Nova Columbia Colonial University, Epsilon City North. He was censured for his role in recruiting students for the GLF, but they couldn't prove that he directly incited violence, and he has tenure, so nothing really happened to him."

I shook my head. "Of course. Did you find anything else?"

"I did. Take a look at this."

I shuffled behind Lily's desk so I could see her computer screens. She had a document pulled up, another page of the missing woman's extensive notes. A quick skim of the text revealed she was researching finds of ancient alien artifacts and their significance.

"The first evidence of an ancient, advanced alien species was discovered in the Trappist-1 system in 2183," she said. "They found what was believed to be the wreckage of a large spacecraft in a solar orbit, estimated to be between sixty and seventy million years old."

"That's the First Antecessor Race, right?"

"Yeah." She tapped the touchpad and brought up a picture of one of them, a reconstruction based on fossil evidence. It had six limbs, like an insect, but stood with an upright posture. They walked on their four hind limbs, with the front two serving as arms. The head had two eyes, each on the end of a stalk. "They've found more evidence of their presence in this part of the galaxy, all estimated to be from approximately the same time frame. It is unknown if they departed this region of space or if they went extinct. Most of what remains is so old that it's decayed beyond repair, but every so often they find something more intact. Did you ever read about the incident at the Medusae Fossae Colony on Mars?"

"Sounds familiar. The colony blew up, didn't it? Some kind of accident?"

"It happened a hundred and fifty years ago. They found some First Antecessor Race artifact in deep space and brought it there for testing, in secret. Then the explosion happened, a five-hundred-megaton blast. All one hundred thousand colonists died instantly. It left a crater that you can see from space."

"Damn. What the hell did they do?"

"Nobody really knows. The responsible parties, including the Martian government, scrubbed all their records after the incident to cover their tracks. The best theory is that they were trying to reactivate an ancient vacuum-energy engine. If Ascension really did find some alien artifact up there and is experimenting on it, they could be putting us all in danger."

"You're not wrong."

"And if they didn't notify the government, all the money and lawyers in the world won't save them from the fallout if they're found out. They might have finally gone too far, Easy."

"Maybe so," I said. "Good work. Keep on it. I'm going to make some calls myself."

CHAPTER 5

It took a day for her to set everything up, but Lily came through for me. She was able to get ahold of her ex, a fellow named Clarence who went by the moniker *Dante*, and convince him to meet with us. As expected, Arcanum was being very cautious about the whole thing. We were to meet on their turf and we'd be swept for cameras or listening devices.

It was a dark and rainy night on the South Side of Delta City. Traffic is usually lighter at night but this town never really goes to sleep. Lily sat in the passenger's seat next to me, quietly, like she was lost in her own thoughts. She was wearing makeup, dark eyeliner and purple lipstick. Maybe it was just so she would blend where we were going; her ex wanted us to meet him at a nightclub in the southeast sector of the city, a joint that, according to Lily, Arcanum owned and operated through a cutout. Maybe she just wanted to look good so that this Clarence cat was reminded of what he wasn't getting anymore. Women are funny like that sometimes.

I was dressed the same way I always was, and Lily said I'd stick out like a sore thumb, especially with the tie. She was probably right about that, but I wasn't interested in playing dress-up to try and convince a bunch of kids that I was hip. Normally I try to be the gray man, not draw attention to myself. That helps a lot this line of work. In this case, though, it didn't really matter. They knew who I was and were expecting me.

"You okay?" I asked, breaking the silence.

"What?" Lily turned from staring out the window and seemed surprised by the question. She could get lost in her own head sometimes, especially when we were working on a case. "Oh. Yeah. I was just thinking about Cassandra Carmichael's notes, Arcanum, all that. Mentally juggling a lot of things right now."

"I know the feeling. Did you find anything else in her files? I know it's the weekend and I don't expect you to work on your days off. I just know you. I'm guessing you kept looking through it."

"I did," Lily admitted with a smile, "but I didn't get too deep into it. There's a ton of material there. Years and years of repots, requisitions, financial analysis, spreadsheets, personnel management, things like that. A lot of it is interesting, but isn't related to this Seraph or Site 471. I think she just downloaded as much data as she could and didn't have time to sort through it."

"Seems reasonable. She looked like she was in in a hurry in that video."

"A lot of her notes are disorganized and haphazard. She was paranoid and wasn't getting much sleep. I *did* find some documentation confirming that terraforming plant site by Mount Gilead is Site 471. There was also a long stop-work put in place up there before a bunch of personnel were cycled out, later replaced by different people, but nothing about why."

"That would seem to corroborate some of what Cassandra Carmichael said in that video."

"Most of the documents describing the dig site are redacted, and I don't think Cassandra was able to find get the unredacted versions. I haven't found anything that specifically mentions this Seraph or finding alien technology yet, and because of all the redactions, simple keyword searches aren't helpful. I have to read the whole thing line by line and try to figure things out from the context. It's a slow process. Right now I think our best leads are still Arcanum and the stepfather."

"I agree, but I appreciate your hard work. That's a lot of information to start with." I was quiet for a moment. "Say, if you don't mind me asking, just how involved were you with Arcanum?"

"Somewhat involved, I guess? I was a member but I never got in too deep. I did some coding and analysis work for them, but I was never really an insider. That takes a long time. You've got to prove you can be trusted."

"Just like the GLF," I said, "I'm getting tired of all this cloak-and-dagger business."

"It wasn't as bad as that. They didn't try and make me do anything wrong. I was just hesitant to get too involved. Last time I did stuff like that, it blew up in my face and I got arrested." She paused, then looked up at me. "I was worried that if I got busted again, I'd be looking at real prison time, given my record."

I gave the sort of half shrug you do when you've got both hands on the steering wheel. "That was a perfectly reasonable concern for you to have, kid. The sorts of people Arcanum likes to take on have a lot of influence. One of the downsides of growing up is that you realize how much trouble your youthful idealism can get you into. It's the same sort of lesson our client learned the hard way."

"I know. It was hard to let it go, though. I admire what they do. There's still a part of me that would like to be part of something like that."

I grinned. "Admittedly our work isn't usually glamorous."

Lily smiled. "I like my job, Boss, don't get me wrong. It's just . . . I don't know. Dante was so passionate about it. I think he felt a little betrayed when I didn't want to go all in for Arcanum. I hadn't been trying to mislead him about it or anything, I just wasn't comfortable with it."

"Sometimes people hear what they want to hear. It sounds to me like this young man wanted you to join Arcanum so badly that he couldn't tell you weren't as enthusiastic about it as he was. I assume this is why it didn't work out between you two?"

"Yeah, mostly. We had a pretty big fight about it. I told him we were done."

"That was probably for the best. The question is, is he still holding a grudge? Will he help us?"

"I think so. Dante was never, like, petty."

"Well, I guess we'll find out."

She was quiet for a minute, then looked up at me again. "You know, you're pretty good at giving relationship advice."

"My ex-wife would argue with you on that." I chuckled.
"Hell, that woman *loved* to argue. Let's just say I've done
so much dumb shit in my time that I know what *not* to
do." That got a smile out of her. I made it a point not to
pry into Lily's personal life. Besides that she's an adult—
she doesn't need me acting like I can run her life better
than she can.

All that said . . . she has a good head on her shoulders,
but she's still so young. Twenty-one local years old, which
is about twenty-four in Terran years. I remember being
that age and what a fool I was. If I can help her avoid some
of the mistakes I made, well . . . all the better.

"Tell me about this guy," I said. "Clarence, Dante,
whatever his name is. What's he like?"

"Do us both a favor and call him Dante. He doesn't like
it when people he doesn't know use his real name. It's kind
of a *thing* with the net-diver community and Arcanum in
particular."

"Did you have a nickname like that when you ran with
those people?"

"Yeah—Lilith, or L-1-L-1-7-H. I know, not super
creative when my real name is Lilian, but I came up with
it when I was a kid. Twelve-year-old me thought it
sounded really mysterious. I didn't even know about the
figure from Jewish folklore until I was older."

She knew more about Jewish folklore than I did.
"How'd you meet Dante?"

"Same way I met all my other friends—on the Net. I
knew him even before I got busted. I never met him in
person until my trial."

"Is that right? He showed up there?"

"He did. Put on a tie and everything to support me in court. My parents took a liking to him, thought it was sweet that he showed up."

"Your parents weren't the only ones who took a liking to him."

"Well . . . let's just say he's not like a lot of the other diver boys I met."

"How were those other boys?"

"You know the type: pasty, awkward, shy. Not great people skills. A lot of them live off of junk food and energy drinks, spend all day jacked into virtual reality."

"So the stereotype of the unhealthy, weird net-diver has some truth to it?"

She grinned. "More truth than a lot of us would like to admit. Not Dante, though. His parents immigrated from Earth, from the African Union. He works out a lot and wasn't a VR junkie. He didn't, you know, act weird because I'm a girl, and he was so polite to my parents."

"Everything a girl could want, hey?"

"He was my first love, my first . . . uh . . ." Lily trailed off. I looked over at her and she was blushing a little. "We were just kids."

"You think he'll help us? I brought some cash in case we need to incentivize someone."

"The money won't help, not with Arcanum. They'll either help us or they won't. If Cassandra Carmichael was working with them, that means she earned their trust. They always look out for their own."

"I hope you're right."

She looked over at me, cocking her head slightly to the

side. "You're not thrilled about talking to the stepfather, are you?"

"I'm not. Cassandra went to him, turned up missing, but he told Dagny everything is fine. It's suspicious. Whatever is going on, he knows something about it. I don't want to tip our hand any earlier than necessary. He already knows Dagny was asking after her sister, but he doesn't know about us yet."

"Yeah," Lily agreed. "I would be hesitant to go to anyone at Ascension unless we know they can be trusted." She looked at the navigation screen. "Hey, we're almost there."

The nightclub was called The Vault and it was not my kind of place. It was, however, the sort of joint I would have hung out at when I was Lily's age: the loud industrial-synth music, expensive shots, a cloud of cigarette smoke hanging in the air despite the best efforts of the ventilation system, and, most importantly, lots and lots of women.

Just inside the front doors was a sort of foyer, the place where you checked in and paid the cover charge. The muffled thump of heavy bass resonated through the walls and floor. A couple of bouncers, big guys in tactical armor vests, stood at the back of the room and surveyed the crowd. Behind a panel of armored glass stood an earnest young woman in a skintight halter top. Half her head was shaved the way young people do these days. I let Lily do the talking, only handing over my ID when asked.

"We've been invited," Lily explained to the other girl. "Dante is waiting for us."

The hostess looked down at a screen for a moment. "There you are. Great! I'll need you to hand over any weapons that you might be carrying. No guns, knives, or other weapons are allowed in the club. You will be checked before going in. You can also check your coats and hat."

Lily took off her jacket and placed it in a big metal drawer before turning to look at me. "Boss?"

"Rules are rules, right?" I took off my jacket and folded it up. Setting my hat on top of it, I placed it in the drawer. The two goons at the back of the room shuffled a little bit when they saw the gun under my right arm, but they didn't say anything. I undid the fasteners that attach the shoulder rig to my belt and took the whole harness off. I looked at the girl behind the glass. "You want me to clear it, too, or should I just leave it in the holster?"

"As long as it's in a holster it's fine." I laid the holster rig on top of my jacket, next to my hat. "Great!" she said.

"Not so fast, kid." Reaching into one pocket, I pulled out the little 9mm snub automatic I carry as a backup, still enclosed in its holster. "You'll want that, too, I expect." From another pocket I drew my auto-opening knife and put that on the pile, too. After that came my multitool, which has a knife blade on it, a flashlight, and spare ammunition for both guns. "I want a receipt for all this," I said to the girl behind the glass.

"Holy shit, Boss," Lily said, putting a hand over her face. Hell, I didn't even wear my body armor that night.

After handing over all my hardware, the two mooks gave me a rough and thorough pat down. Then they swept both Lily and me with electromagnetic scanners designed to detect concealed weapons, tiny cameras, microphones, or other electronic devices. "You treat all your customers like this?" I asked.

"Only the ones who show up loaded for bear, buddy," the one sweeping me said. "You got any cybernetic implants, artificial organs, things like that?"

"Not me, friend. One hundred percent meat except for a metal plate in my head. Little souvenir from the war."

"Oh. Uh . . . thank you for your service, sir," the bouncer said awkwardly.

"Don't mention it."

He looked over at his partner, who had just finished checking Lily. "He's clean."

"You can both go," the other goon said.

"Thank you," Lily said, apologetically. "Come on, Easy. I know where we're going." Past the entranceway was a set of stairs that went down. Being in the basement seemed on the nose for a club called The Vault. "This building used to be a bank," she said, leading the way. "They got the property for cheap at auction."

"So the club takes up the basement," I said. "What about the rest of it? This is a big building."

"They rent it out to generate revenue. There's a big server farm on one floor, and I think a cybernetics clinic on another. It's all on the up and up."

At the bottom of the stairs was an open landing with another set of doors. Lily pushed them open and we were in the club. The music had been turned down and it seemed like most of the customers were getting ready to leave. A pair of women probably the same age as Lily eyed me up and down as they walked past. I eyed them right back—one, with pink hair, was wearing a tight mesh dress. The other was dressed like a schoolgirl from an old porno. They smiled at me as we passed each other.

Lily looked up at me with a grin on her face. "You dirty old man."

"What? I can't help it if women find confidence attractive. Besides, look at the other men in here. A lot of them are wearing as much makeup as the women."

"It's called *glam*," Lily explained. "It's in this year. To be honest, I don't see the appeal, either. If I wanted to make out with a chick I'd make out with a chick, you know?"

I chuckled at that. "So this is where you like to hang out, hey?" Another woman walked past, this one with bright green hair and a pair of enormous knockers barely contained by a corset. "This ain't really my scene, but it's growing on me."

"Easy, you're probably the oldest guy in the place right now."

I laughed again. "Hell, you're probably right. Don't worry, kid, you won't catch me here after work. The eye candy is nice but it's too loud. Anyways I'm not interested in being a vehicle for a girl half my age to work through her daddy issues. I have all the drama in my life that I need just now."

"I don't really come here anymore. Too many people I'd prefer not to bump into."

One wall of the club was lined with semicircular booths, padded benches partially encircling a round table. In one of them four young people, three guys and one girl, were slumped into their seats, heads rolled back like they were passed out. They all wore headsets that covered their eyes and ears. A bulky virtual reality console sat on the table in front of them. Wires led from the console to the back of each kid's head, plugged into their neural interfaces. I shook my head. "Why would you bother to come here and pay the cover charge if you're just going to jack into VR? Can't they do that at home?"

"It's a fad," Lily said, making a disapproving face. "Virtual hookups. People call them *coomers*. They come here, meet strangers, jack into a VR program together, and simulate having sex."

"I'm pretty sure people have been doing that since they invented VR, kid."

"I know, but it's the *in* thing this year. Sometimes people will hookup with multiple virtual sex partners a night. They'll do things that they wouldn't do in real life. Since you meet your partners in person, you know they're really who they say they are." She looked up at me. "That's important to most people."

I shrugged. "At least you can't catch chlamydia that way. I guess I would just prefer to not do it in front of a room full of strangers."

Lily looked up at me again. "You've never tried VR, have you?"

"Of course I have. It just makes me a little motion sick, is all."

"No, I mean *real* VR, with a neural implant."

"Right, right. No. Didn't feel comfortable plugging a computer directly into my brain."

"It can be addictive, very addictive. That's the problem. It doesn't perfectly simulate your body's senses, at least not with a commercial-grade cerebral interface. The more you use VR, the more your brain adapts to it, and the less real it feels. It becomes harder and harder to ignore the sensations from your physical body despite the direct stimulation from the implant. You start to notice the flaws in the simulation more and more, especially if you're using a portable console like that, which has low fidelity. They end up in this ugly cycle of addiction, needing the dopamine hit from VR but finding it harder and harder to get."

I stopped and looked down at my young partner. I'd never seen her use a VR interface. As far as I knew, she didn't even have the neural implant, yet she seemed a little unsettled. "I didn't mean to upset you."

"You didn't, Easy. This . . . this is a big part of the reason I stopped coming here, of why I left this whole world. There are people who try to spend their entire lives online, plugged into the system for every waking hour. Some even try sleeping while plugged into VR."

"Isn't that supposed to cause nightmares?"

"You do it enough it'll cause more than nightmares. You can get hallucinations, psychotic breaks, even brain damage."

"Sounds like you're speaking from experience," I said, delicately.

Lily was quiet for a second. "I . . . let's just say I had problems with VR dependency, and I saw what it did to people I care about. I swore off it, got my implant taken out. I don't even like being around it now. It . . . it brings back to when I was in a dark place. I'm sorry."

"Don't apologize for being honest, kid. It takes real strength to admit you have a problem, even more to actually overcome it." I nodded to the far wall. "Those are the VIP rooms, I think."

"They are," she said, happy with the change of subject. "We're meeting him in number three."

"Right. What do you say we go get this meeting over with then get the hell out of here?"

"Sounds good, boss. And, you know, thank you,"

I patted her on the shoulder. "Anytime."

"Hey, when we get in there, let me do the talking at first, okay?"

"You got it. Lead the way."

Lily slid the double doors open. The VIP room was small and square. There was a low table in the middle and padded couches along the walls. The walls were covered with mirrors. The room was lit by red lights. Dante was sitting on the couch facing the door. Like Lily, and like a lot of the kids in this club, he was decked out in all black. His eyes were hidden, in the dim red light, behind a pair of smart glasses. His hair, curly and black, was cropped short on top and shaved on the sides of his head. A small goatee stuck out from his chin. He had gauges in both his earlobes, too.

He had his arm around a young woman with tanned skin, dark hair, and dark eyes. She wore a short skirt and a tight top, and was snuggled up next to him real cozy-like. Her legs were crossed and her arms were folded across her chest. She gave Lily one hell of a glare as we stepped into the little room. I guessed she was Dante's new squeeze from the way she was mean-mugging Lily.

Lily, to her credit, didn't let the girl's evil eye phase her. "Dante. Thank you for meeting with us."

Dante looked at his girl. "Baby, give us a few minutes. OPSEC." The girl huffed but didn't say anything. She stood up and stalked out of the room, leaving a cold draft in her wake. She closed the sliding doors behind her and the noise of the club was muffled to where we could have a proper conversation. The three of us were alone.

"I, uh, I hope I'm not causing a problem," Lily said, tepidly. She'd been right, this was really awkward for her.

The young man stood up. "No problem. Selena understands operational security." He reached across the table and, looking Lily in the eye, offered her a hand. "It's good to see you again." He was a smooth operator. He then held his hand out to me. "I'm Dante."

I shook his hand firmly. "Easy Novak, private investigator. I appreciate your willingness to meet with us."

"Sit, please," he said, taking a seat himself. "I apologize for the security measures, but we have to be careful, especially when investigators come sniffing around." He looked me in the eye. "No offense."

"None taken," I said.

He looked at Lily. "Haven't heard from you in a long time, Lilith. A couple years, I think. You don't stay in touch with hardly anyone from the old days. You don't come to the club anymore. You ghosted all of us. Then, out of nowhere, you contact me and say you're a detective now and you need my help. You say you have a problem that involves Arcanum. What is going on?"

"It's about Cassandra Carmichael," Lily said. "She disappeared. We were hired to find her."

Dante played it cool. "What does this have to do with Arcanum?" Was it an act or did he really not know? How compartmentalized were these people?

"She was working with you," I said, firmly, "and she's been missing for two months now."

"Is that right?" Dante asked, raising an eyebrow. "Who hired you?"

"Concerned parties," I said, tersely.

Lily put a hand on my arm. "Easy."

I didn't let up. I leaned in so I was a little closer to Dante. "I didn't come all the way down here and get groped up by a couple of goons just to sit here and listen to you play coy. I know you know something whether you want to admit it or not. I'm not asking you to divulge everything about Arcanum. Honestly, I don't give a damn about Arcanum—I got no beef with you people. I'm here to do a job. Cassandra Carmichael is missing and she could be in real danger. Hell, she could be dead already. Either way, I was hired to find her and that's what I intend to do. Will you help us or not?"

It's a gamble using direct pressure like that. It works well on some people, but others will double down and push back even harder. From what Lily told me, though, Dante was basically a good kid, not the type to callously use someone. I figured my best bet here was to appeal to his sense of honor while letting him know how serious the situation was.

The young man took off his glasses and exhaled, heavily. "I was afraid of this. Yeah, she was working with us, and we know she's missing. We had someone check her place to see if they could find out what might have happened."

I looked at Lily, briefly. Dante had just confirmed that Cassandra Carmichael actually was working with

Arcanum. I didn't know yet if it would help us find her or not, but it at least confirmed that she hadn't made the whole thing up. "That explains how her apartment got turned over," I said. "I take it you were responsible for getting the security cameras disabled, too? How'd you manage that without the building super noticing?"

He raised an eyebrow again. It was a tell, something he seemed to do whenever I said something he wasn't expecting. "Sorry, that's kind of a trade secret. We were doing the same thing you are, trying to find any clues as to what happened to her."

"Was it your man who got into the wall safe?"

He was quiet for a moment.

"Dante, please," Lily said.

He sighed. "Okay, listen. I wasn't involved with this at all. I only found out about it after you contacted me. I had to take it up the chain to find out who Cassandra Carmichael was and why we were helping her. Our operative was able to get her safe open but there wasn't anything in there about what she was investigating."

"What did you find?" I asked.

"Personal documents and belongings, like you'd expect. Her passport and birth certificate, some cash, jewelry, things like that."

"So you just took it?" I asked. "Burgled her apartment? Does Arcanum care at all about the people who try to help it, or was she just a means to an end?"

He broke eye contact when I said that, looked down at the table. It must have got to him. I know how to push a guy's buttons when I have to. "You must understand, we have to be careful. It took us a long time to even realize anything was wrong. It was only a week ago that we had her apartment searched. I guess they took the stuff in the safe to scan it, make sure there wasn't a data stick or anything hidden in it. We still have all of it, even the cash. We're not thieves. We were going to give it back if she turned up."

"Okay, now we're getting somewhere," I said. "She told us that she was going to approach Arcanum to help. What sort of help did you offer her? Did she give you any information?"

"If you're familiar with our work then you know what kind of help we offer, Mr. Novak," Dante said. "My question is, how much do *you* know? You wouldn't be here if you didn't need our help. If you want us to disclose anything, you have to be willing to do the same."

"Dante," Lily said, her voice pleading.

I held up a hand. "No, he's got a point. We were hired by her family."

"I see. From what I understand, Cassandra contacted us over encrypted chat. There was a long process of vetting before we got involved. We were able to connect her with other insiders who were willing to talk to us. She wouldn't tell us exactly what she was investigating, just that it was big."

"We did find quite a bit of information from Ascension," I admitted. "I'm guessing your insiders are where she got some of it from."

That piqued his interest. "What did you find?"

"Financial documents, logistics stuff, requisitions, things like that. Some of it related to what she was investigating, some of it not."

"We would be interested in taking a look at what she gave you."

"Why's that? It all came from your source, didn't it?"

"Some of it, but you have to understand, she also *was* a source. She was a high-level logistics coordinator. She had access to a lot of things. Our organization is interested in seeing what she was able to dig up."

"We might be able to come to an arrangement," I suggested.

"Maybe. I need to know I can trust you. I need to know that you're not working for Ascension."

That pissed Lily off. "Are you serious? You think I would work for them?"

"No offense, but like I said, you ghosted all of us. I don't know what you've been up to since then."

I raised a hand to intervene before Lily shot her mouth off. She was normally slow to anger but she did have a temper. "Seems like we have ourselves a predicament, here. I want something from you, you want something from me, but neither of us knows if we can trust the other guy."

"I feel like you're going to make a proposal," Dante said.

"I feel like I am, too. Let's start with a show of good faith. I will give you some of the files on Ascension that Cassandra Carmichael left behind. There are things that don't pertain to my current case, but you might find it interesting all the same. In return, you give me everything that was in the safe in her apartment."

"That ... sounds reasonable. I'll have to talk to some people to get the okay, but I think they'll go along with it. Then what?"

I held my hands up agreeably. "Then, if we're both satisfied with what the other has provided, we move on to the next thing."

"I don't know where she is," Dante said. "I'm sorry. I wish I did."

"We understand that," Lily said. "We're just trying to retrace her steps."

Dante pulled out his handheld and began tapping at the screen. "Hang on a second," he said, not looking up at us. A few moments ticked by without anyone saying anything. He just kept watching his screen. Finally, he said, "I got the okay for this. Where do you want to do the exchange? Do you want to come back here?"

"If it's all the same to you, I'd rather not," I said with a grin. "Lily has informed me that I'm too old to hang out here, and the music's a little loud for my taste. Any reason you can't just swing by my office?"

That caught the kid off guard, like the thought of just coming over had never occurred to him. "Uh . . . I can do that, I guess, if you want. When?"

"We'll be in the office on Monday at zero-eight-hundred. See you there?"

"I'll be there," Dante agreed. We shook on it.

CHAPTER 6

One of the secrets to success as an investigator is building up a network of contacts and informants who will forward information you wouldn't otherwise have access to. I started the business shortly after coming home from the war and spent most of the subsequent decade doing just that. I made a lot of connections while I was in the service and some of them have proven beneficial in my entrepreneurial enterprises.

One such connection was the Baron, a former intelligence officer named Deitrik Freiherr von Hauser. We met on Harvest, where he served as a senior field officer for the Terran Confederation's Security Intelligence Service. My platoon spent several months escorting his team around the battlefield while they collected examples of alien technology.

We all called him the Baron because he technically held that title of nobility in the Pan-European Royal Court back on Earth. His title was nothing more than an honorific in Confederation service, and he seemed almost embarrassed to be referred to by it. Naturally, then, we insisted on addressing him that way.

It was just lighthearted ribbing. He was a good guy and we all liked him. He didn't complain, pulled his own weight, and kept his cool under fire. He was a quiet and reserved man but was unbothered by the off-color gallows humor of the infantry. The Baron, for all the crap we gave him about his lofty title, never complained about having to live and work with us grunts. We respected him for that.

After the war he went back to Earth for a few years before "retiring" on Nova Columbia. To hear him tell it, he left his title, his lands, and his privileges back home in order to open a restaurant on another planet. Now, maybe he always dreamed of being a frontier restauranteur, but one thing I learned about the intelligence world is that there's no such thing as a "former" spook. Once you're in, you're in for life, especially at the levels of access the Baron has.

That's what makes him a good source.

As usual, I met him at his establishment, a restaurant and cocktail lounge called Bauhaus Gaststätte, on the lower north side of the city. He usually refuses to discuss anything over electronic communications, even if it's end-to-end encrypted. If you want information from the Baron, first you have to earn his trust, then you have to meet him in person. The only way to do that is to sit down for a meal at his restaurant. The place is a little pricey for my taste, but damn, the food is good. It probably won't shock you to learn that authentic German cuisine, prepared by a human chef, is hard to come by on Nova Columbia, so I always make the most of my visits to

Bauhaus Gaststätte. Besides, he always gives me a big discount on account of how I saved his life once or twice.

After the server robot cleared the table and refilled my beer, the Baron sat across from me with a glass of wine. "How was your meal, Easy? Satisfactory, I hope?"

"I've never had a bad meal here, Deitrik. I've never even had a mediocre meal here. The Hollander schnitzel was fantastic."

"Good, good," he said, clearly pleased. "I've been training a new chef and it is she who prepared your meal."

"Give her my compliments, then," I said. It was late Sunday evening, near closing time, and I was the only customer in the place. "Also, thank you for seeing me."

"You are always welcome, even if you have questions for me. What are you working on now?"

"I'm looking for a woman named Cassandra Carmichael. She and her stepfather both work for Ascension."

"I see. Have you asked this man where she might be?"

"Not yet."

"Do you suspect him?"

"Maybe. I don't know yet. Her sister contacted him. In response he left a message stating that Cassandra is fine. My client didn't believe him."

"I suppose law enforcement was of no help?"

"They rarely are when Ascension is involved."

"Sadly true. There are many things I love about this world, but there are some things I am less fond of. The cozy relationship certain private entities like Ascension have with the government is unfortunate. Am I to assume that you would like me to place some inquiries as to this woman's possible whereabouts?"

"I would be grateful, but it might be more complicated than that. It seems she took an interest in whatever it is the company is doing up there in Hyperborea, near Mount Gilead."

"I have heard of it. Supposedly it is called Site 471."

Supposedly, he said. Deitrik never carelessly used a word like that. He was probing me, trying to see just how much I knew. I had to be careful what I divulged and what I kept to myself. I trusted him as much as you can trust anyone who works for the government, but his interests and mine didn't always necessarily align. I wasn't about to tell him about my contact with Arcanum, for starters. "Cassandra Carmichael was under the impression that Ascension found some alien tech up at that dig site, something they are trying to keep a lid on."

"It would be unfortunate for Ascension's shareholders if the company was found guilty of such a thing. It would mean the forfeiture of all company assets used to facilitate the crime and the prosecution of everyone involved. It might not be limited to their holdings on Nova Columbia, either. You suspect foul play, then?"

"It's a possibility. The stepfather is the sticking point, though. By all accounts he had a very good relationship with Cassandra. He helped her get her job there. You would have to be a cold bastard to raise a girl from childhood, caring for her for years, only to do something like that just to protect your job."

"Indeed, but he may well be a cold bastard, as you say."

"Maybe. Not much in his history, at least from what I've been able to dig up, that would indicate that, but it seems he is involved in whatever is going on at Site 471."

Deitrik frowned. "I see. Well, that certainly doesn't prove anything, but it does give one pause, doesn't it?"

"Yeah. Like I said, I haven't contacted him yet. Not sure if it would do more harm than good at this point."

"I will see what I can turn up. Perhaps there are some clues as to where this woman has gotten off to that might not be readily accessible to the public. Now . . . am I wrong in thinking that something else is on your mind?"

I was quiet for a few seconds. I wanted to choose my words carefully. "They've built a complex up there, at the dig site. Even if it's mostly underground, it's not the sort of thing that you could hide from a satellite. More than that, they were building a terraforming plant up there, an operation subject to government regulatory inspection. You can't keep them out without starting a bigger investigation. The bureaucracy takes its sweet time, but eventually, somebody in the government is going to ask what you're doing."

"That's a reasonable assumption."

"Sure, you could deflect for a while. You could tie up the proceedings with lawsuits and legal battles. You could buy yourself some time, but sooner or later the government is going to find out what's going on at the site. They'll get a warrant if they have to. Ascension has half the Commonwealth Congress bought off, but the other half campaigned on corporate accountability. There are plenty of crusading politicians, bureaucrats, and prosecutors who would love to be the ones to take Ascension down—illegally withholding the discovery of alien technology is a serious enough crime that they'd actually be able to pull it off."

"That is also a reasonable assumption. The penalties

for such an offense would be severe. It would be the end of the company."

"It would," I agreed. "It would be a huge risk. That leaves me with a bad feeling that maybe the government is in on this whole thing, officially or unofficially."

My host didn't say anything. He just sipped his wine.

"Deitrik, we've known each other a long time. I know there are things you can't tell me. I've never asked you to do anything that would get you in trouble."

"But?"

"But . . . I'm afraid I'm getting in over my head here."

"If what you have surmised is true, that seems unfortunately likely."

"Please don't play coy with me. I don't want to end up in prison for accidentally uncovering some secret military project."

He was quiet for a few moments. He sipped his wine again, his eyes darting back and forth while he chose his words. Deitrik was a deliberate man. He always said exactly what he meant to say and not a word more. "There are other possibilities that may explain the situation."

"Like what?"

"Perhaps there is no alien technology. Perhaps the rumor was started deliberately as a way of exposing leakers' corporate espionage assets. Cassandra Carmichael may have unwittingly gotten caught up in a ruse."

That didn't seem unreasonable. In fact, it sounded like exactly the sort of thing that a company like Ascension would do.

"I'm surprised that you haven't considered this," he said.

Truth be told, I was, too. In fact, at that moment I wanted to kick myself, not because I was certain his theory was correct, but because it hadn't even crossed my mind. Maybe I was getting sloppy. Maybe I just let my desire to help a beautiful woman cloud my judgment. "Even if that's the case," I said, "the fact remains that Cassandra Carmichael is missing. My job to find her, not to bring down Ascension or expose any corporate secrets."

"The safest course of action would be to walk away from the case," Deitrik said. "Regardless of what illegality Ascension is or is not engaging in, they have a lot of money and a lot of power. They have ruined people before."

"I know, but I took the case. I intend to see it through."

My host nodded. "I respect that, Easy. Just realize that this affair could get more complicated than you might expect." He glanced at his wristwatch, an old-fashioned mechanical one that was nonetheless designed for Nova Columbia's twenty-six-hour day. "*Ach*, it's past closing time. I'm going to have to ask you to excuse me."

I stood up to leave, and so did he. "Thank you, Deitrik. I mean that. I'll be on my way. I don't want to keep you any longer. Please let me know if you find anything."

"Of course. Watch for a dinner reservation confirmation. Then come by, enjoy a meal, and we'll talk again."

My conversation with the Baron was on my mind the next morning. It was Monday and I was in the office, waiting for Dante to show up. I sat in my chair, brooding, resisting the urge to fix myself a drink. Dagny was there, too, sitting in one of the chairs across from my desk, smoking a cigarette. She wore a tight black skirt that came down below her knees but had a long slit up the side. She sat cross-legged, the tattoo on her thigh barely visible beneath patterned hosiery. A well-tailored red blouse with an open collar was color-matched with a pair of platform pumps. The shirt and shoes were further complemented by bloodred lipstick and nail polish. She'd even recolored her hair highlights to a fiery red. She was striking to look at and only my professionalism kept me from gawking.

The moment Dagny walked into my office the first time, she brought a whole lot of trouble with her. There were so many pieces to this case: Dagny, Cassandra, their stepfather, Arcanum, and Ascension. The only ones who had the whole picture were myself and Lily. I didn't tell Deitrik about Arcanum, I didn't tell Dagny about Deitrik, and right then I didn't trust Arcanum enough to tell them much of anything.

Being honest with myself, I had to admit that Deitrik was right—the most sensible thing to do would be to just walk away from all this. I could already picture a lot of ways that this case could end badly for me.

I sighed, knowing full well I wasn't going to be able to do that. Despite what you might be thinking, it wasn't because of the woman sitting across from me, all legs, looking as pretty as a picture. When I turned thirteen my old man warned me that the easiest way for a man to get himself in trouble was to do his thinking with his pecker, and I had personal experience to back that up. In this business, that kind of poor judgment can ruin you or even get you killed.

This wasn't just about Dagny, though; it was about her

sister, and the implicit promise I made when I took the case. At least that's what I told myself. She glanced over and gave me a smile that would have melted a glacier, and then I wasn't so sure.

A video chat window popped up on my computer screen. It was Lily, who was at her desk out front. "He's here, Boss," she said.

"Send him in, please." She nodded and closed the window. I looked up at Dagny. "Follow my lead."

She nodded and stubbed out her cigarette.

The door slid open a moment later and Dante strode in. He was dressed in black again, this time with a long coat that went down to his knees and a small messenger bag slung over his shoulder. "Mr. Novak," he said, looking at me through those tinted smart glasses he wore. He noticed Dagny then and did a double take.

"Dagny Carmichael," she said, using her real name. She extended a hand upward to the burly young man.

He removed his glasses, leaned down, and accepted her handshake. "My friends call me Dante," he said, smooth as polished glass. If he was this much of a ladies' man it was no wonder his girl was so jealous.

"Thanks for stopping by," I said. I indicated the empty chair next to Dagny. "Please, have a seat."

"I was not expecting anyone else," Dante said delicately, sitting down. I could tell he didn't want to offend Dagny. Her presence caught him off guard, exactly as I'd hoped. He held the messenger bag in his lap.

"Normally I wouldn't bring a client into this," I explained, "but given the situation, with you returning her sister's effects, Dagny insisted."

"Oh. Of course. I will, presuming that you have the data that you promised."

"I'm a man of my word," I said, producing an inch-long portable drive from my pocket. I reached across the desk and offered it to Dante.

"Is this everything?" he asked, taking the device.

"No, but it's a lot," I assured him. "Like I said, she gathered a whole lot of documentation from Ascension. A good portion of it doesn't necessarily pertain to my case but still may be of interest to your organization."

"I hope you don't mind if I take a look," he said, putting his smart glasses back on.

"Be my guest. I'll wait."

Dante pulled out a bulky handheld, one that looked like it was armored, and plugged the drive into it. He stared into space, his eyes dimly illuminated by the glasses. He touched his thumb to the screen of his handheld and used it to scroll. "Holy shit," he said quietly.

"Lily wanted me to tell you that the authentication tags on all the documents are intact and that you can verify that."

"I see them. Yeah, this looks good." He took off the smart glasses and unplugged the drive from his handheld. "I have some friends who will be very excited to see this." He slid his handheld back into his pocket. He grabbed the messenger bag and offered it to me.

I nodded at Dagny. "Let her have it. Whatever is in there belongs to her sister."

"Right. Sorry." He turned and handed the bag to my client. "Here you are. This is everything that was in her wall safe. Nothing has been taken, not even the cash."

Dagny nodded and took the bag from him. I leaned back in my chair and didn't say anything as she opened it and began setting the contents on my desk. It was the sort of thing you'd expect a person to keep in her wall safe—documents, a passport, a bundle of what was probably a few thousand bucks in cash, and some jewelry. I didn't think any of it would be useful in helping us track down Cassandra Carmichael, but that didn't really matter. This was for Dagny.

"Oh my God," she said, covering her mouth with one hand. In the other, she lifted an ornate silver locket out of the bag.

"Everything okay?" I asked.

"Yes," she said. "It's just..." She trailed off as she opened the locket. A blue glow emanated from the pendant as it projected two small, three-dimensional holographic images, one from each side. The images were of two little girls with dark hair, one maybe a year or two older than the other. She stared at them for a few moments then closed the locket. She looked up at me, tears rolling down her cheeks. "This belonged to our mother. It was us when we were little. Our father—our real father, I mean—got this for her before he died. It... it hasn't worked right in years. She must have gotten it fixed." Dagny looked over at Dante. "Thank you. This... this means a lot to me."

"I, uh, I hope we're able to find your sister," Dante said, awkwardly. I didn't know that the contents of Cassandra's safe would elicit that kind of reaction from Dagny but it couldn't have gone any better if I did. Not only had I upheld my end of the bargain, but the young man was sitting next to a beautiful woman in need of help. Dante was a smooth operator but he didn't strike me as the cold, detached type who uses women and tosses them aside. I could tell he was a sucker for a pretty girl, especially one in distress.

Dagny wiped a tear from her eye and gently closed the locket. She looked up at Dante again and put a hand on his arm. "She said she was working with Arcanum. Can you help us? You got what you need, right?"

"What sort of help do you need? Cassandra never even told us what she was investigating. She just used our network of contacts and informants inside the company to gather information. She would barely tell us anything."

"You let her access your network without even finding out what she was working on?"

"It was a calculated risk," Dante said. "She's an Ascension insider herself, with access to high-level logistics information, which she was giving us before she disappeared."

"Have you heard from any of the other people she was talking to recently?"

Dante shook his head. "No. Since Cassandra disappeared the rest stopped talking to us. We don't want to put any of those people in danger, nor do we want to risk our own people. We've kind of set the whole thing aside for the time being."

"It's possible that was the intent," I said. There was also the possibility that when they got Cassandra, they made her divulge the identities of the people she was talking to, and that they've gone after them, too. I didn't say that part out loud. "That's probably the best move for your organization. Would you be willing to give me the contact info for the informants Cassandra was talking to?"

Dante raised an eyebrow again. "What do you intend to do?"

"Follow up. See if any of them are willing to talk to me. Maybe I can get something out of them."

"Do you really think they would talk to you when they won't talk to us?" he asked.

"Maybe. I'm just a private eye trying to locate a missing person, not a secretive hacktivist organization famous for exposing corruption. I'm not looking to go public with anything."

Dante rubbed his chin. "I hadn't thought of it like that. I will have to run this by the others."

"Come on, have I not established my trustworthiness?"

"I mean no offense, Mr. Novak, but we deliberate on all decisions." He glanced down and rapidly tapped the screen of his handheld with both thumbs. "There," he said, looking up. "I have forwarded your proposal."

I sighed. "How long does this usually take?"

Dante looked down at his handheld again, then back up at me. "Counteroffer: we will share this information with you if you agree to send us anything else you uncover on Ascension."

I only had to think about it for a moment. "Deal. Just remember, if you guys try to burn me I'll burn you right back. Do we understand each other?"

Dante's eyes narrowed. "I think we do." He looked down at his handheld again and tapped the screen. "There. I sent the information to your in-box. It's a list of the people we know of, within Ascension, who had been giving information to Cassandra Carmichael."

Dagny put her hand on top of Dante's and leaned in closer to him. "I can't thank you enough, Dante."

The kid, to his credit, was cool as ice. He slickly put his smart glasses on, then flashed Dagny a confident smile. "It was my pleasure. If you need anything, stop by the club anytime." He stood up and looked at me. "If there's nothing else, I'll be on my way."

With that, he was gone, leaving Dagny and me alone. We were quiet for a minute until I was sure that he'd left the office completely.

"You did good," I said, grinning. "You had that kid wrapped around your finger."

"What can I say?" Dagny said with a smirk. "I know what boys like. Between you and me, it's kind of nice to know that I've still got it, even with men a decade younger than me." I couldn't tell if she was humble-bragging or was genuinely concerned about getting older, but to my eyes she looked amazing. Anyway, thirty-five is still young, especially these days. "Besides," she continued, "I like to get dolled up once in a while. What's our next move?"

"I'm going to follow up on the contacts that that young man gave me, see if any of them can point me in the right direction."

"What if that doesn't pan out?" There was concern on her face now.

"Then I go to your stepfather directly. I'll hound him day and night if I have to."

"That might be risky."

"Somebody's got to do it. I'm sick and tired of how

Ascension can just do whatever the hell they want. Nobody should have that much power. It's past time somebody stood up to them."

"I didn't realize you were so passionate about this, Easy."

I hadn't realized it either, to be honest. Maybe it was just the pressure I was putting myself under, maybe it was how afraid of Ascension everyone was, but I had had enough. "Maybe the problem with this world is we're all too willing to accept an injustice because it's convenient and safe. Sure, we don't like it, but we tell ourselves that there's nothing we can do, or that if we try, we'll just make things harder on ourselves. They have all this power, all this money, and they're in bed with the government, so we just accept it. It's not right."

Dagny gave me a sly smile and rested her chin on her hand. "Didn't you just tell that young man that you weren't out to bring down Ascension?"

"I wasn't, but I'm starting to change my mind."

"You know," she said, cautiously, glancing down at her lap before looking back up into my eyes, "you don't have to do this alone. We make a pretty good team."

"This agency has a policy against getting the client directly involved in the investigatory process."

"Does it now?" Dagny asked, playfully. "What's the point of being your own boss if you can't bend the rules once in a while?"

"I suppose it's more of a guideline than a policy. It's not like I wrote it down or anything."

"Don Quixote didn't tilt at windmills alone. He had Sancho to watch his back."

At the time I didn't get the reference; I went to vocational school, not university, and I'd never read much classical Earth literature. "Alright, then. There might be some things I still have to do alone, but when I can use your help I'll let you know."

"Thank you," she said. "So . . . which contact should we try and track down first?"

CHAPTER 7

It was pouring rain the next afternoon when I swung by Starlight Tower to pick Dagny up. Remembering what happened the last time I was there, down in the parking garage, I stopped my car in the loading zone in front of the building and waited for her there. She came hurrying to the car and quickly climbed in.

"Wow," she said, pulling back the hood of her purple rain slicker. "It's really coming down out there. Oh, sorry, I got your seat wet."

"A little water isn't going to hurt anything. How are you doing today?" I pulled the car into the street while I spoke.

"As well as can be expected, I guess. Where are we headed?"

"We're going out to North Hampton."

"Way out there?" she asked. If you don't know your way around Delta City, North Hampton is a suburb in the northeast quadrant of the Crater. It's a place where people who either don't mind a long commute or can work remotely live if they don't want to be crammed into a hundred-story tower in the city. There aren't a lot of places zoned for single family houses in Delta City, and in those places the cost of living is sky-high. There's only so much room in the Crater and beyond it is the critical farmland necessary to feed tens of millions of people. Space is at a premium.

"Yup," I said. "We're going to have a visit with Dr. Ocean Ivery, a former scientist with Ascension's exobiological research division. Lily got ahold of her yesterday and she agreed to meet us, but only if we could talk face-to-face."

"Exobiological research? Like the study of alien life? This proves it, right, that they really did find something at Site 471? There isn't any alien life on Nova Columbia except for pseudo-moss and that purple slime that causes Kellerman's Syndrome."

"It's not the slime, it's the spores the slime releases into the air," I said. "Another possibility has occurred to me, that this business about alien technology might just be a ploy."

"A ploy? What do you mean?"

"Think about it. It's a sensational enough story to get all of the would-be whistleblowers, do-gooders, and leakers to tip their hands."

"You mean . . . you think Cassie was wrong? That's not like her."

"Anybody can be wrong," I said.

"No, I mean it's not like her to fall for something like that. She's skeptical by nature."

"For a trick like this to work, it would have to be believable enough to convince the skeptics."

"What about this scientist, then? She's an exobiological researcher."

"She is. Remember, though, Ascension's headquarters is on Nova Columbia. They have people from every scientific discipline on their payroll and send them off-world when needed. Dr. Ivery lives here, but from what Lily found, she's spent most of the decade since the war on other planets."

Dagny nodded, but looked dejected. I could tell she didn't like the idea that her sister may have fallen for a scam. "Let's say you're right, and they didn't find any alien artifacts up there. Where is Cassie? Wouldn't they just fire her?"

"That's what's been sticking in my craw," I said. "The only things the company could do to her are terminate her employment, sue her for breach of contract, or have her arrested if she did anything illegal. None of that would have resulted in her disappearing, unless . . ." I trailed off.

"Unless what?"

"It's a long shot, but . . . what if your sister *did* fall for an entrapment scheme, but your stepfather intervened to protect her? Shuffled her off somewhere until the heat's off? Maybe the reason he didn't tell you anything is because he knew his communications were being monitored."

"That does sound like Arthur," Dagny said. "Do you really think this could all be a trap?"

"I don't know what I think yet. We'll see what our contact says today. Something about this whole thing stinks either way. Regardless of whether or not there are any aliens at Site 471, we're going to get to the bottom of it."

"Thank you, Easy. I don't know what I'd do if I had to handle this on my own."

I grinned at her. "I'm just doing what you hired me to do. I'd appreciate it if you left a positive review of the business when all this is over."

That go a laugh out of her. "Deal. Hey, you said this scientist is a *former* researcher for Ascension?"

"Yup. She resigned a couple weeks ago. Lily was able to anonymously query Ascension's employee database to verify."

"You think that's why she's willing to talk? Because she quit?"

"If you're investigating an organization, a good way to get dirt on them is to talk on disgruntled ex-members. You've got to be careful, though, because sometimes people like that will exaggerate or just make things up. This is especially true if they were *fired* from a job, but as near as we can tell, Dr. Ivery quit of her own accord."

Dagny was quiet for a few moments as I maneuvered the car through stop-and-go traffic. "Isn't it weird that after all this secrecy and all these dead ends, someone you approach is suddenly willing to talk?"

"Yeah, it is," I said, nodding at her. "Now you're thinking like a snoop."

"What if they're trying to throw you off? You know, you talk to this scientist who tells you that everything is on the up and up and Ascension hasn't done anything wrong."

I was impressed with Dagny's conspiratorial thinking. "That's a possibility, and one you always need to keep in mind in this business. People who seem very credible will lie to your face. You have to learn to be able to tell when someone is lying, and even with experience it can be tough."

"Aren't there lie detectors you can use?"

"There are," I said. "I have a program called Truthsayer on my handheld. It analyzes voice patterns and face and eye movement to try and guess whether a person is telling you the truth. If you have smart glasses or an ocular implant it can give you real-time analysis as they talk, like a language translator program. I don't use it very much."

"Why not? Wouldn't that make your job easier?"

"Not really. It doesn't work as well as advertised, for one thing. There are so many variables to account for when people talk that even the best software is going to struggle to interpret it. The best lie detection systems require direct biometric data from the person being questioned in addition to voice and facial patterns. That's what the Security Intelligence Service uses for their interviews, for example, but even those are inadmissible in court by law. Too many ways to manipulate or misinterpret the data."

"Huh."

"Besides," I said, "in order for Truthsayer to work, it needs to be able to see the person's face and record their voice. Everyone knows tech like that exists. A lot of people won't talk to you if you're wearing smart glasses. There are hidden fiber-optic cameras, of course, but even those can be detected by a quick scan. People will wear face masks and use voice modulators when talking to you if they think you're going to try and run a lie detector on them. A lot of your professional criminals have been trained to spoof lie detection software, or they'll use drugs that alter the cues the software relies on. Either way, you still need to learn to get a read on people. I guess I just prefer to do things the old-fashioned way."

"Does this stuff ever just give you a headache?" Dagny asked, pinching the bridge of her nose.

I shrugged. "Nature of the business. It is what it is."

It was quiet for a few minutes before she said anything again. "Do you think this meeting could be a setup?"

"I don't know. Maybe they're just sending her to throw us off the trail. Even if she quit they might have gotten her to agree to it. Or, maybe she's genuine and she's willing to talk."

"Cassie told me every Ascension employee signs a nondisclosure agreement as a requirement for working there."

"All an NDA means is that you can be sued if you disclose information you were privy to, with certain exceptions like being deposed in court. You can say whatever you want if you're willing to risk a lawsuit. The worst thing they can do is bankrupt you with legal fees. Besides, reporting illegal activity is protected, regardless of what they made you sign."

Dagny looked down at her lap, then out the window. "I hope this pans out, Easy. I know you're doing everything you can, but each day that goes by I fear more and more than I'm never going to see Cassie again. It's all because I didn't check my blocked messages sooner. That was stupid."

"Don't be so hard on yourself. You didn't know what you didn't know. Let's say you had listened to that message as soon as it arrived. What would you have done with the information?"

"I guess I would have tried to track down Arcanum myself, but I wouldn't even know where to begin. I probably would have ended up in your office sooner or later anyway."

"And you already contacted your stepfather. You did what you could even without the message from your sister."

"Thank you," she said, looking at me with a sad smile. "You're sweet."

"Heh. My ex-wife would disagree with you there."

"You were married?"

"I was, a long time ago. Her name is Marian. We tied the knot right after I got home from the war. We had been, you know, kind of seeing each other before I got shipped out. When I got back I proposed and we shacked up right away."

"Oh. How'd that work out?"

I chuckled again. "Well, she's my ex-wife now, so you can probably guess. Honestly, we were both in too big of a hurry. I was so happy to be home that I just wanted to settle down and have, you know, a normal life. I think she fell in love with the man she thought I was and then was disappointed when I turned out to not be him. The whole thing lasted about two years."

"Do you have kids? I'm sorry, I'm being nosy."

"No kids," I said, smiling. "Anyways, I don't mind. If we're going to do this together, we need to trust each other."

"And what about now?" she asked. "Is there someone you're making jealous by spending all this time with me?"

I looked at her out of the corner of my eye when she said that, while trying to pay attention to the road. I wasn't sure if it was just small talk or if she was interested. I wasn't sure how I felt about that, with her being a client and all, but I was sure that I didn't want to embarrass myself by seeing something that wasn't there. "The only one waiting for me at home is Penny."

Dagny paused for a second, like she wasn't sure how to take that. "Oh. Who's Penny?"

I grinned. "My virtual domestic assistant. She's always happy to see me, she keeps the place clean, she cooks for me, and she doesn't worry if I stay out late."

That got a laugh out of her. "Well, I hope she isn't the jealous type. I'd hate for her to passive-aggressively burn your toast."

"I've got a question for you, too, if you don't mind me asking."

"What is it? I don't mind."

"It's not my business and if you want to keep it that way, that's fine. It just seems like you live on kind of the rough side of town, you don't have a car, and you haven't had the scar on your face repaired."

"But I do have the money to pay you," she said, completing the thought for me. "I was wondering if you were going to ask."

"Like I said, it's not my business. If it's something I'd be better off not knowing, then feel free not to tell me. I'm just curious."

"When we were little, our parents set us up long-term savings accounts, and they were maintained even after Dad died. My mother insisted on budgeting money to put into them all throughout our childhood and teenage years. I didn't have access to the account after the falling out with Mom and Arthur, and I thought for sure that they'd have cashed it out."

"But they didn't."

"No. In fact, Mom kept putting money into it, even while I was running around with the GLF, even while I was in prison. She put more money into it when she got sick. When she passed away, I found out that half her life insurance money had gone into the account. The other half went to Cassie."

"Sounds like your mom never gave up on you."

"She didn't," Dagny said. I could tell she was trying not to get choked up. "I was given access to the account after Mom died."

"But you didn't use it."

"I didn't. Sure, I could have gotten a car or maybe moved into a nicer place, but it didn't feel right. Mom spent years putting that money away for me. It seemed disrespectful to spend it on petty things like that, so I just kind of sat on it. Thought maybe it'd be nice to have a retirement fund."

"You have a day job, then?"

"More of a night job," she said. "I'm a manager at a club called The Luxy in midtown. I've been there for years. Started off as a cocktail waitress, moved up to bartender, and now I'm in management."

"They have human bartenders?" It wasn't unheard of, but it wasn't common. The Arcanum club, The Vault, had actual bouncers and a greeter girl at the door, but downstairs the bartending and cleaning was all automated.

Even the Baron's restaurant used robots instead of human waitstaff.

"We do. That's part of the Luxy experience—real people to take your order, talk with, whatever. The only robots in the place are for cleaning. The pay isn't amazing or anything but I get by. I've been putting money away myself to eventually upgrade to a nicer apartment."

It was interesting to learn that Dagny was so frugal and responsible with money. She looked like trouble, hell, she *brought* a heap of trouble with her, but she seemed to have her head on straight. I had to admit she was growing on me, and I began to wonder if that was clouding my judgment. I thought about what Deitrik had said and had to ask myself, was I doing this for the right reasons? Was I doing it because of the beautiful woman sitting next to me? Does it matter if you do the right thing for the wrong reason?

Was it the wrong reason?

It took another hour to get all the way across the Crater to North Hampton. Dr. Ivery insisted on meeting us in public. There was a big farmers' market set up in a city park and that's where she said she'd be waiting for us. The rain had stopped but the skies were still overcast and gray, pretty normal for Delta City in autumn.

This farmers' market is a biweekly occurrence in North Hampton throughout the summer and into the fall. The well-to-do happily pay top dollar for produce grown by independent farmers outside the city, especially for things that are hard to come by on this planet, like peaches and oranges. There's nothing wrong with the crops mass-produced by corporate farms, despite what the beatniks and the flower children tell you. Efficient industrial farming is the only way a barely terraformed frontier planet like Nova Columbia can feed a population of almost a hundred million. That said, I can't blame the farmers for capitalizing on demand like that. It helps keep the little guys in business.

The market was busy, especially seeing as how this was going to be the last one of the year. It took me a while to find a parking spot and Dagny and I had to walk a few blocks to get to the park. Rows of temporary booths and tents were set up as hundreds of vendors pushed their wares. This late in the afternoon, the crowd had thinned out some, but the market was still bustling with people.

"I don't get out of the city much," Dagny admitted, looking around. "We used to go to these every summer when I was a kid, but I haven't been to one since. It feels a little strange to look up and see nothing but sky." The city skyline could still be seen to the southwest, with its hundreds of monolithic towers disappearing into the low clouds, but the there were no tall buildings nearby. The market was crowded but people were packed in shoulder to shoulder like they were at events downtown. Nobody was wearing a respirator, either, as the native slime molds don't do well in open-air environments that get direct sunlight.

There was still plenty of daylight left, too, when downtown was already being overtaken by the shadows of its own structures. The living green of the grass and trees, the fresh air, and the relative quiet contrasted sharply with the noisy, congested, and often smelly world of ceramicrete, transparent aluminum, and nanotube-steel you can find in the city.

I looked down at my handheld and showed Dagny the screen. I had a map of the market pulled up. "We're here. We're supposed to meet Dr. Ivery over here. I hope this was worth the drive." We made our way through the crowd of suburbanites, between rows of booths and stands that were beginning to close up shop for the day. At the end of the row on the right was a large walk-in tent. The sign out front said they were selling bonsai trees.

With Dagny in tow I stepped into the tent. The short Japanese woman at the entrance welcomed us and said to come find her if we had any questions. I thanked her without really looking at her; I was focused on someone else. At the back of the tent, idly examining one of the little trees, was the person we'd come to meet. "That's her," I said to Dagny.

Dr. Ivery, dressed in white, looked up at us as we approached. She was a tall, fiftyish woman, lanky and androgynous, with skin so fair she looked pale. Her platinum-blond hair, accented by streaks of gray and white, was cropped short on the sides and combed back on top. Cybernetic eyes had replaced her natural ones. The implants covered both her eye sockets and made her look like she was wearing a small pair of goggles. She considered me coldly from behind blue-tinted lenses. "Mr. Novak?"

"I hope I didn't keep you waiting too long."

She looked at Dagny suspiciously. "Who is this?"

"My name is Dagny Carmichael," she said, offering her hand. "Thank you for meeting with us."

Dr. Ivery didn't take the offered handshake. "Walk with me," she said, and strode away. I looked at Dagny, shrugged, and followed after her. The doctor led us out of the farmers' market, down a paved walkway into the wooded portion of the park beyond.

About a hundred yards into the woods she stopped. An unpaved footpath branched off of the walkway and led to an enormous tree. It was a Western Red Cedar, one of the ones planted by the first settlers at Site Delta, and had to be two hundred feet tall. Its huge trunk was covered in moss and ivy and was surrounded by waist-high ceramicrete barriers. Signs were posted at the edge of the footpath warning people not to climb on or carve into the trees.

"Nice day for a nature hike," I said, breaking the silence.

The doctor looked up at the towering tree, like she was contemplating it for a moment, then back down at us. "I apologize. I am merely trying to be cautious. I was not expecting two of you and I do not want to have this conversation in front of strangers."

I looked around. It was a gloomy, rainy day and there was no one else around. "Dagny here is my client. Cassandra Carmichael is her sister. She's gone missing."

"I was afraid of this," the scientist said. "When she first approached me I warned her that it could be dangerous."

"So you were in touch with Cassandra Carmichael. Did Arcanum put you in touch with her?"

"Who?"

"Arcanum? Activist group? Sound familiar?"

Dr. Ivery stared at me like I was stupid. "I have had no contact with any such organization, Mr. Novak."

Interesting, I thought. *Cassandra obviously gave this woman's name to Arcanum, but she's not one of their informants.* "When was the last time you spoke with her?"

"With who?"

"Cassandra Carmichael," I said. "Are you okay, Doctor?"

She looked down for a moment and took a deep breath. "Yes. I am...tired, is all. The last time I saw her was thirty-four days ago."

"Thirty-four days?" Dagny asked. "She's been missing for two months! Where did you see her?"

Dr. Ivery looked perplexed. "She was assigned to Site 471. Her father helped her secure the position there. The company is unfortunately rife with that sort of nepotism these days."

Dagny put a hand on Dr. Ivery's arm. The scientist stiffened when touched but stopped herself from recoiling. "So my sister...she was just transferred up there? For *work*?"

"Yes. Were you not aware?"

"We were not, Doctor," I admitted.

"Arthur was telling the truth," Dagny said, shaking her head. "Wait. This doesn't make any sense. Why would she have left me that message, then? Dr. Ivery, what's going on up there? Where's Cassie now?" She was gripping the doctor's arm tightly now, and I could tell it was making the scientist uncomfortable.

"Whoa, whoa, let's all take a breath here, okay?" Dagny let go of Dr. Ivery's arm and folded her own arms across her chest. I turned my attention to the scientist. "How did you meet Cassandra Carmichael?"

"I was introduced to her when she was assigned to the project," the scientist said.

"Is that Project Isaiah?" I asked.

"Yes. I was responsible for her onboarding process and giving her the required briefings. We did not actually meet in person until after she had arrived at the site."

"I understand you resigned from the company a couple of weeks ago."

"I did. You caught me just in time. I have a flight booked to L5 Station in two days."

"L5 Station? Taking a trip off-world?" L5 Station is Nova Columbia's main port of entry to interstellar traffic. It's where most warp-capable ships will dock between flights.

"I am returning to Earth," the doctor said. "I wish to be far away from this place."

"Forty-six light-years is pretty far," I said. "Why did you quit the company?"

She was quiet again. Her prosthetic eyes glinted in the afternoon light as she studied Dagny and me. She was trying to decide how much to tell us. "How much do you know?"

"Not enough," I said. "They supposedly found something they think might be alien technology. I don't know what it is or anything about it, just that it's called the Seraph. Look, I didn't take this case looking to expose any company secrets. I just want to find a missing woman."

Dr. Ivery looked up a little and stared off into the distance. "The Seraph," she repeated. "When they read me into the program I thought they were being fanciful with the name. When I finally saw it, though . . ." She trailed off, then looked me in the eye. "If anything, a religious reference does not do it justice. It's magnificent . . . and terrifying."

"So it's real?" Dagny said, excitedly. "There really *is* alien technology up there?"

"Indeed," The scientist said. "They found it under Mount Gilead, but it is far older than the volcano."

"It's older than the *volcano*?" I asked, incredulously.

"Oh yes," the scientist answered. "Mount Gilead began forming approximately two hundred thousand years ago. The strata in which they found the Seraph is at least sixty-eight million years old."

"Sixty-eight million years? Is it some relic from the First Antecessor Race?" I asked.

"No," the scientist said. "It is something wholly different. The First Antecessor Race was advanced, of course, incredibly advanced, but they were still carbon-based beings. Like us, they were finite and . . . mortal. They lived, they created, they reproduced, and they died, just like every other life-form we have encountered."

"I don't follow," I said. "Is the Seraph a living being?"

"No," Dr. Ivery said, "and yes. It is not biological life as we understand it. It is something wholly different from anything humanity has encountered thus far. The size of it alone is terrifying."

"What do you mean?" I asked.

"It's massive, larger than any life-form ever encountered. It has been buried here for sixty-eight million years, waiting for someone to find it."

"Wait, it's not dead?" I asked.

"Dead?" She looked at me, her bionic eyes shuttering

closed a couple of times, mimicking blinking. "No, it is not dead, not in the way you mean. It appears to be an inert husk, but somehow it is still . . . aware. Sixty-eight million years and it is *not dead*. I do not know that it *can* die."

"I don't understand," Dagny said.

"Neither do I," the scientist admitted. Her voice cracked a little, like she was going to start crying. "You . . . you would not believe the things I have seen, the things it showed me."

"What *it* showed you?" Dagny said. "You mean the Seraph?"

Dr. Ivery ignored her question and kept rambling. "It is not like anything we have ever encountered. It . . . it is *magnificent* . . . and terrifying. Just looking at it makes you realize how insignificant we really are, how little we understand."

"Doc? Doc!" I said, getting her attention again. "Do you need help? Are you in danger?"

"We all are," she said. "I apologize. I am not . . . I am not myself. I have not been sleeping. I have been taking medication and I still cannot sleep. It is because of the psychological contamination. It strains the mind." She didn't bother to explain what that meant. "That is all I know. I have not been back there. I *will not* go back there."

I gently put a hand on Dr. Ivery's arm. She was shaking. "We're not asking you to go back there, Doctor. I'm just trying to find Cassandra Carmichael. Do you know where she is?"

"I am sorry, I do not."

"From what you told us, it sounds like she left Site 471 before you quit."

"There was an . . . incident," the scientist said, slowly, her voice little more than a whisper. "It was my fault. This is all my fault."

"Slow down, Doctor. Nobody is blaming you."

"We disturbed it. It was . . . I do not know that you can assign human emotions to something so alien, but as near as we could understand, it was . . . it was confused. Lost. Intruded upon. We thought we could . . . we presumed . . . to communicate with it. We used a neural interface. That was my idea. It was successful at first, but . . ." She trailed off, slowly shaking her head. "It quickly became too much. I would not go back in, I *could not*. I refused, but it . . . the Seraph . . . would not be denied. It demanded another . . . so we gave it Cassandra Carmichael."

"What do you mean you *gave* it my sister?" Dagny said, almost shouting at the woman. "What did you people do to her?"

"It was not like that. She . . . she volunteered. Somebody had to. I could not, not again. No one else would."

I held up a hand. "Doctor, listen to me. It seems like you have a lot to say. Will you come with me? Will you go on the record? You can still make your flight. I can keep you safe until you get off-world. The authorities have to be alerted to what's going on up there."

"The authorities?" she asked, tilting her head slightly to the side. "They know. They have had observers on-site from the start."

She confirmed my worst fears. "Who are these observers? What agency or branch?"

"We were told not to ask. I think they are intelligence officers. Off-worlders, I think, guessing from the accents."

"Off-worlders? You mean Terran Confederation?"

"Easy!" Dagny interrupted, tugging on my jacket sleeve. "Look!"

Coming down the path from the direction of the farmers' market were two people dressed alike. One was of average build, the other was a big guy, tall and heavyset. They both wore black protective jumpsuits—the kind with armor plates that motorcyclists like to wear—and bright green jackets with the collars popped up. Their faces were concealed under green-and-black full-face helmets. From the other direction up the path, two more guys approached, dressed in the same getup.

"Who . . . who are they?" Dr. Ivery asked.

"Green Dragons," I said, quietly. That clearly didn't ring a bell for her, so I explained. "They're a street gang from East Central. Come on." Taking her by the arm, I led Dr. Ivery down the trail away from the main pathway and toward the big tree.

"Where are we going?" Dagny asked, following closely behind. "What do these guys want?"

"The barriers around that tree will give us some cover if things go sideways."

"Sideways?" the scientist asked. "What does that mean?"

"It means this might get ugly, Doc," I said, hurrying her along. "When we get to the tree, I want you to take cover and stay there until I tell you it's safe to come out. Do you understand?"

"This cannot . . . this cannot be happening. Are they here to kill me?"

I didn't have an answer for her. If Ascension wanted Dr. Ivery dead, you'd think a company with all their resources would have better ways to do it than hiring a bunch of street hoodlums to do the job. On the other hand, maybe having the Green Dragons do their dirty work for them would give them a measure of deniability. "Just keep your head down," I told her, pushing her behind the closest barrier. "I'll handle this."

As I expected, all four of the Green Dragons turned off the paved walkway and followed us up the footpath toward the tree. They approached in a cluster, all with their hands in their jacket pockets.

Dagny had her handheld out. "I can't get signal to call anybody."

"They might be jamming us somehow. You got that gun on you?"

"Of course."

"Now's the time," I said, drawing my revolver from under my jacket. Holding it at the low-ready, I raised my voice and spoke to the approaching gangsters. "Nice day for a walk in the park, isn't it?"

They stopped maybe twenty feet away, hands still in their pockets. The big guy took a step forward. I snapped my gun up and had it pointed right at his face. The reticule of the little holographic sight was right on the visor of his helmet. He cocked his head to the side a little. "Why so aggro, pops? Can't we look at the trees, too?" His voice was disguised by a modulator in his helmet.

"Yeah," the guy next to him said. "What's this city

coming to where you can't even visit a park without getting a gun pulled on you?"

They all chuckled at his little joke. Dagny had her gun drawn, too, but they hadn't flashed a weapon yet. Keeping my gun trained on the big guy, I asked him, "What are you boys doing all the way out in North Hampton? You're a long way from East Central."

"Maybe we're expanding," the big guy said.

"Or maybe we just like trees," his buddy next to him added. "You got a problem with that?"

"No problem," I answered. "You want to look at the trees, you can look all you want. Just step aside so my friends and I can be on our way."

"We don't want any trouble," Dagny said.

"You hear that?" the big gangster asked. "They don't want any trouble!" They all chuckled again.

A bead of sweat rolled down my temple from under my hat. I was calm but my heart was racing. What were they planning? We had them dead to rights, and none of them had pulled a weapon yet. Why would they corner us like this but let us draw down on them?

I figured it out a second later, but it was a second too late.

"Mr. Novak!" Dr. Ivery cried, grabbing my arm over the top of the barrier. I turned around just in time to see a fifth Green Dragon come up behind her and plunge a short sword into her back.

"Doc!" The gangster shoved the scientist off his blade. Stepping around the barrier I was able to catch her before she fell. The Green Dragon turned to run, but he wasn't fast enough. I shot him in the back as he tried to vault over one of the ceramicrete barriers. He dropped his sword and crumpled to the ground in a heap.

Gunfire echoed through the trees as Dagny opened fire. I was busy lowering Dr. Ivery to the ground behind the barrier, trying to see if there was anything I could do for her. I had a small first-aid kit in my jacket pocket but it looked like the son of a bitch had stabbed her right through the heart. Blood poured out of her wounds and onto the mossy ground.

"Easy!" Dagny cried. She was trying to get behind another one of the barriers when two rounds caught her in the back.

"Dagny!" Transferring my gun to my right hand, I leaned out from behind the barrier. One of the Green Dragons was facedown and another was wounded. All three, including the wounded man, had pistols drawn.

The big guy, the one I thought was their leader, he was closest. I fired twice, shooting him first in the gut and then in the chest. The protective armor of his motorcycle gear was no match for APHE rounds. He shrieked as he fell, his voice distorted by his modulator.

"He got Chud!" another of the Green Dragons shouted. I ducked back behind the barrier as the surviving gangsters started shooting again. Bullets whizzed past, smacking into the barriers and the old tree. Hitting the release lever with my thumb, I ejected the partially expended cylinder from my revolver and grabbed a fresh one from a holder on my shoulder harness. I pushed the new cylinder down and locked it into place.

Dagny had managed to sit up, her back to the ceramicrete barrier. She was bleeding, bad, but she was still conscious. She nodded at me then, reaching up and behind her, stuck her pistol over the top of the barrier and blindly fired. There was no way she'd hit anything like that but she didn't need to. All I needed was some suppressing fire. I didn't want to appear in the same spot twice, so instead of leaning around the barrier this time I popped up over it.

The last two Green Dragons were running away. The wounded man was being helped along by his buddy. I held my gun on them for a few seconds but didn't fire. When they were out of sight, I turned my attention to the wounded.

"We make a good team, Easy," Dagny said weakly as I knelt next to her.

"We sure do. Can you lean forward? I need to see your back."

"I'm okay," she said, but did as I asked. She was definitely not okay. Two pistol slugs had gone into her back. One had struck high, hitting her in the shoulder. The other had gone low, punching a hole into her guts from behind. Both missed the spine, but she was losing a lot of blood.

I opened my first-aid kit and grabbed the shears. "I need to cut your jacket and shirt off," I said. "I need to patch up those holes."

"If you wanted to get my clothes off all you had to do was ask," she said, grimacing through the pain.

I chuckled humorlessly, cutting through her purple raincoat, shirt, and bra strap. "Hold still. This is going to hurt." I cleaned the area around the bullet holes, then injected the wounds with hemostatic foam. She cried out in pain as I did this but didn't move. Once the wounds were filled, I covered each one with a seal. "Okay, that's it," I said, gently lowering her back against the barrier. "I know it hurts but you should sit up if you can."

She nodded haltingly. "Check on Dr. Ivery."

"Yeah. Sit tight." Keeping an eye out in case the Green Dragons came back, I knelt by Dr. Ivery and checked her pulse. It was weak and there wasn't much I could do for her. Even if I could stop the bleeding with what supplies I had left, she'd been stabbed right through the heart. Without immediate trauma surgery . . . well, it didn't look good.

Somehow she was still conscious. She looked up at me, the cybernetic lenses she had for eyes irising. "Am I going to die?"

I was quiet for a second. I hadn't had a conversation like this since the war. "Yes. I'm sorry."

She reached into a pocket of her tunic and grabbed something. She held it out to me in a trembling, bloody hand. It was a plastic wafer, maybe an inch in diameter, infused with circuitry. I looked at her. "What is this?"

"In my home," she gasped, her voice gurgling slightly. "D-Diana . . ."

"Who's Diana?"

Dr. Ivery didn't answer. She was gone. *Damn it to hell.* There was no time to dwell on the situation. I stashed the little disk in a hidden compartment inside my hat and went back over to check on Dagny.

"You still with me?" Sirens warbled in the distance, growing closer.

"Yeah," she croaked. "I'm still here. How's Dr. Ivery?"

"She didn't make it. Listen, I think SecFor will be here soon. They'll get you to a hospital. You hang in there, you hear me?"

Dagny grabbed my hand and squeezed. "Stay with me."

"You got it."

A drone appeared over the trees and descended toward us. The quad-copter, maybe six feet across and painted blue and white, hovered overhead and addressed us through a loudspeaker. "This is the Colonial Security Forces," a synthesized voice said. "Remain where you are. Troopers are en route to your location."

"She needs medical attention!" I shouted, pointing at Dagny. "She's been shot!" I knew the drone was transmitting its camera feed, or would be if it could get past the signal jamming. I crouched next to her, holding her hand, and waited for SecFor to show up.

CHAPTER 8

I spent the next few hours sitting in a jail cell at the North Hampton Security Forces post. They'd confiscated all of my possessions, including my clothes, and gave me an orange prison jumpsuit to wear. Don't get the wrong idea, I'd been well within my rights to shoot those skags. They murdered Dr. Ivery and attempted to do the same to Dagny and me. It was self-defense, but SecFor was still trying to sort out what happened. They never found the radio frequency jammer that the Green Dragons used and I wasn't sure they believed me when I told them our attackers were using one. It had probably been in the pocket of one of the guys who got away.

I wasn't being especially cooperative, either. All I told Security Forces troopers was a statement that we had been attacked, that we defended ourselves, and that I wouldn't say anything else without my lawyer. In my experience, even if you think you're in the right, even if you think you acted lawfully, you should never talk to law enforcement without legal counsel. Don't lie, but don't

volunteer information, either. Keep your mouth shut and
wait for a lawyer, especially if you were found near four
dead bodies in a city park. I didn't tell them about what
Dr. Ivery had given me and was betting that they wouldn't
find it.

When given the opportunity I called Lily and told her
I'd been arrested. I only gave her a quick rundown of what
happened, since I couldn't be sure the call wasn't being
monitored, and told her to get ahold of Dwight Cullender.
When he made the offer to assist me if I ever needed it, I
didn't think I'd be taking him up on it within a matter of
days, but I wasn't going to turn down the help. Even in a
clear-cut instance of lawful self-defense, an overzealous
prosecutor can make your life miserable. Even if you're
eventually cleared, they can still bankrupt you with legal
expenses.

Dagny was in the hospital, so far as I knew. The
responding Security Forces troopers called for an air
ambulance when they got on scene and it arrived a short
while later. I watched the medics load her onto the VTOL
bird as troopers cuffed me and took me into custody. Even
if they decided to charge me, I hoped to hell they didn't
charge her, too. She'd had a bad enough time of it,
between watching Dr. Ivery die, having to kill a man, and
being shot twice herself. She was tough, but that was a lot
for anyone to handle, especially when it all happened in
just a couple minutes. I planned on going to see her
whenever I got released.

In the meantime, there wasn't anything for me to do
but sit on the bunk and stare at the wall. By law, they
could hold me for up to fifty-two hours, after which time

they either had to release me or charge me with
something. Depending on which district you find yourself
in, sometimes they'll hold you for that long just to
inconvenience you. Either way, I thought I might be here
a while. The best thing to do was to get comfortable, wait
it out, and don't let them see you sweat. At 23:00 hours
the lights went out. I rolled onto my side and decided to
get some shut-eye. I'd had a pretty rough day myself and
I was exhausted. It didn't take me long at all to fall
asleep.

I was startled awake some time later when the lights in
my cell came back on. Only a few hours had past and it
wasn't wake-up time yet. I sat up on my bunk, rubbing my
eyes, wondering what the hell was going on.

"Novak, you have a visitor." The voice had come from
the speaker by the cell door.

"What?"

"You have a visitor. Get up and stand against the back
wall of the cell. See the footprints painted on the floor?
Put your feet there." I did as I was told, figuring it was
Dwight Cullender. I was pretty surprised that he'd come
in the middle of the night, but I wasn't going to fault the
man for getting over here as quickly as he could.

Once I was up against the back wall, the door slid open.
It wasn't the lawyer who walked in but the Baron, holding
his fedora in his hands.

"Deitrik?" I asked. "What are you doing here?"

Before he could answer, the door slid shut behind him.
"You got ten minutes," a voice said over the loudspeaker.

"Thank you," Deitrik said, but the intercom had
already turned off. We were alone. "Good morning, Easy,"

he said, taking a few steps into the cell. "I'm sorry to call on you at this hour, but the matter is urgent."

"Yeah, well, I've got time to talk, as you can see. I didn't expect you to visit me. What's going on?"

"The Security Forces are under the impression that I'm an attorney. By law they cannot listen to this conversation, so for the moment we have privacy. Dr. Ocean Ivery is dead. What happened?"

"She is," I confirmed, then got him up to speed on what had gone down, leaving out the part where the scientist gave me the small plastic wafer. "Do you know how Dagny Blake is doing?"

"She's at Mercy Medical Center North and is in stable condition."

"Oh, thank God." I'd done as good a job patching up her wounds as I could, but she'd lost a lot of blood before the medics got to her. Even with the best medical treatment available, a person can still die from complications after being shot.

"Dr. Ivery's death is a tragedy, not only for the loss of human life, but because she had been privy to what was going on at Site 471."

I wasn't sure if Deitrik actually knew that or was trying to get me to confirm his suspicions, but I wasn't in the mood for skullduggery. "She was. She told me as much herself before she was killed. Since I know you're going to ask, no, I don't think it was a coincidence or bad luck. I think somebody put a hit out on her and used the Green Dragons as a cutout to do the deed. The ones who got away will probably end up dead before they ever get paid."

"As a matter of fact," Deitrik said, "the authorities found two dead men, both in their twenties, wearing the colors of the Green Dragons gang. Both had been shot in the head from close range. No cameras or sensors managed to record the murders and they don't have a suspect."

"Of course," I said, shaking my head. "Couldn't leave a loose end like that running around. Deitrik, I think we can safely assume that the activity at Site 471 is not some ploy to unmask informants and industrial spies. They're willing to kill to protect it."

"What did she tell you?"

"Enough. She told me enough. Why are you here? I don't suppose you've come to tell me that you located Cassandra Carmichael?"

"I'm afraid not. My inquiries thus far have been frustrated at every turn."

"Dr. Ivery believed that the government is aware of what Ascension is doing up at Site 471. She said there were observers from the Confederation—intelligence, she thought."

Deitrik didn't say anything for a moment. "Is that so?"

"That's what she told me."

"Interesting. What will you do now?"

"I don't know," I admitted. "I need to talk to Dagny and see what she wants. She could have been killed." I sighed. The whole thing was damned frustrating. "For the time being, it seems like I'm going to stew in here."

"Ah, yes," Deitrik said, as if he'd just remembered something. "About that. I have secured your release and have been assured that the district attorney won't press charges."

"What? How did you manage that?"

He shrugged. "The DA is an acquaintance of mine and a frequent customer at my restaurant. However, there is something I need from you."

"Really," I said, folding my arms across my chest. "What might that be?"

"Six people are dead. The situation is rapidly escalating and we need to get to the bottom of it. You have had much better luck uncovering things than I have had so far. I need you to keep going, broaden the scope of your investigation, and keep me appraised of your findings."

"In what way? I was hired to find Cassandra Carmichael and that's what I intend to do."

"I am aware, and you will of course continue to do so, but this may be more than just a missing person case. You will be compensated, of course. I am a man of means and will make it worth your while."

"You're asking me to compromise my client's privacy in violation of her contract with me."

"I am aware of that as well. I do not take this action lightly, Easy. Whatever is going on merits further investigation, and I want you to pursue it."

"And if I refuse?"

"That would be unfortunate. Your presumed cooperation is what allowed me to convince the DA to let this matter go. Without that, I won't be able to help you. You'll be at the mercy of the justice system."

I shook my head and chuckled humorlessly. "So it's like that, is it?"

"I understand your frustration but I'm trying to help you. I need you to trust me."

That was the trouble with someone like the Baron. As much as you might want to, you can't ever really trust someone like him. His loyalty is with the system, and protecting it will always come first. On the other hand, what choice did I have? The unspoken threat was that if I didn't agree, the DA would press charges on me. I might eventually be vindicated in court, but in the meantime they'd make my life hell, and there was always the possibility that they'd keep me imprisoned until trial. I was also worried about Dagny. With me locked in the clink she was all alone. "Fine. You win. I'll do what you want, on the condition that you also guarantee that Dagny is protected from prosecution."

He seemed satisfied with that. "Consider it done. Thank you, Easy. It will take a little while, but you should be out of here this morning. I will be waiting for you when you are released."

He was true to his word. Within a few hours I had been released and my belongings were returned to me. It was a cool, gray, rainy morning as I left the Security Forces station. The Baron was waiting for me on the sidewalk out front. "Good morning," he said, as I approached.

"As good as a morning can be when you woke up in jail," I said, tersely.

The Baron shrugged. "Most people who wake up in jail will still be there at the end of the day. The district attorney has signed off on the decision not to press charges on either you or Miss Blake, citing a case of lawful self-defense. They have even agreed to waive the impound fee for your car."

"Mighty generous of them. Look, Deitrik, I don't want

you to think I don't appreciate you helping me out, because I do."

"I know you're not happy about the situation. That's understandable. Again, though, please trust me."

"Trust can be difficult sometimes. You're putting a lot of trust in me, you know. What will you do if I don't uphold my end of the bargain now? Try to get the DA to reverse himself and charge me?"

"I don't think it'll be an issue," he said.

"What is your role in all this? Who do you really work for?"

As I expected, the Baron didn't answer. He patted me on the shoulder, turned, and walked away, leaving me standing in the rain.

Between getting my car out of the impound lot and driving across town in morning traffic, it took me a while to get to the hospital. On the drive over I called Lily and brought her up to speed on everything that had happened.

"So that's it?" she asked. "We're just going to give him everything we have on the case?"

"I think it's in our best interest if we go along with this for now," I said, mindful of the fact that my handheld could have been bugged while I was in jail. SecFor couldn't legally do anything like that, but the Baron seemed to operate under his own rules. "We'll talk about it more when I get back to the office."

"You going to see Dagny?"

"Yeah."

"I'm glad she made it. I'm sorry about Dr. Ivery. Did . . . did we get that woman killed, Boss?"

I sighed. It had been gnawing at me, too. "The only ones to blame for her death are the people who murdered her," I said, trying to convince myself as much as Lily. "Besides . . . odds are, they were never going to let her get off Nova Columbia alive. Sooner or later they would have made a move."

"I hope you're right," Lily said. "Give my best to Dagny when you see her."

"Will do. Talk to you later." When I ended the call, my handheld notified me that I had a message from Dagny. She said that she'd just woken up and told me what room of the hospital she was in. I sent a quick reply, telling her that I was on my way over, and asking her to make sure the hospital would let me in to see her. Sometimes they restrict who they allow to see patients.

Dagny's face lit up when I walked into her hospital room. "Easy!" she said, happily. She was sitting up in bed looking at her handheld. An IV tube was sticking into her arm.

"Here, these are for you." I handed her the bouquet of flowers I bought at the gift shop in the hospital lobby.

"You brought me flowers?" She smiled at me. "You're a real sweetheart, you know that? You act tough but you've got a heart of gold. Come here." Before I could say anything, she reached up, wrapped her arms around me, and hugged me. "Thank you for everything. You saved my life."

"Yeah, well . . . I'm just glad you're alright. How are you doing?"

She let go of me and settled back into her bed. "I am

really high," she said with a smile. "They shot me up with a bunch of drugs. I'm not in any pain right now, but they tell me it'll hurt later. I was lucky. They were able to surgically repair the tissue and bone. It'll take me a few weeks to heal but I should make a full recovery. No infections."

"Let's be grateful for gangbangers who can't shoot worth a damn," I said. "How long are you going to be in here?"

"They want to keep me overnight for observation. I should be released tomorrow morning. What happened to you? Where did you go?"

I closed the door, sat down in a chair next to her bed, and held my hat in my hands. "I spent the night in jail."

"Oh wow."

"Eh, wasn't the first time."

"What for? We were defending ourselves!"

"It's complicated." I took a few minutes to explain to her everything that had happened to me the night before, including my encounter with the Baron. I explained who he was, how we met, and how he came to be involved in the case. "He didn't want me to tell you any of this," I said, "but keeping it from you didn't seem right. You're the client. This is your case. You have a right to know that my investigation is . . . well, it's compromised, in a manner of speaking."

"Wow," Dagny said again. "This is a lot to take in."

"I was worried that if I didn't go along with it, they'd come after you as well. I never should have brought you with me out there. I'm sorry. I screwed up and you could have been killed. Listen . . . it might be time to let this go."

"Are you saying we should just give up? After coming this far?"

"Knowing when to hold and when to fold isn't just good advice for poker," I said. "This isn't just a case of a missing person anymore. These people are playing for keeps, I've got someone from the Security Intelligence Service breathing down my neck, and I can't guarantee client confidentiality anymore. I know you want to find your sister, but that won't happen if you're dead."

She looked up at me angrily. "Why did you tell him any of this? Why did you get him involved?"

"He's been a good source in the past, especially for cases like this. He's never tried to butt in like this before, either. You know, though, if not for him, I'd still be in jail and both of us might be looking at criminal charges. I couldn't risk that happening to you. I'm sorry."

She reached over and squeezed my hand. "It's okay, Easy. I understand. I was the one who wanted to be there, remember? I'm a big girl. I can make my own decisions."

I smiled. "I never doubted that for a second."

"I thought about this a lot last night, while they were prepping me for surgery. I don't want to let this go, not even after what happened. They *murdered* Dr. Ivery and tried to kill us! They can't get away with it. It's not right."

"It's not, no, but sometimes that's how the world is."

"That doesn't mean we have to just lie down and accept it," she said, firmly. "No, I'm not giving up now." She looked up at me again. "Are you still willing to be my detective? You risked your life trying to protect me and a woman you didn't even know. I've brought you nothing but trouble, got you arrested, almost got you killed, and what do you do? You come to see me in the hospital and you brought me flowers. Even if you do have this Baron guy on your back there's nobody I trust more right now. I want to see this through to the end, whatever that might be, if you're willing."

I was quiet for a few moments, thinking real hard about what to say next. The smart thing to do would be to walk away. I'd pushed my luck far enough, and given how the case was spiraling out of control, it seemed less and less likely that this would end with a teary reunion for Dagny and her sister.

"I've never backed out of a case," I said, looking her in the eye. "I don't intend to start today."

Dagny nodded. "Thank you, Easy. You're a good guy."

I felt myself blushing a little. "I'm a lousy poker player, though."

"Hey, can I ask you something?" Dagny asked. "How did you become a private detective? It just seems like an odd job choice for someone who went to school to be an automated systems technician." I glanced over at her, surprised, when she said that. "What?" she asked. "You have the certificate on your office wall."

Impressive attention to detail, I thought. I chuckled again. "To be honest, it wasn't my idea. The agency was founded by my friend Victor Redgrave."

"He was your, um, sergeant, in the war, right?"

"The same."

"You said he bequeathed you that big gun you carry. He passed away?"

I sighed. "He did. Eight years ago now."

"How did he die?" Dagny asked, matter-of-factly. Her

openness and lack of candor was likely a product of whatever painkillers they had her on.

I was quiet for a few seconds. I hadn't told anyone about this in years. "He was murdered."

Dagny's eyes went wide. "Oh no! I'm so sorry. What happened?"

"Red had this idea to start a detective agency when he got home. Apparently he had an ancestor who did it back on Earth and he was in love with the idea. I thought the idea was kind of dumb, to be honest."

"But you didn't have the heart to tell him," Dagny said.

"Huh? Oh no, I told him. I was pretty blunt about it, too." That got a laugh out of her. "He didn't listen to my naysaying, though. Told me that if he got his agency off the ground, he'd hire me when we got home. After my divorce from Marian, I was looking for a change, so I gave him a call. He was good to his word, hired me on and started training me. About a year later he made me a full partner."

"But he was murdered?"

"He was. We got hired by an off-world businessman, a rich Japanese fellow named Murayama Masahiro. We provided protection for him and investigated potential threats. It was good work and he paid us well."

"Was somebody after him?"

"Oh yeah. The Yakuza were after him."

"What's a Yakuza?"

"Japanese organized crime syndicates. They go back to the seventeenth century on Earth. You'll find them everywhere there's a Japanese population."

"Oh wow. That's crazy! What happened?"

"We were escorting Masahiro while he inspected one of his properties, a casino he was building, when the Yakuza made their move. It would have worked, too, if they weren't so damned old-fashioned about how they operate."

"Old fashioned? How do you mean?"

I chuckled humorlessly. "They tried to kill him with a sword."

"A sword? The guy who killed Dr. Ivery had a sword!"

"He did," I said, vividly recalling the look on her face when she'd been stabbed through the heart. I knew right then that that image would be with me the rest of my life. "The Green Dragons are just a bunch of punks, though, petty thugs who like to mimic Chinese crime syndicates. The Yakuza? They're professionals. They're dedicated like few other criminal organizations are. When one of them screws up bad enough, his boss might ask for his life in recompense."

"His life? You mean . . . ?"

"Yeah. He kills himself. They go through with it, too. It protects their families, sure, but mostly it's dedication. They care a lot about loyalty and tradition. That's why they use swords, even in the modern world. When they came after Masahiro, they had guys with guns, but those guys were focused on me and Red. The actual assassin tried to cut our client's head off with a long, curved sword called a *katana*. It's a design that originated from Earth, specifically medieval Japan. They used to make them by folding steel onto itself over and over again. Now they have self-sharpening, nanotech blades with cutting edges only a few molecules wide. You can slice a man in half with one of those swords, with ease."

"Holy shit. You sure know a lot about swords."

I shrugged. "I watched them try to murder a man with one of these things. I felt like it was worth reading up on." It was strange talking about this. The only one I'd ever told all this to was Lily. "Anyways, Red held them off while I got Masahiro into the car. He shot and killed the guy with the sword, with this revolver"—I tapped the gun butt under my right arm—"but he'd been shot several times himself. I tried to stop the bleeding, but . . ."

I trailed off, then looked over at Dagny again. "It was a hell of a thing. We got through the entire Harvest Campaign together, from beginning to end, and Red never got a scratch on him. Believe me, there were a few times when we didn't think we were ever going to make it home. We saw things that nobody ought to see. The Ceph were absolutely vicious. Their soldier class doesn't even understand the concept of surrender. They'd fight to the last every single time and never took prisoners. When we finally wiped the bastards out on Harvest, we thought we were going home, but then we got orders for 220 Colfax-B."

"I've heard stories about that campaign," Dagny said.

"The Confederate fleet bombed the planned landing sites for weeks before the invasion, but the Ceph, they'd hide deep underground and ride out the attack. There were still six million colonists trapped down there, too, so they wouldn't just, you know, drop a big asteroid on it and wipe everything out. The only thing to do was land and retake the planet. Operation Sovereign, the biggest planetary invasion in history. Over a million troops were involved in the initial drop, including our unit. A hundred thousand men died in the first six hours."

"Oh my God," Dagny said, quietly. "It's one thing to read about this. It's another to talk to somebody who was there."

"A couple years back I heard that the colonists on 220 Colfax-B finally settled on a proper name for their planet. They voted to name it Sovereign, after the operation. Our unit was rotated home after securing that initial foothold, and that was the end of my part in the war. All that, all that carnage and death, and Red comes home to be murdered by some assassins from a crime syndicate." I shook my head. "Seems like such a waste."

"That's how you came to have a detective agency," Dagny said.

"Yeah. Quite a tale, ain't it? I thought about quitting, but the agency was something Red built. He didn't have a wife or children. It's his legacy. Somebody had to maintain it. Masahiro was so grateful that he paid for all of Red's funeral expenses on top of the very generous fees he'd agreed to. He even lobbied to make sure Red was buried in the Colonial War Memorial Cemetery with full military honors."

"Has anyone ever told you you're an interesting guy?" she asked with an uneven smile.

"Not too often. I don't talk about this stuff much. Everybody's got a sob story. A million other guys went through the same things we did and worse. It is what it is."

"Well, thank you for telling me."

I smiled. "What can I say? You're easy to talk to. You had Dante eating our of your hand the other day, and now me."

To my surprise, that actually made Dagny blush a little bit, and smile. What a smile it was, too. I was forced to admit to myself that I wasn't doing all this just to do right by a client, not anymore. I got out of jail and the first thing I wanted to do was see her, before I even went home. *You big idiot*, I thought. *This won't end well.*

"Easy?" Dagny asked. "Are you alright?"

"Huh? Yeah."

"You kind of zoned out there for a second."

"Sorry. I'm just tired."

"I'm really glad you came to see me."

I nodded and smiled. "I'm glad, too."

"What will you do now? What's our next move?"

I was quiet for a moment while I thought about that. "The first thing I need to do is see if I can't have a look around Dr. Ivery's residence. After that, I'm not so sure. Your sister left some other contacts that we could try and track down, but now I'm worried that doing so will put them in danger. I think . . ." I trailed off.

"What do you think?"

"I think I need to get ahold of your stepfather, see if he'll talk. Dr. Ivery told us he was involved and that he got your sister a position up there. If anyone knows what's going on, it's him."

"Are you sure? Won't that, I don't know, expose us?"

"You caught two bullets in your back just a few hours ago," I reminded her. "If you don't want to go this route, I won't, but I think it's the best way forward."

She looked thoughtful for a few seconds, then frowned. "No, I think you're right."

"Do you have a way of contacting him directly? A private number or personal account?"

She shook her head. "No, sorry. When I went to him before I looked up his contact information on the Net and called his office."

"That's alright. I'm a detective, I'll figure it out."

"When can we get started?"

"Not so fast. I want you to sit this one out." I held up a hand. "It's not that I don't think you can take care of yourself. You handled a dangerous situation like a pro, but you could have been killed. I want to find your sister, too, but I'm not willing to sacrifice your life to do it. Leave the snoop work to me. As for your stepfather . . . it might be better if I can talk to him man-to-man. Having his estranged stepdaughter there might set him off, given your history."

I could tell she wasn't thrilled with being left behind, but she didn't argue with me. I was glad—I didn't want to put her in any more danger. "Yeah. He wouldn't talk to me before. Maybe he'll talk to you now."

"We'll see. It might take me a while to get into Dr. Ivery's place and track your stepfather down. In the meantime, I'm going to go home and take a shower. We both had kind of a rough night."

"We did," she agreed. "Come here." Still sitting up in bed, she held out her arms like she wanted another hug. I stood up and awkwardly bent down to hug her; she surprised me by throwing her arms around me and kissing me, deeply, her tongue teasing my lips just a little. "That's for saving my life," she said, softly, into my ear.

"It was, uh, my pleasure," I said, standing up, trying not to blush again and failing miserably. I grinned. "Probably gonna need to make that a cold shower, now."

She laughed. "I'm going to rest now. Call me later?"

"You got it."

CHAPTER 9

I went home after leaving the hospital. It felt good to shower, shave, get breakfast, and put on some clean clothes. I got back into the office a while later and brought Lily up to speed. She went through the files left to us by Cassandra Carmichael and found personal contact information for her stepfather—his address, a private number, things like that. Assuming that information was still valid, getting ahold of him would be pretty straightforward. Whether or not he actually wanted to talk to me was another matter.

If he didn't? I could confront him face-to-face. That carried a certain amount of risk, though. I had to be careful how I went about it. There's a fine line between persistence and harassment, and more than one overzealous P.I. has been brought up on stalking charges. The risks aside, under normal circumstances, tracking a guy like that down wouldn't be too hard. He was a corporate executive, the type who pays his taxes and has a good credit history, not some professional con man who knows how to drop off the grid. Most corporate executives don't have a remote high-security facility that they can flee to, though. If he was at Site 471, he was out of my reach.

I figured calling him up was my best bet. I just had to be careful about how I confronted him. Telling him I knew about Site 471 and his missing stepdaughter would probably get me slapped with a restraining order before it got me a meeting. If he *was* willing to talk, he'd probably need to be discreet about it, given the secrecy surrounding Project Isaiah. I called Lily into my office to see what she thought. Yeah, I'm the boss, but a good boss listens to his people, and Lily was a sharp kid.

"We can do this two ways," she explained. "You can just call him directly from your work number if you want, but then he'll know who you are and where we are."

"True," I said, "but that might show we're on the up-and-up. Or it could scare him off, assuming he's even willing to talk in the first place."

"Otherwise we can use one of the burner accounts and contact him anonymously. We can even spoof the global positioning system and wireless network triangulation so they don't know where the call is coming from."

I grinned. "I don't pay you enough."

"You don't," Lily said with a smirk. "The problem with this is, who answers an anonymous call? Depending on the filter settings on his handheld, he might not ever know that we contacted him."

"That's a good point. If his personal handheld is being monitored, he won't talk to us either way. If he knows who we are, he might be willing to find some other means to talk to us."

"Or they might just send some goons to kill us like they did with Dr. Ivery."

I chuckled humorlessly. "If they want me dead, they're going to have to do better than some street skags like the Green Dragons. But..." I looked at my assistant for a moment, choosing my words carefully. "Listen, I want you to take some time off. You haven't had a vacation this year."

"Time off? Now? In the middle of our biggest case ever?"

"Yeah. Maybe get out of the city for a couple weeks. Your folks live down in Epsilon City, don't they? When's the last time you were home?"

"Last Christmas, but what does that have to do with anything?"

"Weather's a lot nicer down there, too."

"Boss, what are you talking about? Do you... do you not want me on the case anymore?" She looked hurt.

"It's not that," I said, looking down at the desk. "You know I couldn't run this agency without you." I looked up at her again. "It's just... I don't know who's pulling the strings in all this, but like you pointed out, they're willing to kill. They killed Dr. Ivery, they nearly killed our client, and they tried to kill me. It might not safe to be around me. If anything happened to you?" I shook my head. "I couldn't live with it. I'd never forgive myself. You're young, you've got your whole life ahead of you, and this job ain't worth getting killed over."

Tears welled up in Lily's eyes. "I'm not leaving. If you want me gone, you're gonna have to fire me. Our client is counting on you and you need all the help you can get."

Lily always was a good kid. She worked hard, she didn't complain, and she was as loyal as any of the men I served in combat with. I didn't have the heart to force her to go, and even if I did, that was no guarantee that she'd be safe. She was right, too, I needed all the help I could get. "You know I'm not going to fire you."

"Good," she said, sniffling. "I hate job hunting."

She actually got a laugh out of me with that. "You got guts, kid. Maybe I'm making too much of this, but I would feel better if you would at least make some contingency plans."

"What kind of contingency plans?"

"Have a plan to get out of town if something happens to me, or if I tell you that you need to go for your own safety. Pack a bag. Have cash on hand. Be ready to leave on short notice, and figure out places to go ahead of time. Maybe that means you go to Epsilon City to your parents' place, maybe it means you go stay with a friend."

"I can do that, I guess."

"I won't tell you to go for nothing, so if I say that you need to get out, you need to leave right away, no hesitation, no arguing with me. Same thing if something happens to me, like I go missing or turn up dead."

I could tell this was rattling her a little. *Good,* I thought. If she wanted to stick it out through this one, she needed to understand the risks and take them seriously. *She's no quitter, though.*

"Okay," she said, nodding slowly, thinking over what I said. "I can do that. Do you . . . You don't think it'll really be necessary, do you?"

"Well, I sure as hell don't *plan* on dying," I said, "but

this one could get dicey. Hell, it's already dicey. I'd feel better if I knew that you had a safe place you could go, even on short notice."

"I'll talk to some friends. I wouldn't be the first person to turn up needing a place to lay low."

"Good. Thank you for humoring me on this. I don't think it'll come to that, but it's always better to have a plan. Now . . . let's talk about Dr. Ivery's house. Where is it?"

"She lives in a townhouse in North Hampton." She brought up the address on her tablet and showed it to me. "Won't SecFor have been there by now?"

"Probably, and that'll make getting in difficult even if they haven't already taken whatever it was she wanted me to find." I held up the electronic wafer that the scientist had given me in her final breath. "This might be an access key to something, but she didn't say what. She mentioned someone named Diana."

"Family member?" Lily asked.

I shook my head. "Dr. Ivery lived alone. She might not have been referring to a person, but to something else."

Lily tapped at her tablet screen. "Diana is a fairly common woman's name on Nova Columbia. It's also the name of the Roman goddess of the hunt, going back almost three thousand years." She showed me several depictions of the deity, including paintings and sculptures. The goddess was usually portrayed as a strong-looking woman with a bow. "The more pressing question is, how are you going to get in and look around if SecFor is there?"

"I'll have to wait until they leave, then try to get in. If we're lucky, they'll just lock the place up and leave it for her estate to sort out. Given that she was murdered, though, they probably went over the place in detail, taking everything they thought might be related to the case. They might even have left security on the house."

"What will you do if they have security?"

I grinned. "Depends on the security. I have ways."

"It sounds risky."

I nodded. "It is, no doubt about it. I'm still going to try. In the meantime, let's give Mr. Carmichael a call, shall we?"

I called him from my work handheld without bothering to hide my identity. He didn't answer, so I left a voice message. I explained who I was and that I was hired to find Cassandra Carmichael. I didn't mention anything about Project Isaiah or Site 471, but I did tell him that Dr. Ocean Ivery was dead and that Dagny was in the hospital with multiple gunshot wounds. I told him that I feared Cassandra might be in grave danger and that I hoped he could help me get her to safety. I concluded the message with my contact info.

"That should do it," I said, ending the call. "Now we'll see if we hear back from him."

"What if we don't?" Lily asked.

"Then I hit the street and try to find him the old-fashioned way. If that doesn't work, then I don't know."

"What about the Baron? Why don't you ask him for help? If he wants to be involved in the investigation he can make himself useful. Maybe he can get in touch with Cassandra's other contacts without putting them in danger."

"I thought about that. I just don't know how much I

can trust him. Dr. Ivery thought that there were Terran Confederation intelligence people at Site 471. Deitrik used to work for the SIS. Something like the Seraph would be of particular interest to them."

"If he's still working in some capacity for the Confederation, and they already have their people at Site 471 . . ." She trailed off. "I don't get it. Why did he bail you out of jail and tell you to keep investigating? If he's with them, why would he be helping you?"

"I don't know and it's bothering me. I don't like being a pawn in somebody else's game."

"I don't like *any* of this," Lily said.

"I don't either, kid."

The rest of the day ground by slowly and we heard nothing from Arthur Carmichael. I tried to be productive; I read through the files that Cassandra Carmichael had left and studied the blueprints of the block townhomes that Dr. Ivery had lived in. I was tired and found it difficult to concentrate. I did manage to get a technician over to fix the auto-nav on my car, so I at least accomplished something for the day.

After that, I sent Dagny a message, asking her how she was doing. I didn't mention trying to contact her stepfather. I'd be lying if I said the kiss she'd given me wasn't on my mind, but I tried to be realistic about it. She had just suffered a traumatic experience, was injured, and had been shot up full of painkillers. Sometimes surviving a dangerous encounter makes people act impulsively, gives them the desire to do something pleasurable and life-affirming. Nothing that happened meant she was in love with me.

Even if she was, I was forced to ask myself how I imagined things could possibly turn out. Did I really think she was going to settle down with me, that we were going to get married and live happily ever after? *Get real*, I told myself. *Whatever infatuation she has with you will be gone if her sister turns up dead, and you know damn well that's probably what's going to happen.* Besides, I thought, getting romantically involved with a client is unprofessional. Besides *that*, what was *I* after? There was no denying that I was attracted to her, but she was drop-dead gorgeous and I'm only human. I hadn't seriously dated anyone since my divorce. Did I really want to start now, or was this because of the stress I was under?

Hell, I thought, shaking my head, *I'm acting like a damn teenager, getting led around by hormones and emotions.* What I really needed was a meal, a drink, and a good night's sleep. It was still hours away from close of business, but I told Lily that we were going to take an early day. I left the disk that Dr. Ivery had given me in the safe in my office and drove Lily home. After dropping her off, I headed back to my own apartment across town. I parked in the underground garage and made my way to the elevators.

I have to admit, my mind was on other things, like Dagny, food, and my bed, and not on my surroundings. I was tired, too, and wasn't as alert as I should have been. That's probably why I didn't notice the two big guys in suits coming up behind me until it was too late.

They shoved a shock baton into my neck before I could pull my gun or even turn around. Every muscle in my body locked up and I fell to the pavement. They stopped zapping me long enough for one of them to give me a good, hard kick in the guts. Even with my body armor resisting the blunt force trauma, it hurt like hell and knocked the wind out of me. The guy kicked me again, flipping me onto my back, and his partner shocked me with the baton one more time.

Lying on the pavement, twitching, gasping for air, I finally got a quick look at my two assailants. The one with the shock baton was younger and looked more athletic. He was black, with short-cropped hair, tinted smart glasses, and looked real slick in a well-fitted suit. His partner was built like a freight truck, probably close to seven feet tall, with thick arms and a body like a tree trunk. He was older, white, and had serious cybernetic augmentation. The suit he wore had to be custom tailored, because nobody with shoulders that wide could wear off-the-rack shirts.

The clanker grabbed me by the collar and hoisted me to my feet. He clamped a huge titanium hand around my throat while his partner restrained my arms behind my back. They patted me down, quickly and efficiently, and stripped me of all my weapons and possessions. They then roughly pulled a black bag over my head and forced me into a car.

The whole thing only took a minute. They injected something into my neck and, as I started to lose consciousness, I hoped to God that Dagny and Lily were alright.

I awoke with a start. My head was pounding and my vision was blurry, but I realized that I was strapped to a metal chair in the middle of what looked like a storage room. Shelves of boxes lined the walls, but I couldn't make anything out clearly. The floor was bare ceramicrete and the lights were dim.

"Wakey wakey," a man said, his voice a deep baritone. It was the big clanker, Truck, and he roughly patted me on the head. His partner, Slick, stood next to him.

"Oh good," I slurred, "you two are here. Gah!" I gasped as Slick stuck another auto-injector into my neck. "What the hell did you dose me with now?"

"Just a stim to help you focus," he answered. "It will neutralize the effects of the sedative. Your vision should clear up in a minute."

I coughed, sending pain shooting up my side. "If you were gonna just knock me out anyway, did your big friend there have to kick my ribs in, too?" That seemed to please Truck, whose face split in a mean grin.

Slick chuckled. "Your reputation precedes you, Mr. Novak. We know what you did to those Green Dragons. We weren't going to take any chances. You understand."

"Yeah, sure," I said. I had been stripped down to my pants and undershirt. They took my shirt, my jacket, my hat, hell, even my shoes and socks. Seemed like a lot of hassle if they were just going to kill me. "What do you fellas want?"

"What do *we* want?" Slick asked. "You're the one who wanted to speak with Mr. Carmichael."

"Be careful what you wish for," Truck said with a smile.

"Holy hell, all he had to do was call me."

"You and I both know it's not that simple," a new voice said. I heard a door close behind me. Slick stepped back and an older man appeared in front of me. He had silver hair and a neatly trimmed mustache. He wore an expensive-looking, double-breasted suit with a smart-screen eyepiece over his right eye.

I was still groggy from the drugs and it took me a second to catch up to what was happening. "Arthur Carmichael?" I recognized him from Cassandra's files.

"Yes," he acknowledged, taking the eyepiece off, "and you're Ezekiel Novak, the private investigator hired by Dagny." He sounded like the whole situation annoyed him. "I have enough going on without that damned girl injecting herself into the matter."

"Oh, I'm sorry," I said, laying on a little sarcasm. "We were nearly killed trying to find your stepdaughter, but I do apologize if we inconvenienced you. Will you listen to yourself, man? Your goons kicked the shit out me, kidnapped me, and now you got me strapped to a chair. But sure, let's talk about how bad *your* day was."

"You've got a mouth on you, don't you?" he said, like a teacher scolding a schoolboy. "Clearly you don't appreciate the gravity of the situation you're in, Mr. Novak, so allow me to explain it for you. Nobody knows where you are. From the moment you were taken, you've been surrounded by EMF shielding. Even if you have a tracking beacon stuffed up your nose, its signal can't get out of this room. Bluster and bravado aren't going to get you out of this."

My vision having cleared up, I took another glance around the room. It looked like a pretty ordinary storage or maintenance room to me. Past the shelves, there was a utility sink on one wall. Opposite that, a Mrs. Tidy cleaning robot was parked in a charging station. Maybe he had this room shielded, maybe he was just bluff. It didn't really matter because I had no way of calling for help.

"If you wanted me dead I'd be dead already," I said, "so the question isn't what I want. What do *you* want? Why are we having this conversation? What could you possibly want from me that you think you'll get by abducting me? All I'm trying to do is find Cassandra."

"I *know* where Cassandra is!" he snapped. He regained his composure and straightened his tie. "Dagny should have left it alone."

"Does she really strike you as the type to leave things alone?"

"She ignored her family for years. All she had to do was act like she used to. Now I don't know if I can protect her."

"Your company hired some gangbangers to kill her. If that's your idea of protecting her, I can see why she never liked you."

His eye twitched when I said that. That got to him. "You don't understand anything!" he said, raising his voice a little. "You don't know what I am willing to do to protect my family!" Slick and Truck both took a step forward, but Carmichael waved them off. He leaned down and looked me square in the eyes. "Dagny was . . . a disappointment, in a lot of ways, but do you really think I want her dead? I raised her from when she was a little girl! I loved that girl!"

"You had a funny way of showing it. She came to you for help, wanting to know where her sister went, and you told her to kick rocks."

He didn't have a retort for that. It must have gotten

under his skin, I thought. I realized then how tired he looked. He had dark circles under his eyes and that strung-out look you get when you're using stims to make up for a lack of sleep. It was the same look that Cassandra and Dr. Ivery both had.

"I know," he said, his tone softer now. He stood up straight and put his hands on his hips. "I didn't know what else to do. Keeping her away from the whole thing was the only way I could think of to protect her."

"I know about the Seraph, Mr. Carmichael," I said slowly, "and Site 471. I don't care about any of it. All I want is to be able to tell Dagny that her sister is okay."

"You know about the Seraph?" He chuckled, then leaned in again. "No, Mr. Novak, you do not. Whatever it is you think you know, whatever Ocean told you, the truth is beyond your comprehension. It's beyond any of us."

"That may be the case, but you brought me in for this little chat for a reason. I'll ask you again: What is it that you want from me?"

"I told them this was too risky," he said, ignoring my question. "I told them it would be impossible to conceal something like this. They wouldn't listen. That damned old fool wouldn't listen."

At that point I wasn't sure he was even talking to me. "What old fool?" I thought about it for a second. "You mean Xavier Taranis? I got the impression he was running this whole thing."

"I don't know how you figured this out," Carmichael said, "but you even being here proves I was right. Did Ocean tell you all this? I warned her. She didn't listen to me, either."

"She told me some things," I said, "but I figured a lot out on my own. I'm pretty good at what I do."

"Yes, I suppose you are. What do you know about the Cosmic Ontological Foundation?"

"I know Xavier Taranis is one of their biggest supporters."

"The people running Project Isaiah, half of them are COFfers who think they've found a holy relic. The other half just see alien technology they can exploit for profit. None of them know what they're playing with and it . . . well . . . it leaves me in a difficult position, doesn't it?"

Whatever was going on with him, he was agitated and clearly under a lot of stress. He looked like he hadn't slept much. That seemed to happen to everyone from Ascension who got involved in this mess. Instead of antagonizing him some more, I softened my tone. "I asked you twice what you want from me."

"Yes, you did," he said, slowly. "I think we might be able to help each other." Truck and Slick looked at each other, behind Carmichael's back, when he told me that, but neither of them said anything.

I wasn't sure what he was going to ask of me, but I wasn't in any position to argue with him. "I'm listening."

"You want to find Cassandra? I can help you with that. I know precisely where she is."

"Well, I would sure like to know that. So would Dagny. Can I assume, then, that she's still alive? Is she okay?"

The question seemed to surprise him. "Alive? Yes. Okay? No, Mr. Novak, she's not okay. She's anything but okay."

Despite how badly my side and head hurt, hearing that

Cassandra Carmichael was still alive was a relief. "Where is she now? What's her condition?"

"I don't know for sure," he said, distantly. "She's being held for observation at the Ventura Medical Research Center."

"Let me guess: that's a company-owned outfit."

"Of course," he said. "It's a wholly owned subsidiary, and that's part of the reason she's there. They are outside of my area of responsibility. I can't access their records, their security systems, any of it. They don't know that I know where she is, you see. They won't tell me where she is or let me talk to her."

"Then how are you so certain she's there?"

"I've been doing this for thirty-two years and I'm good at my job, Mr. Novak," he said, as if I had just asked a dumb question. "I know how the company handles its business. Thirty-two years and they think they can pull this on me!"

He was getting agitated again, so I tried to sound calm. "The company is holding Cassandra and they won't let you see her? Why would they do this to one of their own people?"

Carmichael looked down at the floor for a moment. "I know what people think of Ascension. I can tell you from personal experience that most of the stories you hear are false, nothing but urban legends. The company helped *build* this colony. This? This isn't corporate politics. This is Xavier Taranis. He came back when he learned of the discovery at Site 471. He just . . . he just showed up and took charge as if he hadn't been retired for decades. He has no official position at the company but somehow he's running it again, just like that. Him and his damned COFfer flunkies."

I don't think he realized how tone-deaf he seemed, talking about all the great and noble things Ascension did to a guy he had kidnapped and tied up, but I decided to leave that alone for the moment. "You didn't answer my question," I said. "Why do this to you?"

The company man was quiet for a few moments. "Three reasons. One, she's valuable to the project." He didn't elaborate on what that meant. "Two, she's out of my reach there. Had they left her at Site 471, I'd be able to see her, maybe even get her out, and they know that."

"And three?"

"Three? Three is *leverage*. They don't have to worry about me so long as they have her."

"Do they *need* to worry about you?"

"You don't get to this rung of the corporate ladder without learning a few things," he said. "People at this level always have their contingency plans, their escape paths, if you will. I'm no different."

Despite the fact that I was in pain and being held against my will, the things he was telling me were damned interesting. I wanted to keep him talking. "I guess that begs the question, why not just get rid of you like they did Dr. Ivery?"

"They're afraid of what those contingency plans might be. They're afraid of what I might be able to do, even posthumously. They're right to be afraid, too," he said, starting to pace around. "If anything happens to me, a lot of company secrets are going to become public knowledge. Ocean? She was not the sort of person to think like that. She was ... she was brilliant, but she was a bookish scientist, hired for her expertise. She didn't have to fight her way up the ladder or play the political games."

"Let me make sure I have this straight, then. They're holding Cassandra to keep you from exposing the whole operation, and you're being blackmailed into cooperation? Is that what you're telling me?"

Carmichael fidgeted some more. "Yes. I lost her mother to cancer. I lost Dagny to political radicals. Cassandra is all I have left, and those bastards know it."

"Why did they bring you in in the first place if you're such a security risk?"

"I wasn't a security risk, at first, and I'm very good at what I do. The site security manager, Blanche Delacroix, specifically requested that I be brought in as her number two. I had no idea what I was getting into until I had been read into the project. Once I realized the scope of it, I grew concerned. I thought about blowing the whistle. Then Cassandra got wind of it. She started digging. I pleaded with her to leave it alone, told her that we had it under control, but she just wouldn't listen. She was putting herself in danger."

"You brought her in to protect her."

He nodded. "Yes. If I could keep her close, I could keep her safe, that was my reasoning. It worked, too. It worked too well. She wanted to help me. She ... she's brave. Very brave." He was quiet for a moment, then looked up at me again. "That's where you come in, Mr. Novak. We can help each other. You help me get my daughter back, and I'll tell you everything you want to know about Project Isaiah. Once she's safe, I don't care what happens to me."

"This sounds like a rescue mission. I'm just a snoop. Surely you can find someone better suited for this than me?"

"Maybe I could, but maybe you're also downplaying your own talents. I looked at your service record."

"Is that right?"

"Don't look so surprised. What, you think I didn't know about you until you tried to contact me? I've been watching you since Dagny hired you. I thought it was only a matter of time before you abandoned the investigation, especially after the run-in with those hired guns, but you've proven more capable and more resilient than I guessed. You're clearly resourceful. Not too surprising for a man who ran black-ops with the SIS."

"I can neither confirm nor deny that," I said. He didn't seem to know about the information that Cassandra had left Dagny, nor did he seem to know about her network of contacts. She had managed to keep that secret from him, even after she went to work at Site 471. "Even still, I've never done a hostage rescue before. Why me?"

"Because, Mr. Novak, there's nobody able to do the job who I can trust. Everyone capable I know has ties to Ascension or has worked for them before. If I try to bring any of them in, Blanche will find out, and that'll be the end of it. You? You're an outsider, hired by a third party, and you don't seem like the type to be bribed or intimidated into silence. It gives me plausible deniability."

"Won't they suspect you as soon as someone tries to get her out of the hospital?"

He shrugged. "Perhaps, perhaps not. They will likely keep the fact that she's been rescued from me. This may buy us some time."

"Have you thought about just calling the Security Forces? Kidnapping *is* illegal."

"The Security Forces," he scoffed. "And what will I tell them? That a person I trust told me my missing daughter is being held against her will in a company hospital? Even if I could convince them to investigate, word would get back to Blanche. The company has plenty of informants in the Security Forces Corps. By the time they could get a warrant and gain access to the facility, Cassandra would be gone, as would my only hope of getting her out of this situation."

"Maybe so, but your other idea still seems like a huge risk to me."

"It is, but my daughter's life is at stake and I'm short on good options right now. You coming along may well be just the lucky break I need."

"And you're just assuming I'll go along with this? Do you have any idea how crazy this sounds?"

"I do, yes. It is crazy, but I think you will go along with it. Right now, my people and I are the only ones who know about you, but sooner or later, Blanche and Taranis will find out. When that happens, you, Dagny, and your assistant will all be in danger. Believe me when I say that I am the only thing restraining them." That could have been a threat but it sounded more like a warning. "I can also make it worth your while."

"Generous of you. Tell me, what are they doing up there that they're willing to be so brazen to protect it?

This all has to be a huge risk. Even with all their pull, there's a limit to what Ascension can get away with."

He didn't answer that question. "Get my Cassie back and I'll tell you everything. I can cover our tracks after to protect all of us, but we have to hurry. Do we have a deal?"

"Seems to me I don't have much choice."

"Neither do I. What else would you have me do? This is the only way I can think of to protect both Cassie and Dagny."

"Alright, then. You got yourself a deal. I'd shake on it, but I'm still tied to this chair."

"Right." Carmichael looked over at Slick. "James! Release him. Stephen, please get Mr. Novak's effects and return them to him." He turned his attention back to me as the straps holding me to the chair were undone. "Thank you for this."

"Yeah," I said, rubbing my sore wrists, "don't mention it. Now listen, I may need your help to pull this thing off. You said you'd be able to cover our tracks, but you need to be ready. You're going to be the prime suspect once we try to get Cassandra out of there. Whatever contingency plans you have, whatever threats you've made, they might just decide that they're willing to risk it and have you taken out just like they did with Dr. Ivery."

"I know," he said, quietly. "It doesn't matter, so long as the girls are safe."

I nodded. "Understood. But first we need to talk about how you're going to make this worth the risk."

His eyes narrowed. "I came prepared. What do you want?"

"One hundred thousand dollars, cash. Fifty grand up front, the other fifty if and when I deliver Cassandra safely to you."

"If? You want fifty thousand dollars up front and you're telling me *if*?"

"You're asking one man to try and pull off a job that would be tough for a team of specialists. If you want guarantees you need to go somewhere else."

He breathed through his nose a few times, not saying anything. He clearly wasn't happy with the situation, but I think he was backed into a corner. "If only you knew what was at stake," he said, shaking his head slowly.

"I *do* know what's at stake, Mr. Carmichael: my life and my freedom, along with those of my assistant and client. You want me to risk all that, I'm willing, but it won't come cheap."

"I will get you your hundred thousand dollars," he said. "Half will be cash, the other half will be crypto."

Cryptocurrency is, for some purposes, even better and harder to trace than cash. It's been banned on some colony worlds but is widely accepted on Nova Columbia. "Deal. I also need to know everything about this research facility, their security, their schedules, everything."

"You'll have whatever I can get for you." Truck came back into the room, carrying belongings in a plastic bin, like the kind you put your stuff into when you go through security screening.

"You have my private contact information," Carmichael said. "I trust you'll use it with discretion."

"Discretion is my specialty," I assured him, then took the bin. It contained my hat, coat, shoes, and shirt, but not my guns or my handheld. I looked up at the cyborg. "What gives? Where's the rest of my stuff?"

"You'll get your weapons and handheld back after we drop you off," Truck said with a growl.

"Thank you, Stephen," Carmichael said. He then looked at Slick. "James, go get Mr. Novak his money."

"Yes, sir," the bodyguard said, and left the room. Truck stepped back but was watching me like a hawk as I dressed myself. I sat back down in the chair, moving slowly so as not to spook the clanker. He'd already kicked my ass once today and I didn't want him to think I was going to take a swing at his boss.

Slick came back in a couple minutes later, carrying a bundle of cash. He handed it to Carmichael, who handed it to me.

"That's fifty thousand dollars in cash," Carmichael said. "As I said, the second part of the payment will be in cryptocurrency. Believe me when I say that if you don't uphold your end of the deal, you'll regret it."

I didn't bother to count the money—that's always perceived as an insult. I shoved the fat stack of five-hundred-dollar bills into my coat pocket. "If I was the type of guy to cut and run, I'd have done it after I almost got killed yesterday. I'll uphold my end of the bargain."

"See to it that you do," he said. "My men will show you out."

"Put this bag on your head," Truck said, holding up a black sack.

I looked at Carmichael. "Is this really necessary?"

"We're not going to drug you, if that's what you're worried

about," the businessman said. "As for the bag ... for fifty thousand dollars cash, I think you can indulge me."

Truck roughly pulled the bag over my head before I could protest any further.

Getting my car fixed when I did proved to be good timing on my part. After my "meeting" with Arthur Carmichael, Slick and Truck couldn't be bothered to take me back to my apartment tower. They dropped me off in the industrial part of the city, way over at the southeast side of the Crater, with fifty grand in cash weighing down my coat pocket. It was midafternoon now and it was raining again.

My handheld was fully synched with my virtual domestic assistant, so I was able to message Penny and have her send my car to my location. She told me it would take more than an hour for my car to get to me so I hiked a couple blocks over to a lunch counter, one of those fully automated ones with outdoor seating. I sat at a round, metal table under an awning, nursing a cup of coffee, and called Lily.

"Holy shit, Boss!" she said, after I explained everything that went down. "Are you okay?"

"I still got a headache from whatever they injected me with. Aside from that, I'm fine."

"What are you going to do now?"

"I got my revolver back, but I'm going to swing by a vendor and pick up a new handheld, first. Then I'm going to go home and get some sleep."

"You worried they put a tracker in it?"

"It doesn't look tampered with, but I don't know if they

accessed it while I was out, or even opened it up and put a chip in it. Better safe than sorry."

"Smart thinking. What should I do until I hear from you again?"

"Call your friend, the one we spoke to the other night. Tell him we might have something for him."

"Got it. Anything else?"

"Check on the client, please, but don't tell her what happened. I need to figure some things out first."

"Understood. Be safe, Easy."

I chuckled. "Hell, kid, I'm trying. I'll call you later."

CHAPTER 10

Late that night, after catching up on my sleep and having a big pot of coffee with my dinner, I made my way back to North Hampton. I went about it differently this time, seeing as how I was planning on a little breaking and entering, and wanted to minimize the chances I'd be identified. For one thing, I left my car at home and used the monorail network to get there. I paid in cash for a day pass instead of using one that would be linked to my ID.

I also made it a point to disguise my appearance. I put on some black cargo pants, a hooded sweatshirt, and a well-used jacket that was loose enough to conceal my gun under my arm. A worn work cap and a used pair of sneakers that I'd picked up at a secondhand store finished the ensemble. I kept a supply of these kind of clothes for just such an occasion, and when dressed I looked like a vagrant. A little bit of theater makeup on my face made me look like I'd been living on the streets for a while. I put in contact lenses that would spoof most retinal scanners and change my eye color.

The last thing I put on was a particulate filter mask that covered my nose and mouth. It had a built-in electronic voice modulator that would thwart most attempts at voice-matching.

It was past midnight when I made it to North Hampton. Unlike Delta City proper, this part of town was pretty dead at night. Traffic was light and only a few people could be seen on the streets or walkways. Instead of the imposing towers downtown, this neighborhood consisted mainly of very expensive one- to three-story family homes and rows of somewhat-less-expensive attached houses for those who traded less maintenance for less privacy. I couldn't afford a townhouse like Dr. Ivery had on my income.

It was about a mile from the nearest monorail station to the street where Dr. Ivery's home was. The streets were well lit and these houses would all have security cameras. I had my hood up, my mask on, and kept my head down. Sometimes in these richer neighborhoods, private security will stop and hassle people out on the streets at night, citing city vagrancy laws, so I kept moving and tried not to draw attention to myself. It must have worked, because a security drone buzzed overhead without even stopping to scan me.

Dr. Ivery's house was in the middle of a block-long row of townhomes across the street from a small municipal park. I stayed on the sidewalk on the far side of the street and did my first pass by the house. There was no law enforcement around that I could see, not even a robot or an aerial drone. I held a small screen in my hands and stared at it, as people often did. In my case, though, I wasn't playing a game or scrolling feeds on my handheld. In fact, I'd left my handheld at home (you should *never* have your handheld on you if you're up to something shady; they can track you that way). I had a discreet optical and radio-frequency detector in the pack slung over my shoulder, with the sensor cluster barely poking out of the top flap. It scanned in multiple spectra and looked for things like radio transmitters, the reflection of camera lenses, and infrared sensors. The screen in my hands was the scanner's display.

I kept walking without stopping, going around the park, analyzing the results of my sensor sweep. There were, as I expected, security cameras on every home in the row of townhouses, including Dr. Ivery's. Since this was kind of an upscale neighborhood, there weren't any security cameras mounted to posts like you see in the rougher parts of town. The people who live in North Hampton have enough money to successfully lobby the City Council to respect their privacy and not put cameras everywhere.

After lapping the park, I kept going, following a side street. The rows of townhomes were built back-to-back, with a narrow service road running between them. This road was gated off at either end, and all of the homes had an eight-foot privacy fence around their backyards. Still, as near as my scanner could tell, there weren't any cameras back there, nor were there any streetlights, so that seemed like my best option.

There *was* a camera on the security gate itself, though, looking down at it from an eight-foot pole on one end. It was a remote camera with a signal transmitter antenna and its own power supply. I had two options: one was to ignore it and hope it wasn't being monitored in real-time. This is how most security cameras are set up—they're more for deterrent and evidentiary purposes than for catching criminals in the act. On the other hand, in a neighborhood like this, there was a chance the camera feed was being monitored by an AI, and that it would notify the authorities right away if it saw me climbing the fence. Then it became a race to get in and out before the private security or even SecFor showed up to investigate, because they would probably first check the house they knew was empty and was involved in a recent murder investigation.

The other option was to disable the camera. A camera going down on a monitored network would usually result in an automatic maintenance request, but it would probably be the next morning before anyone showed up to look at it. Some systems are set up to put in an emergency call if anything happens to the cameras, but that's usually only when a place has high-end private security, and that North Hampton neighborhood wasn't *that* rich. SecFor isn't going to respond every time some AI reports that a camera isn't functioning in a city of thirty million people. If a technician or even a security guard *did* show up, I'd be in Dr. Ivery's place before they got there, and they weren't going to search the empty house like SecFor would.

It was still a risk, but of the two options, disabling the camera was the less risky. I come prepared for that possibility. Sometimes you can jam the camera's broadcast transmission, but these days you see more and more systems using frequency-hopping encryption regimens that makes that difficult without very powerful equipment. Other times you can just cut the power cord, but this one had its own internal power supply. You can blind the camera with a laser, but the laser itself might draw the attention of a security drone.

There is one method of disabling a camera that works every time, though. First, I grabbed a small can of aerosol paint from my pack, then I shimmied up the pole the camera was mounted to, staying out of its field of view. Reaching around, I sprayed the camera lens, covering it completely. Stuffing the paint can into my pocket, I swung around the pole, climbed over the gate, and dropped down on the other side. I jogged down the service road into cover of darkness. The lack of security on the place made my job a lot easier, but I'd still have to be quick. There was at least one security drone patrolling the neighborhood and the darkness wouldn't hide me from its thermal cameras.

Dr. Ivery's place was the fifth house on my left. The tall fence around the backyard didn't have a gate in it, but I didn't need one. I jumped up and grabbed the top of the fence. Using my feet to help me climb, I hoisted myself over and dropped down into the yard. I hurried across the grass and onto the ceramicrete patio at the back of the house. There was what looked like a glass door there, but it was actually one of those security doors made of insulated safety transparency. I'd have been there all night trying to cut through it, so instead I went for the lock. It was a standard electronic residential door lock. I had my locksmithing tools with me and within a few minutes I was in the house.

The interior of the house was dark enough that I pulled out my flashlight. The place looked like one of those display homes with the ultramodern furniture, glass tables, and abstract art on the walls. A Mrs. Tidy robot was in its charging station against the wall, and just like at Cassandra Carmichael's apartment, the drives had been pulled. In fact, as I looked around it became obvious that SecFor had already been there and conducted a search. There was a home office on the main floor that had also been cleaned out—no computers, no paperwork, and nothing that the little electronic wafer the scientist had given me would go to. The good news was, the home security system had been disabled, too. Whatever cameras were in and around the home were no longer functional.

I didn't find anything useful downstairs so I headed to the second floor, being careful not to shine my light across any windows. The upstairs was even more sparsely decorated than the ground floor. At the top of the stairs there was a sunroom with nothing in it, not even any chairs to sit in. I noticed, too, that there were no pictures or personal effects hung up anywhere. The house was a rental, and I don't know who, if anyone, the late scientist had listed as her next of kin, but her few belongings were still in the house. I was willing to bet the furniture had come with the house and that she hadn't even bothered rearranging it. Whatever other eccentricities she may have had, Dr. Ivery seemed to have a lived a solitary life.

Down the hall were a small bedroom, a bathroom, and a master bedroom at the end. I decided to start with the master bedroom and work my way back out. I wasn't entirely sure what I was looking for. It was possible that whatever device the electronic wafer went to had been taken by SecFor and that I was wasting my time.

The bedroom door slid open with a tap of the touchpad on the wall. At the center of the room was one of those therapeutic smart beds, complete with a retractable dome in case you wanted to sleep at higher or lower than normal air pressure. The dresser was a built-in, automatic one, the type that connect to the laundry. They're nice, if you can afford one—toss your dirty clothes into the laundry chute, and the system will wash, dry, press, and fold your clothes before putting them away for you.

There was one thing in the room that really stood out, though. In fact, it seemed out of place given how impersonal and bland everything else in the house was. In the corner by the closet door was a statue on a pedestal of rough-hewn stone. The statue was metal, real bronze from the look of it, and stood four feet tall. It was the striking figure of a woman, dressed in flowing robes, hair braided and tied up. She had an arrow drawn back in a bow, ready to strike. "Diana," I said aloud. "Just the woman I've been looking for." I was sure this is what Dr. Ivery had been talking about—a statue of the Roman goddess Diana.

Leaning in, I studied the statue closely. The column it stood upon was about two feet tall and felt solid. It took a lot of effort just to move the sculpture; between the stone pedestal and the solid metal figure, it must have weighed several hundred pounds. My scanner didn't detect any electromagnetic or radio-frequency emissions from it, and there didn't seem to be any kind of a slot to stick the wafer into. No seams, compartments, or doors were apparent.

While the sides of the pedestal were roughly hewn, the top of it was polished smooth. A Roman coin was embedded into the stone at the goddess' feet. On the coin was the profile of a man's head and the letters M. AGRIPPA.L.F.COS.III. It was covered with a laminate so that the surface of the pedestal was completely flat. Touching it did nothing, so it wasn't a button or a control, but I realized it was the exact same size as the little disk that Dr. Ivery had given me.

Could it be that simple? I placed the disk directly on top of the coin. It seemed to align itself perfectly and was held in place with a small electromagnet. A blue light on top of the wafer lit up, and with a loud beep, the entire sculpture started to lift itself up on hydraulic pistons. It raised up about a foot, revealing a compartment. In it was a cylindrical metal canister with a screw-on end cap.

Well, I'll be damned, I thought. The statue was a hidden safe. I'd seen these before, of course, but ones like that were all custom-built and unique. They're shielded to conceal the signatures of their power sources and some are even lined with lead or tungsten to frustrate X-ray attempts. You'd have to cut the thing open to even be able to tell it's a safe, and that would take time and require power tools. It was too big and heavy to move easily so you couldn't just make off with the whole thing. I wasn't surprised that SecFor had missed it. Hell, without the key and the clue that Dr. Ivery gave me, I wouldn't have known what it was, either.

I grabbed the canister and unscrewed the top. It hissed as I broke the seal and equalized the air pressure. Inside, wrapped in a silk handkerchief, was an oblong object three inches long, an inch wide, and maybe half an inch thick. It was silvery white in color and seemed to shimmer in the light. The material was hard as steel and had no give to it, but the object was as light as a piece of dried wood. One side was smooth as glass. The other side had the texture of tree bark. One edge was jagged, like fractured iron. I couldn't tell what it was made out of, some kind of metal I thought, but like nothing I'd ever seen. It was cold to the touch.

There was a small plastic card in the canister with the object. On it was a matrix barcode, along with the Ascension logo and some text. It read:

<ext>
<ext>Project Isaiah 24880421NC32448
<ext>Object SERAPH, Sample 36A
<ext>WARNING: ANOMALOUS MATERIALS
<ext>Proprietary Information//TOP SECRET//COSMIC
<ext>PROPERTY OF APHG
<ext>

I had the strangest sense of unease, holding that thing in my hand. I wasn't sure what they meant by *anomalous materials*, but began to wonder if the thing was toxic or maybe radioactive. My scanner didn't pick up any emissions from it, though. In fact, I couldn't even get the scanner to lock onto it for a detailed examination. It was like it couldn't differentiate it from the background.

I didn't have time to screw around anyway. I'd found what Dr. Ivery wanted me to find and needed to get out of there. I carefully wrapped the white shape back up in the cloth and inserted it into its canister. I felt a little better once I had the lid screwed back on. I put the canister in my pack and removed the electronic key from on top of the embedded coin. The statue quietly lowered itself back to the floor, locking into place with a click, and that was that. Maybe they'd realize it was a safe before it went to the estate auction, maybe not.

I left the house the same way I'd come in, locking the door behind me. I climbed the fence and started the long trip home.

Later that morning I got to the office a little earlier than usual—before Lily, something that rarely happened. She was surprised when she came in just before 0900, to find me already there and making a pot of coffee.

"I didn't expect you to be in so early, Boss," she said, sitting at her desk. "You messaged me at, like, oh-four-thirty that you made it home. I figured you'd sleep in a little."

"That was the plan," I said. "I had a hell of a time falling asleep. It was like I couldn't relax or unwind." In truth I had gotten maybe three hours of fitful sleep. "So I, you know, came in a little early."

"You look like crap," Lily said, bluntly. "You sure you're not sick?"

"I'll be alright," I told her.

"So? What did you find? All your message said was that you were home safe."

Being a private detective doesn't give me license to break into people's houses. What I had done was illegal, but sometimes, that's what the job requires. We're always careful about things like that—we don't discuss any details over electronic communications unless absolutely necessary, and then it's via end-to-end-encrypted chat and we delete the conversation logs afterward. Lily and I hadn't talked about my trip to North Hampton over the handheld and she didn't know what I had found. It was easier to show her than to try and explain it.

"Maybe you'll make more sense of it than I did," I said, nodding for her to follow me into my office. I knelt down in front of my safe and began to unlock it, using two-factor authentication. It required both a combination number and my biometric data. A light diode turned green as it accepted the authentication, and the safe beeped as it unlocked. I retrieved the canister, carried it over to my desk, and unscrewed the lid. I gently emptied the contents onto my desk and set the canister down.

Lily reached for the silver-white fragment. I grabbed her hand to stop her before she touched it. "Don't hold it in your hand," I said.

"Is it dangerous?"

"I don't know. This is all I know about it," I said, handing her the plastic card it came with.

"Anomalous materials," Lily read. She looked at me. "What does that mean?"

I shrugged. "Your guess is as good as mine. I'm assuming it means they weren't able to figure out what it is."

"Should we be keeping this here? Is it dangerous?"

"It's not emitting any radiation," I said, "at least none that the scanner could detect. It's not emitting anything at all. It's just, I don't know, maybe it's not safe to handle."

"What are you going to do with it?"

"I don't know yet," I admitted. I scooped the fragment

up and sealed it back into its canister. "I need to talk to Deitrik. Will you call and make me a dinner appointment?"

"You got it, Boss."

CHAPTER 11

A few hours later I drove across the city, fighting through afternoon traffic as I went, headed for the Bauhaus Gaststätte. I took the canister from Dr. Ivery's home with me, stuffed in a small satchel.

When I walked into the restaurant I was greeted by an actual human hostess, something you see only in the fancier establishments in town. She was a pretty thing in a black dress, college-aged I thought, with her bright blue hair done up nicely and sparkly earrings hanging from her ears.

"Good afternoon, sir!" she said, bubbling with authentic-sounding enthusiasm. "Welcome to Bauhaus Gaststätte! Can I have your name?"

"Ezekiel Novak," I said, taking off my hat.

She glanced at the transparent eyepiece over her right eye. "I see you have a reservation for one."

"I do," I said. "Say, are you new? I'm something of a regular here and I haven't seen you around before."

"I just started!" she said. "Do you have a seating preference?"

"I'd like a private booth, please, and give my compliments to *Herr* Hauser, if you would."

Something must have clicked when I said that. "Oh. Oh, I see. We have a private booth available. Just follow the robot."

I thanked her and let the robot lead the way. It was a tall, slender machine, a conical body balanced on a thin central shaft that ended in a single, big wheel. It rolled quietly across the carpeted floor as it led me to the booth in question. "Here you are, sir," it said, in a tinny, synthesized voice.

I nodded at the robot before I could stop myself and sat down in the booth. It was a big pod built into the back wall, with a padded bench circling a round table in the middle. The door slid closed and the noise from the rest of the restaurant was muted. It was so quiet it could have doubled as one of those little closets they stick you in to test your hearing. You could choose from a selection of music if you wanted, but I didn't mind the silence.

I was famished though, not having eaten since breakfast, and I figured getting some food in me would help with the headache. I ordered from the provided tablet and sipped at a glass of room-temperature carbonated water. My meal, sauerbraten with a side of rotkohl, arrived at the same time the Baron did, about fifteen minutes later. He stood aside as the server robot placed the dishes on the table, then sat down across from me. The door slid shut and we were alone in silence.

"I did not expect to hear from you so soon, Easy," he said, cautiously, "or on such short notice. Are you alright?"

"You mind if I eat?" I asked. "I'm starving." He waved me on so I dug in, only talking after I'd swallowed a bite. "I wasn't planning on meeting you this soon either, but it's been a hell of a couple of days. To answer your question, no, I'm not alright. Yesterday morning, I got jumped by a couple of Ascension corporate security types."

He raised his eyebrows. "You were attacked?"

"They used me for soccer practice before drugging me and shoving me in their car, but I'll live." I aggressively sawed another piece off of my beef roast and ate it before speaking again. "Last night, I made a house call to the late Dr. Ivery's residence."

"I see. Did you find anything?"

I wiped my mouth with a napkin. "The food is fantastic, as usual."

The Baron sipped his wine before speaking and took a deep breath. "I'm afraid you'll have to fill me in on what's happened since we last spoke. Start with these Ascension security people and tell me what happened."

"I decided the best way forward was to have a talk with Arthur Carmichael, so I contacted him directly. Turns out he wanted to have a talk with me, too, and sent a couple of his boys to fetch me. They weren't gentle about it, but he and I came to an understanding, I think. More importantly, I know where Cassandra Carmichael is."

It was obvious that he was not expecting me to say that. "I see. Am I to assume that she's still alive, then?"

"She is. At least, that's what I was told."

"That is good news. Where is she?"

"According to her stepfather, she's being held at the Ventura Medical Research Center under a false identity.

They won't let him see her and apparently don't know that he knows where she is. They're holding her as leverage to keep him in line and he wants me to get her out. If I can, he's willing to spill everything he knows about Site 471, Project Isaiah, and the Seraph."

"I see."

"I need a way to get into that place and get her out without ending up in prison."

"He expects you to do all this?"

"It seems nuts, right? I asked him the same thing. He's desperate. He doesn't have access to anyone who could pull off such a job that wouldn't rat him out to the company. He doesn't have any concrete proof that she's being held there, either, just the word of people he trusts. He won't go to the Security Forces because he thinks they either won't believe him or that word will get back to the company if he does."

"And you agreed to this?"

"I did, and I need your help."

"What makes you think I can help you gain access to a private research facility?"

I sighed, loudly. "Deitrik, please. I know there are things you can't and won't tell me, and normally that doesn't bother me too much, but this has been a hell of a couple of days. I have reason to believe that my client and my assistant are both in danger. You convinced a district attorney to not press charges on me. I don't understand your exact place in all this, but you obviously have some pull."

"*My* place? You came to *me*."

"That's true, I did . . . and then you used the threat of

jailtime to get me to agree to feed you information, so here I am. Doc Ivery believed there were observers from Confederate intelligence at Site 471. Cassandra Carmichael, on the other hand, didn't think that the proper notifications to local and Confederation authorities were made when the Seraph was found."

"How do you know this?"

"I'm a detective, Deitrik. This is what I *do*. I need to be honest, it's getting to be a little insulting how everyone is surprised that I'm competent at my job."

"I didn't mean it like that, Easy. It's not like you to act this way."

"Yeah, well, in the last couple of days I've been shot at, watched a woman die, spent the night in jail, got kicked in the ribs, and was drugged, kidnapped, and strapped to a chair. My business, my friends, and my life have all been threatened. You'll have to forgive me if I'm a little short with you, but I have questions I need answered."

He studied me for a moment as if contemplating what to say. "What do you want to know?"

"Do you still answer to the SIS?"

Deitrik took a long swing of his wine and closed his eyes for a moment. "Yes, I still report to the Security Intelligence Service. As far as public records are concerned I'm retired, but my status can better be described as in reserve. One of my roles is to serve as a sort of auditor, watching the watchmen, ensuring operational security and legal compliance."

"Are you aware of any SIS involvement with Project Isaiah?"

"No. Believe me when I say that if this were an SIS-run operation I would not have brought you in. What is it that Dr. Ivery told you? You wouldn't tell me before, except for that she thought there were intelligence people on-site."

"The doc told me that the Seraph is real. I couldn't get a lot of specifics about what it is, exactly. She said it's a life-form of some sort, somehow not dead after sixty-eight million years."

Deitrik raised his eyebrows. "Is that so?"

"Yes. It was found buried under Mount Gilead and they were able to communicate with it somehow. They killed her to stop her from going off-world. They wouldn't have done that if she was just making things up."

"Someone killed her, yes, but even if Ascension was behind it, that doesn't mean that anyone from the SIS is involved. Dr. Ivery may have simply been mistaken about who she saw."

That *was* a possibility, even if I didn't want to admit it. "Well, if you want my investigation to go forward, we need to get Cassandra Carmichael out of that facility. Finding her was what I was hired to do. You help me do that and I'm your man. I'll dig into whatever you want me to dig into. This has to come first, though."

"Easy," the Baron said, softly, "that is, as they say, a *big ask*."

"I realize that, but it's necessary."

"Do you have any evidence that she's there?"

"Her stepfather is a career security manager for Ascension. He located her."

"And you think you can trust him?"

"He was willing to pay cash up front. If this is some

kind of a setup, it's the most elaborate one ever. Why contact me at all, much less pay me, if the goal was to keep me from finding her?"

"Arthur Carmichael may not be the one setting you up. He may be the intended target."

"That's a possibility, but given the stakes, I'm willing to take the risk. Aren't you? Whatever the Seraph is, it's alien and it could be dangerous. They might be putting the whole colony at risk."

Deitrik sipped his wine again. "When alien artifacts are found anywhere in Confederation space, there is a reporting procedure established by treaty, specifically the Conventions on the Discovery and Control of Alien Technology, Organisms, and Remains. These were ratified after the Medusae Fossae incident on Mars. You've heard of it, I trust?"

I nodded.

He continued, "Such finds must be reported to Confederation authorities, who then come to oversee the find and secure it, if necessary. Nova Columbian law has similar, parallel reporting requirements. In fact, the Confederation cannot legally keep it secret from the member government if the artifact is found on one of the colonies. This is expressly prohibited by the treaty."

I kept eating and let him talk.

"The process is supposed to be quite transparent and such finds are not kept from the public. In certain specific cases the find can be kept secret, but the reporting requirements remain in place. I have been aware of Site 471 for some time, but no report of the discovery of alien artifacts ever crossed my desk."

"Why do you want me to report my findings to you if you don't believe anything is going on?"

"I never said I don't believe anything is going on. In any case, it's not a question of what I believe; it's a question of what I can *prove*. Helping you break into private property is illegal and carries a high risk of exposure, not just for myself, but for the entire organization. There are ways it can be justified and sanctioned, but only as an emergency contingency operation. If I back you on this and you're wrong, we could *both* end up in prison. The word of Dr. Ivery and Arthur Carmichael isn't enough for me to act on, at least not in such a brazen fashion."

"I figured you might say that," I said, reaching into my satchel. "Here, I brought you something." I handed him the canister containing the shard.

"What is this?" he asked, taking it into his hands.

"I got it from a hidden safe in Dr. Ivery's home. The last thing she did before she died was give me the key. See for yourself."

Deitrik slowly unscrewed the lid of the metal canister and removed it. He reached in and withdrew both the shard and the little card that came with it. He set the fragment down on the table and read the plastic card.

I watched the color drain from his face. "Anomalous materials," he read. He set the card down and looked at the silver-white object on the table. "Fascinating." The shard caught the light in odd ways. It didn't emit light on its own, but appeared brighter than it should in the ambient light.

"It seems Doc Ivery smuggled this out of Site 471 and

was intending on taking it off-world with her. Maybe that's why they had her killed."

"I'll have to have it tested," he said, hesitantly, not taking his eyes off the fragment as he spoke. "To verify its authenticity."

"Whatever you do, do it carefully. I don't know what the hell that thing is made of, and I don't think Ascension does, either." Having finished eating, I wiped my mouth with a napkin. "The food was excellent, by the way."

"Dinner's on the house tonight, Easy," he said, still looking at the fragment.

"You sure? I'm good for it. I've got a wad of Arthur Carmichael's money burning a hole in my pocket."

"I'm sure, it's no trouble." He looked up at me again. "You should go. I'll have the security recordings scrubbed. You were never here."

"Of course."

"I will contact you with more information after the analysis." He put the fragment and the card back into the canister, sealed it, and placed it in his lap under the table.

"Alright, then," I said, standing up. I could tell that he was taking this seriously, which was what I needed. I tapped the control to open the booth; the curved doors slid open with a quiet hiss, and the sounds of the restaurant dining room could be heard once again. "I'll wait for your call." I paused at the door. "Deitrik? I wouldn't take too long. I've got a feeling we don't have a lot of time to sort this out." I closed the door and was on my way.

It took a few days and a little diplomacy on my part, but I managed to arrange a meeting with the folks from

Arcanum. We weren't down in their club this time, but were instead using a secure conference room in the same building, sitting around a big table. It was late at night and Lily and Dagny were both with me. Representing the activist organization was Dante, an elderly gentleman they called Doc, and a woman named Mi Kyong. I understood that the rest of the leadership of Arcanum was watching the meeting over video.

I went over everything that had gone down since I took the case, leaving out only a few details to protect Dagny's privacy. I didn't name the Baron, either, but I made it clear that I expected support from the Security Intelligence Service and an insider at Ascension. My hosts were not thrilled with this.

"If you would have asked me last week if I'd be contemplating an operation involving not only Ascension but the damned SIS, I'd have laughed at you," Doc said. "Yet here we are." He was bald and had to have been in his eighties. Despite his age (or maybe because of it), he commanded great respect from the others at Arcanum. His left arm was a clunky-looking cybernetic prosthetic and he wore a smart visor over his eyes. Lily told me that he was one of the founding members of the organization.

Mi Kyong spoke next. She was a petite Asian woman, maybe the same age as me, who stood no more than five foot two. She carried herself unpretentiously, wearing jeans and a T-shirt, with no makeup. "This entails significant risk," she said, speaking clearly and precisely. "What assurance do we have that this isn't all an effort to infiltrate our organization?"

"Are you serious?" Lily asked. "I used to be one of you! Look at the information we gave you!"

"You *used* to be one of us, yes," Mi Kyong said, coldly.

"The files they gave us on Ascension have all been authenticated," Dante pointed out. "They've been on the level with us so far."

"Let me ask you something," I said, calmly. "If the SIS or Ascension were trying to infiltrate Arcanum, don't you think there are better ways of going about it than through a private eye who straight-up *tells you* he's got a contact with ties to the SIS? I've been pretty transparent from the get-go. I didn't *have* to tell you about my contacts. Why would I tip my hand if I was trying to pull one over on you?"

Mi Kyong was unmoved. "A liar will always insist he is being honest with you," she said.

I sighed, trying not to get frustrated. "If I was trying to infiltrate your organization on behalf of the SIS or Ascension, I'd say I've already done a pretty good job, don't you think? Here I am, having a face-to-face meeting with Arcanum leadership. You weren't worried about it until I told you about their involvement."

Mi Kyong narrowed her eyes. "Some of us were worried about it." She turned to Doc. "We are already more exposed than we should be. I think we have gone far enough."

Doc looked thoughtful for a moment, sighed, and looked at me across the table. "My colleague is as blunt as a baseball bat, but she's not wrong. It was one thing to exchange information with you. It's another matter altogether to actively help you break into an Ascension-owned facility and abduct a patient. Even if you ignore the possible involvement of the SIS, that's still a long list of felonies we'd be abetting, if not committing. Kidnapping. Breaking and entering. Conspiracy. There are a lot of things that can go wrong, a lot of risk. As if that wasn't enough, you told us that they had one of their own scientists *killed*."

"Dante, come *on*," Lily said.

Dante took off his smart glasses and looked at her apologetically. "We're hackers, activists, information brokers. This? This is secret agent stuff."

"And I have a secret agent on the team," I said.

"So you claim," Mi Kyong said, "but you have not explained what it is this secret agent of yours can do for us."

"He got me out of jail once," I said, "and convinced a district attorney not to press charges on me. He's got a network of contacts in the city and colonial governments as well in the intelligence services. He's willing to stick his neck out on this one, provide us with some top cover, keep SecFor off us if things get sideways."

"Assuming this is true," Mi Kyong asked, "what about Ascension's corporate security?"

"I've got an in with them, too," I reminded them. "Arthur Carmichael."

"And you risk exposing us to them as well!"

"I can't believe what I'm hearing," Lily said, arms folded across her chest. "Arcanum is afraid of Ascension security now? Holy shit, Dante, things have changed since I left."

"A lot has happened that you don't know about," Dante said, defensively.

"It is not your concern," Mi Kyong added. She *really* didn't like Lily. If looks could kill, my assistant would have dropped dead right there.

Doc held up a hand then, quieting everyone down. There was some bad blood at the table and he was trying to keep things calm. "It's not a matter of being afraid, Lilith, it's a matter of risk." He turned to me. "What you are suggesting is not only illegal, Mr. Novak, it entails a litany of serious offenses, and all we have to go on is your word."

"I've been completely honest with you people from the start," I said.

"I believe that to be the case," Doc said, "but there are other possibilities to consider. One is that I might be wrong about you. Another is that you're unwittingly being used in a sting operation to entrap our people. A third possibility is that you sincerely believe things that aren't true. You have come to us with an incredible story— Ascension experimenting on some ancient alien artifact and that they were willing to kill a scientist to keep their secrets. It's a compelling story."

"It's not a story, it's the *truth.*"

"I would ask you to consider this from our perspective. Extraordinary claims require extraordinary evidence, and you have presented us with no evidence so far. We have only your word, and you, by your own admission, only have the word of a handful of other people—someone in the SIS, an Ascension security manager, and a dead scientist."

I hadn't told them about the object I recovered from Dr. Ivery's home. The fact that I handed it over to Deitrik would only make my mentioning it seem more suspicious.

"You also have my sister." Everyone turned to Dagny, who had spoken up for the first time since the meeting began. "Her name is Cassandra. Remember her? You people had no problem encouraging *her* to take personal risks when it benefitted *you*. You asked her to trust you to protect her identity. What proof did you give her that *you* were trustworthy? Huh? All she had to go on was your word and your reputation. It looks to me like that reputation is overblown, because as soon as she needs *your* help, you want nothing to do with it. Do you treat all your sources this way? Do they know that you'll abandon them as soon as they're no longer useful?"

I could tell that what Dagny said got to Dante. He was looking down at the table now. Even Doc was bothered by it. He was trying not to show it, but I could tell wanted to help. Mi Kyong, though, she wasn't having it. "Most of our sources don't expect us to break them out of secure facilities!" she snapped.

Dagny pushed against the conference table and stood up. "Nobody's expecting *you* to do anything, bitch!" Mi Kyong's eyes flashed with anger and she stood up, too.

I put a hand on Dagny's arm and gently squeezed, getting her attention, and raised my voice. "Let's everybody calm down, hey?" I turned my attention to Doc. "We're not asking you to break anyone out of that place. If anyone goes in it'll be me."

"How do you propose to do this?" Doc asked. Both Dagny and Mi Kyong sat back down and looked daggers at each other across the table.

"I'm not sure yet," I admitted. "Before I come up with a plan, I need to know what tools I have at my disposal.

Do you think your hackers could disrupt their security? You know, unlock some doors, disable some cameras, maybe trip a fire alarm?"

"It's possible," Dante said, "but there's no guarantee we'd be able to get into their system from the outside. Our best bet would be to upload our programs to their internal network. You could load them into one of their computers from a removable drive, maybe, or, I don't know, do a hard line splice and access it directly. Both would require physical access to the building, though."

"I have ways of getting into places I'm not supposed to be," I said. "Say I was able to successfully upload these programs of yours to their system. What could you do then?"

"Assuming their internal network architecture is typical, it should give us full control of their networked systems. It depends on a lot of factors, though. I'd have to see a map of their network to be able to say for sure." He looked over at Doc. "I request that I be allowed to help them do this. I'll go it alone to minimize the exposure to others, if necessary."

"Thank you, Dante," Lily said. I nodded at the kid.

"A decision like this requires a vote," he said, then turned to me. "Is there anything else you want to say to make your case?"

"Yeah. If everything I've learned is true, the entire colony could be in danger. It's big enough that even Ascension, with all their money and lawyers, couldn't get away with it if exposed. Whatever information I'm able to obtain about the Seraph, about Ascension's internal operations, I'll share all of it with you."

"You think your benefactor with the SIS will allow that?" Mi Kyong asked, sarcastically.

"Why don't you let *me* worry about that?" I replied, then looked at Doc again. "What do you say?"

"We will vote," he said, then fell silent. Mi Kyong looked down at a tablet in her hands. They didn't speak again for almost a minute.

"Well?" Dagny asked. "Will you help us?"

"I'm sorry," Doc said. He hesitated for a moment. "It has been decided. We cannot risk our people being implicated in something so risky, not when there are so many outside actors involved."

Before Dagny could say anything, I put a hand on her arm again. She looked at me and I shook my head slightly. There was no point in getting into it with these people again. "I understand," I said. I pushed my chair away from the table and stood up. "Thank you for hearing us out."

"Thanks for nothing," Dagny said. "Come on, Easy, let's get out of here."

"Yeah."

"I'll show them out," Dante said. Kid looked like he'd been gut-punched. I could tell he wasn't happy with Arcanum's decision. No one spoke until we were back out on the street. It was the middle of the night; traffic was light and the sidewalks were mostly empty. A light rain sprinkled down on us, and it was just cool enough out that you could see your breath.

Dante walked with us to the small parking lot behind the building, where my car was. He hung back and talked to Lily as Dagny and I got into the car. I couldn't hear what they were saying from where I was, but the conversation got a little animated. Lily lost her usually cool demeanor and was yelling at the poor kid. After some more angry hand gestures and raised voices, Dante walked away, head down. Lily came up to the car window, arms folded across her chest. She was trying really hard not to cry.

"Get in," I told her. "I'll give you a ride home."

"Thank you," she said with a sniffle, "but I'm fine. I'll get an auto-taxi."

"You sure? I don't feel great about leaving you out here by yourself. It's no trouble."

"I'll be okay, Boss," Lily said. "This is my old stomping grounds, remember? I'll hang out by the club entrance until my ride gets here. I just kinda want to be alone right now. Take Dagny home."

"Alright," I said. "Thanks for coming out with us. It was worth a shot, even if it didn't pan out."

"You mind if I come in a little late this morning?"

I looked at the clock on the dashboard. "You know what? Take a day."

"You sure?"

"Yeah, I'm sure. I'm not going to keep you up half the night and then tell you to show up at work eight hours later. Besides, I need to figure out what our next move is, and we can't really do anything until we hear back from Deitrik."

"Thank you," she said.

"Sure thing, kid. If you think of any good ideas, you let me know, okay?"

"I will, Boss. Have a good night."

"You too. Be safe. I'll see you tomorrow." With that, I drove off, leaving Lily behind.

"You really think she'll be okay?" Dagny asked.

"She can take care of herself," I said. "Besides, Arcanum has enough security around the building that she'll be safe there."

"What now?"

"Hell, I don't know. I need to stew on this for a while. The Arcanum people weren't wrong, though, this whole scheme carries a lot of risk. I can't really blame them for not wanting anything to do with it. In the meantime, let's get you home. It's been a long day."

She was quiet for a moment. "I don't want to go home. I don't . . . I don't feel safe there. I don't like being alone there anymore, not since . . . well, you know."

Getting shot is more traumatic than most people realize. It's not like hurting yourself by accident. Even if she makes a quick physical recovery, as Dagny did, having someone try to murder you can leave a person in a bad way.

"I'm sorry," she said. "I'm being silly."

"No, you're not. You've been through a hell of a lot since this whole thing started." I was stopped at a traffic light, not sure of which way to turn. "Where would you like me to take you? Do you have a safe place you can go?"

"I don't know," she said.

"Tell you what," I said, making a right turn. "You can stay at my place if you want." I hoped she wouldn't take that the wrong way. I just didn't know where else to bring her, short of getting her a hotel room someplace.

"I'd like that," she said quietly. "Are you sure it's no trouble?"

I grinned. "No trouble at all."

❋ ❋ ❋

It took me another hour to get home, and Dagny fell asleep in the car on the way. She was quiet in the elevator up to the 109th floor and during the walk to my apartment.

"Excuse the mess," I said, unlocking the door. "I wasn't expecting company."

The lights turned on as we stepped into the apartment. Penny automatically activated. "Welcome home, Easy," she said, in her polite, synthesized voice. "I see you have a guest."

"This is Dagny," I told her, hanging my coat up. "She'll be staying with us for a while."

"Hello, Dagny," Penny said.

"You hungry?" I asked Dagny.

"I'm starving."

"Help yourself to the kitchen," I said. "There's plenty of stuff that Penny can make for you. Sit, relax, put on some music. I'll go scare up some towels so you can take a shower."

We had dinner together and didn't talk much. While Dagny was showering I grabbed myself a pillow and a blanket and tossed them onto my big armchair. It was plenty comfy, especially reclined, and I'd slept in it plenty of times before. Dagny protested, insisted that I didn't need to give up my bed, but I told her she was getting the bed and that's all there was to it.

A while later I was settling into my chair when Dagny called me from the other room. "Easy?" she said, her voice muffled through the door. "Can you come in here, please?"

I got up and walked to the bedroom. I tapped the button and the door slid open. "What do you . . . need?"

"You," Dagny said. She stood at the front of my bed, naked as the day she was born. Her hair, highlighted blue again, hung carelessly over her bare shoulders. Her smooth skin was only blemished by a few scars, like the one on her face. The serpent tattooed on her left thigh continued up over her hip, with its head protruding down her pelvis. She stepped forward, pressing her perfect breasts against me, and threw her arms around my neck. "I need you," she repeated, looking up into my eyes.

Sleeping with a client is about the most unprofessional thing a detective can do. It's bad form, it can compromise your investigation, and it can lead to complicated, entangled relationships with someone you're in a contractual business agreement with. It's something I'd never done before, something I never even considered doing.

This case had me doing a lot of things I never considered doing before. I knew in the back of my mind that this was going too far, that the smart thing to do would be to back away. My God, though, she was beautiful. I slid my hands down her back, across her tight butt, and grabbed the backs of her thighs. She gasped, then giggled as I picked her up, wrapping her legs around me as I carried her to the bed.

I woke up late the next morning feeling like a million bucks. I disentangled myself from Dagny, who was softly snoring, dead to the world, and quietly left the bedroom. I took a shower while Penny made breakfast and brewed a pot of coffee.

I was sitting at the kitchen table, nursing a cup of coffee, and scrolling on my tablet when Lily called on an end-to-end encrypted connection. Her face appeared on my tablet screen when I accepted the call.

"Good morning, boss," she said. "I hope I didn't wake you."

"Nah, I've been up for a while. Did you have any trouble getting home last night?"

"No, it was fine."

"You're looking a little rough there, kid. Did you get any sleep?"

"Some. I stayed up pretty late turning all this over in my head, you know?"

"I'm open to ideas."

"That's why I called. I just got a message from Dante. He told me he'll help us."

"He did, huh? Did Arcanum change their minds, then?"

"He said he quit."

"Is that right? Lily, I think that boy is still sweet on you."

She blushed a little. "What? You think that's why he's doing this? He has a girlfriend."

I shrugged. "I'm not saying he doesn't genuinely want to help, but I'd bet my hat that he wouldn't be doing this if not for you."

"Oh, God. Am I using him?"

"You didn't ask him to quit Arcanum. He's an adult, he can make his own decisions. If he really wants to help, we could sure use him."

"You really think we can pull this off?"

"That depends on what Deitrik decides. No matter how we approach this, it's going to entail some pretty serious risks. You sure you still want to be a part of this?"

"I'm with you no matter what, Boss," Lily said. "You know that."

I smiled. I like to think I'm pretty good to work for, but I couldn't think of anything I'd done for Lily to garner this kind of loyalty from her. I considered it my responsibility to not let that loyalty get her in trouble. She trusted me and I didn't want to lead her astray. "I know you are, kid, but we're going to be smart about this. We all need to sit down together and come up with some ideas."

"You want to meet at the office?"

"Let me contact Arthur Carmichael first. We're going to need his help to pull this off, so he should be in on the planning. Unless something comes up before then, don't worry about going into the office until the usual time Monday morning."

"Understood. You want me to call the client and tell her what's going on?"

"That's not necessary. I'll tell her."

"Okay." Lily paused, looking at me quizzically. "Wait a second. Is she there with you? Did she go home with you last night?" I tried to fumble through a non-denial, but Lily saw right through it. "Oh my God," she said, smiling coyly at me. "You sly dog! I knew there was chemistry between you two, I could tell the first time I saw you together."

"Listen, this wasn't something I, you know, planned, it just kind of happened. It's a breach of professional conduct."

"Uh-huh. I want details. Tell me everything. What's she like? Easy, are you blushing?"

I did feel my face getting flush, as a matter of fact. "If

you're done giving me a hard time, how about you call Dante?"

"I'm sorry, Boss. I'm just happy for you! You haven't gone out with anyone in a long time. It's cute."

"Cute," I repeated.

"It is! You're a great guy. You deserve to be happy."

"Yeah, well, I just hope I didn't make things worse. This case is already complicated enough."

"Of all the things we have to worry about right now, that's something I'd worry about the least. Besides," she said with a smile, "life is short. Sometimes you have to take a chance. Maybe she's worth it!"

I looked up when I heard my bedroom door slide open. "Easy?" It was Dagny, wearing nothing but a pair of panties and my shirt. Unbuttoned, it was way too big for her, but damn, she looked good all the same.

I turned back to the tablet. "Maybe she is. I'm going to let you go."

"Will do," Lily said. "Have fun!" She winked at me then disconnected the call.

I shook my head, set the tablet down, and turned to Dagny. "Good morning, beautiful. Want some coffee?" I was curious to see how she'd act. You can get a pretty good idea of how a woman feels about having slept with you by how she handles herself the next morning. If she quickly gathers her things and leaves, that's probably not a good sign. It usually means that it was nothing but a one-night stand. She might even regret the whole thing. If she stays, though? Then it might go somewhere.

"I would love some coffee," she said. She padded into the kitchen, barefoot, and kissed me on the cheek.

I grabbed a mug from my cupboard and poured her a cup of coffee. "How'd you sleep?"

"Like the dead," she said. She took the mug and sat down across from me at my small kitchen table. "What time is it?"

"It's almost ten," I said. "I've only been up for about an hour."

"You could have gotten me up."

"Eh, you looked comfortable. I figured I'd let you rest." I took another sip of coffee. "I heard from Lily. Her friend Dante decided to help us after all."

"Really? That's great!"

"It's just him, though, not Arcanum proper. He's doing it on his own."

"So we're really doing this? We're going to try and rescue Cassie?"

"A lot of it depends on what my SIS contact says. Look, I need to level with you. All those concerns the Arcanum people had last night? Those are legitimate. There is a lot of personal and legal risk that we will be undertaking if we do this, even if we are somehow sanctioned by the SIS. We could both end up in jail or dead."

"I'm not afraid," she said. "Cassie is all the family I have left. If you're not willing to risk it all for your own sister, what kind of person are you?"

"I admire your guts. I just want to make sure you understand what we're getting ourselves into here. We're way past any normal case."

Putting an elbow on the table, she rested her chin in her hand and grinned at me. "I think we went way past a normal case last night. Either that or you really go the extra mile for your clients."

There was that smile again, that dangerous smile that could make a man contemplate damned near anything. It was disarming, too; despite the seriousness of what we were discussing, I actually chuckled. "Heh. No, that is definitely not included in my normal investigatory process. In fact, it's never happened before."

Dagny raised her eyebrows. "Really? Not once?"

I shook my head while I sipped my coffee. "Not once. I've had a couple clients make advances now and again. I always politely declined."

"That's interesting. How come?"

"Mostly it was just prudent. One time a rich man's wife hired me to find out if her husband was cheating on her. When I confirmed that he was, she tried to jump me right in my office. Revenge sex. I didn't want any part of that."

"Ew, no. That's just asking for trouble."

"It is. I got to be honest with you, what happened last night was unprofessional of me, especially while the case is open."

"I wouldn't call it unprofessional," she said with a twinkle in her eye. "You were more than competent."

I tried hard to stop myself from blushing but I don't think it worked. "That's . . . not what I meant."

"I know. You don't regret it, do you?"

"I don't," I said, honestly.

"Good, because I don't, either. Believe it or not, I don't sleep around much, and it's not for a lack of men trying to get in my pants."

"I didn't try to get into your pants."

"I know. You were nothing but professional. You believed me and were willing to help when no one else was. You risked your life to protect me. You saved my life. Now you're talking about doing something crazy and illegal to rescue my sister."

"I hope you don't think I did all that to try and get you into bed," I said.

"I don't. Not at all. It just made me realize what a good guy you are. So stop worrying about me, okay? It's sweet, but I'm a big girl and I know what I'm doing."

"Fair enough," I said.

"This SIS contact of yours, any idea when you'll hear from him?"

"It's hard to say with him. Our interactions are strictly off the books and he usually doesn't trust electronic messaging, even if it's encrypted."

"Then how will he get ahold of you?"

"He has his ways. In fact, let me check something." I picked up my tablet again and scrolled through my calls and messages. There hadn't been any calls overnight, but I had one new message in my inbox. Penny didn't alert me to it when I got up because it wasn't from one of my saved contacts. It was from an unknown account and I was surprised that it made it past my junk mail filter. I tapped the screen to open the message.

Easy:

Come to the restaurant ASAP. Most urgent, do not wait for normal business hours. Come alone.

"What is it?" Dagny asked.

"My guy at the SIS," I said, setting the tablet down and

standing up. "I'm going to get dressed. I need to go meet him."

"Do you want me to come with you?"

"He told me to come alone."

"That sounds sketchy. Are you sure?"

I smiled at her. "Don't worry, I've known this guy for years. You, uh . . . you don't have to go home if you don't want to. You're welcome to stay here."

A wicked little smile appeared on Dagny's face. "The sex was good, Easy, but don't you think it's a little soon to ask me to move in?"

Once again I tried not to blush and failed. All I could do was chuckle and shake my head.

"I'm just teasing you," Dagny said. She stood up and threw her arms over my shoulders. "Go do what you need to do. I'll be here when you get back. Be safe."

Then she kissed me and, for a brief moment, things didn't seem so bad.

CHAPTER 12

The Bauhaus Gaststätte restaurant was closed when I arrived there an hour or so later. That wasn't surprising; they were never open on Sundays. What was unusual was the Baron wanting to see me outside of normal business hours. I figured he liked to keep up the appearances of me just being a fan of the restaurant (which was true, I loved the food). Having me come over when they were closed was more suspicious, though. I could only assume that whatever testing he had done had verified the authenticity of the Seraph fragment.

I parked around back, by the staff entrance, and got out of my car. It was a cool but clear day, a pleasant break from the normal rain and gloom of autumn in Delta City. The door slid open with a quiet hiss as I approached and closed behind me. One of the server robots was waiting for me inside.

"Please come this way, sir," it said. Without another word it pivoted around and rolled away. I followed the bot across the restaurant and was led to Deitrik's private office. He was waiting for me inside, sitting behind a large desk that appeared to be fashioned from real wood.

"Thank you for seeing me on such short notice," Deitrik said. He didn't stand up to greet me. He looked tired, like he hadn't gotten any sleep. He motioned toward a plush chair facing his desk. "Please, sit down."

I took my hat and coat off and held them in my lap after taking a seat. "Why do I feel like I've been called to the principal's office?" I asked, only half-jokingly.

The Baron didn't smile. He took a deep breath and exhaled slowly. His hands were folded together on the desk in front of him, almost like he was praying.

"Deitrik, are you alright?"

He slowly shook his head. "No, I am not." He looked up at me. "I had the object you brought me tested in a laboratory. They were unable to identify what material it is made from, and it displayed properties that they described as . . ." He trailed off.

"Anomalous?" I said, finishing the statement for him.

"Yes. I did some more checking. I wanted to make sure I had investigated every possibility before reaching a conclusion. For example, it is not illegal for a corporation to have small samples of alien technology to study. There is a process which allows for this outlined in the Conventions on the Discovery and Control of Alien Technology, Organisms, and Remains, and it was possible that Ascension had acquired the sample legally. That might have also explained why Dr. Ivery was apparently planning on smuggling it off-world."

"An artifact like that would be immensely valuable on the black market."

"Indeed. However, Ascension has *not* requested nor been granted the legal authorizations to acquire and keep a sample of alien technology for research purposes. Nothing of the sort is to be found in any of the company's records, going back a decade."

"If they didn't acquire it legally, that means it was either brought to Nova Columbia off the books or they found it here."

He nodded. "Correct. The information encoded onto the identification card included with the fragment lists when and where it was found. It was excavated from Site 471."

"Well, then," I said, "isn't that all you need? That's proof, right? Can you expose this whole thing?" He didn't answer. "Deitrik?"

"I sent a routine query to the station chief of Nova Columbia's SIS detachment. I didn't mention you or what you found. I stated that I'd heard in the news that an Ascension scientist was found murdered, and that sources are reporting unconfirmed rumors of possible alien technology at Site 471."

"I see. What did they say?"

"I was told that they had also heard of the rumor and investigated it thoroughly. SIS investigators were invited to go inspect Site 471, which they did, and that no evidence of alien technology was found. I was assured that Ascension was quite forthcoming and turned over reams of documentation, which they also sent me to review if I wanted to. Dr. Ivery's death was, in their opinion, a coincidence."

"Is that right? Seemed pretty conveniently timed to me."

"Yes, well...this puts me in something of a predicament, doesn't it? I have, on one hand, the assurances of the local SIS station chief that there is no alien technology on Nova Columbia, and that the matter was investigated thoroughly. On the other hand, I have physical evidence of alien technology found on Nova Columbia."

"It's a pickle, that's for sure. Seems to me that either this station chief really doesn't know about it, or that he's in on it."

"Do you remember what we discussed before, about how difficult it would be to hide such a find?"

"Yeah?"

"It is theoretically possible that SIS officers inspected Site 471 and somehow missed the excavation site. It is also theoretically possible that what Dr. Ivery said about that wasn't true."

"She was right about everything else so far."

"I know. All of this information is leading me to the conclusion that the local SIS office is in fact conspiring with Ascension to keep secret the discovery of advanced alien technology, in violation of Commonwealth law and the Conventions."

"That's a big deal, Deitrik. Are you sure?"

"Objectively? No. Subjectively? My gut tells me something is very wrong, and that I can't trust my own agency."

"You didn't answer me before. Can't you expose all this now? Take what you have to the Colonial government?"

"You don't understand the gravity of the allegation, Easy," he said, looking down at the desk again. "Never in the history of the Security Intelligence Service has an entire branch office actively conspired to break the law like this. There have been scandals, yes, but nothing of this magnitude. I also can't rule out the possibility that this isn't limited to Nova Columbia, and that the Service itself may be compromised. Even an artifact like the one you gave me can be explained away, especially if it's just my word against both the SIS and Ascension. I also don't know to what extent Nova Columbian government officials are involved."

"I need to ask you something. Are you absolutely sure that this is a rogue operation? Is it possible this is all being done in accordance with the letter of the law, and that you've just been kept out of the loop for some reason?"

"I have considered that possibility. I was up most of last night considering it, as a matter of fact. I spent hours reviewing procedures, regulations, and the law, trying to find a way for this to not be what it looks like."

"No luck?"

He shook his head. "There is no procedural or regulatory mechanism for such a find to be kept hidden from someone in my position. To do so would be to defeat the entire purpose of my being here. I have been delegated powers from the inspector general. Attempting to conceal operations from me is in of itself an actionable violation of SIS regulations."

"What can you do, then?"

"There isn't much in the way of set procedure for a situation like this. What I'm supposed to do is report my findings to a higher office and await instructions."

"Do you *have* a higher office on Nova Columbia?"

"No. There is only the Embassy of the Terran Confederation, and they are not in my chain of command. If I bring this to them, they may start an investigation, but it will be a ponderously slow affair, working through the bureaucracy, and most likely that won't even begin until they send a message to and receive a response from Earth."

"Hm. May as well cut out the middle man and call Earth yourself, then."

"I am putting together a communiqué, but even then, the response will be slow. Assuming I could get the message uploaded to a ship leaving immediately, it'll take seven weeks of local time for it to reach Earth, and another seven weeks for the reply to get here, not including any time headquarters has to spend deliberating on the matter."

"So months, basically."

"Yes. Given incidents like Medusae Fossae, I don't know if waiting for months is prudent. As you have pointed out, they could potentially be putting the colony at risk. Even if I sidestep the normal chain of command and bring this all to the Colonial government, I still don't have much evidence. The fragment may not be enough by itself. The person who seemed to know the most about Project Isaiah, Dr. Ivery, is dead."

"There are other people who know what's going on," I pointed out. "Arthur and Cassandra Carmichael. It seems to me we can help each other. I need to get Cassandra Carmichael out of that facility. You need testimony from witnesses. If I'm able to recover Cassandra, her stepfather will talk. Cassandra herself might be able to testify. I also have some Ascension records she left for her sister, nothing definitive, but it might help. Hell, I'll do you one better—you help me with this, and I'll testify about what Doc Ivery told me."

"You don't happen to have a recording of it, do you?"

"'Fraid not. People are hesitant to talk to a snoop to begin with. You get a reputation for secretly recording them when they do talk, you'll be out of sources in short order. But I'll still go under oath and give my account, if you need me to. Dagny Carmichael was with me, she can vouch for what I say."

"Desperate times call for desperate measures," Deitrik said, more to himself than to me. "Do you really think you can get her out of there?"

"I don't know," I said, honestly, "but I'll try. I've got a few aces up my sleeve, and Arthur Carmichael is willing to help me."

He nodded. "Very well." He swiveled around in his chair and grabbed a book off of the bookcase behind his desk. It was a leather-bound Bible, and he set it on the desk in front of me. He then reached over to his computer and tapped the screen to wake it up. He rotated a camera so that we were both in its field of view, then addressed it directly.

"My name is Deitrik Freiherr von Hauser," he said. "I am the adjunct inspector general for the Security Intelligence Service, Nova Columbia branch. My badge number is three-three-six-two-four-zero one." He then turned to me. "I am now going to swear you in as a temporary deputy officer of the Terran Confederation. Do you understand and consent?"

"Uh, I do," I said.

"If you care to, please place your hand on the Bible." I did as he asked. "Now repeat after me. I, state your name."

"I, Ezekiel Novak . . ."

"Do solemnly swear to support and defend the Articles of the Terran Confederation, against all enemies, human and alien; that I will bear true faith and allegiance to the same; that I take this obligation of my own free will, without coercion, reservation, or false purpose; that I will faithfully discharge the duties of the office on which I am about to take; so help me God."

"So help me God," I repeated.

"Ezekiel Novak, by the power vested in me by the Articles of the Terran Confederation and the Charter of the Security Intelligence Service, you are hereby legally sworn in as a temporary officer of the Terran Confederation. This post is voluntary, uncompensated, and you may resign at any time. Do you understand?"

"I do."

He reached across the desk and shook my hand. "Welcome to the SIS, Easy." He glanced over at his computer. "End recording."

"Now what?" I asked.

"Now we consult with the other concerned parties and come up with a plan to rescue Cassandra Carmichael."

I was able to arrange another meeting with Arthur Carmichael for Monday evening, the next night. As you can imagine, he was pretty anxious to get going, and for the money he was paying me the least I could do was be prompt. He sent me directions to a place he described as a safe house on the southwest side of the Crater, a large home he rented through a shell company. Dagny, Dante, Lily, and I all piled into my car and set off across town.

His two security men, the always-cool Slick and the imposing Truck, were waiting for us at the house. I still didn't like these guys, on account of them kicking my ass and then kidnapping me, but Carmichael seemed to trust them. He must have been paying them pretty well to get them to stick by him as he went up against the company, or else maybe he had something on them. They greeted the four of us politely when we arrived, then showed us to what they said was a secure conference room. They asked us to leave our personal devices in the hall and let us in, closing the doors behind us.

Arthur Carmichael was waiting for us inside, sitting at the far end of a conference table with a portable holographic projector on it. He stood up slowly when we entered and locked eyes with Dagny. Nobody said anything for a few awkward moments. "Dagny," he said, trailing off slowly. "It's been a long time."

"It's . . . good to see you, Arthur," she said, stiffly. "Thank you for this."

He smiled at her, sadly. "There's so much I want to talk to you about, but now isn't the time. Just . . . thank you for doing this."

I glanced over to Dagny to see how she'd respond. She looked down at the floor for a moment, then back up at her stepfather, and nodded. With the family reunion out of the way, we all sat down and I introduced Carmichael to Lily and Dante.

"These two are both experienced hackers and net-divers," I said. "Lily's worked with me for years, and she can vouch for Dante here."

"I see," Carmichael said. "And what is it that you two can do?"

Dante answered his question with a question. "You don't happen to have access to the Ventura Medical Research Center's systems, do you?"

"Not directly, no," Carmichael admitted. "It's a subsidiary company and is outside of my normal scope of operations. They have their own security manager who doesn't answer to me and I can't directly access their network. If I try, they'll know that I've located Cassandra. Surprise is the only advantage we have right now." He looked thoughtful for a minute and rubbed his chin. "However . . . as of four months ago, all of the company's subsidiaries were required to standardize on Ascension's network architecture, to streamline interoperability, consolidate personnel files, things like that. I *do* have current, proprietary network blueprints and security protocols for the company. As a senior security administrator I have access to all of this information. Will that work?"

Dante's eyes went wide. "Y-yes," he stammered.

"You're willing to give that to us?" Lily asked. "Couldn't you get in trouble?"

"Trouble?" Carmichael chuckled and shook his head. "I could end up sued to bankruptcy and thrown in prison for corporate espionage. I don't care about any of that anymore. The only thing that matters is getting Cassandra back. I'll give you whatever you need. What do you plan on doing with this information?"

"We might be able to create a worm," Dante said, "one that will allow us to take over their entire system."

"It's possible," Carmichael said, "but it might be difficult, even with the information I can give you."

"Trust me," Dante said, grinning, "we're *really* good at this."

"Why all the security for a medical research lab?" Dagny asked. "Is this just because they're keeping Cassie there?"

"Not exactly," Carmichael said. "The Ventura Medical Research Center is a Biosafety Level-5 laboratory that primarily focuses on the study of, and developing treatments for, life-threatening conditions brought on by exposure to non-terrestrial organisms," Carmichael explained.

"Like Kellerman's Syndrome?" Dante asked.

"Yes. It's also researching conditions that occur on other colonized worlds. In fact, it's the only lab on Nova Columbia to possess samples of some of the organisms it does. Some of them are quite rare, and effective treatments for them, once patented, would be very valuable. That's why Ascension bought VMRC.

"However, because of the dangerous nature of the organisms being studied, and the potential value of the proprietary information the lab produces, it's a high-security facility. A breach will trigger a response."

"From SecFor?" Lily asked.

He shook his head. "No. The first response will be from corporate security. Ascension has four active Special Response Teams and one is on call at all times. If the alarm goes out, they'll send a jump-jet full of heavily armed operators who will shoot first and ask questions later. If that happens, our odds of success aren't good."

"Okay," Dante said, looking thoughtful. "Could we possibly disable the alarm, stop the call for help from going out?"

Carmichael leaned in and rested an elbow on the table. I wondered if, despite the serious circumstances, he wasn't enjoying the scheming. Doesn't everyone fantasize about screwing over their boss from time to time? "You won't be able to stop them from triggering the alarm, but you might be able to cut off their intranet so the alarm doesn't go out."

"Won't they realize something is wrong?" I asked.

"They will eventually," Carmichael said, "but this might buy us some time. Typically, the sort of emergency call for help that triggers a response from a Special Response Team is similar to a silent alarm in a bank. It's designed so that employees can activate it without the assailants realizing it, so they don't panic and start hurting people. The company has a policy of always responding to these alarms, even if it turns out to be nothing. They're designed so as to be difficult to trigger accidentally and don't require any further feedback from the person calling for help. The trick is to make their intranet think the call for help went out as intended."

Lily chimed in. "I think we can do that. A false feedback algorithm."

"This won't stop them from calling someone by other means," I pointed out.

"It won't," Carmichael said, "but realistically, we're not going to be able to steal Cassandra out from under their noses without them realizing it. The best we can hope for is to give you enough time to get in and get her out."

"How are you going to get this worm into their system in the first place?" I asked. "You can't hack into it remotely, can you?"

"Probably not," Lily said. "Ascension's encryption and network security protocols were always tough to crack."

"We haven't had a successful hack of our networks in several years," Carmichael said. I could tell that, even now, he was proud of the work he'd done.

"Right," Dante said. "The way you usually gain access to a system is by getting someone who does have access to the network to install your program for you. You can send a message with the worm encoded in it, or figure out the password of someone with network access. That's usually all it takes."

"If they weren't watching me the way they are, I could send an official email from my office with your worm embedded in it. I don't think that will work, the situation being as it is. I'm being watched. If I try to do anything involving the Ventura Medical Research Center, they'll know, and we'll be compromised."

"You don't have anyone you trust who could maybe do it for you?" Lily asked.

Carmichael shook his head. "Once you get assigned to Project Isaiah, nobody talks to you anymore. It's a black hole. Even if I were to create an alternate account and send it, there's a very good chance it'll get picked up by our protection software, or that the message will be flagged. Internal correspondence is heavily monitored. There's no guarantee that this will gain us access to the system."

"Okay," I said. "We're going to have to do a recon of the building to see if we can find a way in."

"Let me show you the building in question," Carmichael said, tapping at a tablet in his hands. The holo-projector lit up and generated a three-dimensional image, a trio of tall buildings somewhere in the city. Each tower was perfectly triangular if viewed from above, and they were arranged in a big equilateral triangle, with a point facing inward toward the center. A massive circular platform was suspended in midair between the three buildings, near their tops. Below that, many covered walkways and tramways connected the towers. At ground level, between the three buildings, was a cluster of lower structures.

"This complex is called Research Towers," he continued. "It's a hub for numerous industrial and commercial scientific concerns, as well as being the main campus of the Delta City Institute of Technology."

"The university?" Dante asked.

"The same," Carmichael confirmed. "The three towers each have one hundred and thirty floors. The platform in the center is a landing pad for aircraft, complete with parking space and automated traffic control. DCIT is in the Southwest Tower. Among the smaller buildings at ground level are a hotel and a convention center, as well as a station for the city monorail system."

The hologram zoomed in, focusing on one of the three buildings, and he kept narrating. "The Ventura Medical Research Center is here, in the North Tower, on the north side of the eighty-fifth floor. The research center has forty-five employees and operates during normal business hours on weekdays. At any given time during the day, anywhere from one hundred and fifty to two hundred thousand people are working at, living in, or passing through the transit hub of Research Towers."

"Jesus," Lily said, looking at the hologram. "This is where they're keeping Cassandra Carmichael? Talk about hiding in plain sight."

"Indeed," Carmichael agreed. "I never would have guessed that this is where she is being held, had my contacts not told me so. The company has several, ah, black sites, at which they can hide things that need to be hidden."

"But you would have probably found out if she was at one of those sites," I pointed out. "How certain are you that she's even there?"

"As certain as I can be," he answered. "There was a direct flight to Research Towers from Site 471 shortly after . . . well, let's just call it *the incident* for now. This flight corresponds to when I think my daughter was removed from Site 471. My contact, who works in logistics, was able to get a look at the cargo manifest and flight log before it was scrubbed. Mind you, I was still at Site 471 at this time, and had no access to outside networks. I learned all of this later."

"That's some compartmentalization," Dante said.

"As I said, Project Isaiah is a black hole. This cargo manifest listed one nonambulatory patient, an Ascension employee whose name was supposedly redacted for privacy reasons, being brought to VMRC for observation. This patient's age, sex, and description match Cassandra's."

"Nonambulatory?" Dagny asked. "What happened to her?"

"I'm not going to get into it right now," he said. "The last time I saw her she was in a medically induced coma. I will have a doctor here to safely revive her when the operation is complete."

Carmichael's lack of candor was frustrating, but I couldn't blame him for not being entirely forthcoming. In any case this information was important to know. Cassandra wouldn't be able to walk out on her own.

Carmichael continued, "She was transported from the landing pad to the Research Center in a medical isolation pod, and was logged as having contracted Kellerman's Syndrome. I was able to cross-reference that information with Ascension's accident and incident reporting system; no cases of Kellerman's Syndrome have been reported in almost four years."

"That's all you have to go on?" I asked.

"Yes," Carmichael said, curtly. "For the money I'm paying you, I'm afraid it will have to suffice." He looked me in the eye. "If you want my cooperation on exposing Project Isaiah, this is what I require."

"The whole colony could be in danger!" Lily said.

"You have no idea," Carmichael replied, coldly. "But if I do anything before Cassandra is safe ... I don't know what will happen to her. If there's a chance, even the slightest chance, that I can get her back safely, then I must try."

"I understand," Dagny said softly. "I'm with you, Arthur. Whatever it takes to get my sister back."

I shrugged. "Well then, I guess we better figure this out," I said.

"I know it's daunting," Carmichael said. "If this goes wrong we could all end up in prison."

"I have gotten us some overhead cover on that," I said. Now was as good a time as any to tell him. I pulled out the credential wallet the Baron gave me and opened it for him to see. Inside was a laser-cut titanium badge, coated in platinum, bearing the shield of the SIS. Below that was an identification card he had made for me. "This operation has been greenlit by the SIS under an emergency contingency provision, as a matter of urgent colonial security."

Carmichael's eyes went wide. "What? You're serious? The Security Intelligence Service? *You?*" He was angry.

I held up a hand. "Calm yourself, Mr. Carmichael. This isn't a setup. I got roped into it same as you. It's good news for us, though, because it means we have a better chance of pulling this off and not getting arrested for it. Just know that the SIS expects to fully debrief you when this is over. I told them you'd cooperate if we got Cassandra back."

"This doesn't make any sense," he said. "The SIS has been on the ground at Site 471 for months! What in the hell are you trying to pull, Novak?"

Aw, hell, I thought. *Probably shouldn't have told him.* "Look, something is definitely screwy here. My SIS handler thinks the local office has gone rogue. I don't know all the details, but whatever you people are doing up there has not been authorized through the proper channels."

Carmichael sat back in his chair, looking defeated. "Unbelievable."

"You're telling me. Listen, I don't know what all is going on with the SIS. I'm just a private eye; these spy games are above my pay grade. All I know is that I have a high-level SIS intelligence officer willing to help me get your daughter back if you're willing to talk to him after. We need all the help we can get if we're going to pull this off."

He nodded. "I suppose we're committed, aren't we?" He sighed. "Let's get to it, then. How do we get you in, and, more importantly, how do we get you and Cassie out?"

I looked at the holographic projection of the building and rubbed my chin. "Our biggest problem is that the moment they think we're up to something, they'll call for a security response team. What if . . ." I trailed off for a moment, then looked back up at Carmichael. "Hypothetically speaking, what would the response look like if there was an incident? Not a security breach, but some other kind of emergency? A hazardous materials leak, or maybe a fire? They'd have to move her, right?"

"I think I see where you're going with this," Carmichael said. "Research Towers has numerous laboratories of different specialties, and they work with all manner of hazardous materials: biological, chemical, even radiological. Several entities in the complex have their own emergency response teams, and the complex has an in-house fire department." He looked down at the electronic tablet in his hands and tapped at the screen a few times. "There's a mutual response agreement in place. If the leaseholder doesn't have its own response capabilities, or the incident exceeds their ability to contain it, the other teams in the complex will respond as quickly as they can. For anything major, the fire department, which has its own hazard containment team, will respond.

If that fails, Public Safety and the Metro Fire Department will respond."

"Would the company send a response team for this kind of emergency?"

"They shouldn't, not right away, if they're following standard operating procedure. Ascension has high value assets all over the city. The SRT won't deploy unless there's an alarm or a direct report of a breach of physical security. They don't respond to things like fire alarms."

"That makes sense," I said. "It would be too easy to cause a diversion that way." I was quiet for a moment, turning some things over in my head. "Okay, here's what I'm thinking."

Planning a heist is the easy part; actually getting away with the goods is where things get complicated. There are a lot of variables and not all of them are under your control. You have to account for as many as possible while knowing that you can't possibly account for them all.

It took a few days for our little band of strange bedfellows to get the operation started. Using the network blueprints and security protocol information that Carmichael had given them, Lily and Dante spent the time tailoring their malicious computer program while I began reconnaissance on the building itself. The architectural plans for Research Plaza were publicly available, but blueprints don't tell you much about the day-to-day workings of a place. You actually have to get eyes on your target if you want to understand the patterns, the comings and goings, and the general state of physical security. That was my job.

Dagny offered to help, but given her relationship to Arthur and Cassandra Carmichael, I was worried that she was on Ascension's radar and would tip them off if facial recognition software was able to ID her. I opted instead to take Dante along, since two of us could cover more ground in one visit.

Working in our favor was the fact that the complex was open to the public and bustled with activity during the day. Tens of thousands of people, from students, to scientists, to office staff, came and went constantly. It made it much easier to move around without raising suspicion.

The Research Towers complex had its own maintenance and building security staff, supplemented by a fleet of robots for the menial tasks. Security cameras in the public spaces, such as corridors and plazas were common, but each individual suite or office was on a separate network. The complex's employees wore badges that granted them access to different areas of the buildings, and there were enough of them that they weren't likely to all know or be able to recognize one another.

Wearing a hidden camera, I gathered footage of their uniform attire, their routine, and how they generally presented themselves. I made it a point to hang out by doorways, allowing the radio-frequency decoder in my pocket to record the signals broadcast by the card readers and ID badges as employees accessed them. The badges were passive, only activating to broadcast a signal when pinged by a reader. That made things easier—some places use active broadcasting ID, allowing them to track every single badge-wearer at all times, and that would have complicated the plan.

Once the RF decoder had scanned the transmission of several card readers, it was able to duplicate and broadcast those signals over short distances. This allowed me to ping and receive information from numerous employees' ID badges as I wandered throughout the building. Dante was doing the same thing in a different part of the complex. The buildings' access codes didn't seem to change or rotate throughout the day, and none of the access readers used by building staff were equipped with frequency-hopping or other security features.

Lackadaisical security is the norm in most places, especially in public commercial facilities. What security they did have was mostly for crowd control and getting them a discount on their insurance. This all worked in our favor. Using the signal data that Dante and I gathered, Lily was able to program smart access badges, ones that could use any of the access codes we'd gathered. She also set them to use different sets of credentials as often as possible, so that anyone looking at the access logs wouldn't have a clear pattern of where we went.

Before leaving, I made my way to the eighty-fifth floor, where the Ventura Medical Research Center was located. The research center had a lobby that was accessible from one of the main public corridors, but I thought it was too risky to go in, even just to look around. Being owned by Ascension, they would definitely have good security, including cameras with facial recognition software. We weren't going to be able to get past the lobby with the access codes we had been collecting, but Dante thought that there might be another way.

A couple days later he and I made our second visit to

the Research Towers complex, this time disguised as maintenance technicians. The uniforms the techs wore were common work coveralls with the Research Towers logo printed on them. Having a couple sets of those fabricated for us at a small clothing shop only took an hour or so. We each wore ID badges that Lily had encoded; between the maintenance, security, and vendor personnel we had gathered data on, we could get almost anywhere in the complex.

They would not get us into the Ventura Medical Research Center, but Dante didn't think we needed to in order to gain access to their computers. After studying building blueprints he was able to locate a telecommunications junction box in a network closet off a maintenance corridor near our target. We *did* have access to that corridor and to the closet. There wasn't any security on the junction box except a normal commercial electronic lock, which I was able to get open with my locksmith tools.

"What now, kid?" I asked, looking at Dante. The junction box was mounted on the wall. The closet was warm and there was barely enough room for both of us to fit into it.

He reached into his pocket and pulled out a tablet computer. It was a bulky, ruggedized device, with multiple ports and several different cables. "I need you to keep a lookout while I do this. It might take a few minutes." He pulled a retractable cable from the tablet and plugged it into the junction box's access port.

"What are you going to do?"

"These are high-bandwidth network lines," he said, nodding at the junction box. On the inside of the door was a diagram, showing which vendor each hardline belonged to, including the Ventura Medical Research Center. "This is the portal between the VMRC intranet and the planetary network." He paused long enough to draw another cable from the device and plug it into a port embedded in his skull, behind his right ear. "With the network architecture and security protocol information Carmichael gave us, I should be able to get our malware into VMRC's systems without them realizing it. Then, unless they disconnect their intranet from the planetary network entirely, we should be able to access it remotely whenever we want."

"You sure you want to plug this thing into your head like that?"

"It'll go much faster using a direct neural interface. I'll just be zoned out while I'm working, so I need you to keep an eye on me. It can be disorienting doing this standing up. Don't let me fall over."

"What am I supposed to do if we need to leave?"

"I'm not going in that deep. I'll still be able to hear you, but you may have to give me a good shake to get my attention."

"Got it. Good luck, kid."

Dante grinned. "Luck's got nothing to do with it," he said, putting his smart glasses back on. "I'll be back in a few."

He leaned against the wall and fell silent. I quietly closed the door to the closet in case somebody else walked past. It got damned hot in there and sweat started to trickle down my brow. Dante was sweating, too, but I didn't think he would even notice. Plugged into the system as he was, he seemed oblivious to everything around him. His neck and facial muscles twitched as he did his thing.

After ten minutes of this I was starting to get worried. I was just about to give his shoulder a shake when he lurched forward, stumbling into me. I caught him before he fell and asked him if he was okay.

"I'm fine," he said, breathing hard. "I'm fine." He took off his glasses and looked around. "It's hot in here."

"How'd it go? I was starting to think you got lost or something."

He grinned again. "Mission accomplished. Sorry it took so long. Their network has an algorithm that automatically scans for malignant code at regular intervals. I had to disable that before I could install the worm."

"Are we good to go, then?"

"Oh yeah. Carmichael's security administrator access paid off. Once the worm was installed, I took a snapshot of the network and told the algorithm that this is what it should look like."

"So when the algorithm scans the network again, it'll think the program you installed belongs there."

"Exactly," Dante said. "I created several hidden accounts for us. We can remotely access their intranet and poke around at our leisure. Lily's false-feedback algorithm is installed, too—we can cut off their network access and they won't realize we're capturing all of their outbound communications. They won't even know they've been compromised until it's all over."

"Good job, kid. Come on, let's get out of here."

The malicious program that Dante and Lily cooked up worked like they said it would, but we were still limited on what we could access. A lot of the work going on at the Ventura Medical Research Center was compartmentalized, even within their own internal network. The accounts that Dante created couldn't get into the encrypted data storage to see what kind of research they were conducting.

This didn't mean that embedding the kids' malware into the Research Center's intranet had been a waste of time; far from it. They had reported to Research Towers that they were currently hosting one in-patient who was the subject of a study. In the event of an emergency, she was to be evacuated in an isolation pod and moved as quickly as possible to another approved medical facility. They had a memorandum of understanding in place to allow her to be taken off-site without being held up by the building authorities.

No further identifying information on this patient was given, allegedly due to medical privacy laws, but our inside access allowed us to pull up a confidential document about her. With that we were able to confirm that Cassandra Carmichael was there. She'd been checked in under a false name, June Davis, but there were photographs. Both Dagny and Arthur Carmichael positively identified her, and my facial recognition software matched her with ninety-seven percent confidence.

At last, I'd found her. We couldn't determine what her status was, if she was ambulatory or not. Carmichael said that she was in an induced coma when they evacuated her from Site 471, so I assumed I was going to have to wheel her out of there.

Our access to the VMRC intranet proved useful in other

ways, too. We were able to have a look at their administrative database. From that we learned the names, addresses, and contact information of everyone who worked there. We knew what their schedules were, we knew how much they got paid, and we could even read their employee evaluations. Their internal communications were end-to-end encrypted, so we couldn't read anybody's private messages, but we got a very good picture of how the place operated from day to day.

That was all good information and it would definitely be useful, but the real prize was gaining access to their emergency reporting and response system. Their research data was encrypted and out of our reach, but the climate control, communications, security, and fire suppression systems were not. The kids were able to pull up live feeds from security cameras and said they'd be able to shut them down when the time came.

Even better, they were able to capture ID badge data from every employee who worked at the VMRC. This meant that they'd be able to duplicate that information and encode it into my own badge, giving me complete access to the facility. I would try to talk my way in, at first, but if that didn't work I had other options.

After seeing what we had to work with, we all sat down and refined the plan. Our best bet was still to try and trigger an evacuation and use the confusion to get in and out. The facility had two armed security officers on site at all times; a direct approach would probably lead to a dangerous confrontation. Carmichael said that they would likely have an emergency lockdown protocol, too. A triggered security alarm would immediately disable all badge access and close and lock every door. The only way this function could be overridden was if there was an ongoing emergency that required evacuation. By design, the security system couldn't lock people in to die during a fire or biohazard leak.

There was one more decision we needed to make, too, and that was when to attempt the operation. The Research Towers multiplex was operational twenty-six hours a day, seven days a week. It was less busy at nights and on weekends, but at no point was the towering commercial campus deserted.

There was a case to be made for going during the day. If Ascension corporate security got tipped off, there was a good chance their special response team would come in guns blazing, and my odds of getting out of there alive dropped considerably. Ascension, for all the politicians and judges they owned, still had some powerful enemies and couldn't be too brazen. Having a big enough crowd of bystanders and witnesses could make even the biggest corporation on the planet show some restraint.

Trying to pull off the operation during business hours had some pretty big drawbacks, of course. More witnesses also meant more people scrutinizing what I was doing. It increased the chances that bystanders might interfere or even get hurt. Most importantly, the Ventura Medical Research Center was only operational during the day. At night, the lab was minimally manned—two security guards, an attendant to monitor Cassandra Carmichael, and sometimes a couple scientists working overnight. A handful of people would be a lot easier to manage than dozens. Nighttime it was, then.

When everything was decided, I contacted Deitrik on an encrypted call and briefed him on the plan. He was the one signing off on this whole thing, after all, so he had a right to know what we were doing. He was, needless to say, relieved that we had actual confirmation that Cassandra Carmichael was on-site, and gave me permission to go ahead with the operation to extract her. He asked me to do everything in my power to keep the collateral damage to a minimum. If I had to, I had permission to flash my SIS credentials and interface with law enforcement. As an absolute last resort, to protect my life or the life of another, I, and I alone, had the authorization to use deadly force.

I told him that I hoped it wouldn't come to that, and I was being sincere about it. I had my fill of killing during the war. Sometimes violence is necessary and can't be avoided. As we used to say in the service, the enemy gets a vote, too. That doesn't mean you should be too quick on the trigger, though. The problem with trying to fight your way out of every bad situation is that sooner or later, your luck is going to run out. In my experience, a little bit of restraint can go a long way toward keeping you out of trouble.

Deitrik brought more to the table than just some legal cover. He was providing an aircraft for our extraction, an autonomous rotorwing VTOL that would pick us up off the landing pad at the Research Towers and take us to a designated rendezvous point. It wasn't like a normal air-taxi, either—this one was an SIS asset that Deitrik had access to, programmed to purge its records after each mission.

Having an aircraft waiting for us made pulling off this crazy operation a hell of a lot more likely. If not for that I'd have had to have found a way to get Cassandra Carmichael down more than a hundred floors to a waiting vehicle, and there are a million things that can go wrong when you're trying to get away in a car. Something as mundane as a fender-bender or a traffic jam can ruin everything.

It took a few days, but we got everything set. We made all the preparations we could, had a plan of action, and had an escape route. Now all we had to do was pull it off.

CHAPTER 13

I was nervous the night of the rescue operation. Uncertainty can be contagious, and a lot of people were counting on me, so I tried to not let it show. I assured Deitrik and Carmichael both that we'd accounted for every contingency that we could. I was on my own this time; I wasn't going to risk Dante or anyone else going in with me when we tried to pull this off. Technically, I was the only one who had been sworn in by the SIS, so I was the only one who had real legal protection for what I was about to do.

I returned to Research Towers, once again wearing the jumpsuit of a building maintenance technician. I had a tiny earpiece in, connected to my handheld, which allowed me to talk to Dante and Lily in real-time.

"I just got confirmation that your ride is in place," Lily said over comms. "It set down on the Research Towers landing pad twenty minutes ago, broadcasting that it was experiencing engine trouble. It's been parked in the northwest quadrant of the pad."

"Roger," I replied. "How long do I have?"

"Don't worry about that," Lily answered. "It was programmed to tell traffic control that it's waiting for its owners to send a tech to look at it. As long as the fees are paid it can sit there for up to three days."

"Acknowledged," I said, quietly. Having the egress aircraft in place ahead of time was good thinking on Deitrik's part. We intended to set off some emergency alarms for our heist, and once they were activated, traffic control would automatically start waving off any aircraft trying to land on the pad. Carmichael told me that the Ascension Special Response Team would ignore such orders, though, so it wouldn't keep them off our backs. It would just make getting away that much easier.

I took the elevator to the eighty-fifth floor, doing my best to give the impression that I was supposed to be doing what I was doing. In my hands was a computer tablet and over my shoulder was a small duffel bag. In the bag I had my lockpick kit, cutting tools, a flashlight, a trauma kit, and my revolver. I switched out the upper receiver of the piece to the one with the integral sound suppressor, and it was loaded with subsonic, nonexplosive ammunition. I didn't normally carry it in this configuration because the suppressor added weight and bulk to an already big gun, but for a job like this? Suppressed was the way to go.

An actual maintenance tech rode the elevator with me part way, and she and I made small talk until she got off on the seventy-ninth floor. I kept my cool during the conversation and she was none the wiser—the knockoff uniforms we'd had made did the trick, as did the fake ID cards Lily printed up.

My first stop on the eighty-fifth floor wasn't the Ventura Medical Research Center. I was headed for an emergency response staging room on the same level. There were many such rooms scattered throughout the complex, and they could be accessed by most employees. Given the presence of a Bio-Safety Level 5 lab on the floor, this one was stocked with hazmat response gear in addition to the usual first-aid and firefighting equipment. There was just one problem: there was someone already in the room when I entered.

He was a young man, in his late twenties at most, lying down on a bench. He had earbuds in and darkened smart glasses over his eyes. He was either asleep or engrossed in watching something. I had to get rid of him, so I tapped him on the shoulder.

He sat up in a hurry and took off his glasses. "Holy shit," he said, wide-eyed. "You scared the crap out of me." He looked up at me, but I just glared at him and didn't say anything. "I'm on break!" he said, defensively, as he stood up. I could tell from the way he was acting that he wasn't supposed to be in here goofing off.

"Uh-huh," I said. "Is this where you're supposed to take your break?"

"N-no," he answered. "Wait, are you new? I don't think I've seen you before."

"That's probably because I don't hide in emergency response lockers to take naps."

"I'm on break!" he repeated, even more defensively this time. "Look, I know I'm not supposed to be in here, okay? I just needed some peace and quiet. You're not going to be a dick about this, are you?"

"Hey, I don't care what you do on break, but you should get going. I need to do an inspection of this equipment."

He tilted his head slightly. "Already? We just did one a couple weeks ago, I thought."

I improvised. "It's some new requirement from the city. They don't tell me the details, they just told me to come to the North Tower and inspect all the emergency response lockers."

The young man nodded, knowingly. "That's always the way it goes, isn't it? They never tell us shit. My break's over anyway, I'm gonna take off."

"Take it easy," I said. The young man left the room and closed the door behind him. I exhaled, heavily.

"Nice bluffing, Boss," Lily said into my ear. "Dante says he's ready to go when you are."

"Roger. Let me find what I need. Wait for my signal." At the back of the room were several sets of hazardous materials handling suits and the self-contained breathing apparatuses that went with them. I found a suit, overboots, gloves, and SCBA mask that would fit me and began to get suited up.

"Tell him to go ahead with Phase One," I said.

"You got it," Lily replied. "He's executing."

This part of the plan was Arthur Carmichael's idea, one he came up with after Lily and Dante's malware gained them access to the VMRC's intranet. One of the things the utilities network had control over were half a dozen huge freezers. These were used by laboratories to keep biological specimens intact and had to be maintained at -80° centigrade. He suggested that they would start scrambling to respond if the freezers were to shut down, especially since a lot of their specimens came from off-world. Dante did one better: he didn't just shut them off, he told them to start doing a thaw cycle.

Dante spoke over my earbud next. "Oh man, they just realized something is wrong. They're starting to send messages asking for help, but our worm is stopping them from going out. Mr. Carmichael says that they'll be trying to find portable freezers to store their samples in, but won't have enough on site for everything, so they'll be trying to save the most valuable first. They aren't authorized to request outside assistance until they get the go-ahead from corporate."

"Sooner or later they'll stop sending messages and start making calls," I said. We couldn't do anything about the employees of the Ventura Medical Research Facility making calls over their personal devices. Using a communications jammer would make it obvious that this wasn't just a system malfunction.

I pulled the suit's hood up over my head, then donned the mask. I checked the seal and verified that I had positive airflow. The SCBA mask covered my nose and mouth, which would help conceal my identity. "Give them a few minutes and stand by." I sat on the bench and fidgeted while I waited. Having everything go wrong at once might be suspicious, but we couldn't wait too long, either. After five minutes ticked by, I said, "Start Phase Two."

"Executing," Lily said.

This was the part where we *really* gave the VMRC a headache. With their scientists and lab technicians rushing to figure out which samples they could stuff into portable freezers and save, the odds of them having an accident went way up. All it would take was for one person to drop or spill the wrong thing, and they'd have a full-blown emergency on their hands. We weren't leaving it to chance, though. Phase Two meant sending out a biohazard containment failure alert to the rest of Research Towers, triggering an evacuation of the entire eighty-fifth floor and a response from every available emergency service in the complex. This alarm would be allowed through by our malware and we could turn it off whenever we wanted.

A loud, buzzing alarm began to echo throughout the building and red lights in the emergency response locker began to flash. That was my cue. "I'm en route," I said, taking my data tablet and duffel bag with me. "Stand by to execute Phase Three." I stepped into the hall and began making my way toward the Ventura Medical Research Center.

The building was huge and it took me a few minutes to reach my target. Each level in the North Tower had a wide central corridor with offices on either side. In several places it opened up to a large common area, like a food court or an indoor park complete with trees and UV lights to sustain them. Scattered groups of people were hurriedly leaving the floor. An automated voice spoke over the public address system, asking everyone to remain calm and evacuate. I wasn't sure if they were going to clear out just this floor or the entire building.

We weren't done yet, either. Phase Three was setting off their fire alarms.

See, the kids had discovered something interesting while poking around the VMRC's intranet: they used an inert-gas fire suppression system. It made sense—a laboratory full of expensive equipment and valuable samples would be a total loss if it used a water deluge system. By sealing rooms and flooding them with an inert gas, this kind of system starved a fire of its oxygen and would put it out with minimal collateral damage.

The problem was, sucking down nitrogen would starve a *person* of oxygen, too, and could cause rapid asphyxiation. If the fire alarm were activated, everyone in the VMRC who hadn't already evacuated would be forced to do so unless they had oxygen masks they could wear. There would be emergency oxygen masks available, Carmichael said, but protocol would be to evacuate.

This part *was* a risk, because I needed to get Cassandra Carmichael out without her choking to death, but I figured the one-two punch of the biohazard and fire alarms would get damn near everybody out of the lab and cause so much confusion that I'd be able to slip away with the girl.

I rounded the sixty-degree corner at the apex of the North Tower and the Ventura Medical Research Center came into view. Groups of people were still making their way into the corridor from different offices, some moving with more urgency than others. I hadn't seen any other emergency response personnel yet, but they would be coming soon.

"Lily," I said, "Execute Phase Three."

"Roger. Stand by . . . done." Another alarm rang out, a shrill whooping on top of the obnoxiously loud buzz of the biohazard warning. "Pandemonium ensuing," Lily said into my earpiece. She was enjoying herself.

"I'm making my approach," I said.

The sliding, transparent doors to the lobby of the Ventura Medical Research Center were locked open, to facilitate quick evacuation, as I got close. A group of about a dozen VMRC employees was milling around in the corridor, not moving with any urgency, and they didn't seem to be leaving.

"What's going on here?" I demanded, my voice amplified by a speaker in the mask. "We've got fire and biohazard alarms going off! Why aren't you evacuating?"

"It's a mistake," someone said. He was a balding, middle-aged man in a lab coat. "There's no fire and there hasn't been any containment breach. We're having a system malfunction."

I had to think fast. "Listen up!" I shouted, using the old command voice from my days as an NCO in the Defense Force. "Everyone needs to clear this corridor! Proceed to your designated accountability points immediately!"

"But there's no fire!" another VMRC employee insisted. She was a stocky woman with her hair done up in a tight bun. "We need to go back in to preserve our samples!"

"Proceed to your designated accountability points *immediately*!" I repeated. "Fire and hazmat response teams are inbound! Clear this corridor before I get security up here!"

That got them moving. The small crowd, obviously confused, started moving down the corridor.

The balding scientist persisted. "I can't just leave!" he insisted, shouting to make himself heard over the blaring alarms. "Our freezers are down as well! We have valuable biological samples that we *must* preserve. I'm not supposed to leave them under any circumstances! As soon as the fire suppression system cycles, I must return to the lab!"

I looked down and glared at him through the visor of my mask. "Sir," I said firmly, "we have a real emergency happening right now. Multiple alarms are going off in the North Tower, not just yours." That wasn't true, but he'd have no way of knowing that. "If you don't leave right now, the fire department will drag you out, and then you'll be arrested for obstructing an emergency response. Do you understand?"

"Y-yes," he stammered.

"Thank you for your cooperation," I said. "Now please move out."

"Of course," he said, and headed down the corridor.

"Another nice bluff, Boss," Lily said.

"That guy is probably calling corporate right now, if he hasn't already," I said. "I'm going to head into the lobby, tell any stragglers to clear out."

Carmichael chimed in, speaking into my earpiece as well. "Their security personnel won't be shooed off so easily," he said.

"Roger," I said. "I'll figure something out." That's when I saw four people in hazmat suits, riding in a small electric cart, head toward me from up the corridor. I flagged them down. The cart came to a stop near me and the four people disembarked. Their suits were the fully encapsulated kind, all in a blue-and-white color scheme with reflective strips and visibility lights. They weren't from the fire department.

The one who had been driving the cart, a woman it turned out, approached me. All I could see of her face was her eyes. "We're from VersaLife Bio-Engineering. You the on-scene response coordinator?"

"I just got here first," I said.

"I don't know if anyone else is going to respond because of the fire alarm," the woman said. "I think everyone is going to leave this one to the fire department."

"Shouldn't you be evacuating, too, then?"

She shrugged in her suit. "Our lab is just down the hall and it's a slow night. How can we help?"

I pointed at two of the VersaLife employees. "You two, take up positions in the corridor and make sure everyone evacuates. When I got here they were trying to say it was a false alarm and that they wanted to go back in. Keep everyone out until the fire department gets here, and let them know we're inside if we're not out by the time they get here." I looked at the woman again. "You two," I said, nodding toward the man standing next to her, "come inside with me. They said their freezers went down and they're trying to save samples. We need to make sure everyone evacuates."

"Got it," she said. "If we see fire we're supposed to evacuate ourselves, but we'll help as much as we can."

"Alright, then. Let's go."

The lobby of the Ventura Medical Research Center was large, and had that same slick, sterile, corporate look as a million other offices. There was a deserted receptionist desk in the center of the room. Off to the side were a couple of couches and a few potted plants. Large screens on the walls were still playing advertising videos, but they had been muted. A pair of uniformed security guards, both wearing masks and oxygen tanks, approached us as we entered. I noted that they were both armed and wearing body armor vests.

"What's the situation?" I asked.

"You're from building maintenance?" the taller of the two asked, his voice tinny over his mask's electronic voice amplifier.

"I am," I said. "I'm the emergency response coordinator."

"We're from VersaLife," the woman who'd come in with me said. "Emergency Response Team. We were close by and thought you might need help."

"The situation is under control," the shorter guard said, tersely. Both of them seemed tense.

"There is no fire and there has been no biohazard containment breach," the taller security man said. "We're having a massive system failure."

"If there's no hazard, what's with the oxygen masks?" the woman from VersaLife asked.

"When the fire alarm tripped it automatically engaged the nitrogen/argon fire suppression system. The labs are still filled with it and we can't get the HVAC system to cycle."

"Okay, but what are *you* still doing here?" the VersaLife woman said. "You need to evacuate per emergency response protocols. The fire department will be here any minute."

"That's none of your concern," the short guard snapped. "We have the situation under control and do not require assistance. You need to leave."

That snippy comment set off my new friend from

VersaLife. "Are you serious? We suited up and trudged all the way over here to help you people, and you're telling us to piss off?" She squared up with the security guard.

Her companion put a hand on her shoulder. "Janice, let's just go. They're owned by Ascension now."

"Unbelievable," Janice said. She looked up at the security guard. "Is there something in your corporate bylaws that requires you to be pricks?"

I held my hands up and tried to calm things down. "Okay, okay, everybody relax." I looked at Janice. "I appreciate your help even if they don't. Head back outside and link up with your teammates. Let the fire department know what's happening."

"Fine," she said, turning to leave. "Believe me, they're going to hear about this in my after action report."

With the VersaLife team gone, I was alone with the two VMRC security guards. "She wasn't wrong, you know. You people need to clear out for the fire department. What are you waiting for? How many people are still in here?" That sounded like something an *emergency response coordinator* would want to know.

They didn't answer at first. I pressed them. "Listen, fellas, I'm just trying to do my job and get everybody out safely. I need to know how many people are still inside."

"Five total," the shorter guard said, "including us. We have a patient in the lab who is being prepped for transport in an iso pod."

"Where do you need to get her to?"

"Up to the heliport," the taller one said. "She's got some rare condition and needs to be sent to a hospital. An air ambulance is on its way. Look, I'm not trying to be a dick.

That's all I'm at liberty to disclose, and that's all I know. There's a lot of proprietary research going on here. Since this all started, they've been screaming at us to maintain containment and not let anyone in."

"Understood," I said. "I'll head back outside and let the fire department know when they get here." It was hotter than hell in the lobby, made all the worse by the suit I was wearing. The heat and all of the walking I'd done were overwhelming my suit's rudimentary temperature regulator and sweat was starting to pool in my boots.

The two security men thanked me and I turned around as if to leave. Turning off my voice amplifier, so that the guards wouldn't hear me talk, I spoke into my earpiece. "Dante, button this place up."

"You got it," the hacker said. A few seconds later, armored shutters dropped from the ceiling and slammed to the floor. They covered the entrance to the Ventura Medical Research Facility, the glass wall of the lobby, and all of the exterior windows. I stopped, making a big show of looking startled.

I turned back around and switched my voicemitter back on. "What's going on, fellas?"

"What the hell?" one of the security men said.

"Did you hit the alarm?" the other asked him.

"No! It shouldn't be able to go into lockdown when there's an evacuation order anyway!"

"Are we trapped in here?" I asked.

The security guards didn't answer me. They hustled across the lobby to have a closer look at the metal shutters. "Try the manual override," one of them said. The other entered a code into a keypad on the wall.

"That won't work," Lily said, into my earpiece.

"It's not accepting my code!" the taller of the two guards said.

"Let me try mine," the other said, frustrated, breathing hard in his mask. "It's no good!"

The guards had their backs turned to me now. I quietly opened the duffel bag, placed the data pad in it, and wrapped my gloved hand around the grip of my gun.

"Call corporate and tell them we can't move the patient until they get us out of here!" the shorter guard said. "The fire department is going to have to cut the doors open."

"Hold it right there, boys," I said, my command amplified by the amplifier. The two VMRC security officers turned around to find themselves looking down the barrel of a .44. "Drop the handheld. Do it!"

"Holy shit," the taller guard said, raising his hands.

The shorter one dropped his handheld to the floor. "It's a setup!" He put his hands up, too.

"Now you," I said, pointing the big revolver at the tall one. "Take out your handheld and drop it on the floor. Only use your left hand. Your right hand so much as twitches and I'm going to plug you, you got it?"

"Yeah, I got it!" he said. Did as I asked, slowly taking his handheld out of his pocket with his left hand. He dropped it to the floor and raised it back over his head.

"Now turn around, both of you!" I ordered. "Keep your hands up!"

"Do you know whose lab this is, pal?" one of them asked. "Do you have any idea who you're fucking with?"

The other guard looked over his shoulder at me as he

turned around to face the door. "If you surrender yourself now, you might actually make it to prison alive."

"It's not my life you fellas need to be worrying about right now. Face the wall! Now listen to me. You, on the left. With your right hand only, reach down and draw that pistol. Slowly, goddamn it! Either of you so much as twitches and you'll be dead before you hit the floor." He did as I asked, pulling his pistol out of the holster and holding it up in his right hand. "Good. Now clear that weapon." He hit a release lever with his thumb. The rectangular body of the pistol hinged open and the ammunition cassette ejected, clattering to the floor.

"Good," I said. "Now toss the gun over to your left, as hard as you can." He did as he was ordered and threw the gun across the lobby. It hit the floor and slid under a chair. "Now you on the right! Do the exact same thing your partner just did. Keep facing the goddamn wall, I'm not going to tell you again!" Sweat was drizzling down my face and back now, both from the heat and from the stress. The second guard did as he was told and unloaded his pistol. "Toss it over to the right! Throw it hard! Keep facing the wall!" He followed my command and threw the pistol. It hit the floor off to my right and skittered into the hall. "Now turn around! Put your hands on top of your heads."

"You're never going to get away with this, asshole," the tall one said. "You're a dead man and you know it."

"That's my problem, not yours. Now shut your mouths, both of you." Keeping the gun trained on them, I sidestepped to the right. "Take me to her, now!"

"Who?" the short guard said.

"*Her!*" I snarled. "Your *patient*."

"Wait, you're here for her?" the tall one asked. He shook his head. "Why?"

I put a round into the floor near the guard's feet, causing both of them to jump back. The big gun was surprisingly quiet with the suppressed upper, but the fat slug still blew a small crater in the marble floor. "I told you to shut your mouth! Now, you can either take me to her or I can kill you and find her myself. Your call."

"Okay, okay!" the short one pleaded. "Don't shoot! Holy shit!"

"Good. Get moving. Keep your hands up."

"Steady, Boss," Lily said, into my ear. "We don't want to hurt anyone if we don't have to."

I switched off the amplifier again so the two guards couldn't hear me. "Don't worry, I'm calm. I'm just putting on a show for these boys. If they don't think I'm serious they might try something stupid." They led me past the reception desk to a set of double security doors. A sign read LABORATORY ACCESS and AUTHORIZED PERSONNEL ONLY. "Open it," I commanded.

Doing as I ordered, the security officer on my right reached over and waved his badge near the reader on the door. A red light turned green and the doors slid open. Beyond it was the main corridor of the laboratory complex. "Take me to her," I said. "Move!"

Keeping their hands up, my two prisoners led me down the hall, toward a bend. The glossy flooring and swank décor of the lobby were replaced with a much more sterile, utilitarian design. Red emergency lights illuminated the corridor. Labs and offices on either side of the hall were sealed, with warning lights indicating a low oxygen environment inside. With the HVAC system shut down, the facility was still flooded with inert gasses. Around the bend, we came to another set of closed security doors.

"Is this it?" I asked.

"Yeah," the taller of the two security guards said.

"Open it. Now!"

The guards looked at each other for a moment, and I was worried that they were about to try something, but instead they did as I commanded. The one on the right once again waved his ID badge near the reader. The doors hissed open, revealing what looked to be an observation room. Through a window on the far wall I could see a medical isolation room, basically an especially clean jail cell. It was separated from the observation room by a small airlock. A man and a woman, each wearing VMRC lab coats and emergency oxygen masks, were awkwardly pushing a mobile medical isolation pod out through the airlock. The stopped when they noticed the two security officers standing there with their hands up.

"What are you two doing back here?" the woman asked, sharply, her voice raised to make herself heard over the persistent alarms.

The security guards looked at each other, then pointed a thumb back at me. The woman stepped around them to see what they were pointing at, only to freeze when she found herself looking down the barrel of a gun. Her eyes went wide and she started to scream.

"Shut up!" I shouted, silencing her. "All of you, get your goddamn hands up. You, too, buddy," I said to the man who was still standing by the isolation pod.

"What…what's happening?" the female scientist asked.

"What does it look like is happening, Dr. Ankari?" the tall guard said, sarcastically. "We're being robbed."

"That's right," I said. "Listen to me very carefully. Do exactly as I say and nobody gets hurt, understand?" The frightened scientists nodded. "Good. Push that medical pod this way. Stay back there, push it from that end, toward me. Any of you takes a step in my direction and I'll shoot you dead."

"Y-you can't take her!" the woman named Dr. Ankari protested. "She'll die without proper medical attention!"

I was running out of time and losing my patience. I pointed my gun directly between the scientist's eyes. "*You're* going to die if you don't do as I say, Doc. Now push that pod this way. Last warning."

She relented and nodded at the other scientist, the man who still hadn't said a word. He carefully pushed the isolation pod in my direction. Keeping the gun trained on my prisoners, I stepped aside to make room for the pod. When it was within reach, I grabbed the handle on the near end and pulled it closer to me.

"Good. Now, empty your pockets. Drop everything on the floor. I want to see your handhelds, your ID badges, every last thing you've got in a pile right there. Do it!"

"This is insane," Dr. Ankari said as she tossed her handheld and access badge onto the floor. "Do you really think you'll get away with this?" The other scientists followed suit, and the security guards dropped their badges as well.

She was right about one thing: it *was* insane. "All four

of you, get into that isolation room." I turned off the amplifier and spoke to Lily. "As soon as they're in there, lock them in."

"You got it, Boss," she replied. "Good thinking."

I kept my weapon pointed at the four VMRC employees until they had all been sealed into the room they'd been keeping Cassandra Carmichael in. I stuck my gun back into the duffel bag and checked the isolation pod. It was like a gurney on wheels, but with a hard composite top, its own air supply, and a touchscreen displaying the occupant's vital statistics.

Arthur Carmichael spoke into my earpiece this time. "Do you have her? How is she?"

I slid open the cover of one of the pod's observation windows. "Yeah, it's her," I said. "She's breathing. The readout says she's sedated and stable."

"Thank you for this," he said.

"Thank me later. I still need to get out of here. Dante, are you there?"

"I'm here. What do you need?"

"I'm going to wheel her out now. I want you to lock the door to the observation room behind me. Once I'm back out in the lobby, lock every interior door in the place."

"I can do you one better. I'll secure them then scramble the access codes. None of their badges will work, and there is no way to manually open them. They'll have to cut through the doors to get in."

"Good. When I'm back out in the lobby, can you open only the front security door, so I can get out, but keep everything else locked down?"

"We can do that," Lily chimed in.

"Okay. The second I'm clear I want you to drop the front security doors again. Wipe everything you can from their system, then unplug."

"On it," Dante said. "Good luck."

When the heavy security gate covering the lobby entrance lifted, I was immediately met by a bunch of bewildered-looking firefighters in full hazmat gear. The moment I stepped out I told Dante to drop the gate again, before any of the firefighters could get inside the lobby.

"Security gate secured," Dante said over the radio. "Access codes scrambled."

"The fire department is here," I replied. "I'll have to talk my way past them."

Carmichael spoke once more. "You must hurry. I just got an alert on the company security network that the Special Response Team has been released. They're preparing to deploy as we speak. You've got fifteen minutes at most."

"Did the alarm get through?"

"No," Lily said. "Somebody probably made a call and said this is suspicious. Get moving, you need to get out of there."

"I'm going as fast as I can," I said, as one of the firefighters approached me. "Stand by."

"Who are you?" the firefighter asked. "Are you with Ventura? I'm the on-scene commander, Research Towers Fire Department."

"I'm a lab technician," I said, betting that the firefighters weren't familiar with who worked at this particular lab. The responders from VersaLife were gone, and none of the real VMRC employees were around to dispute my story.

"What the hell's going on in there? Why are we locked out?"

"We're having a massive systems failure caused by a network attack. We have no control over anything."

"How did you get out, then?"

"I was waiting in the lobby in case the doors opened. When they did, I took the opportunity."

"Where are you going?" the fire commander asked me. "Who is this?"

"She's a patient we've been keeping for a long-term study. She needs to be transported to another medical facility immediately."

"That checks out, Chief," one of the other firefighters said, showing the commander a tablet screen. "They have an MOU to evac her in the event of an emergency."

"An air ambulance is coming to collect her. I need to get her to the helipad," I said.

"Fine. Real quick, what's the situation in there? Can you confirm a fire or a biohazard containment breach?"

I shook my head. "I don't know."

He didn't like that answer. "You don't know? How can you not know?"

"Every alarm is going off at once. Our freezers went down first and we were trying to get samples into emergency coolers. Something may have gotten dropped in the confusion, but I didn't see anything. I didn't see a fire or any smoke, either, but the fire suppression system activated. I didn't check the whole lab. My job is to get her to the heliport. I need to get her up there right away!"

"Is there anyone else in there?"

"I think so. Don't know how many or who got out.

Every door in the place was locked and wouldn't accept our badges."

"Can you get her to the heliport by yourself? We're going to have to cut these doors open." I told him I could. "Okay. When you're done, report back here. We'll get you checked out and debrief you."

"Understood," I said. "I'll come right back as soon as she's loaded onto the bird. It will be here soon if it's not already."

The firefighters stepped aside and let me past. I wheeled the isolation pod down the now-deserted corridor to the nearest elevator. My forged Research Towers access badge would allow me to access the elevator's emergency override, so it wouldn't stop at any other floor on my way up to the heliport.

The heliport wasn't accessed from the top floor of the building, but instead from ten stories below, on the 120th floor. I was still on the north side of the building and needed to make my way to the south side in order to access the pad. Pushing the medical isolation pod ahead of me, I hustled down the wide corridors as quickly as I could. I was soaked with sweat and was sucking oxygen through my mask. My air tank was running low, but I didn't want to stop to doff the hazmat suit.

Luckily, the 120th floor was mostly deserted. Many of the office spaces hadn't even been leased out. I did get strange looks from a few people as I rushed down the hall, but nobody got in my way or tried the stop me. At least, not until I got to the heliport terminal on the south side of the building.

"Aw, hell," I said aloud, into my radio. "Security Forces."

Lily responded. "Shit. Are you sure?"

"Affirmative," I acknowledged. There were two Security Forces troopers in the terminal, standing near the exit to the helipad itself. They were wearing gray flight suits and helmets, and each had a pistol slung in a chest holster. "Probably an air unit that responded to the emergency alarms. I'll see if I can talk my way past."

"Good luck," Lily said.

Pushing the isolation pod ahead of me, I approached the exit to the helipad, but the troopers stopped me before I could get to the doors.

"This is a patient from the Ventura Medical Research Center," I said, breathing hard. "She needs to be medevaced right away!"

"We are aware of the situation," one of the troopers said. She was a stocky woman with bronze skin and a stern expression. "We are in contact with Ascension. They have an aircraft en route. We were given an ETA of eight minutes."

"Wait here with us," the other trooper, a wiry man with a ruddy complexion, said. "It's cold and windy out there. Do you need that gear on, or can you take it off?"

"Oh, shit," Lily said, into my earpiece.

"There must be some mistake, guys," I said. "The air ambulance is already here."

"I can check," the female trooper said, "but the word we got was that an aircraft from Ascension is on its way."

"Yes," I said, "that's a security team. They're coming to investigate the incident downstairs. The medevac aircraft is waiting for us and I need to get her on board immediately!"

"Sounds like there was a miscommunication somewhere," the trooper said. "Don't worry, when the Ascension team lands, we'll get this straightened out."

"Trooper, please," I pleaded. "I need to get her onto that aircraft!"

"Is she going to die in the next ten minutes?" the male trooper asked. He leaned, glanced through the pod's viewport at Cassandra Carmichael. "She looks stabilized to me."

"Why don't you take that gear off?" the woman said.

"Easy!" Lily said into my ear. "These two are on the take! They're stalling you! You need to get out of there!"

I looked around the terminal. There was no one else around except for me and the two SecFor troopers. "I didn't want to do this," I said into my radio, and reached into my bag.

"Hold it right there!" the woman shouted. She and her partner both had their guns drawn now. "Get your hands where we can see 'em!"

"Show us your hands!" her partner said.

I wasn't reaching for my gun. From my duffel bag I produced the SIS badge and credentials that Deitrik made for me when he swore me in. I held them up in my left hand so that both troopers could see them. "This woman is a critical witness for an ongoing SIS investigation. She was being held down there under an assumed name against her will. This is a rescue operation."

"What?" one of the troopers asked, lowering his gun slightly. "Are you serious?"

The woman, scowling, stepped forward to look at my

badge. "Let me see that," she said, holding her gun muzzle-down. She held up a mini-tablet and scanned the badge. "Holy shit," she said, looking back up at me, eyes wide. "This is real."

"It is," I said, once again calling upon my old command voice, "and you two are impeding my investigation. What are you doing here, anyway?"

"We picked up the alarms coming from the Ventura Medical Research Center on our scanner. We told Dispatch we'd land and see if they needed help."

"Good to hear," I said, looking down a the female SecFor. "For a minute there, I was worried that you two might be doing a little side job for Ascension." The pair glanced at each other, but didn't say anything. "I'm glad I was wrong."

They stood aside and let me push the isolation pod to the exit doors and out onto the helipad. Cassandra Carmichael and I were aboard Deitrik's rotorwing and in the air before the Ascension Special Response Team arrived. Somehow, our crazy plan had actually *worked*.

CHAPTER 14

It was nearly dawn by the time I got back to Arthur Carmichael's safe house. It was too much of a risk to have SIS aircraft take us straight there. Instead, we flew past the outskirts of Delta City, out of the Crater itself, and set down on a rocky flat near a lonely stretch of highway. There, Carmichael's two security men and his doctor were waiting for us with a van big enough to carry the medical isolation pod. It took us a couple hours of driving to get back to the safe house.

Once there, I showered, changed back into my regular clothes, and got some food. Stepping out onto a balcony, I called the Baron over an encrypted connection and gave him a quick rundown of everything that went down.

"I'm sorry I had to flash my credentials," I said. "I didn't see another way."

"Easy, you did the right thing," Deitrik said. "It will be much easier for me to explain this to my superiors, when the time comes, than to explain two dead Security Forces troopers."

"It may have tipped our hand. I think those SecFor clowns were dirty and were there to stop anyone from trying to get Cassandra Carmichael out. I'm willing to bet there were more doing the same thing down at street level, and at the monorail hub. If they blab to Ascension about what happened, they'll know the SIS is involved."

"So, too, will the Nova Columbia SIS office," Deitrik said. "There's a risk but it was one we needed to take. What's happening now?"

"Cassandra Carmichael is in an induced coma, apparently has been for some time. Arthur Carmichael has a doctor here who's going to try and bring her out of it."

"Excellent. Well done, Easy. As soon as you're able, I need you to debrief Arthur Carmichael. Get everything you can from him on Project Isaiah, Site 471, and the Seraph. We took great risks to get his daughter out of that place and it's time for him to uphold his end of the bargain."

"I think he will. I can't imagine that he'd try to pull something now."

"For his sake, he'd better," Deitrik said coldly. "Keep me apprised of the situation."

"Will do. I'll talk to you later." I ended the call and went back inside.

That's when I heard the screaming.

I raced to the second floor, taking the stairs two at a time. Around the corner and down the hall was the large bedroom where they had taken Cassandra Carmichael, and that's where the commotion was coming from. I was ready to burst into the room with my gun drawn, but one of Carmichael's bodyguards was standing in the hall. It was the big clanker, the one I called Truck. *Stephen*. His real name was Stephen.

"What's going on in there?" I asked.

"They woke her up," he explained, curtly. "Caught me off guard, too. I went in to check. The doctor said she's in shock."

"Is Dagny in there?"

"Yes," he grunted. "Mr. Carmichael said you can go in if you want."

"I'll do that. Uh, thanks." The hulking bodyguard stepped aside and touched the door control switch. The heavy faux-wood door slid open, quietly, and closed behind me. I found myself in a large bedroom that had been converted into a makeshift infirmary. Cassandra Carmichael was in bed. Dagny sat next to her, holding her sister as Cassandra sobbed into her shoulder. The doctor, a middle-aged black man with gray hair, hovered nearby, monitoring his patient's vitals.

Arthur Carmichael turned and realized that I was in the room.

"How's she doing?" I asked, taking my hat off. "I hope I'm not intruding."

Carmichael stuck out his right hand. I took it and we shook, firmly. "I can never repay you for this," he said, his voice wavering. I could tell he was struggling to keep his composure and I didn't want to embarrass him.

"You've paid me plenty, Mr. Carmichael," I said. "I'm just happy we were able to pull it off." I looked over his shoulder at his two stepdaughters. Cassandra was still crying, clinging to Dagny tightly. Dagny was in tears, too, as she held her sister in her arms. "I came when I heard the screaming. Is she going to be alright?"

"Physically, she's fine," Carmichael said, quietly. "Her mind is another matter. Dr. Larson gave her a mild sedative to calm her down. It seems to be working."

"What happened to her? What did they do to her up there?"

"We," Carmichael said, correcting me. "This is what *we* did to her." His face was ashen. I could see the regret and the shame in the man's eyes. "Do you have kids, Mr. Novak?"

"Me? No."

"Usually when a father fails his children as completely as I have, he doesn't get a second chance. I have one, thanks to you and Dagny."

"Like I said, I'm happy I was able to help, but we're not done yet."

"Of course," he said. "I will tell you everything I know about Project Isaiah. Can you give me a little while? This is the first time I've seen Cassandra in weeks. I wasn't sure if she'd be lucid enough to talk."

"Sure thing. I'll be in your conference room. I have a long case report to write and I need to get started. Stop in when you're ready and I'll debrief you there. If possible, I'd like to interview Cassandra as well."

"I don't know if she will be able to today."

"I know this isn't ideal, and I'm not trying to pressure her after she's been through so much, but time is of the essence, here. I need to gather as much eyewitness testimony as possible."

"I understand. I'll talk to her about it later on."

"Thank you, Mr. Carmichael. I'll leave you alone with your family now." He nodded, and I left the room as quietly as I'd come in.

To my surprise, the big cyborg was gone. In his place by the door was his young partner, the one I called Slick, looking cool as ever in a fitted black suit and dark glasses. His real name was James.

He surprised me when he asked me a question. "Is she gonna be okay?"

"What?"

"Mr. Carmichael's daughter," the bodyguard said. "Is she going to be okay?"

"She's alive, conscious, and in one piece," I said. "I don't know what that girl's been through, but all things considered it could be a lot worse."

He nodded. "Thank you."

I nodded back and turned to walk away. I didn't get five steps down the hall before someone else called out my name. I turned to see Dagny hurrying after me.

"Hold up," she said, putting a hand on my arm. "I wanted to thank you." She hadn't left her sister's side since we got back to the safe house and we hadn't really talked. Judging from the circles under her eyes, she hadn't slept, either. "You risked so much and you found her. You did the impossible."

I wasn't sure what to say. Turns out I didn't have to say anything; she threw her arms around my neck, reached up, and kissed me, deeply. I could see James over her shoulder. The bodyguard raised an eyebrow and gave me a knowing nod. "All in a day's work, I guess," I said, looking back into Dagny's eyes. "It was worth the risk."

She looked up at me and smiled. "You're a very sweet man, Ezekiel Novak."

"Don't go spreading that around," I said with a grin. "It'll ruin my reputation."

"I need to get back to Cassie," Dagny said. "I just wanted to thank you."

"Come find me later," I said. "I'll be debriefing your old man. If you're up for it, I'd like to get something on the record from you, too. Just to, you know, back up my account of things."

"I will," she said. She squeezed my arm, turned, and headed back up the hall.

I set everything up in advance so I'd be ready when Arthur Carmichael arrived. I placed a holographic camera on the conference table, set up so that it would be able to record both of us at once. A tablet was on the table in front of me, a list of notes and questions I wanted to ask displayed on the screen. We sat across from each other at one end of the rectangular table, so we could talk without having to raise our voices. We both had bottles of water nearby. With Carmichael's permission, I began recording.

"My name is Ezekiel Novak," I began, speaking clearly into the camera. "I'm a licensed private investigator in Delta City, on the colony world of Nova Columbia. I have been deputized as a temporary officer of the Terran Confederation, on the authority of Adjunct Inspector General Deitrik Hauser of the Security Intelligence Service." I looked up at Carmichael. "Please identify yourself, for the record."

"My name is Arthur Carmichael," he said. "I'm a senior

security administrator in the Technology Development branch of Ascension Planetary Holdings Group."

"How long have you been with the company?" I asked.

"Thirty-two years. Local years, I mean. That's . . ." He trailed off, doing the math in his head. "About thirty-five Terran years."

"What is it that you're doing for the company right now?"

"I'm the assistant security manager for Project Isaiah. My immediate superior is Blanche Delacroix. We both answer directly to Xavier Taranis. Supposedly he answers to the Board of Directors, but I've seen no evidence that they are engaging in any oversight of the project."

"What is Project Isaiah?"

Carmichael was quiet for a moment. He glanced at the tablet screen on the table in front of him. I could tell he'd been contemplating what to say ahead of time. "Isaiah is the project name for an ongoing effort to study and communicate with a previously unknown extraterrestrial entity. It was found last year, buried deep beneath the Mount Gilead volcano in southwestern Hyperborea. We call it the Seraph."

"What *is* the Seraph?"

Carmichael shook his head slowly. "I don't know. You could describe it as a life-form, but it's not life as we understand it." He looked up at me. "Technically speaking, it isn't *alive*. It isn't even organic. It's made of an anomalous quantum metamaterial that they've not been able to identify."

"Did you know that Dr. Ivery was able to smuggle out a sample of the Seraph?"

"She did, huh?" He smiled, knowingly. "She was more clever than I gave her credit for."

"Next question: How old is the Seraph, in your estimation?"

"We have no way of knowing how old it is. We do know that it's been there since before Mount Gilead formed. Judging by the layers of rock it was found in, we believe it has been in place for approximately sixty-eight million years. That puts it in at least the Late Cretaceous period on Earth. Geological surveys indicate that the spot we found it in was on the surface at that time, but Hyperborea has been seismically and volcanically active for millions of years. Over time it was buried, sealed in a tomb of volcanic rock."

"How did it get there?"

"We don't know. It had to have come from off-world, that much is certain, but we have no information regarding its true origin. The COFfers thought we'd found a god."

"Could you, uh, elaborate on that?"

Carmichael sighed. "Xavier Taranis is a major funder of the Cosmic Ontological Foundation. He brought as many members of the COF into Project Isaiah as he could, using what I believe are illegal discriminatory hiring practices. The Board did nothing."

"Okay, but why a god?"

"It makes a certain amount of sense from their point of view. One of their core tenets is that all sentient life in the galaxy was artificially created by ancient, advanced beings billions of years ago. In studying the Seraph you can see how the superstitious would conclude it's one of their mythical star gods." He scoffed at the idea. "They're fools."

"I see you don't put much stock in their theories."

"Their theories are unfalsifiable pseudoscience. There is zero evidence that the development of sentience in life on Earth or anywhere else required an external origin. The COFfers mock religion but invented their own creation myth."

"Can you recount the discovery of the Seraph? Were you there when it happened?"

"No. I was brought in after, as the security for the facility was ramped up. I have seen it, though."

"Tell me, why do you call it the Seraph? Can you describe it?"

Carmichael didn't say anything at first. "It's huge." He looked at me. "A leviathan."

"Can you be more . . . specific?"

He chuckled knowingly. "I know how this sounds, Mr. Novak. The Seraph is difficult to describe, and I don't have the talent to draw it for you. The body is nearly two hundred meters long from end to end."

"I see. Why do you call it the Seraph?"

"We call it that because of the six elongated wings protruding from it, like the seraphim described in the biblical Book of Isaiah. They're not *actually* wings, mind you, but they bring them to mind."

"If they're not wings, what are they?"

"They don't know. One theory is that they're heat radiators for whatever energy source could power something that big. Another is that they're some kind antennae. Really, they're just guessing." He paused, took a sip of water, then continued. "The most striking thing about it, though, are the Spears."

"The Spears," I repeated. "Can you, uh, elaborate?"

"Yes. When they excavated the Seraph, they discovered that it had been impaled by a pair of hundred-foot-long spikes, made of an unknown black metallic substance. The spikes protrude all the way through it. They call them the Spears because that's what they resemble."

"What do they do?"

Carmichael shrugged. "As far as I know, neither their purpose nor what they're made out of has been ascertained."

"Huh," I said quietly, typing notes into my tablet. "Do you have any recordings of any of this? Pictures, video, anything?"

"No. All recording equipment is strictly monitored and accounted for. When they finally let me leave Site 471, I was subjected to a full search and body scan. I couldn't risk trying to smuggle anything out."

"That's okay. That's a lot for them to chew on already. Tell me, what happened to your daughter?"

He took a deep breath and looked down at the table for a moment before looking up at me again. "How much did Ocean tell you?"

"She said you tried to talk to it via a direct neural link. I've got to be honest, that sounds insane."

"It was insane," he said. His hands curled into fists. "It was utter madness. It started when they tried to remove the Spears."

"That . . . sounds dangerous."

"Indeed. We don't know what they do or why they're

there, but let's yank one out and see if anything happens. Another brilliant idea from Xavier Taranis."

"Holy hell. What happened?"

"The Seraph was found lying on its side. They dug a side tunnel from the primary excavation pit and constructed a huge, powered winch-and-pulley setup. It took a few tries but they dislodged one of them, pulled it out. That seemed to, I don't know, wake the Seraph up. Shortly after, they began to detect trace electromagnetic radiation coming from it."

"Well, how about that?"

"Yeah," Carmichael said, knowingly. "Like I said, madness. They left the other Spear in place but started probing deeper and deeper into the Seraph. The signals became more active and more frequent. Eventually the technicians noticed a pattern, like a very basic binary language. We were *communicating* with it. Somehow it's still able to do that, despite the state it's in."

"So they decided to try and plug a neural link into it? Whose idea was that?"

"Xavier Taranis's, of course. It became an obsession for him. The more we interfaced with it, the more of a response we got, as if it were slowly gaining awareness. We could send signals and get responses, but we couldn't interpret what it was trying to tell us. That wasn't good enough for the old man. He wanted to actually *talk* to it, as you said."

"I already know that didn't go very well."

Carmichael slowly shook his head again. "The first person who interfaced with it was a communications technician. After two sessions, he had an aneurism and died. After that, no one else would do it, so Dr. Ivery connected to it herself. She had better luck, but..." He trailed off, then looked me in the eye. "There were side effects. You spoke with her, you know what I'm talking about."

The scientist hadn't seemed right in the head, that was a fact. "She told me she couldn't do it anymore and quit."

"That enraged Taranis. He was going to refuse to let her leave, threaten her, force her if he had to. I talked him out of it. I convinced him that she'd come back, but she just needed time to recover, given the side effects. He let her leave, and we were going to pause the project for a while, but..."

"But what?"

"It demanded someone else to talk to."

"What did? The Seraph?"

He nodded slowly. "Yes. It was able to penetrate our computer network through the interface we connected to it and send a message."

"What did it say?"

"One word, over and over again: *Communicate*. Taranis was going to force somebody else to do it. Cassandra volunteered so that no one else would have to do it."

"That took courage."

"Yes. She was always selfless like that. I tried to stop her, of course. I told her I'd go in her place. She wouldn't have it. She actually wanted to try. We were making history, after all. I should have done more. I should have restrained her if I had to. I failed her."

"Was she able to communicate with it?"

"Yes, but after a few sessions she started having increasingly severe neurological side effects. They put her in an induced coma to prevent brain damage, and transported her off-site to be monitored."

"There's something else I need to know," I said. "Am I to understand that the Security Intelligence Service was at Site 471 during all this?"

"Not the whole time, but yes," he said. Carmichael was sweating despite the fact that it wasn't especially hot in the conference room. The conversation was stressful for him. "The normal reports of finding an alien artifact were not sent out—that much I can confirm. I believe Xavier Taranis contacted the SIS through some back channel, but I don't have any details on that. Several people with SIS credentials visited the site. I memorized their names and will send them to you. The one who was there every time was a man named Leonard Steinbeck. Do you know him?"

"Never heard of him, but I'll pass it on. Let me ask you one last thing, then we'll take a break. Why is old man Taranis so hell-bent on talking to this thing? It's already a huge discovery and he's already the richest man on the planet. What more does he hope to gain?"

"Something all the money in the world can't buy you," Carmichael said. "Life. The old man is dying."

"Xavier Taranis is dying?" I asked. "From what?"

"From what?" Carmichael repeated, looking at me like I was stupid. "Old age, of course. His body is riddled with inoperable cancers. Half his organs have been replaced with artificial ones. He sleeps in a life-support pod. Despite having the best medical care available anywhere, his health is failing and he doesn't have much time left. He's convinced that the Seraph holds the secret of immortality."

"Immortality? That's nuts."

"Is it? The Seraph is a form of life that we don't understand. Despite being buried for sixty-eight million years, it isn't dead." He paused, then looked up at me. "It isn't alive, either, not by our current definition of the word, but it is . . . conscious. The science team believes, or at least claimed to believe in their reports, that one of the potential benefits of understanding it was what they called radical life-extension technology."

"I think that will be enough for now," I said, and turned off the holo-recorder. "This report is going to be strange enough as is. Thank you for sitting through all this questioning. I'm sure it's not easy."

"In a way it feels like a weight off my shoulders. I haven't been able to tell this to anyone."

"Believe it or not, I hear that a lot in my business."

"What now?"

"I'm going to finish this initial report, then send it up the chain. After that, I don't know what they'll want you to do. I've never been a secret agent before."

"Are you sure you can trust your SIS handler?"

"As sure as I can be," I admitted.

"If that's all, then, I'm going to go check on Cassandra."

"I'll be here if you need me," I said, looking down at my tablet. "This is going to be one hell of a report."

He paused by the door. "There's one more thing. After they took Cassandra away, the Seraph didn't want to talk to anyone else. Others tried to talk to it via neural link and it was unresponsive. It established, I don't know, some kind of *bond* with her."

"I see. You think Ascension will try to recover her?"

"They will. They need her. I need to move her soon, get her off-planet, if I have to. I suppose you're going to tell me that I should wait, work with your SIS handler."

"My employment with the Security Intelligence Service is a temporary expediency, Mr. Carmichael. You do what you need to do to keep her safe. That said, I will relay to him that you thinking getting off-world might be the safest bet. We'll figure something out."

Carmichael looked tired. "I hope you're right, Mr. Novak." He stepped through the door, leaving me alone in the conference room.

After sending off my initial report, I managed to find a spare bedroom and catch a few hours of sleep. I was out, completely dead to the world, and didn't wake up until the early evening. After getting some food and a couple cups of coffee in me, I went to Arthur Carmichael and asked about Cassandra. He told me that the doctor still had her on some mild sedatives, but that she was awake, coherent, and eating. This was the first opportunity I had to speak with her and I couldn't pass it up.

When I walked into the infirmary, Cassandra was sitting up in bed, slowly eating from a yogurt cup. Dagny had taken her shoes off and was sitting cross-legged at the end of the bed, facing her sister. She looked over her shoulder when she heard the door open.

"Easy," Dagny said, smiling at me. She swung her legs over the side of the bed and stood up. "I'd like you to meet my sister, Cassie. Cassie, this is Ezekiel Novak, the detective who helped me find you."

Cassandra considered me for a moment without saying anything. "It's . . . it's nice to finally meet you," she said, slowly. She looked like hell. Her skin was sallow and there were dark circles under her eyes. It was clear that she'd lost a lot of weight while in her induced coma. "I understand you went to a lot of trouble for me. Th-thank you."

"I couldn't have done it without your sister and stepfather. I'm just glad that we were able to pull it off and get you home."

"You have questions," she said.

"I do," I admitted. I had my tablet in one hand and the portable holo-recorder in the other. "If you're up for it. It shouldn't take too long."

Cassandra smiled weakly. "You can ask me whatever you want."

Dagny looked at her sister. "Are you sure? You don't have to do this if you're not ready. You've been through a lot and you've only been—"

She fell silent when Cassandra put a hand on her arm. "I'll be okay," she said. She looked back at me, her smile faded. "I can't promise you'll understand the answers to your questions."

I shrugged. "Been dealing with that a lot lately."

"I want to stay with you while you talk to him," Dagny said. She looked up at me. "Is that okay?"

"Of course," I said. "It'll just take me a minute to get set up."

A couple minutes later we were ready to begin. There

was a wheeled cart next to the bed, serving as a nightstand, on which I set the holo-recorder. I dragged a chair from across the room, sat down in it, and began the interview. As before, I stated who I was, and had both Cassandra and Dagny do the same. I then had Cassandra recount, as best she could, the story of how she became involved in Project Isaiah and ended up at Site 471. Her story matched up with events of the case from when I became involved. She described leaving the drive in the safe deposit box, slipping the key in Dagny's pocket, and her attempt to send her sister a message, all while being harassed and stalked by people she assumed were working for Ascension. Her testimony backed up the version of events Arcanum gave me, too, so it seemed like they had been telling me the truth.

In discussing Site 471, she corroborated much of what Arthur Carmichael told me, taking into account that she wasn't involved with Project Isaiah for nearly as long as he was. It was when I brought up the Seraph itself that she became hesitant. That's the best way I can describe it. She reminded me of a trauma survivor recounting the traumatic event. Her voice wavered. She blinked more frequently. Her hands fidgeted.

"D-did Arthur tell you about Dr. Ivery?" she asked. "He told me she's dead now."

I looked at the floor for a moment. "She is. I was there when . . . well, when it happened. She was murdered."

Cassandra closed her eyes tight, but tears leaked out anyway. Dagny squeezed her hand.

"I know this isn't easy," I said. "I wish I could have done more for her. But . . . well, without her I wouldn't have gotten this far. She provided the evidence I needed to get the kind of support that made getting you out of there possible. I guess what I'm saying is, it wasn't for nothing."

"I know she came across as strange to most people," Cassandra said. "She didn't have great people skills. She was very kind, though, and...brave. She was brave. She volunteered to connect her neural link to the Seraph even after someone died because of it. She did it for as long as she could."

"Arthur told me that after Dr. Ivery quit, they were going to suspend the program, but Xavier Taranis changed his mind. Do you know why that happened?" I was hoping that she would corroborate what her stepfather had told me. If she didn't, I was going to have to have another talk with him, and I really wanted this whole mess to be over.

"The Seraph wanted someone else to talk to," she said, quietly, looking down at her lap. "We woke it up after millions of years and it didn't want to be isolated again."

"How do you know this?" I asked.

"It told me," she said, quietly. "It told me a lot of things."

"Okay, let's back up a second. You volunteered to connect directly to the Seraph with your neural link, is that correct?" She nodded. "How is that possible?"

"I don't know," Cassandra admitted. "When we started probing it, it became...aware...of us. Slowly, over time. We...disturbed it...when we pulled the first Spear out. The substance it's made out of, the silver-white stuff? Have you seen it?"

"I handled a small fragment."

"It's adaptive. It responds to stimuli. You must

understand, we didn't communicate with it. It realized we were there and decided to communicate with *us*."

"You're saying the Seraph initiated contact?"

"Yes . . . in a manner of speaking. I don't think it was fully aware at that point. It was . . . it was dreaming, I think."

"What means did you use to connect to it, exactly?"

"We used a high-fidelity, commercial-grade virtual reality headset with a neural link. It was Dr. Ivery's idea, after the first person who linked to it . . . after he died. She thought it would be able to make itself understood better visually and that this might reduce the neurological strain. She was right. It worked."

I paused for a moment. I knew what I wanted to ask next, but I wasn't exactly sure how to word the question. "What . . . what did you talk about? You and the Seraph, I mean."

Cassandra didn't answer me at first. She stared off into space, blinking more often than seemed normal, her eyes rapidly darting back and forth. She fidgeted more.

Dagny leaned in and put a hand on her sister's shoulder. "Cassie? Are you okay?"

Cassandra looked back at me. "Do you have a cat, Mr. Novak?"

I raised an eyebrow. "No. Why do you ask?"

"If you had a cat," she continued, "what would you talk about with it?"

"I don't understand," Dagny said.

"You can talk to a cat, but you can't talk *with* a cat," Cassandra said. "You're too different. Even if you could understand the cat perfectly, the cat will never be able to understand you. It's just not on your level."

"So . . . it was like talking to a cat?" I asked.

"In a way," she said, "except I was the cat."

"Okay, I see what you're saying, I think."

"It wasn't even fully awake and its mind was so . . . so vast. Deep like the ocean, older than our entire species. It was like meeting a god."

"A god? You, uh, wouldn't happen to be a member of the Cosmic Ontological Foundation, would you?"

"I thought they were just misguided fools until I touched the mind of the Seraph. Now?" She slowly shook her head. "I understand how a person could look upon something like that and believe it to be divine. But . . . it's not a god. It's not mortal, but it's not a god."

"Uh, noted," I said.

"After the first couple sessions it learned how to communicate with me in a way that I could understand, in a way that was safe. It was . . . gentle . . . with me, with, you know, my mind. It slowed down to where I could almost keep up with its thoughts. It asked me questions, and I asked it questions. Not . . . not for long. I could only go in for a few minutes at a time. More than that and it's just . . . it's just overwhelming. Y-you start to lose your sense of self."

"Is . . . is that what happened to you, why you were put into the coma?" Dagny asked. "Did you stay connected for too long?"

"Yes," Cassandra said, nodding. "I . . . lost track of time. They tried to pull me out, but I wouldn't wake up. They were afraid to just sever the connection."

I tapped notes into my tablet as quickly as I could. This was without a doubt the most interesting conversation I'd ever had. "Why did you stay linked for so long? What did it ask you?"

"It asked me what I was. That's kind of a big question, you know? How do you explain what a human being is to something that's never seen one before? I summarized as best I could. I think . . . I think it understood. Then I asked it what *it* was. I asked it if it was a god." She smiled. "That's how I know it's not, because it told me so itself. Instead, it described itself as a *vessel carrying a soul.*"

"Huh. I suppose we all are."

"I asked it why it was there. It told me it wasn't sure where it was, so I uploaded a bunch of astronomical data for it to process. I think . . . I think it realized then how long it had been there. It was . . . it didn't like that."

"It didn't like you answering the question?"

"That's not it. It was . . . upset? That's my best guess."

"Upset? At you?"

"No, no, not at me. I think . . . I think it has an affinity for me, actually. It told me we achieved *stable synchronicity*, but it was upset that it had been there for so long. Frustrated, perhaps, maybe even . . . I don't know, sorrowful? It's like it forgot what happened to it and then remembered the truth."

"Oh my god," Dagny said. "This is incredible."

"Communicating with the Seraph *is* incredible," Cassandra agreed. "It's almost like . . . I mean, I've never had a religious experience, but I imagine that's what one feels like. It was so easy to lose track of time. It showed me so much."

"What did it show you?" I asked.

"It told stories visually, presented its memories in a way

that I might be able to understand. There was . . . there was a war, long, long ago. A war across space and time, over millions of light-years. It expressed this to me as the *War of Wrath*."

"Who was fighting who?"

"I . . . I don't know. The Seraph only described its side was *we*, so we started referring to them as the Seraphim."

"My God," I said. "That's a huge discovery all by itself."

"The enemy, the thing the Seraphim were fighting, it called *the Constrainer* and the *Void Tyrant*. I'm sorry, I don't know what that means, either. I don't understand what they were fighting over, or why. It didn't show me how it where or how it started."

"Well, what *did* it show you?"

"Destruction on a scale you can't comprehend. Worlds burned to ash, stars collapsed into black holes, the fabric of space-time itself was torn open. They fought for eons, across the galaxy and beyond, backward and forward in time. Battles would end before they began, history rewritten over and over. The war came to a standstill because there was almost no one left to fight."

"Who won?" I asked.

"It doesn't know. It . . . fell, in battle. The Spear was the final blow. It didn't kill it, because the Seraph can't die, but it . . . it . . . ." She trailed off, struggling to find the right words. "The Spear *binds* it. It leaves it not dead but not alive, its soul trapped in a prison it can't escape from. It was left here, for millions of years, all alone, trapped in the darkness of its own mind."

Cassandra's eyes were wide. She was breathing heavily

and sweating. "In the last session, it told me to remove the second Spear, to set it free. It commanded me. It begged me. I . . . I tried." Tears were trickling down her face now. "I tried. I couldn't make them understand. We need to set it free. It might be the last of its kind."

"I think that's enough for now," I said carefully. She was getting too worked up.

Cassandra surprised me by grabbing my wrist. "You don't understand," she said angrily, her eyes glazed over. "It was lost in its own mind. It allowed itself to forget, so it wouldn't go mad. The Spears restrained it, trapped it in its own body, not letting it live and not letting it die. It's in pain, in agony, suffering in silence. Imagine needing to scream but not having a mouth, having an itch you can never scratch, horrendous pain that never subsides. Imagine being alone in the darkness for so long you forget the light. The Seraph is trapped in its own hell and has been for sixty-eight million years!"

"Okay but . . . are you sure setting that thing free is a good idea?"

"The Spears were there to bind it. Both are needed for this, one isn't enough. It will take a long time, maybe years, but sooner or later it will grow strong enough to overcome the remaining Spear. Imagine what it'll do if we torture it for years and years and then it gets free?"

Her heart-rate monitor was beeping at a rapid pace. "Cassandra, I need you to try and remain calm."

No matter how you phrase it, telling a woman to calm down never works. "It's capable of such wrath, such terrible wrath. That's what happened to the First Antecessor Race! They sided with the enemy and they

were wiped out, every last one of them, forever. This is a
test, don't you see? A test of our character!"

"I . . . think I have enough for now."

Cassandra clutched her hands together, close to her
breast, and kept ranting. "I tried to tell Taranis, I tried to
tell him. He wouldn't listen. He's a frail old man, afraid to
die. He thinks the Seraph will bargain with him, will grant
him immortality. That's not how it works! I tried to tell
him, that's not how it works! It's not a genie to grant our
wishes. It can't give him what he wants. It's not . . . it's
not . . ."

The poor girl broke down sobbing and buried her face
in her hands. Dagny wrapped her arms around her sister
and held her tight.

"That was rough," I said. "I'm sorry about this."

Dagny looked shaken. "I-it's okay. What now?"

"Now I go sit down, write another report, and send it
up. After that, I don't know. The whole thing might be out
of my hands from now on."

Dagny looked up into my eyes as I stood up. "I'll come
find you later."

I smiled at her as I packed up the holo-recorder. "Sure
thing. I'll be around."

CHAPTER 15

Another full day went by without any word from Deitrik and I was beginning to get concerned. I tried not to let myself get too worried, though. After all, I'd dumped a pretty fantastic couple of reports into his lap, and I was sure it would take him a little while to process it all.

I was also going a little stir-crazy. I figured it was too much of a risk to come and go from the safe house any more than was absolutely necessary and I hadn't left once since the night I got there. Don't get me wrong, the house was nice and I didn't mind availing myself of Carmichael's hospitality, but I hadn't slept in my own bed in a while and I really just wanted to go home.

Alone in the small bedroom I'd been using, I put in an encrypted video call to Lily. I'd made it a habit to check in with her regularly since the operation at Research Towers went down. Her face appeared on the screen and she greeted me with a smile, just like she always did.

"Easy!" she said.

"Are you well?" I asked. I didn't normally talk like that,

but it was a challenge phrase. We'd taken to using it as a way of letting the other know if one of us was under duress.

"All's right in the world," she said, answering the challenge correctly. "How've you been?"

"Getting tired of sitting on my butt."

"Aren't you glad you packed extra clothes like I said?"

I grinned. "I sure am, kid. You doing alright?"

"It's been quiet here," she answered. At my insistence, she'd gone to stay with friends and was laying low until this whole thing blew over. I didn't know who she was with or where she was, and I didn't ask. "Dante and I have been monitoring network traffic and the infostreams for any word on what happened."

"Oh? Hear anything interesting?"

She shook her head. "Not much, Boss, at least on anything we can access. They reported the incident at the Ventura Medical Research Center as a robbery."

"A robbery? That's their story, huh?"

"Yup. A press release from Ascension stated that high-value biological samples from off-world were stolen, and that their security was hacked. Nothing about a missing person or a kidnapping."

"That's interesting." I rubbed my chin. "Did they say anything about me walking out with her in the medical pod?"

Lily smiled. "You're going to love this. When you took her out? They said that was them doing that."

"Is that right?"

"We got ahold of a message sent to the management of Research Towers. They claimed that, per protocol, their patient was evacuated to another facility when the VMRC's systems went down. Either everyone is buying their cover story or they're too scared to start asking questions, but there's been nothing further about the incident. I'm sure they're going nuts wondering where Cassandra Carmichael is, but it seems like they want this kept quiet."

"Sure seems that way, doesn't it? Anyway, how are you getting on? Been spending a lot of time with Dante, have you?"

Her fair skin flushed just a little and she smiled the way girls do when they're in love. "Is it that obvious?"

"I told you he was still sweet on you. Say, what happened to what's-her-name?"

Lily's eyes narrowed a little when I brought up the other girl. "Selena dumped him the moment he quit Arcanum."

"I'm not surprised. By the way they acted together I could tell it wasn't a serious thing. You're the one he wanted to be with."

She smiled again. "Yeah, well, we're taking it slow, you know? Seeing what happens. It's been good, though. Better than before."

"I expect you've both grown up a little since then."

"Now it's your turn to dish, Easy. How are things with Dagny?"

"Eh . . . being honest, I haven't seen much of her since we got here."

"Oh no. I hope everything's okay."

I shrugged. "She's been taking care of her sister and reconciling with her stepfather after everything we've been through, and we're all stuck in the same house together. It's got to be overwhelming. I'm giving her some space is all."

"Yeah," Lily agreed, "that's the best thing to do. Still, I hope she comes back to you. It's her loss if she doesn't, especially after everything you did for her."

"It ain't like that. I did what needed to be done for the client."

Lily actually rolled her eyes at me. "Sure, Boss, you'd have risked life and limb and prison for any rando who wandered into the office with a sob story." She giggled. "You can fool yourself but you can't fool me. I could feel the chemistry from the moment you two met."

I hadn't thought too much about what would happen between Dagny and me once this whole thing was over. I told myself that too much was going on right now to try to make any big plans for the future, but deep down I think I was scared to get my hopes up or see something that wasn't there. You strike out as many times as I have and you learn to keep yourself at a safe distance.

Still. "She's a hell of a woman," I admitted.

"You should tell her how you feel. I mean it. Don't let her go without taking your shot. You'll regret it forever if you do. You know I'm right."

It's weird for a man to take romantic advice from a girl half his age, but Lily was hitting pretty close to the mark on this one. Her earnestness was cute, too, and it made me chuckle. "Okay, okay, you win. I'll talk to her when the time is right."

"You deserve to be happy, Boss, that's all."

Before I could answer, my handheld vibrated in my hand. "I need to let you go," I told her.

"Everything okay?"

"I have another call coming in. Work-related."

"Understood. Keep me posted." With that, Lily disappeared from my screen and I accepted the incoming call.

"Hello, Easy," Deitrik said. The screen was black except for the words AUDIO ONLY.

"Deitrik! I'm glad to hear from you. I was getting worried."

"I'm sorry it took me so long. I've had to be very careful about whom I discuss this with."

That didn't sound good. "How bad is it?"

"It's a worst-case scenario," he said, gravely. "The local office of the SIS is compromised. The name you gave me, Leonard Steinbeck? He's the station chief for Nova Columbia."

"Well, shit," I said. "So they really *are* in on this."

"They are. I can only speculate on their motives and I've been unable to get a lot of specifics. My routine queries have been ignored."

"That's a bad sign, isn't it? Do they know that you're onto them?"

"I am sure they do."

"I'm sorry, Deitrik. I was afraid this would happen when I flashed my credentials to those SecFor troopers."

"You did what you had to do, Easy. I have prepared for this contingency."

"Are you in danger?"

"I don't know if they're willing to be that brazen, but I can't rule it out. They may just be hoping to stonewall me as a way of buying time. They know that I will have to contact Earth and how long that will take."

"Buying time for what? Sooner or later this whole thing is going to get found out, right? They have to know that."

"I'm afraid I don't know what their endgame is, or what they intend to do with the Seraph."

"The Carmichaels both told me that Xavier Taranis thinks he can gain immortality from it somehow. Do you think that's what did it?"

"Perhaps. Men have been driven to do terrible things for lesser prizes."

"Do you think the SIS itself approved this?"

"No, at least not officially. If it were, they would have brought me in on it or replaced me with someone more amenable to what they're doing. I don't know how far this conspiracy goes, but I intend to find out." There was a finality in his voice that told me he wasn't just talking tough. "In the meantime, we need to move Cassandra Carmichael. I agree with your assessment that she's in danger and I have every reason to believe that they will try to recover her."

"Where can we move her to? Can we get her out of the city?"

"Arthur Carmichael had the right idea: we need to get her off-world."

"That's a serious move."

"It's the best option. I can't unravel this alone and I can't guarantee her safety here, not with the limited resources I have available. I need to bring in higher authority on this."

"That could still take months. If what Cassandra told

me is true, the Seraph . . . that thing could put the whole colony in danger."

"I know, Easy, I know. There's nothing I can do about that from here, not by myself."

"What about the Commonwealth government? Can't we go to them, take the evidence we gathered?"

"I'm afraid that Leonard Steinbeck has prepared for that possibility, and has informed the local authorities that I have gone rogue. I don't know if they genuinely believe his story or if the officials he contacted are in on the whole thing, but the Colonial Security Forces are looking for me, now. They raided the restaurant last night and have now staked it out, hoping I will return there. They will be disappointed."

"My God, is your wife safe?"

"Yes. She's with me."

"Good, good. What about Cassandra? Are they looking for her now, too?"

"No. No mention of her has been made. They want her found, yes, but they do not want the local authorities questioning her . . . I suspect they know I had accomplices, but as of yet have not named any of them, including you."

"That's a relief. What now?"

"I have secured off-world passage for Cassandra, Arthur, and Dagny."

I paused for a second. "I . . . see," I said levelly. It made sense. It was the right thing to do. They knew who Dagny was and these people were dangerous. It was the only way to make sure she was safe, and right then I didn't have time to get spun up over how I felt about her leaving.

"There's something else you should know," he said. "I intend to leave as well, with my wife. I have a duty to keep pursuing this matter, wherever it leads me, for however long it takes," he continued. "I also have a duty to my wife, and I cannot protect her if I'm gone. It's not an ideal solution, especially on such short notice, but it's the best option I have."

"Well, damn, man. I don't mean to get all sentimental, here, but . . . you know, it's been nice working with you."

"I want you to come with us, Easy. I would not have uncovered any of this if not for you. You have proven to be an invaluable asset and I could surely use your help."

He caught me by surprise with that one. It made sense, once I took a second to think about it, but still. "You want me to just drop my life and walk away from it with no notice?"

"I know it's a big ask, but I don't know how deep this thing goes and I need people I can trust."

"I need to think it over."

"I understand, but please don't think too long. Time is not on our side. In the meantime, I'm sending you the relevant information about the travel arrangements. Unless the Carmichaels have any objections, they'll be leaving late tonight. Whether you choose to come with me or stay here, I have one final task for you, if you're willing."

"Tell me what you need."

"I need you to ensure that Cassandra makes it to her flight safely. I cannot risk the exposure of trying to arrange transportation to the departure location. Can you do this for me?"

"Sure thing. I'll brief Arthur and come up with a plan."

"Thank you, Easy."

Later that evening I found Dagny alone on the house's western balcony, smoking a cigarette. Her figure was silhouetted against the dying light as Scorpii sank below the mountains beyond the edge of the Crater. There was a cold wind in the air that night and I was wearing both my hat and coat.

I stood next to Dagny and took in the view myself. It was a little fuzzy on account of the one-way privacy screen that ran from the awning above us to the railing we were leaning on. The last light of Nova Columbia's short autumn day was failing, giving way to the long night to come. Below us was the house's small courtyard and driveway, surrounded by an eight-foot security wall.

"Come here often?" I said, lightly, looking out into the distance. Not long before I had briefed everyone on the Baron's plan to evacuate them all off-world, and surprised them when I explained that I would be staying behind. I hadn't told Deitrik yet, but that was my decision.

Dagny took a long drag off her cigarette and exhaled the smoke into the cold breeze. "I'm sorry I hurried off after the meeting. I just ... I just needed some time to think. It was a lot to take in." We were heading out that night, off to a small commercial spaceport outside the Crater. The Baron had arranged a shuttle to take the Carmichaels up to a waiting starship, and even had armed security waiting for us. All we had to do was get there. Carmichael's two bodyguards were out renting armored vehicles for us as a last-minute precaution.

"It is," I agreed. "Believe you me, when you first walked into my office, I never imagined that this would end like this."

"You really think this is the end of it?" she asked. "That thing is still up there at Site 471. What if Cassie is right? They're going to keep poking it and prodding it, pissing it off. What if it breaks free? She said they wiped out the First Antecessor Race."

There was fear in her voice. It was understandable; humanity has been in space for a few hundred years now, and in all that time we only encountered a couple intelligent alien races. The only one that proved to be a threat so far is the Ceph, and we walloped them pretty hard in the war. The First Antecessor Race was far more advanced than either us or the Ceph; if the Seraphim really did exterminate them, then we wouldn't have a ghost of a chance.

There wasn't anything to be done about that just then, so I tried to be comforting. "It's been there for sixty-eight million years, it can wait a few more months. Besides, this isn't the end of this matter. I have no doubt that Deitrik will sort things out, and there'll likely be hell to pay for Ascension and the SIS when he does."

"You should come with us," Dagny said, her eyes locked onto mine. A man could lose himself in that gaze.

I smiled. "Deitrik said the same thing. He wants to hire me on permanently until this whole mess has been put to bed. I thought about it, too, I really did."

"But you decided to say," she said, regret in her voice.

"I did. This miserable rock is my home. I was born here and I intend to be buried here."

"That's not the real reason you're staying."

"It's not," I admitted. "The agency is Victor's legacy. I also can't up and leave Lily behind, not after dragging her into this mess, and I know that girl won't leave no matter what I say. Besides, I promised my dad I'd help him look after my mom as they got older."

"You don't have to explain yourself to me, Easy," Dagny said. "I respect your decision no matter what."

"It wasn't an easy one to make. Part of me wants to see this thing through to the end, no matter where it takes me." I hesitated for just a moment. My heart was racing. I gazed down into Dagny's eyes. "And . . . watching you leave will be hard."

"I'll stay if you ask me to," she said, quietly, stubbing out her cigarette on the top of the banister. I could tell by the look in her eyes that she meant it, too. For just a moment I let myself imagine what that life would be like, having her in my arms every night. Would we grow old together? We made a good team and she'd be a hell of an asset for the agency. I'd been alone since Marian left. Oh sure, there was a woman here or there, but nothing real, nothing that meant anything. I almost couldn't picture it, picture me in a healthy relationship like a normal person.

Then I came back to reality. "I can't ask you to do that," I said. "It wouldn't be safe for you here, not with you being Cassandra's sister. I'd be a hell of a hypocrite, too, telling you to leave your family behind while I stay near mine. That's not fair to you."

"I guess it isn't," she said. "It's decided, then."

"Yeah." I didn't say anything for a few moments. "This is for the best, but . . . I want you to know something." I looked into her eyes again. "I will always wonder how things might have turned out, if circumstances had been different. I think... I think being with you would have been pretty great."

Dagny closed her eyes, stood up on her tiptoes, and kissed me. We wrapped our arms around each other as we embraced. After the kiss, she turned her head to the side and rested it against my chest. A tear trickled down her cheek, and I held her tight. "I'll never forget you, Easy Novak."

"Hey, if you ever end up back on Nova Columbia, look me up. You know where to find me."

"I wonder where we'll end up?" Dagny asked, still holding onto me.

"I don't know. Earth, probably. That's where SIS headquarters is."

"Have you ever been to Earth?"

"Me? No. Harvest, Sovereign, Amethyst, and San Martin, but never Earth. I've heard it's nice."

Dagny let me go and stepped back. "I've never been off of Nova Columbia. Neither has Cassie."

"It's good that you'll be there for her, then," I said reassuringly. "She's been through a lot and she needs her big sister."

"I know. I just..." She trailed off, reached up, and gently caressed the side of my face with her hand. "I'll always wonder, too. Thank you for everything you've done for us... for me."

I grinned. "Think you could leave the agency a positive review before you leave?"

That got her to laugh. "Of course. Five stars. Dedicated

detective, pretty good in the sack. I'm sure it'll bring in a lot of business."

The compound's front gate opened, and two black, armored sport/utility trucks rolled through the courtyard and into the garage. "Looks like our ride's here," I said. "Guess we should go get loaded up."

"Yeah," Dagny said. She squeezed my hand, took one last long, lingering look into my eyes, and walked away.

I was right; it was hard to watch her go.

It was the dead of night when we rolled out of the safe house. The two armored trucks that Carmichael had rented were the well-equipped sort that politicians and VIPs use, with plush interiors and a smooth ride. Carmichael's bodyguard James was driving, his usual suit replaced with an armor vest and combat pants. Cassandra was in the back seat. She didn't say much and I didn't blame her. I'm sure all this was a hell of a lot to process, and she was still recovering from her ordeal.

I was in the front passenger's seat, also wearing body armor, with my .44 holstered under my right arm. The bodyguards had provided me with a weapon, a commercial clone of the Mk.211 rifle that the Nova Columbia Defense Force used. These rifles fire 8mm explosive, armor-piercing ammunition and are accurate as hell. I was issued one of these during the war and being handed one was like shaking hands with an old friend.

The other vehicle took the lead. This one was being driven by Stephen and was carrying both Dagny and Arthur Carmichael. I opted to ride with Cassandra, not only because she was the primary mission objective, but because . . . well, I'd already said my goodbyes to Dagny. There was no sense dragging it out with a long, awkward car ride. I didn't need the distraction.

After the first half hour or so the stifling silence started to get to me. Everyone was on edge and I wanted to break the tension some if I could. I looked over at James. "If you don't mind me asking, what's going to happen to you boys once Carmichael leaves?".

James shrugged a little without taking his hands off the steering wheel. "Not sure yet. I've been working for Mr. Carmichael for five years now. We're both getting a pretty generous severance package, so we should be set for a while. It's just kind of sudden, you know?"

"You don't work for Ascension, do you?"

"No, we work directly for Mr. Carmichael."

Cassandra spoke up from the back seat. "Arthur hired Stephen and James after he helped break up a criminal theft ring that was stealing from the company. The ones who didn't go to prison tried to kill him."

"That makes sense," I said. "I'm just surprised that he didn't get security directly from the company."

"Oh, they offered," James said, with a knowing grin. "Not to brag, but Stephen and I are a lot better trained and equipped than your typical corporate security dregs."

"Arthur wouldn't trust anyone from Ascension anyway," Cassandra said. "If you have company security protecting you, you can be sure they're reporting on everything you do corporate."

"It's kind of funny that he worked for Ascension for more than thirty years but doesn't trust them," I said. "Not that I blame him."

"He didn't trust them *because* he was a career company man," Cassandra replied. "There are a lot of people in the company like that."

I looked back over at James. "You aren't worried that somebody from Ascension will come after you?"

"They're welcome to try," he said with a chuckle. "No, I'm not worried. I'm sure they'll come by asking questions and offering bribes, but I won't have anything useful to tell them. I don't know where Mr. Carmichael is going."

"I'll be sticking around, too," I said. "You mind doing me a favor? If I give you my contact info, will you let me know if they come sniffing around? I'll return the favor, of course."

"That's a good idea," James said. He nodded. "Yeah, I will."

We followed Route 2 through the southern outskirts of the city. Traffic was light that night, especially for a six-lane highway, and we made good time. After another thirty minutes we climbed the long upward slope and left the Crater behind us. The highway stretched out into the arid, rocky plains beyond.

Things were quiet and everything seemed to be going according to plan. We would be at the departure location in another hour, and after that? Well, my part in this whole thing would come to an end. Dagny had paid me in full, I'd received a nice chunk of cash from Deitrik, and had a hundred thousand dollars from Arthur Carmichael filling up my accounts. I would be all set for a while. I could give Lily a raise and maybe take my first-ever real vacation.

The proximity sensor in the dashboard of the truck started beeping then.

"What is that?" Cassandra asked, nervously.

"Incoming aircraft," James said, glancing at the display screen.

I closed my eyes tight for a second, and took a deep breath. *That's what I get for thinking positive*, I thought.

"Mr. Novak," the bodyguard said, "he's coming from behind and on our right."

"I don't see it yet," I said, ducking down a little to try and scan the night sky through the armored window. "Notify the other vehicle that we're being pursued."

"Hold on," James said. I was pushed back into my seat a little as he stepped on the accelerator. The armored sport/utility truck had a big motor and was surprisingly fast for how heavy it was.

I turned back to Cassandra. I could tell she was scared, but to her credit she was maintaining her composure.

"What are we going to do?" she asked. She was wearing a ballistic armor vest that was a little too big for her.

"We're going to keep going," I said. "My SIS contact has people waiting for us. These assholes aren't taking us without a fight."

"Easy, I'm scared. I just feel so . . . so powerless."

"I know, but we're not going to let anything happen to you." I thought for a second. "Say, you know how to shoot?"

"What? Yeah, I guess. I did marksmanship in Frontier Scouts when I was a kid. Why? I don't have a gun."

I reached back toward her. In my hand was my backup, the little 9mm snub pistol. I handed it to her butt-first and was pleased to see she carefully kept her finger off the trigger when she took it.

"You're giving me a gun?"

"Yes. It holds ten rounds but the bullets won't penetrate armor. If you need to use it, aim for the head and make your shots count. Keep it hidden in your pocket unless you need it."

She hesitated and looked down at the small weapon in her hands. "Are you sure?"

"Yeah, I'm sure. Keep it with you until you get safely aboard the ship."

"Thank you."

"Don't mention it," I said, and turned back around. Truth be told, there probably wasn't much Cassandra could do with that little pistol if things went sideways, but I figured not feeling helpless would keep her from panicking.

The truck's threat warning system sounded another warning tone. "What now?" James asked. We were driving fast, weaving around the few other cars on the highway, and he didn't take his eyes off the road.

"It's another aircraft," I said, looking at the display. "This one is coming up on our left. Shit."

"Can you see them?"

I peered out the window again. To our right, coming in low over the highway, was a boxy VTOL, its fuselage briefly illuminated by each streetlight as it flashed past them. "Yeah, I see it. Three o'clock high. It's matching speed with us."

We were speeding along at nearly a hundred miles per hour. "I don't think this thing will go much faster," James said.

"We can't outrun them," I said. "Keep going. Let

them make the first move. They might just follow us to the departure point, and they'll be in for a surprise if they do."

"How did they know where we are?" Cassandra asked, from the back seat.

"I don't know," I said. "Strap yourself in."

"There's the other one," James said, quickly shifting his glance between the road ahead of him and the driver's side window. "It's matching speed also."

I covered my eyes as a blinding light shined in my window, so bright it caused the window to auto-tint. It was a spotlight from the jump-jet on our right. The one on our left was shining one on the other truck. We continued to speed along for a few moments until Stephen, driving the truck ahead of us, stepped on the brakes and began slowing down.

"What the hell is he doing?" I asked. "Why is he slowing down?"

"I don't know," James said. "He—oh shit!"

The lead truck swerved violently into the left margin, scraping against the ceramicrete barriers before straightening out back on the highway. It continued to slow down.

A voice emanated from the truck's tactical radio. "James," it said. It was Stephen, who was driving the other vehicle. "Do you read me?"

James spoke into his headset. "Loud and clear. What's going on? Are you okay?"

"Everything is going to be fine," he said, calmly. "Listen to me very carefully. It's over. You need to exit the highway and come to a stop."

"What? What are you talking about?" James asked.

"There's no getting out of this unless we cooperate," Stephen said. "Don't worry, I made us a deal. You and I will be set for life. Do you understand what I'm telling you?"

"He sold us out," I said, bitterly.

I could tell by the death-grip he had on the steering wheel that James was seething with anger. He replied over the radio, "Just like that, huh? After all these years you just stabbed Carmichael in the back?"

"You're damned right I did," Stephen said. "It's nothing personal. I just got offered a better deal. Do I have to remind you that he was about to leave us behind? He and his family get to safety, but what about us? You know we'd be the first ones the company came looking for."

"God damn it!" James snarled, slamming the steering wheel with the palms of his hands.

"James," Stephen continued, "you need to be smart about this. All we need to do is stop and let them take the Carmichaels. By tomorrow we'll each have two million dollars in our pockets. Are you really going to risk your life and become a fugitive from the SIS just to protect our last client? Think, James, *think*."

James looked over at me. His usual emotionless demeanor was gone. I could see the pain on his face. "What do we do?" he asked.

"We're going to keep driving," I said.

"We can't leave Dagny and Arthur behind!" Cassie protested.

"Yes, we can," I said, coldly. I looked back at her. "I'm sorry, kid, but you're the priority here." I looked back at

James. "Keep going." He nodded, stepped on the accelerator, and sped around the other vehicle.

Stephen spoke over the radio again. "James, I wish you wouldn't do this, but you're not leaving me any choice. If you don't pull over and come to a stop right now, I'm going to kill the old man first, then the broad. Am I making myself clear?"

"Don't do it!" It was Arthur, shouting in the background. "James, get her to—gah!" He fell silent.

"Don't make me hurt them," Stephen said. "I don't want to, but I will."

"He always was a cold son of a bitch," James snarled.

"You have to stop!" Cassandra cried. "Please! Don't let them kill my dad and my sister!"

"No," I said. I was sweating. My heart was racing. I knew I was signing Dagny's death warrant. "We have to keep going. That's the mission."

"James," Cassie said. I looked back at her again. She had the gun I'd given her extended in her right hand, pointed at the back of the driver's head. Tears were streaming down her face. "Stop this car right now or I swear I'll shoot you. I mean it!"

"Cassandra," I said.

She didn't let me finish and pointed the gun between my eyes. "Shut up! How can you leave Dagny to die like that? You bastard, she loves you! She *trusts* you!"

"I know, damn it, I *know*! I don't want to do this, but my job is to get you to safety above all else. You're the key to all of this! Now put that gun down, you're not going to shoot me."

"You're right," Cassandra said, lowering the gun. "I

can't hurt anybody else." Leaning back against the back seat, out of my reach, she raised the little pistol to her right temple. "But I *can* kill myself."

"Time's running out, James," Stephen said, over the radio.

I held my hands up, really slow. Her eyes were wide and she was breathing rapidly. Sweat and tears both trickled down her face. "Cassandra," I said, as calmly as I could, "this isn't the answer. Please put the gun down."

"Shut up! This is all my fault!" Her right eye twitched and she began blinking rapidly. "I tried to tell it that this would happen, I tried to tell it! This is the only way!"

"It's not the only way," I said. "James? Start slowing down. Tell them we'll stop."

"Are you sure?"

"Pull over or I'm going to blow my brains out!" Cassandra cried. She was scared, desperate, and quickly growing unstable.

I couldn't risk calling her bluff. "Yeah, I'm sure," I said. I tapped the controls and linked my own headset to the radio so I could talk to Stephen. "Alright, you bastard, you win. We're coming to a stop."

"You made the smart choice, Mr. Novak," Stephen said. "I'm going to pull back in front of you and you're going to follow me. There's an off-ramp coming up, County Road Four. Exit there and turn right. We'll head away from the highway, then come to a stop. You're going to disarm and get out of the truck with your hands up. Do exactly what they tell you and you'll live through this."

The Baron needed to know what was happening. I pulled out my handheld and went to send a secure message, only to discover that I had no signal. "Damn it," I snarled. "Comms are being jammed."

James looked surprised. "What? We were just talking on the radio!"

"One of those birds has an advanced electronic warfare suit. Probably SIS. They can pick and choose which frequencies to let through and which to jam. Hell, they can probably pinpoint every device in this vehicle."

The exit for County Road 4 was coming up quickly. James looked over at me with a worried face. "You really think they'll let us live?"

"They need Cassandra. Us, not so much."

"They will!" Cassandra said. She still held the pistol against her head despite her shaking hands. "I'll make sure they will! I'm sorry!"

I thought for a moment before speaking again. "James, there's no reason both of us have to take this risk."

"What are you talking about?" he said.

"When we get to the end of the off-ramp, I want you to come to a stop. Cassandra and I will get out. As soon as we're out of the vehicle, you step on it and don't stop for anything. Get to the meeting point. Tell Deitrik, my SIS handler, what happened." I handed him my handheld. "Give him this. I've been recording everything. He'll know it's not a trick."

To his credit, the young bodyguard seemed hesitant. He barely knew me and had no personal connection to Cassandra, but it was clear he didn't feel good about just leaving us behind. "I don't like this," he said.

"I don't like it either, kid, but there's no reason you have to let them take you."

"You really think they'll just let me go?"

"They might pursue you, but they'll need some pretty heavy firepower to stop this thing. Why risk that kind of exposure once they have their prize? My gut tells me that as soon as they have Cassandra they'll be satisfied. For now, anyways. They'll come after you eventually, but Deitrik will make sure you're protected. Don't believe your partner's promises about that money, either. Two bullets cost a hell of a lot less than four million dollars."

"I don't know what to say."

I patted him on the shoulder. "It's alright. It was nice working with you. Get to Deitrik as fast as you can. Tell him what happened. He'll know what to do."

"Easy, you should go, too," Cassandra said, quietly. "Just let me get out."

Being perfectly honest, I thought about it. It was tempting. It seemed prudent. There was a chance that James and I would both make it to safety. The only problem was, I wouldn't be able to live with myself. "I can't," I said, shaking my head. "I promised Dagny I'd see this through to the end. I can't leave her, not like this."

"Easy, please," Cassandra pleaded. "You don't have to do this."

"You don't have to do this either, kid. You made your choice, I made mine. We'll go through it together." We exited the highway and headed down the ramp. I unbuckled my safety restraint. "This is it. Remember, as soon as we're out the door, you go. They're not going to risk a traffic camera recording them blasting you on a public highway. Get to the spaceport as quickly as you can."

"I will, Mr. Novak, I promise."

"Thank you, James," I said, as we slowed to a stop. The other vehicle had already made the turn, but paused to wait for us. The two VTOLs hovered nearby, engines screaming, one of them still shining that damned spotlight on us. I set the rifle aside, opened the door, and stepped out. Cassandra followed suit.

A second later, the truck's tires squealed as James hit the accelerator. The armored truck sped off. It climbed the on-ramp and got back on the highway, disappearing from sight. As I guessed they would, both aircraft remained overhead. The other armored truck flipped around on the road and pulled up to where we stood. It stopped a few yards away, blinding us with its headlights. The driver's side door opened and Stephen stepped out. Even a truck that large was cramped for the big man, and it noticeably lifted on its suspension when he got out.

I looked over my shoulder at Cassandra. "Get behind me. Stay close. We might still have a chance. Don't do anything crazy."

Without saying anything, Stephen opened the back door of his truck, reached in, and pulled Dagny out by the arm. She was kicking and struggling but was no match for the strength of the cyborg. He had a large gun in his other hand, pointed at her head.

"Easy!" Dagny cried. It hit me like a knife to the gut. Her face was bloodied.

"Shut up, woman," Stephen snarled. He looked up at me. "What game are you playing, Novak? Where's James?" His raised his voice to make himself heard over the roar of jet engines. One of the aircraft stayed aloft, illuminating us with a spotlight, while the other began to descend.

"He decided he didn't trust your new friends here," I shouted back. "Where's Arthur Carmichael?"

"He's alive, if that's what you're wondering. The old man's just taking a nap right now because he thought he'd be clever and grab the wheel. Your girlfriend here's a feisty one, too. She tried to pull a gun on me."

A hundred yards or so away, the second jump-jet touched down, kicking up a huge cloud of rocky dust as it settled onto the pavement. It was facing away from us. A cargo hatch in the rear slowly opened, revealing several people inside, backlit by red interior lights. The group disembarked as soon as the ramp was down and began heading our way.

"Hand over Cassandra Carmichael," Stephen commanded, "and I'll send this one over to you." He squeezed Dagny's arm, causing her to wince in pain. "Cassandra is coming with me either way. Your choice."

A pulse of anger shot through me. My muscles twitched and I had to deliberately stop myself from pulling my gun. I stood there, jaw clenched, raging on the inside, but completely helpless.

The bodyguard kept his pitch up. "Your only chance of getting out of this alive is to cooperate. Ascension and the SIS are willing to make a deal with you. You two can still walk away from this with a fat bank account. We all can."

"Get off of her, you bastard!" It was Arthur! He lunged out of the truck, grabbing at the cyborg's right hand. His face was bloody and bruised but the old man had some fight left in him. Struggling for the gun, Stephen shoved Dagny to the ground, turned, and punched Arthur in the side of the head with all of his mechanical strength.

"Arthur!" Dagny screamed.

In a flash, my gun was drawn, extended in my arms, and pointed at Stephen. I fired off a snap shot. The bullet struck him in the left side, under his arm, detonating with a small flash. I don't know if it managed to penetrate his armor vest or not, but the cyborg winced in pain and staggered back. He looked up at me with a surprised expression on his face.

Time seemed to slow to a stop. I fired again.

The gun barked and recoiled in my hand. I hit the bodyguard right between the eyes and, while it didn't exactly take his head off, the explosive .44 slug sure made a mess of him.

I didn't waste a second. "Come on!" I said, and grabbed Cassandra by the wrist. I pulled her along with me as I ran to Arthur.

Dagny scrambled over to her fallen stepfather. "No," she cried, holding his head up in her arms. "Oh God, no!"

Cassandra fell to her knees and wrapped her arms around her sister. I knelt down to take a look at Arthur. One punch from that clanker was like getting hit in the head with a metal baseball bat.

"He's dead," I said. "Come on, we have to go."

"We can't leave him here!" Dagny protested. Cassandra was sobbing uncontrollably now.

"We have to go, now!" I shouted, pulling Dagny to her feet. "Get in! Both of you, get in, now!"

"Stop right there!" an electronically amplified voice boomed. We were too late. The people from the landed VTOL had caught up with us. There were six armed men pointing weapons at us and they had us dead-to-rights. "Drop your weapon, now!" the voice ordered.

I closed my eyes and exhaled heavily. So close. So damned close, but almost succeeding still means you failed. I dropped my gun and slowly turned around, raising my hands over my head as I did so. The armed men moved closer, into the aircraft's spotlight so I could see them. They were dressed head to toe in black tactical gear and body armor, their faces concealed under helmets. Ascension Special Response Team, I guessed.

The next thing I knew, Cassandra moved in front of me, placing herself between me and the shooters. "Stop!" she said, shouting to be heard over the noise. She had my backup pistol in her hand, the muzzle jammed up under her chin. "Everybody stop or I'll kill myself!"

The tactical team stayed where they were. They hadn't expected that.

"Stay back! I'll shoot, I swear to God!" The top of Cassandra's head only came up to my chin, so she wasn't exactly a human shield, but the Ascension goons stayed where they were. I figured they were under orders to bring her back alive.

"Drop your weapon!" one of the security men shouted.

"You drop *your* weapon!" Cassandra shouted back, defiantly.

"Enough of this!" It was a woman's voice this time, dusky and authoritative. She stepped into the light from behind the tactical team. She was an older woman, mid-fifties maybe, dressed in a brown overcoat that came down to her knees. She had fair skin and gray hair pulled back into a tight bun. I recognized her from Carmichael's files—it was Blanche Delacroix, the security manager for Project Isaiah.

"Lower your weapons," she commanded. One of the security men protested, but she wouldn't have it. "Do as I say! She's no good to us if you stress her into a relapse!" She turned toward us and took a couple steps forward. "Cassandra, there's no need for this," she said. She was trying to sound soothing but still had to raise her voice to be heard over the noise of the aircraft hovering nearby. "We're not going to hurt you."

"Shut up!" Cassandra screamed. I was worried I was going to get a front-row seat to a young woman blowing her brains out. "You killed Arthur! You murdered him!"

Delacroix took a couple more steps forward, holding her hands up so we could see them. "That wasn't us," she said. "He was under specific instructions not to harm either of you. I didn't want this. I'm sorry."

"You—you're *sorry*?" Cassandra protested, anger resonating in her voice. "You kept me prisoner then killed Arthur and now you think you can just say you're *sorry*?"

"We were keeping you *alive*," the older woman said. "It's a miracle they didn't give you brain damage when they brought you out of that coma."

"Stop lying, you bitch!" Cassandra shrieked. She was breathing rapidly, like she was about to hyperventilate, and her hands were shaking. "Take one step closer and I pull the trigger!"

"Okay, okay," Delacroix said, stopping where she was. "Let's talk, then. What do you want?"

"I'll go with you," she said, "but you have to let Easy, Arthur, and Dagny go."

"Cassie, no!" Dagny protested.

Cassandra ignored her. "Let them drive away in that truck and I'll come with you."

"I can't do that," Delacroix said.

"Bullshit!" Cassandra snarled.

"You see that VTOL, the one with the spotlight?" Delacroix asked. "That's an SIS aircraft. Your friends are wanted criminals who conspired with a rogue SIS officer and committed a long list of felonies. Detective Novak there just killed an SIS asset. You're lucky they didn't fire on you."

"That's not true!" Cassandra screamed. "You're twisting again, twisting!"

"What else did they tell you?" Delacroix asked. "Let me guess: they said the Security Intelligence Service was somehow illegally conspiring with Ascension. They claimed that your abduction was a rescue and not a kidnapping. They crafted a convincing story where they're the heroes. Am I getting close?"

"Shut up, shut up, *shut up!*" Cassandra said. She was crying now. "You're confusing me!"

"I didn't want anything to happen to Arthur. For God's sake, I worked with him for months and knew him longer than that. It wasn't supposed to happen like this, and wouldn't have, if not for Mr. Novak."

My eyes narrowed but I didn't say anything.

"We can still work this out," Delacroix continued. "Just come with us, all of you. Mr. Novak, you were being used as a pawn by a corrupt SIS officer looking to line his own pockets, but the shooting that just happened was still clearly justified. All of you are victims in this, don't you see? Nobody else has to get hurt. Cassandra, put down that gun. This is madness."

I knew what she was saying was bullshit, but her spiel really wasn't for me. They were trying to talk Cassandra down, but it wasn't working. The girl was barely holding on and my gut told me that when it became clear Delacroix wouldn't give her what she wanted, she'd pull the trigger. I looked over at Dagny, who was looking back at me. She didn't say anything, but she read my face. She nodded.

I put a hand on Cassandra's shoulder. It startled her and she turned to that she could see me. Her eyes were wide, she was blinking rapidly, and she was sweating despite the cold night air. "It's okay, kid. Put the gun down. I don't want you to hurt yourself."

Dagny moved closer. "Cassie, listen to Easy. You don't have to do this for us. I'll never forgive myself if you commit suicide trying to help me. I just lost Arthur, I can't lose you, too."

Cassandra teared up. "I'm sorry. I tried."

"I know," I said. "You got guts. Sometimes there's no just good way out."

She nodded at me, then turned back around. "I'll come with you, Blanche." The pistol clattered on the pavement as she dropped it. "Just don't hurt them. I'll cooperate, I'll do whatever you want, just don't hurt them."

"Of course, dear," Delacroix said. I had to hand it to the old hag, she could feign sincerity like a pro. "You have my word." She held out a hand. "Please, come with me."

Cassandra took one last look back at Dagny and me,

then walked over to Blanche Delacroix. The older woman put an arm over her shoulder and led her toward the landed jump-jet. She said something to the security team as she passed. I didn't hear what, but I figured it out a few seconds later.

Dagny and I were thrown to the ground and handcuffed. A black bag was pulled over my head yet again. Restrained and unable to see, we were led to the waiting aircraft.

CHAPTER 16

A few hours later I was sitting in a holding cell, something that was becoming an all too regular occurrence. It was maybe ten feet by twelve, with a cot on one end and a latrine on the other. The toilet had a built-in sink and water fountain like the ones in prison. There was a shower nozzle on the wall above a drain in the floor. A camera, surrounded by a protective bubble, was trained on me at all times. I could use the can or wash myself at my leisure, but I got no privacy.

The walls were eggshell-white ceramicrete and the door was reinforced metal. Most workplaces don't include a brig in their floor plan, but a company like Ascension has different priorities. They took away my clothes and shoes, scanned me, searched me, and confiscated all my possessions. They even took my jacket and hat, the thieving bastards. At least they didn't leave me naked; I was given a blue coverall, undergarments, socks, and a pair of shoes, all fresh from the fabricator.

I was in that cell for quite a while, nearly two weeks, I

think. Every night (at least, I assume it was night, I didn't have a window) the lights would dim, and they'd come back maybe eight hours later. A loud air circulation fan ran constantly. The white noise helped me sleep, but it also meant that I couldn't hear anything from outside the cell. There was nothing for me to do, so I slept a lot, at first from exhaustion and then from boredom. There was a compartment in the wall that would open up every so often and supply me with rations to eat and, once, a fresh set of clothes identical to the ones I was wearing.

When they loaded us onto that aircraft, I figure their plan was to get us away from Cassandra, put a bullet in each of us, and toss our corpses into the volcano. The executioner never came, though, and neither did an interrogator. As a matter of fact I didn't so much as see another human being the entire time I was in that cell. I called out sometimes, but no one answered. My cell seemed to be soundproofed.

I was being taken care of better than I had hoped, but it begged the question: why? After a while it started to wear on my nerves, and I wondered if that wasn't the plan: keep me in that hole until I cracked, then milk me for information. I wasn't sure if I believed Blanche Delacroix when she said that Carmichael's dead bodyguard was an SIS asset, but he was obviously a mole who had been feeding them information. The only information he wouldn't have had access to was the identity of the Baron, but Deitrik himself told me that they were already onto him.

What was the point, then? If they were trying to get me to talk, what did they think I knew that they hadn't already figured out? If they weren't trying to soften me up for interrogation, why were they keeping me alive at all?

More importantly, what had they done with Dagny? Was she okay? What was going on with the Seraph? I had no way of knowing and there was nothing I could do. I tried my best to keep calm and levelheaded. Whatever was going on, my situation wouldn't improve by me losing my cool.

I didn't get to see much of Site 471 on the way in, but I was able to learn a few things. Not much of the originally planned terraforming plant had been built when they discovered the Seraph and construction was halted after. As we were being escorted in from the landing pad, I caught a glimpse of a huge structure built into the base of the volcano. That was probably where the dig site was, where the Seraph was entombed. What little else I saw consisted of dozens of buildings connected by a tram system. The whole site was surrounded by twelve-foot walls, and there was a lot of security present.

Well into my second week in that cell, something new happened: the lights went out and I was plunged into darkness. It wasn't the normal evening dimming of the lights; it was a power failure. Even the fan stopped turning. A few seconds later, a red emergency light came on, but the main lights and the fan stayed off. It was odd, because a place like that had to have emergency backup generators in addition to their main reactor. Why weren't they activating? Whatever the reason, I sat in the dark for at least an hour before the power was restored.

A short while after that, the wall compartment that supplied me with my meals hissed and beeped, the little light on it turning green. It didn't feel like it was mealtime yet, so it had me curious. I opened the door and slid out the tray. Instead of food it was a change of clothes, but not another coverall like the one I was wearing. It was a suit, charcoal gray, with a white shirt and a plain black tie. Included was a pair of synthetic leather shoes.

Curious, I lifted up the suit jacket. It was double breasted but unlined, and with plastic buttons. The material felt cheap and, like the coveralls, I could tell it was rapidly fabricated. What I didn't know was why in the hell they were giving me a suit to wear, but I didn't have to wait long for an answer.

"Please get dressed, Mr. Novak," a synthesized baritone voice ordered.

"Gah!" I exclaimed, every muscle in my body tensing up. I hadn't heard a voice other than my own in over a week and it startled me. The voice emanated from the camera in the corner of my cell; seems it had a speaker on it, too. Setting the suit jacket on the bed, I walked over to the camera and looked up at it. "What's this all about?"

"Please get dressed," it repeated. The artificial voice was flat and dispassionate. "You will be having dinner with Mr. Taranis."

"Wait, what?"

"You will be having dinner with Mr. Taranis," the voice said again. "Please get dressed."

"Why does he want to have dinner with me?" There was no answer. I didn't know what the hell was going on, but I also hadn't been out of my cell in days. If the old man wanted to talk, it couldn't hurt to hear him out.

It only took me a couple minutes to change. They had

scanned me when I was brought in so the suit fit pretty well. The door buzzed and slid open just as I finished buttoning the jacket. Two security men entered my cell, and it sounded like there were a couple more in the hall. They were wearing gray fatigues, body armor, and helmets, with their faces concealed behind polarized visors. Each was armed with a shock baton.

I backed away slowly, raising my hands. "I got dressed as fast as I could, fellas. It takes me a little longer to do a Windsor knot without a mirror."

"Come with us," one of the guards ordered. His voice was distorted by an electronic modulator. "We're taking you to see Mr. Taranis."

"Where's Dagny?" I demanded.

The other guard held out his shock baton and hit the switch. It crackled loudly in the cell. "Be quiet and come with us."

"Alright, alright," I said. "Don't get your panties in a bunch. Lead the way."

I was marched out of the cell and into a corridor. The two guards with the shock batons fell in right behind me. Behind them were the other two, both armed with shotguns. There were four cells in total, two on each side of the corridor, with a security office at the end. Dagny and I had been separated after arriving and I didn't see which cell they'd put her in, or if they'd taken her somewhere else. How many prisons did one corporate worksite need?

Past the security office was an indoor station for the tram system that interconnected Site 471. The cars were small, each having only eight seats, but there was enough room for me and my surly entourage. I was shoved to the back of the car and told to sit down. My escorts sat nearby and didn't say anything as the tram left the station.

I looked out the window as the tramcar followed its track around the site. It wasn't very fast, maybe twenty-five miles per hour, but the site wasn't that big. The sun, dimmed by the black smoke rising angrily from Mount Gilead, hung low in the western sky. It was late afternoon, then. As we passed into the shadow of the mountain, I got a closer look at the huge structure at its base, the one I assumed they built to conceal the excavation site. It resembled a giant aircraft hangar, easily big enough to contain four football fields at once. There were large vehicle doors at its base and rock tailings piled into massive heaps behind. Heavy earthmoving equipment was parked nearby, currently idle. Had they dug it up completely, then?

The site was arranged in a large, uneven ring at the foot of Mount Gilead. The cone of the volcano marked the western end while a smaller, rocky plateau stood at the east. In the center was the landing pad, hangars, and a yard full of stacked cargo modules and parked vehicles. A single road led out of the site, to the south.

The plateau on the eastern end of the site was dwarfed by the volcano, but still appeared massive and imposing. It had to be a couple hundred feet high, with an elevator running up the rocky face of it, and more buildings at the top. The tram pulled into a station at the base of the plateau and came to a stop.

"This is where we get off," one of the mooks escorting me said. "Move."

I didn't make a stink as they pushed me out of the tramcar. There was a security checkpoint at the tram station, manned by four more armed guards and a hulking, bipedal combat robot. It had digitigrade legs and walked like an eight-foot, armored chicken. Two stubby arms protruded from its main body, each equipped with a gun pod at the end.

Past the checkpoint, the five of us piled into the elevator. I was shoved into the back corner and told to face the wall. The elevator took only a few seconds to make the climb, and sounded a chime when we reached the top. The doors opened and the guards filed out, never taking their eyes off me, never giving me a chance to make a move.

From the elevator station there was an enclosed walkway with an arched, transparent roof. Snow was blowing in the cold wind outside, but the passage was maintained at room temperature. That's when I first got a good look at the building on top of the plateau. It wasn't just another utilitarian structure; it was a large, multistory house, surrounded by several smaller outbuildings and with a nearby landing pad. The house had been assembled from prefabricated sections, probably the only practical way to do it, given where it was built, but looked as nice as anything you'd see in Delta City. I guess when you're an old trillionaire with more money than you can possibly spend in your remaining lifetime, you spare no expense for your own comfort.

The interior of the mansion was palatial. The floors were polished wood—*real* wood, from the look of it— covered by fancy rugs. Paintings and sculptures decorated the foyer and hallways, and it seemed that old Taranis had brought his personal housekeeping staff with him. I was led up one wide staircase then another, to the third floor. The quartet of security men marched me down the hall toward an ornate set of double doors.

There were three people waiting for us at the end of the hall. Two men, both wearing black suits, stood by the doors, one on each side. Their faces were concealed behind tinted smart glasses and filtration masks. They watched me in silence and regarded me wearily. *Taranis's personal bodyguards*, I thought.

The third man stood in the middle of the hall, hands folded behind his back. He stepped forward as I approached. "Good evening, Mr. Novak," he said, politely. He was a tall, slim fellow, maybe in his fifties, and he was a sight. He was dressed traditionally, in a waistcoat and vest, with pressed slacks and polished shoes. He was the baldest man I'd ever seen; he not only lacked hair on his head, he didn't have eyebrows or eyelashes, either. "Thank you for joining us," he said, stiffly. His breath had an antiseptic smell to it, like he'd just gargled a mouthful of cleaning solvent.

I glanced at the baton-wielding, armor-clad men on either side of me. "How could I say no to an invitation like this?"

He ignored my sarcasm and looked to the four men escorting me. "Thank you for fetching Mr. Novak, gentlemen. You are dismissed." The guards nodded and left, and the man in the fancy coat turned his attention back to me. "I am Mr. Wainwright, Mr. Taranis's majordomo. You are one of his dinner guests this evening. A member of my staff will show you to your seat momentarily. Drinks and appetizers will be served first, followed by the main course of the meal. When Mr. Taranis enters the room, you are to stand and remain standing until he has taken his seat. You may talk with the other guests but do not use inappropriate language. Do not address Mr. Taranis unless he addresses you first."

"Okay..."

"I wasn't finished," he snipped. "At your seat, you will find a disposable filtration mask next to your napkin. If you feel the need to cough or sneeze, you must don the mask first. Under no circumstances are you to cough or sneeze without covering your face. After you have used the mask, a member of the staff will collect it from you and provide you with a replacement. Do you understand?"

Seemed like the old man suffered from mysophobia. "Sounds like a real fun party."

"Dining with Mr. Taranis is an honor. There are many wealthy and powerful people on this planet who would kill for such an opportunity. It is in your best interest to be respectful. Now," he said, turning toward the doors, "you may enter the dining room." The heavy wooden doors quietly swung open. Wainwright stood aside and gestured for me to enter.

Beyond the double doors was a large, ornate dining room, with a roaring fireplace on one end and wide, floor-to-ceiling windows on the other. A half dozen more bodyguards in dark suits were posted along the walls. I couldn't see their faces through the glasses and masks, but I could feel their eyes on me as I entered. A comically long dining table was positioned in front of the windows and was lit by two low-hanging chandeliers.

A servant approached me from the back of the room. He was a young man, dressed in a spiffy white jacket. His eyes were visible but, like the security men, a filtration mask covered his nose and mouth. The entire staff, except the majordomo, had their faces covered like that. "Right this way, sir. I'll show you to your seat." I followed him to the table. There were a handful of people already seated on either side, clustered near one end of the table, though the big chair at the head was still empty.

There were three men at the table, all of them facing me, but I didn't recognize any of them. Blanche Delacroix was there, too, seated with her back to me, wearing an ugly gray pantsuit. I only realized it was her when she turned to speak to the woman next to her. The other woman wore a black dress and had her hair done up in a tight bun with two sticks shoved through it. She noticed me as the servant led me to the table, looking over her shoulder.

"Easy?"

"Dagny!" I said, heart suddenly racing.

She stood up, hurried over to me, and threw her arms around me. "Oh, Easy," she said, "I'm so happy to see you."

I held her tight. "I'm glad to see you too, beautiful," I said, quietly. She was wearing a long, black dress with a slit that went up the leg. It looked good but felt like it was made of the same rapid fabrication material as my suit. "Are you okay? What the hell is going on?"

The servant cleared his throat to get our attention. "Sir, madam," he said, "if you'll both take your seats, we're about to begin serving drinks."

"Alright, alright," I said, stepping back from Dagny's embrace. "I'm getting hungry anyway." The servant held the chair to the right of Blanche Delacroix as Dagny sat back down in it. He pulled out the chair to her right and indicated that that's where I was supposed to sit but didn't hold it for me as I sat down.

The table being situated by the windows made for a spectacular view from where I sat. Almost all of the site was visible from up there, including the giant structure covering the excavation site. The cinder cone of Mount Gilead stood like a smoldering monolith against the failing light.

I leaned over to Dagny as more servants appeared, pouring glasses of water and wine. "Have they been treating you alright?"

"Yeah," she answered. "Where were they keeping you?"

"In a prison cell."

"This whole time?"

"Yeah. What about you?"

"They put me in a dormitory near the dig site. It's where Cassie's quarters are."

"That hardly seems fair," I grumbled. "How come you got the luxury treatment and I got to sit in the cooler?"

"It was all Cassie's doing. She demanded that she be able to see me, and they need her to cooperate, so they went along with it. I'm sorry, I couldn't get them to let you out."

I reached over and squeezed her hand. "Don't sweat it. How's your sister?"

"She's ... managing," Dagny said, but didn't elaborate further.

"You know what this little dinner party is all about?"

Blanch Delacroix leaned forward so that she could see me and spoke up before Dagny could answer. "Mr. Taranis simply wanted to meet you, Mr. Novak. He thinks you're an interesting person and wants to meet the man who caused him so much trouble."

"You know what?" I said. "I think I'd like to meet him, too." I took a sip of my water.

The man across the table from me sipped his wine and leaned in closer. "I've been looking forward to making your acquaintance as well." He looked to be about the same age as me, but had more of a slick, polished look to him, from his expensive suit to his neatly styled hair.

"And who might you be?" I asked.

"Leonard Steinbeck," he said, with a smug grin. "I'm the Security Intelligence Service station chief for Nova Columbia. I'd like to sit down with you one of these days, go over a few things."

I sat back in my chair, chuckling, and took another sip of water. "And here I was worried that this dinner party was going to be boring."

His smile was impeccable but his eyes were hard. "It's not like that," Steinbeck said. "Oh! I'm being rude." He indicated the man sitting directly to his right. That fellow was an older man with a wild shock of white hair sticking out of his head, bushy eyebrows, and an even bushier mustache. Instead of a suit jacket he wore a black-and-purple robe, kind of like the ones you get when you graduate from college. He looked like a wizard. "This is Professor Zephram Farseer, Distinguished Scholar of the Cosmic Ontological Foundation."

The man with the crazy hair and silly robes bowed his head to me. "I am intrigued to have you among us." Around his neck, in place of a tie, was an ornate amulet, several inches across, hanging from a gold chain. It was a golden disk with a triangular section cut out from the middle. Inside the triangle was a representation of an eye, the iris made up of a small black stone surrounded by a larger blue one. All around the triangle were four-pointed stars made from laser-cut diamond. This was the symbol of the Cosmic Ontological Foundation.

Steinbeck leaned farther forward so he could see around the space wizard, and held out a hand toward the man sitting closest to the head of the table. "And over there is Dr. Arjun Mao Sarkar, head of the Advanced Research Division for Ascension and lead scientist for Project Isaiah."

The scientist looked over at me, gave me a curt nod, then went back to ignoring us. He was a stern-looking guy who didn't seem any more excited to be at this party than I was. He clasped his gloved hands together and rested his elbows on the table, like he was brooding over something. His eyes were hidden behind a smart visor that plugged into neural links grafted to his head, just above his ears. The visor was tinted red and made him look angry. He had black hair and a matching black goatee.

"You'll have to forgive Dr. Sarkar," Steinbeck said. "He's been working very long hours recently."

Appetizers were served, an odd but tasty mix of hors d'oeuvres and sushi. Nobody said much and I got the impression that all the people at this table didn't necessarily like one another. I had a lot of questions that I wanted to ask Dagny, but this wasn't a good time. The food was better than anything I'd had in days, though, so I took the opportunity to stuff my face.

A set of doors behind the head of the table swung open and Wainwright, the majordomo, strode in. He touched a control on the big chair at the end of the table and it quietly slid back. He put his hands behind his back once more, then addressed the room. "Ladies and gentlemen, please rise for the master of the house, the honorable Xavier Taranis."

The cronies at the table all stood at once. Dagny did, too, leaving me as the only one seated. The majordomo loudly cleared his throat and shot me an angry glare, so I stood up. This seemed to please Wainwright, who stepped aside and bowed.

I wasn't sure what to expect. I knew what Xavier Taranis looked like, at least, what he *used* to look like. The only publicly available photographs of him were decades out of date. He became a recluse after his retirement and, from what I'd heard, hated having his picture taken.

Heralded by heavy, mechanical footsteps, he appeared in the doorway and entered the dining room. The 131-year-old man got around by way of a full-body, robotic exosuit, under which he wore a blue velvet jacket, white shirt, and a formal ascot. A clear plastic tube ran from under his collar to his nose, likely supplying him with additional oxygen. His face was wrinkled and aged, his skin covered in liver spots, and he only had a little gray hair left on top of his head. His eyes were sharp, though, piercing. It took me a second to realize they were prosthetics.

Taranis positioned his exosuit in front of his chair and gently lowered himself into it. The chair, a mechanical contraption built to accommodate his robotic frame, slid forward to the table. "Please, everyone," he croaked, "take your seats." As we all sat back down, the old man looked over at his majordomo. "Mr. Wainwright, we'll be taking dinner now."

"Of course, sir," the majordomo said. He bowed and disappeared back through the double doors at the end of the room. Dinner was served promptly after, and it was probably the most expensive meal I'd ever had in my life. There was more food than the handful of us at the table could possibly eat: roast duck, filet mignon, and plenty of sides. Taranis himself only ate a little. A man his age can probably only take so much rich food, I thought.

I was told not to speak unless spoken to, so I didn't say anything as I ate. Taranis made a little small talk with the people at the table but ignored Dagny and me. They didn't discuss anything significant, and I got the distinct impression that everyone in the room was afraid of crossing the old man.

Everyone except the SIS man, that is. Steinbeck ran his mouth almost constantly, laughing at his own jokes, oblivious to the fact that the other guests weren't interested in what he had to say. The old man seemed to like him, though, and they chatted about the politics of the Terran Confederation for a long time. Taranis's wheezing voice started to give out after a little while, so he activated an amplifying voice modulator that allowed him to speak easily.

More drinks were poured after the remains of dinner

were cleared away. Taranis surprised me by acknowledging my presence for the first time. "I hope you've been enjoying my hospitality, Detective," he said. You could just barely hear his actual voice, little more than a whisper, over the one projected by the modulator. "I've been impressed by your work and am pleased to finally meet you face-to-face. Have you been well taken care of?"

I'd had about enough of this dinner party charade. All the expensive food on Nova Columbia didn't change the fact that I was being held prisoner and that Dagny had watched her stepfather die just days before. I kept my cool, though. The only hope I had of finding a way out was to humor the dusty old mummy until an opportunity to escape presented itself. "The food was outstanding, of course. I, uh, don't mean to complain, but have to say my accommodations are a little lacking."

He laughed at that, and as soon as he did, so did everyone else at the table except Dagny. "That's one of the things I want to discuss with you this evening. Your arrival here was unpleasant and contentious, I know, but I believe we can come to an understanding that benefits all of us."

I smiled. I was at his mercy but would be damned if I gave him the satisfaction of thinking he intimidated me. "An understanding, huh? I've watched two of your employees get murdered in the past few days, Dr. Ivery and Arthur Carmichael. I think you're used to being able to buy whatever you want, including people. When you can't, it offends you so much that you're willing to kill over it. We just met, Mr. Taranis, but I think I understand you pretty well already."

Everyone in the room was instantly silent. Dagny looked over at me, wide-eyed. "Easy," she said, her voice little more than a whisper. The other dinner guests shuffled uncomfortably. Taranis looked shocked for a moment and didn't say anything. He was clearly not used to being talked to like that. He stared me down and I stared right back. A few seconds later he laughed, showing a bright white set of perfect artificial teeth. His flunkies at the table nervously laughed along with him, except for Steinbeck, who was watching me intently. The color had drained out of Dagny's face.

"Do you know how refreshing it is to have someone talk to me without fear or flattery?" Taranis asked. "The only other person at this table who will tell me what he truly thinks without censoring himself is Mr. Steinbeck. It's an endearing quality to me."

"I have a way of growing on people," I said.

"Allow me to address your concerns, Detective. Mr. Carmichael's death was not my intent. In fact, I had very strict instructions that all of you were to be brought back here unharmed. Arthur was a valuable member of this project for a long time and a dedicated employee of more than thirty years. I deeply regret his murder and I'm glad you dispatched the thug responsible. Rest assured, his daughters will receive his full pension and assets. As for Ocean . . ." Taranis said, his voice modulator lowering to a somber tone. "Her death was a tragedy. She was the most brilliant mind on Nova Columbia and her absence is sorely felt." Dr. Sarkar, who had barely said a word this entire time, twitched at that comment but remained silent. Taranis continued, "It's unconscionable, such a mighty intellect snuffed out by petty street criminals. Believe me when I say that I had nothing to do with that."

He sounded so sincere that I almost wanted to believe he didn't have that woman killed. Was he a master manipulator or did he really not order it? I noticed that when he said that he very briefly glanced over at Blanche Delacroix. Was she the one who was responsible?

Taranis continued, "From what I understand, you and Miss Carmichael both risked your lives trying to protect her. I thank you for your courageous efforts."

He was shrewd, no doubt about it. I couldn't get a read on him at all. Not surprising, considering he'd been practicing his word games for longer than I've been alive. "What's this all about?" I asked. "Why are we here? What is it that you want from me?"

"I like this guy. He's a straight shooter," Steinbeck said to Taranis before turning to me. "The truth is we could use your help."

"My help? What could I possibly help you with? More importantly, why should I?"

Taranis nodded at the SIS man. "Mr. Steinbeck, will you fill him in on the *why*, please?"

"Happy to," Steinbeck said. He was a smooth talker, like a salesman or a con artist. I'd met the type before. "You see, Mr. Novak, you're in a bit of a predicament here."

"I figured as much when I was kidnapped at gunpoint and thrown in your private jail," I said, flatly.

Steinbeck leaned in, elbows on the table, gesturing with his hands as he talked. "Trust me, you're better off here than where you would have ended up otherwise.

Your friend Deitrik Hauser? The *Baron*, as he likes to be called?" He made finger quotations when he said the word *Baron*. "He's in SIS custody now. We're going to ship him back to Earth to answer for his crimes."

"Is that so?" I said. "What crimes are those?"

"Aiding and abetting a kidnapping, illegal misuse of Confederation property, abuse of his office, theft, and conspiracy to obtain and release classified information. If you'd been with him, you'd be looking at some pretty serious charges yourself. Kidnapping. Felony trespassing. Impersonating a Confederation officer. Theft of intellectual property. Illegal disclosure of classified information. Armed robbery. Shall I go on?"

I glared at him and didn't say anything.

"However," the SIS man continued, "I believe there to be some seriously extenuating circumstances in all of this. You were lied to and manipulated by a public servant, an adjunct inspector general of the Security Intelligence Service. You had every reason to believe what Mr. Hauser was telling you. His specialty used to be turning people into intelligence assets, knowingly or otherwise, and he was damned good at it. One of the best. Given your personal history with him, I can easily see how you'd have fallen for his game."

I didn't believe what Steinbeck was saying and I was pretty sure he knew it, but that wasn't why he was giving me this spiel. He was offering me a way out in exchange for whatever it was he wanted, and this was the cover story he'd use.

He kept on. "Despite what he may have told you, his office didn't grant him access to every classified program.

Project Isaiah is sanctioned by the SIS and Ascension Planetary Holdings Group is a trusted industry partner. The government of the Commonwealth of Nova Columbia knows as much as they need to know and they don't have jurisdiction here."

I didn't bother bringing up the Conventions on the Discovery and Control of Alien Technology, Organisms, and Remains, which said otherwise. Hell, he could be telling the truth about that part—intelligence agencies always have ways of circumventing the letter of the law, and the secrecy they operate in allows them to get away with it. The legality of the matter was irrelevant at the moment.

"I'll ask again," I said, bluntly. "What is it that you want from me? What is the point of all this?"

Dr. Sarkar spoke up this time. "There's no need to further mince words. Mr. Novak, Cassandra Carmichael insists on seeing you. We're making incredible progress in studying the Seraph, but that progress is contingent on the bond it has formed with her."

"At first she wished to have her sister with her," Taranis said, "but now she is quite insistent on your company as well."

"This was her way of making sure they kept up their end of the deal," Dagny said to me.

So *that's* why they hadn't just put a bullet in me. Cassandra had a little bit of leverage over them and she was using it. "There's got to be more to it than that."

Steinbeck looked at Taranis with a smug grin. "See? A real straight shooter, just like I said. No nonsense, right to the point."

The old man tried to speak but had a coughing fit. An aide approached his seat but was waved off. "Please excuse me," Taranis said. "I'm not as young as I used to be." He looked at me. "Detective, I will be blunt with you if that is your preference. What Cassandra is doing is unprecedented. No human has ever had a direct neural link with an alien before, much less a life-form as incredible as the Seraph. There is so much we can learn from it."

Professor Farseer piped up, interrupting Taranis. "We need to prove to it that we are worthy of its wisdom." There was reverence in his voice.

"We need it to talk to us," Dr. Sarkar said. "We can only glean so much from observation. At first it seemed content just to have someone to communicate with. When our test subject—"

"That's my sister," Dagny said, sharply, interrupting the scientist. "She's not a test subject."

"Yes, yes," he replied, dismissively. "When *Cassandra* had to be hospitalized, the Seraph refused to communicate with anyone else. It will talk to her and her alone."

"How do you know that it won't talk to anyone else?" I asked.

"Because we tried," the scientist said. "Several different individuals attempted the neural link and received no response. Instead it sent a message to our computer system demanding that we return Cassandra."

"It was imperative that we got her back," Taranis said.

"Let me guess. You keep it happy and it keeps talking?"

"Essentially, yes," Dr. Sarkar said. "The Seraph has been requesting information from us just as we've been requesting information from it. After we resumed communications sessions with Cassandra Carmichael, everything was going smoothly until this afternoon."

"You mean the power outage earlier? Is that why I'm here?"

"Yes," the scientist said. "Our probes and sensors allow us to both send and receive information in binary code. Today it used that linkage to temporarily take over the Verdant-646 supercomputer that manages this facility and cut off the power supply from the reactor."

"You gave it unlimited access to your network without isolating it?" I said. "That seems sloppy of you."

Dr. Sarkar frowned. "Its access was limited to the database by a series of encryptions and firewalls. They didn't work. The Seraph is capable of quantum computations beyond our understanding. A Verdant-646 is one of the most powerful supercomputers on the market and the Seraph overtook its AI on a whim. Encryption and firewalls mean nothing to it."

"That's something," I said.

"Oh, there's more," Dr. Sarkar said. "After software isolation failed, we physically disabled the wireless network relays, completely cutting off its access to anything but the monitoring station. This will suffice for the time being, but real-time AI analysis of its signal output is crucial to our research, and for that we need the supercomputer."

I chuckled. "Sounds like it's got a temper. What did you do to piss it off?"

"Surely a being so ancient and unfathomable is beyond such petty primate impulses," Farseer said.

"You sure about that, Professor?" I said. "Even God has wrath."

"The incident earlier today was not the doing of the Seraph, not entirely," Dr. Sarkar insisted. "It's Cassandra. She's been wanting to see you since you got her. As an experiment, we've been denying her request, to see if the Seraph would react or if she was bluffing. You saw how that went."

I chuckled to myself, but didn't say anything.

"It's incredible," the scientist continued. "She's reached such a level of synchronicity with it that she was able to use its power for herself. Through it, *she* cut off the power to the facility until we acquiesced to her demands."

Blanche Delacroix spoke up for the first time since the conversation began. "This is why I insisted upon the security systems being controlled on a separate network, Arjun. I told you this could happen from the moment it started accessing the Verdant-646."

"Yes, Blanche, you were prescient," Dr. Sarkar sneered, his voice laced with sarcasm. "Thank you."

"It does put us in a spot, doesn't it?" Steinbeck said to me. "That's why you're here, Mr. Novak."

I realized then that they were *scared*. They woke that thing up and now they weren't sure they could control it. "What is it you want me to do, exactly? Tell the Seraph to simmer down? If it won't listen to all of you, why would it listen to me?"

"The Seraph isn't the one who needs to listen, Easy," Dagny said, quietly. "It's Cassie."

I looked back at her. "What?"

"Miss Carmichael is correct," Taranis said. "The issue

here isn't with the Seraph, but with Cassandra. She does not agree with how we're handling the project, and we're concerned that she may be attempting to influence it in a negative way."

"'We'?" I looked over at Dagny. "Are you in on this?"

"It's not what you think," she said, averting her gaze. She then looked me in the eye. "You haven't seen the things I've seen. You haven't seen *it*. This is bigger than us."

Her answer hit me so hard it was worse than when the clanker kicked me in the guts. Was this a ploy, or had they really gotten to her? I shook my head. "I get it, now. You want me to help you keep Cassandra under control so you can keep milking the Seraph for information."

"It's not like that!" Dagny insisted.

"It's not like that at all!" Farseer said. He was flustered and fidgeted with his gold amulet. "This is a test, don't you see? Before the Seraph will impart its wisdom upon us, we must prove to it that we are more than ignorant, squabbling apes. It has chosen Cassandra as its Avatar for a reason. We must first prove our worth to her, one of our own kind, before we can prove our worth to a higher form of life."

"That's not how your *avatar* sees it," I said. "She warned me that the Seraph is not, quote, *a genie that grants wishes*. She seemed to think that you all are screwing around with something you don't understand. That's how it looks to me, too, and you could be putting the whole damned colony in danger."

I think they were surprised by how much I knew. "We have taken every reasonable precaution," Taranis said. "Cassandra believes, or is being led to believe, that we should remove the second Spear. Doing so, she claims, will fully resurrect the Seraph and free it."

"If that's what it wants, why don't you just do that? Maybe it'll be more inclined to talk to you if you help it out?"

"Cassandra is suffering from moderate-to-severe psychological contamination," Dr. Sarkar added. "You can't take everything she says literally or at face value. We record her neural interface sessions with the Seraph and have both a team of scientists and the Verdant-646 AI analyzing the data we receive. Her subjective interpretation of the communications is only one factor that we must consider."

"You went to a lot of trouble to get her back," I said, "and you're not even listening to her because she isn't telling you what you want to hear."

"It's not that simple!" the scientist insisted. "This isn't like you and I having a conversation. We're dealing with a radically advanced and completely alien life-form that's unlike anything we've ever encountered before. The data we get from it is often fragmented and disordered, sometimes contradictory. Its mind, if you want to call it that, is orders of magnitude more complex than ours. It thinks on a quantum level, and seems capable of dividing its consciousness in a way that we don't fully understand. We don't even think it was really aware of us when we first started receiving signals from it."

"Cassie said it was dreaming," Dagny said, distantly. She gazed out the window and didn't look at me.

"I think Cassandra has a better understanding of that thing than you're giving her credit for. You didn't hesitate to pull out the first Spear."

"That was before we were aware that it was somehow still functional," Taranis said. "We thought we were conducting an autopsy, but removing the Spear was the key to accessing its mind."

"Then why not do what she says it wants and pull out the second one?"

"Because we have no idea what those Spears actually do, what they're made of, or how they work," Dr. Sarkar said. "For all we know, the Spear is the only thing sustaining it and pulling it out will kill it."

"There could be other unforeseen consequences, Detective," Taranis said. "This is why I am asking for your cooperation. Cassandra trusts you, just as she does Miss Carmichael. She will listen to the two of you. You help us convince her that we have her best interests, and the best interests of humanity, at heart."

"Sure," I said flatly. "What is it you hope to learn, exactly?" I asked. I'd heard the speculation of others but I wanted to see what Taranis would admit to.

Dr. Sarkar spoke up first. "We believe that the Seraph is powered by an internal vacuum-energy engine, and this is another reason we're hesitant to remove the second Spear. If the Spear is interacting with or stabilizing the engine, there's a possibility that removing it could upset that equilibrium and trigger a catastrophic resonance cascade."

"A what?" That was a new one for me.

"That's what we believe happened at Medusae Fossae," Taranis said. "It was indeed catastrophic."

"There are risks," Dr Sarkar said, "but those risks can be mitigated by caution and further study. If we could learn how to construct a functional vacuum-energy engine, that in of itself would be the biggest technological breakthrough since the warp drive, the internal combustion engine, or maybe since the invention of agriculture. Unlimited energy, anywhere in the universe."

"Think of what such an ancient and immense mind could teach us," Professor Farseer said, wistfully. "It may be the key to unlocking the history of the cosmos, of understanding the true origins of life itself."

"There are even greater possibilities," Taranis said. "The Seraph is at least sixty-eight million years old, likely far older. It must be capable of nearly infinite self-rejuvenation."

There it was. "So Arthur Carmichael was right," I said, flatly. "You're dying and you think that thing will grant you immortality." I looked around to the others at the table. "That's really what you're all after, isn't it?"

"Is that so wrong, Detective?" Taranis asked. "It's no secret that I don't have much time left. I have pursued the science as far as it will go, thrown billions of dollars into medical research, and I've exhausted the capabilities of modern medicine. For all of my efforts, all those years and all that money spent, death is still coming for me, as it does for us all. But . . . what if it doesn't have to be this way? I have always believed that death itself is akin to a disease, a biological failing, nothing more. The Seraph's very existence proves that it can be overcome. Don't you see?"

I glanced over at Dagny. She was looking down at her lap and didn't say anything. "I see, alright," I said. "All this, all the violence, the deaths . . . it's all because you're afraid to die."

"*Everyone* is afraid to die!" Taranis snapped. Raising his voice sent him into another coughing fit. After regaining his composure, he lowered his electronically enhanced voice to a more conversational tone. "Lives have been lost. I regret that, I truly do, but you must keep perspective. This has the potential to save not just *my* life, but *every* life. All of humanity stands to benefit. For the first time since our earliest evolutionary ancestors crawled out of the ocean, we have the opportunity to conquer *death itself*. There is no greater good one could hope to achieve. It must be pursued, no matter the cost."

The old man took a few seconds to catch his breath. "I know how this must sound to you. I assure you I'm no madman. This truly is the single most important endeavor ever undertaken by the human species. We are close, *so close*, to achieving it. We've gotten such promising data. I don't want anyone else to die, ever, and I'm asking for your help. You can be assured that you will be rewarded for your efforts. I can make you both very, very rich. If Project Isaiah is successful, I promise you that you will reap the full benefits of any breakthroughs it achieves."

"Or," Steinbeck said, "you can refuse. Your choice, but if I were you, I'd choose potential immortality over a long prison sentence. Make no mistake, if you're not going to be useful here, then you are going to prison. You and Miss Carmichael both, actually, probably for fifty years." He shot me a grin that made me want to knock his teeth out. "Maybe for life."

Dagny looked me in the eye again. "Please, Easy . . . I don't like it either, but it's the only way."

I hated to admit it, but she was right. If I wasn't useful

for them I was nothing but a liability. I wasn't even worried about going to prison—if they decided they didn't need me I doubted I'd live long enough to ever see the inside of a cell. A choice like that is no choice at all. I sighed, heavily.

"Fine. I'll do what you want," I said.

CHAPTER 17

I know what you're thinking: *Easy sold out to save his own skin.* I admit that's what it felt like I was doing, and I hoped that's what it *looked* like I was doing, but it was subterfuge, not surrender. I was in a bad spot; cooperating with them, at least for the time being, was the only hope I had for finding a way clear of the whole mess.

That night, they didn't send me back to my cell. I was escorted to the housing unit Dagny told me about. It was attached to a larger research complex in a fenced off compound near the Canopy, which is what they called the huge structure built over the excavation site. The interior was laid out like a small dormitory. We each had our own rooms, but we shared common areas and the bathroom. The place had half a dozen bedrooms, but Dagny and I seemed to be the only ones staying there. More rapidly fabricated clothing was waiting for me in my assigned bedroom. In what I guessed was an attempt to get on my good side, they returned my hat and my jacket. I was happy to have them back. I've had that hat for years, and that jacket is made from real cowhide leather and it wasn't cheap.

The residence was nice enough, furnished about like you'd expect from a budget motel, but we weren't allowed to leave. The windows were made of heavy industrial safety transparency and the doors were metal. There was an exterior balcony we could go out on, but the gap between the roof overhang and the railing was covered by a heavy mesh material. Even if I'd been willing to brave the three-story drop to the ground, I couldn't get through that without power tools.

It was quiet in the residence that evening. Dagny and I hadn't said much to each other and Cassandra was nowhere to be found. On top of everything else going on, I figured the place was bugged and that we were being monitored. We were not allowed access to any electronic devices save one big video screen with a library of shows and a couple of e-readers full of books.

I laid on the bed in my room, listening to the howling wind outside, trying to figure out what in the hell I was going to do next. The exterior temperature was below freezing again, and snow was mixed in with the dust and grit buffeting the side of the building. Dagny was in the living room and was watching a show on the video screen. She had the volume turned up too loud for my taste so I'd left the room.

I was surprised by a knock on the door. Dagny was waiting for me when I opened it. "I'm going out for a smoke. You want to come with?"

"A smoke? In this weather?" I caught myself and

thought for a second. Dagny knew I didn't smoke. "Yeah, sure, let me get my coat."

"I'll be waiting for you on the balcony." She turned and left.

I found her out there a couple minutes later. The wind was blasting the balcony from the front, and I had to hold my hat down to keep it from being blown off my head. Coarse, volcanic dust stung my skin. Dagny had the collar of her coat turned up and was facing the wall, smoking a cigarette.

"Hey," I said, quietly, huddling up next to her. With my face inches from hers, we could barely hear each other over the wind. I figured that's why we were out here, why she had the volume turned way up on the screen inside— all that background noise would hinder attempts to listen to what we were saying, and we could speak freely for a few minutes.

She puffed her cigarette and looked at me. She had dark circles under her eyes. "I'm sorry, I haven't . . . I haven't been sleeping well. There's so much I want to tell you, but we have to be careful what we say."

"I get it," I said. "Where's your sister? I thought you said she was being kept here."

"She is, but they keep her in a separate room, under guard, in a lower level. They don't let her into the common areas very often or for very long."

"What's going on? What did they do to you while I was in that cell?"

"They didn't do anything," she said. "It was the Seraph."

"I don't follow."

"They took me down into the pit to see it, to be with Cassie while she was interfacing with it." Another puff of the cigarette. "It's a monster, a weapon more powerful than we can even understand."

"Slow down. They took you into the pit. What happened then?"

"There are VR headsets where you can watch some of the interaction, even if you don't have a neural link. It isn't the same without the link. Most of it is raw data that doesn't translate very well into a visual medium, but sometimes it shows you things."

"Like what?"

"I-I don't know. Cassie thinks they're memories. They might just be it thinking about things. They think it deliberately chooses what to show us."

"Okay. What did it show you?"

Dagny looked up into my eyes again. I could see the fear in them, and I put an arm over her shoulder. "Cassie was right about what they did to the First Antecessor Race. I saw it. It showed us what happened. Th-they wiped them out, all of them, exterminated their entire race. I saw...I saw planets being burned from space, oceans boiling away, alien cities being reduced to dust. I...I heard them screaming as they died. That's why they aren't around anymore. The Seraphim hunted them to extinction."

"Good God. Did it say why?"

"They picked the wrong side in the war, the war Cassie told us about. They sided with the enemy. The Seraphim showed them no mercy."

"Is that why you're doing this, working with Taranis?"

"I didn't want to. I still don't want to. But . . . after what I saw, we can't risk setting that thing free, ever. Cassie says it was a memory, but I think it was also a threat. They need to bury that thing and never let anyone dig it up again."

I held her a little tighter. "We're going to find a way to get out of this mess—you, me, and Cassie."

"You don't understand," Dagny said. "Cassie . . . that thing has infected her mind. They call it psychological contamination. She says she's fine, but she's not fine. She's not the same. She's not well. Since we got here they've had her run interface sessions with the Seraph three times already and I think . . . I think it's using her, making her dance like a little marionette." She looked up into my eyes again. "I'm scared, Easy. I don't know what to do. I don't want to lose my sister again, but Taranis is desperate. Sooner or later he's going to offer to pull the second Spear out in exchange for immortality. If that happens, that thing could kill us all, the entire planet, and it might not stop there."

"I understand," I said. I tried to sound as reassuring as possible. "We'll figure this out. Come on, let's go back inside. I'm freezing."

The next morning I was woken up by Ascension security guards pounding on the door of my room. They told me that they were running an interface session that morning and that Cassandra wanted me there to observe. Not that I had any choice, but I was excited to go. I wanted to check on Cassandra and wanted to finally see the Seraph for myself.

Once I had my coat and hat on, the two guards

escorted me through the laboratory facility and out to the parking lot. The wind had died down to a light breeze with occasional gusts. The sky was overcast and snow had drifted up against the side of the building, and black smoke rose angrily from Mount Gilead. A mix of snowflakes, fine, gray dust, and volcanic ash blew in the wind. The security guards were wearing respirators but didn't give me one.

My escorts led me to a parked truck and told me to get in the back seat. They climbed in the front and off we went, leaving the lab complex behind and heading directly toward the Canopy. There were multiple entrances into the gigantic structure, including a huge set of doors that must have been for the heavy earthmoving equipment. We turned toward a smaller but heavily guarded entry control point and parked in a gravel lot nearby. My escorts got out of the truck and told me to follow them.

It took us a couple minutes to get through the security checkpoint. Despite technically being a prisoner I was still scanned for recording devices, including going through a full-body X-ray. Past security was another set of doors that led into the main chamber.

I found myself in the biggest room I'd ever been in. The Canopy was larger than I'd estimated to be from the outside and easily had a bigger footprint than the largest stadium on Nova Columbia. It rose maybe a hundred feet over the excavation site, creaking and groaning in the wind. The roof, supported by steel arches and buttresses like a bridge, had large, opaque sections and let in some natural daylight. It was slightly warmer in there than it was outside but the air was no less dry.

I was so distracted with my gawking that I didn't see Professor Farseer and his entourage approach. "Mr. Novak, so good to see you!" the space wizard said. He had on a coverall like the rest of us, but over it wore a long, flamboyant coat with a fur collar. A top hat completed his bizarre outfit.

"Professor," I said, giving him a nod. He had a couple flunkies with him, as well as three more armed security guards. They all wore Ascension coveralls, but these guys carried themselves a little differently than the others did. They were more deferential to the professor and seemed almost suspicious of the guards who brought me in. I realized that all of them were wearing little pendants with the emblem of the Cosmic Ontological Foundation.

One of the two guards who escorted me in gave me a tap on the shoulder. "He's all yours," the guard said, as he handed me off to his counterparts in the professor's entourage.

"Please, come with me, come with me!" the professor said, gesturing for me to follow him. "I'm so pleased you agreed to come today, Detective! I can't wait for you to see it for yourself."

"I didn't exactly have a choice," I muttered, but the professor paid me no mind. There was an eight-foot wall around the rim of the excavation site, blocking it from view as we approached a large elevator. It was one of those ones you usually see at construction sites, a metal cage with a steel floor and no frills.

"We descend!" Professor Farseer said, as the six of us piled into the elevator. "Prepare yourself." The shaft was covered with paneling and I was beginning to think I wasn't going to get a good look at the thing. As we descended, however, the shaft opened up, and I got a bird's-eye view of the entire dig site.

The pit itself was gigantic, easily five hundred feet deep, cut in layers and steps like a quarry. A long ramp, big enough for heavy equipment, spiraled around the outside wall of the hole to its floor. Above it was an array of lights and half a dozen large cranes.

I'll never forget that moment for as long as I live, and I'd already seen a lot in my life. I fought the Ceph on two planets and even saw the ugly, tentacled bastards up close a couple times. I thought having encountered aliens before would prepare me for what I saw that day, and I was absolutely wrong. I never felt so small and insignificant as I did when I first laid eyes upon the Seraph.

Professor Farseer put a hand on my shoulder. "'There are more things in Heaven and Earth, Horatio, than are dreamt of in your philosophy,'" he said, quietly. "Isn't it magnificent?"

Arthur Carmichael had been right when he called it a leviathan. The Seraph was huge, bigger than I imagined it would be. Its body, made almost entirely of the silver-white metal, caught the light in strange ways despite being covered in dust. Like the small sample I observed, it seemed to shimmer more than it should in the ambient light. As the elevator descended, changing the angle of my observation, the Seraph's carapace seemed to shift slightly.

It looked both artificial and organic at the same time. Some parts were angular and faceted, like cut gemstones, where others were smooth and curved. The Seraph appeared to be lying on its right side, its visible appendages positioned like it was sleeping. The right-side appendages were still hidden beneath the rocky floor of the pit. From the proportions of the limbs, I guessed that it walked upright, but that was only a guess.

Its shimmering carapace was segmented, comprised of distinct sections like a suit of ancient plate armor, and they all fit together perfectly. In the gaps between plates there was a black material that I imagined had to have been more elastic, so the thing could have moved. A long tail stretched away from the main body in the direction of the volcano. Along its back were rows of spines, which varied in size and shape from spikes to something reminiscent of an airplane wing. The neck was armored and segmented, like the tail, but was shorter. It curved forward as if the Seraph had been curling into the fetal position when it fell.

What I assumed to be its head was lying on the floor of the pit at the end nearest the elevator. Half buried, it was wedge-shaped and angular, with a crown of horns around it like you see on some lizards from Earth. There were no discernable facial features, no nose or mouth, only five dark holes in a staggered row on the side. Were they eyes, or something else? I didn't know.

On its back, between what may have been its shoulders, was a bulbous, roughly teardrop-shaped apparatus. It was made of a different material from the rest of the body and was dull gray in color. Protruding upward out of the Seraph's left side were three tapered "wings." The other three, the ones on the right side, were still buried in the black volcanic rock.

Just as the Carmichaels had said, one of the two Spears was still embedded in the Seraph's body. The Spear, made of a dull, black material, had been plunged into the being's chest between its shoulders and was protruding out its back. As we neared the bottom, I got a good look at the massive mechanical pulley system they had used to pull the first one out. It was connected to the second Spear by a pair of heavy cables. The first Spear, the one they removed, had apparently been taken out of the pit because I couldn't see it anywhere.

"As you might imagine," the professor said, "when we realized that removing the first Spear elicited a response from the Seraph, my colleagues were hesitant to remove the second one. In fact, the controls for the apparatus we removed it with are locked out, and cannot be accessed remotely."

"What do you think about all this?" I asked. "You've heard what Cassandra said, right? That the Seraph wants you to pull out the second Spear?"

He was quiet for a moment as the elevator came to a stop at the bottom of that pit. "From what Cassandra reported, it had been, on some level, conscious the entire time, trapped in its own . . . its own quiet hell . . . for eons. It would have remained buried here for billions of years, until 18 Scorpii itself expanded into a red giant and consumed the planet, if Ascension hadn't stumbled upon it."

He looked up at the imposing alien as we stepped out of the elevator onto the rocky floor of the pit. "If that is truly the will of the Seraph, I would see it done, but I believe it's not so simple as it seems. We are being tested," he insisted. "My colleagues can be contrarian but their concerns are valid. We must proceed with the utmost caution."

Two more people were waiting for us at the bottom of the pit, a man and a woman. Both of them wore Ascension coveralls and had COF pendants around their necks. I guessed they were the drivers for the pair of open-top 4x4 trucks parked near the elevator shaft.

"This is our ride," the professor said. "They will take us to the Lambda Facility."

"What's that?" I asked.

"Forgive me, it's the research lab where Cassandra conducts the interface sessions with the Seraph." He pointed across the floor of the pit to a cluster of buildings near the Seraph's head. "You can see it, there."

"Lead the way," I said, and got into one of the trucks. As we approached, the posture of the Seraph suddenly made sense: its body was in the position it was because it had been impaled by the Spears. The thing had been curling in agony, maybe trying to pull them out, when it fell. It laid there, frozen in something resembling death, for tens of millions of years, helpless as it was slowly entombed by volcanic rock.

It was a lot to process. I found myself gazing up at the incredible bulk of the Seraph as we drew near, wishing for a drink.

"It's incredible, isn't it?" the professor asked. He was holding his hat in his hands so it wouldn't blow off his head. "Sometimes I'll sit out here for hours, pondering it, meditating, wondering what secrets it can teach us."

A few moments later we came to a stop near the

Lambda Facility. Like everything else at Site 471, it wad made out of prefabricated building modules, linked together and stacked on top of one another. A thick cluster of cables ran from the facility, along the floor of dig site, up the wall to the surface.

Being close to the Seraph really drove home how huge the thing was—it had to be hundreds of feet long from end to end. There was more to the feeling than just the being's immense size; it had an overwhelming presence, somehow, that I could feel in the back of my mind. I understood, for the first time, how the COFfers could look upon the Seraph and believe it to be holy. Professor Farseer led the entourage as we entered the Lambda Facility.

In the very back of the building, through yet another security checkpoint and a set of reinforced doors, Cassandra Carmichael was waiting for us. "Easy!" she said, happily, her voice transmitted over a speaker. Her eyes lit up but the girl looked like hell. She was dressed in sweats and sneakers. Her head had been shaved and there were dark circles under her eyes. "I'm so glad you're okay."

They had her sealed in a large room with a big observation window at the front. "I owe that to you, kid." I leaned in and put my hand on the glass as I spoke to her. "They treating you alright?"

She forced a weak smiled onto her face. "They're taking good care of me," she said. She motioned at the room behind her. "As you can see, I have top-shelf accommodations."

"Good morning, Miss Cassandra," Professor Farseer said, bowing his head slightly.

"Good morning to you as well, Zephram," Cassandra said with a smile. "Thank you for bringing Easy to see me."

"It was my pleasure," the professor said, beaming.

I knocked on the glass. It was thick, probably ballistic-rated. "What's with this setup? Are you locked in there?" In the center of the room behind her were two reclining chairs, the kind you'd see at a dentist's office, except there were restraints for the arms, legs, waist, and head. Each chair had a bulky virtual reality headset sitting on the seat, and through a mess of cables was connected to a monitoring station off to the side. That station consisted of a couple of desks cluttered with multiple computers and half a dozen screens of different sizes.

Cassandra glanced past me, the professor, and his entourage. "It's for safety. We just finished conducting some calibration tests. I told them I wanted them to bring you here to see me when we were finished."

"Is there anything else I can do for you?" the professor asked.

Cassandra stepped closer to the window and put her hand on the glass. "As a matter of fact, I have a favor to ask."

"Name it, my dear, and it shall be done."

"Leave us for just a few moments, would you?"

That surprised him. "Leave . . . you?"

"Yes, Zephram, if you please. Take your attendants and leave the test chamber. Only for a few minutes. I get very little privacy as is and I want to assure Easy that I'm being treated well."

The people in the professor's entourage looked at one another anxiously. "I, uh, we're not supposed to do that," he said, holding his hat in his hands and nervously fiddling with it.

Cassandra smiled again. "Oh come on, it'll be fine. I was in here alone until you arrived. There's security right outside the door and my vitals are being monitored. I would just like a few moments to speak with my friend."

"I was ... I'm sorry, I was told not to leave him unsupervised."

"Oh, Zephram, it'll be fine. He'll be under *my* supervision, and you'll be right outside. Don't worry so much. If you can do this for me, then tomorrow you will join me in the session."

That got his attention. "As an observer?"

"No, silly," she said, "as a participant. You will be in here with me."

Farseer's eyes went wide and he dropped his hat. He stepped closer to the glass. "Truly?"

"Truly," Cassandra said. "I've been telling it all about you and the Foundation. It is ready to commune with you, if you're willing, via your neural interface. I believe your eyes will be opened."

For a moment I thought the old man was going to faint. "*Deus ex stellaris!*" he said, happily. "Come, everyone, let us leave the Avatar with her friend. Mr. Novak, when you're ready to go, use the touchpad by the door. It will be secured from the outside but we will open it for you." With that, the professor and his entourage filed out of the room and sealed the door behind them. I was alone with Cassandra.

"I was beginning to worry that wouldn't work," she said.

"Can we, uh, talk? In here?"

"Yes. There are no cameras or audio recording

equipment here. They are brought in only during interface sessions and are physically removed the rest of the time. My vitals monitor is the only device in here that is currently connected to the outside. After what you managed to do, they're even stricter about information security than they were before. There is one uplink to the planetary network on-site, and its use is strictly controlled."

"How do you know that?"

"Because I asked the Seraph to see if it could access the outside world. No luck."

"You, uh, really have a rapport with that thing, huh?"

"I don't know that it experiences emotions in the way we do, but it seemed pleased to have me back."

"Well, you're certainly using it to get what you want."

She gave me a weak smile. "I assure you, I'm harmless. Hey . . . you want to see something *really* interesting?"

"Uh, sure."

Cassandra walked to the back of the room, where a thick plastic curtain hung from the ceiling. She pulled it to the side, revealing the back wall of the chamber. It had an odd shimmer to it. It took me a couple seconds that I was looking at the carapace of the Seraph itself. It was the very edge of one of its massive external plates. The cables from the monitoring station ran under the edge of the silver-white metal and disappeared into the black substance behind it.

"Holy hell," I said, quietly. "They just ran the cables right into it, huh?"

"The soft tissue, if you want to call it that, under the exoskeleton is much easier to drill into," she explained. "This connection is how I am able to communicate with the Seraph." She closed the curtain and came back to the window. Her smile faded.

"Are you doing okay, kid? You look like hell."

She took a deep breath and her shoulders slumped. "I'm tired, Easy. I don't sleep much. I've been having memory problems. They're keeping me under for longer sessions and making me do them more frequently."

"They're going to kill you."

"They might," she said, matter-of-factly. "The Seraph itself studied my neural signature and said I was in danger."

"The old man wants his immortality and doesn't mind killing you to get it."

"He's wasting what little time he has left. The Seraph can't grant him his wish. With enough time, years, maybe we could come up with life-extension technology based on stuff we learn from studying the Seraph, but it won't be of any use to him. It sustains itself through direct vacuum energy. It's not biological. It doesn't have cells that decay or neurons that die."

"All of this for nothing."

"It's not for nothing, Easy. We can still do the right thing."

"I'm going to level with you, kid. They told me that you want them to pull the second Spear out, but they're worried it'll cause an explosion or something called a resonance cascade."

"I told them it won't."

"Can you blame them for being cautious?"

"They don't under*stand*!" she snarled, slamming a fist onto the thick glass. Her demeanor changed so quickly it startled me. "They keep making me do this but they don't listen to what it's telling them!" She relaxed her fist, lowered her head, and leaned on the glass, breathing heavily.

"You alright?" I asked.

"I'm sorry," she said, looking back up at me. There were tears in her eyes. "This has been . . . hard . . . . for me. I'm holding on as best I can but I can't do this much longer. I told them they need to stop and they won't listen. It's suffering, you know."

"The Seraph?"

She nodded her head, slowly. "It wants to die if it can't go free. The Spears, both of them were needed to imprison it. Together, they forced it to stay alive while imprisoning it in its own mind. We disturbed that equilibrium when we removed one."

"So . . . if we don't set it free, it will die here? I don't mean to sound harsh, but is that really so bad?"

That set her off again. "This is what is wrong with humans!" she barked, her spittle hitting the glass as she spoke. "We are willing to kill anything that isn't convenient for us!"

"Hey," I said gently. "I didn't mean it like that. It's just, you know, wouldn't that be the safest thing? Just put it out of its misery?"

She regained her composure once again. "If it dies, the vacuum-energy engine is no longer contained. There's no telling what it will do. It might just shut down or it might be ripped open and cause an uncontrolled reaction."

"Good God. The whole planet really is in danger."

"It could be. That's why you have to help me. Nobody else will listen, not even Dagny."

"She's afraid. She told me you had her down here to observe one of your sessions, and that the Seraph showed them exterminating the First Antecessor Race."

"I know. To be honest, it frightened me, too."

"Are you sure freeing this thing is the right choice? What if, I don't know, it comes back in a hundred years and decides we're the enemy now? Like you said, it's capable of wrath, and we haven't exactly been endearing ourselves to it."

"I told you what will happen if it dies. I don't know what else to do."

"Are you sure it was telling you the truth?"

"What?"

"Just hear me out. Dr. Ivery told me she wasn't sure it could die at all. It's been sustaining itself somehow despite being buried for sixty-eight million years. What if it's just telling you that to try and scare you into letting it go?"

"No. It wouldn't. I mean . . ." She held her head in her hands. "I can't think straight half the time. I'm so tired. This isn't fair."

"I know it's not, kid. It's a hell of a thing, what they're making you do."

"I'm going to have you come back tomorrow to observe the session. I want you here. Dagny won't come back, not after last time. Professor Farseer and I will go under. There are VR headsets there in the observation room that will allow you to watch what I see. You won't get the full experience, not being neurally linked, but you might see some interesting things."

"Like what?" I asked.

She shrugged again. "I don't know. Depends on what

it feels like talking about. Sometimes I get nothing at all. Sometimes it shows me a lot. Very often, what it tells me doesn't really translate without a neural link, and even then I don't always understand it."

"They're going to let me watch while you plug the professor into that thing?"

"That's right," Cassandra said. "Xavier Taranis is getting desperate. He grants me almost anything I want now, except the one thing I really want."

"Why don't you bring *him* down here? Let the Seraph talk to him itself?"

"He won't do it. At his age, the neural strain would kill him."

"Why not just tell him that if he removes the second Spear, he'll get what he wants? That's what Dagny's worried about."

"It won't work. He's too shrewd to give up his only leverage."

"You're probably right about that," I said. "Anyway, what am I supposed to do while observing?"

Before Cassandra could answer, the door behind me beeped and slid open. Dr. Sarkar angrily strode into the room, his red smart visor making him look like a cyborg. Professor Farseer was right behind him, as was his entourage.

"I'm sorry, Miss Cassandra," the professor said. "He insisted on coming in."

"It's alright, Zephram. Good morning, Arjun."

"What are you doing?" Dr. Sarkar demanded. He pointed at me. "What is he doing in here alone with you?"

"We were just talking, Doc," I said. "What, you worried she's going to run off? She's locked in there."

"This is against protocol," the scientist said. He pointed a gloved finger at Cassandra. "You know what the rules are."

Cassandra's eyes flashed angrily and she lunged at the glass, pounding on it with both fists. "I don't give a *damn* about your rules!" she shouted. "You keep me locked up like a fucking animal! Is it too much to ask that I have ten minutes to myself?"

Dr. Sarkar pulled a small tablet from his pocket and checked the screen. "Cassandra, I need you to calm down. This much strain isn't good for you."

"Fuck you!" Cassandra screamed.

"Telling a woman to calm down never works, Doc," I said.

"Why are you still here?" He turned to the security men. "Get this man out of here."

"I want him down here tomorrow," Cassandra said. Her face was so close to the glass it fogged up every time she exhaled. "To observe. The professor will be going under with me."

The scientist didn't like that. "What? Absolutely not."

"How dare you!" the professor said. He got in Dr. Sarkar's face. "The Seraph has requested that I commune with it! Who are you to deny its will? Have you forgotten why we're here?"

"We're here to study it!" Dr. Sarkar said. He was agitated. "To conduct scientific research, not your pseudoscientific, mystical nonsense!"

That comment outraged Professor Farseer and his

entire group, who were all COFfers. "I will be taking this up with Mr. Taranis at once!" he said, huffily, and turned to leave.

"Take Mr. Novak back to his residence," the scientist said, dismissively.

CHAPTER 18

I was escorted back down to the observation room the next morning. It was bustling with activity, in stark contrast to the day before. I sat in one of the chairs facing the armored glass window and waited for someone to tell me what to do next. Professor Farseer sat nearby and he was positively giddy. The man was visibly fidgeting with anticipation. He nervously rubbed his hands together and wouldn't stop talking.

"This is such an honor, such an incredible honor," he said, excitedly. "She is the chosen Avatar of the Seraph and now I will get to join her!"

"Since we're both here, I assume that Taranis told the doc to do what Cassandra said?"

"Oh yes. If I'm too reckless, then Arjun is by far too cautious. He doesn't view the Seraph for what it is. To him, it's just a thing to study, like a germ under a microscope. The audacity!"

"You're pretty excited about this, huh?"

"Oh indeed. It's what I hoped for from the moment we

realized it was conscious. I would have taken Cassandra's place if I could have. To think she was initially reluctant!"

"I think that might have something to do with the fact that the first guy got his brain melted and died, not to mention Dr. Ivery going crazy. Seems like there are a lot of risks to what she's doing."

"There are dangers, there's no denying that," he admitted. "Still, can you honestly say it isn't worth the risk? You're an investigator by trade, surely you have a sense of curiosity. Would that alone not drive you to make the attempt?"

"All things in moderation, Professor, curiosity included. This is as interesting to me as anyone else, I guess, but that doesn't mean I'm looking to connect my mind to an ancient alien . . . being, life-form, whatever you want to call it. Especially not after what happened to the others who tried." I pointed to the side my head, "I don't even have a neural link. I was never excited by the prospect of plugging a computer into my brain."

"Really?" he asked, eyebrows raised, then frowned. "I understand your point of view, but for me? There is nothing I would not have given for such an opportunity, and at last I will have my chance! I have so many questions, so much I hope to learn in the communion."

Communion sure was an interesting choice of word. "You're hoping for immortality, too, then? Can't say I blame you. I just hope it's worth it in the end."

He frowned again. "I assure you it's not like that," he said, defensively. "At least, not for me. Xavier has long been the Foundation's biggest and most generous supporter on Nova Columbia, but he and I don't . . . well, we don't necessarily agree on the goals of the project."

Interesting, I thought. "Is that right? How so? If you don't mind me asking."

He hesitated for a moment, then leaned closer to me. "Truth be told, I fear we are being too presumptuous with the Seraph, that perhaps we are daring to ask too much."

"Fortune favors the bold," I said.

"Certainly! However, there's a fine line between boldness and impudence," he said, voice lowered. "There is much I'm willing to ask of the Seraph, but I worry that Xavier may be crossing the line from *asking* to *demanding*. It is not our place to make demands."

There was reverence in his voice, like a preacher talking about God. "Have you, uh, brought this up with him?" I asked.

"Of course. Xavier thinks I may be projecting my own feelings onto the Seraph, which in and of itself would be an audacious act of hubris. I will admit that sometimes our passions can cloud our judgment, and interpreting the will of such a vast intellect can be difficult."

"Cassandra compared it to a cat trying to understand the mind of its human owner."

"A fitting analogy," the professor said, "but perhaps too generous. Replace the cat with an insect and it may be closer to the truth."

"Let me ask you something, Professor. Why haven't you interfaced with the Seraph yourself? Before today, I mean. You don't seem scared."

"It's not a simple as all that," he said. "I tried such a communion after Cassandra left to recover."

"Didn't go so well, hey?"

"It didn't go at all," he said, regret in his voice. "I was ...
rejected. In Cassandra's absence it would accept no
others. It has stable synchronicity with her. The
connection goes both ways, you know; you touch its mind
and it touches yours. There is a very real danger of losing
yourself."

"Is that what happened to Dr. Ivery? She seemed a
little ... off."

"Indeed, and yes. Until now, Cassandra remained its
sole chosen Avatar. The best we could do was witness from
afar. As you will see, the observation equipment here
allows us to analyze the audiovisual feedback we receive.
Much of what it shows us is ... how shall I put this?
Enigmatic. Up for interpretation, if you will. It fell to that
young woman alone to decipher the will of the Seraph for
us, as she was the only one whose mind it would touch.
You understand now why we needed her back so badly."

"I guess."

"That changes today, though," he said. "Today everything changes."

"What are you going to ask it?"

"There are so many things I'd like to know. I think to
begin I'll tell it how grateful I am for the opportunity,
thank it for finding me worthy of sharing its wisdom."

"Opening with flattery can be a good strategy," I said.

The heavy door to the test chamber slid open. A
technician in a gray-and-orange coverall stepped out and
approached us. "Professor Farseer, we're ready for you
now. Please follow me."

"Splendid!" he said, standing up.

"Good luck in there, Professor," I said.

The technician turned to me. He was a young man, early thirties at most. "Mr. Novak, over there you'll find the four observation stations. You're the only one using them today, so choose any one you like. We will begin in a few minutes."

"You got it," I said. As the technician returned to the test chamber and sealed the door behind him, I found the nearest observation station and sat down in it. It was a big, padded, reclining chair, with a bulky VR headset on a stand next to it. I adjusted the chair to my liking but didn't put the headset on just yet.

Dr. Sarkar was in the test chamber, watching as a pair of technicians strapped the professor into the chair next to Cassandra. He stood out because of his smart visor and his stark white lab coat. The others were dressed in the gray-and-orange coveralls. Aside from a pair of armed security guards by the door, I was now alone in the observation room. I noticed that none of the personnel currently present wore the insignia of the Cosmic Ontological Foundation.

"Five-minute warning," one of the technicians announced over a loudspeaker. The professor, like Cassandra, was plugged in now, his face concealed by a virtual reality visor. With nothing else to do and no one to talk to, I put my own headset on and settled in. It was a full-face helmet type with a panoramic display. At first there was nothing but darkness and silence. It was so quiet I could hear myself breathing, as the earphones did an excellent job of canceling out all external sounds. Headsets like this were designed to allow you to talk in the simulation without bystanders being able to hear you.

After about a minute the blinked on, white text on a blue background, as the system went through it's boot-up cycle. That completed, the display read STAND BY for several minutes, followed up by CONNECTED.

Then the panoramic display lit up, filling my field of vision with bright, silver-white light that, as if through a prism, split into an entire spectrum of colors. A timer at the bottom of the screen started counting down from ten minutes. My ears were filled with deep, pulsing reverberations, strange sounds I can't describe, rising to a crescendo then receding again. It was like an audio playback of natural radio signals from deep space, except a thousand times more complex. Gradually the noise coalesced into a series of discernable patterns, like unearthly music. The longer I listened, the more layers I realized there were to the sounds. The hair on my arms and the back of my neck stood up, and I felt a chill go down my spine.

I was startled when a synthesized rendition of Cassandra's voice sounded in the earphones. "What you're hearing are the electromagnetic signals emanating from the Seraph," she said. She was speaking to me through her neural link, her mind creating an approximation of what she thought her voice should sound like. "It can be translated in a variety of ways, but I've found that listening to it is the most impactful. You're hearing the music of its thoughts, echoes from the depths of its mind. It's beautiful, isn't it?"

She was right; it was. It was haunting and ethereal,

awe-inspiring and unnerving at the same time. In my imagination I was able to feel its presence.

"We can't stay connected for too long," she continued. "The neurological strain can be dangerous. Today, I'm going to ask the Seraph if it remembers how it got here, if it can convey to me what happened, and see if it wants to answer that. Any visual feedback we get will be translated onto your displays. After that, I will ask it if it will tell us why the Seraphim seemingly wiped out the First Antecessor Race."

The screen went dark for another full minute, and the celestial music faded into the distance. The timer counted down and I wondered if it wanted to answer those particular questions. Asking someone how he died and why he committed genocide might be a touchy subject.

All at once a scene came into focus. I was hundreds of feet in the air, a gray, rocky wasteland laid out before me. The sky was overcast with dark clouds and smoke. I realized then that what I was seeing was from the point of view of the Seraph, and my jaw fell open in awe.

A hole opened in the sky and a horrendous creature poured out of it, a black mass of limbs and spikes. It was as big as the Seraph, with what looked like a single great, red eye. As the first monstrosity landed on the ground, kicking up a huge cloud of dust on its four legs, another appeared, landing next to it. In their unnatural-looking appendages each of the creatures held one of the two Spears.

The Seraph seemed to focus on the first one and, holding one of its forelimbs out before it, produced a blinding beam of white light. In a flash one of the two hideous creatures was hit, blasted apart by the beam, and disintegrated to ash. Its crab claw–like arm incinerated, the Spear fell to the ground, disappearing into the dust and smoke.

The Seraph transitioned its attention to the second creature as it lunged forward with a shrill, piercing scream, moving faster than anything that big should be capable of. It had a grotesque tentacle wrapped around the second Spear and tried to impale the Seraph with it. The ancient being held both its forelimbs up and conjured a transparent barrier, some manner of energy shield, and blocked the attacker's thrusts.

Seemingly enraged, the black creature shrieked again and stabbed at the Seraph wildly, each blow failing to penetrate the shield. Behind it, three more of the terrifying black creatures materialized, each one an unnatural corpus of limbs, tentacles, and claws, differing in size, shape, and quantity. They all had that same unblinking eye, though, red and angry.

The Seraph was able to push the attacking creature back, send it flailing to the ground in a huge impact. Somehow levitating up into the sky, the Seraph pointed its limbs downward at the toppled creature, brought them together, and obliterated it in another beam of pure white light. When the smoke and dust cleared there was no sign of the creature, just a bowl-shaped crater in the ground.

In a splash of darkness in the sky, one of the hostile creatures appeared in the air, above the Seraph, clutching one of the Spears with its bony limbs. The black mass came down upon the Seraph, its red eye blazing, emitting an ear-piercing, unnatural scream as it fell. I watched, helplessly, as the Seraph tried to raise its shield, but it was too late. The Spear plunged into the Seraph's carapace. Whatever force was holding it aloft failed and the Seraph fell to the primordial surface of Nova Columbia.

The images were blurrier now. The Seraph managed to stand up as the three huge, black monsters moved in. Shakily raising one forelimb, it produced a third light beam and blasted one of them, vaporizing the creature's top half. The remainder of it crumbled to dust as it died.

Then the second Spear was plunged deep into the Seraph's body. It looked down at itself, weakly trying to pull long, black harpoons out of its body, but its strength failed. It fell to its side, impacting the ground in one final eruption of dust and ash. The remaining hostile creatures, their red eyes smoldering as the Seraph's vision faded to black, screamed in harmonious unison at their victory.

The scene, the memory, whatever it was, ended, and I was again alone in the quiet darkness of the VR headset. I could feel my heart pounding in my ears. I was sweating and breathing faster. Even without the direct neural connection, it had felt so vivid, so real.

Before I was ready the display activated again. The first image it showed me was what had to be a member of the alien species we called the First Antecessor Race. It didn't look exactly like the image of it that Lily had shown me before; its exoskeleton was infused with technological devices, though I could only guess at what they did.

The image rapidly zoomed out, away from the alien, until an image of one of their starships filled the screen. It resembled the ancient hulk discovered in the Trappist-1 system centuries ago, but was intact. It was an ugly monstrosity, vaguely organic in appearance, its exterior covered in lumps and protruding spines. The image continued to zoom out, showing first dozens, then hundreds, then thousands of similar ships of different shapes and sizes.

Through these images the Seraph told a fragmented story about the First Antecessor Race. Cassandra had told me that the enemy of the Seraphim was something they called the Void Tyrant. Whatever it was, First Antecessors seemed to worship it as a god. In its name, they crossed the cosmos, wiping out all life before them. It was the unseen enemy that engineered them, indoctrinated them, gave them advanced technology like vacuum-energy engines, and unleashed them on the universe. Countless life-bearing worlds in our galaxy and beyond were burned and rendered lifeless.

Then, as quickly as they had begun, the images ceased and I was once again left in darkness. I'd had about all I could take, and was about to remove the headset, when I heard the facsimile of Cassandra's voice in my ears again.

"Easy, please listen carefully," she said. "Neither the Seraph nor Dr. Sarkar are aware of this conversation. It's just me. I can speak freely, but I don't have much time. I need your help."

"What . . . what do you need?" I said, hoping like hell the VR helmet's sound dampening worked like it was supposed to.

"When the session is over, Professor Farseer will be a devoted, unquestioning acolyte. His mind is receptive to suggestion and the indoctrination is nearly complete."

"My God, what are you doing to the man?"

"The Seraph is giving him what he desperately wants: a god he can believe in. I've been thinking about what you said yesterday. What . . . what if everything the Seraph is showing us is all lies? What if Dagny is right, and as soon as we let it go it'll kill us all?"

"I guess that's a possibility."

"We have a plan to set the Seraph free. The professor will help us after this. He will do anything I ask him to do, at least for a while. I just . . . I need to know if I'm doing the right thing, Easy. Dagny is afraid. Everyone else here is manipulating me. The Seraph, as close as I feel to it, could just be manipulating me like it is Professor Farseer. It's suffering and it will do whatever it can to escape. You're the only one I can talk to who doesn't have his own agenda."

Is this really happening? I wondered. *Is it really all going to come down to me?* "I'm just a detective, kid, I can't decide the fate of the world."

"Easy, please," Cassandra pleaded. "I'm scared and I'm losing my mind and I don't know what to do." I could hear the fear in the synthesized rendition of her voice.

"Okay, okay, just let me think for a moment. Alright, look at it logically. If the Seraph was just lying to you, why hasn't it been telling you what they want to hear all along? *Sure, I'll give you immortality, just pull the Spear out!* Why did it decide to talk to you and not somebody easier to manipulate, like the professor? Why would it have even shown you anything about the destruction of the First Antecessors? Doing that only gave us cause to be afraid of it."

"That . . . that does make sense," she said.

"I'm not qualified to analyze an alien mind, but reason and logic still matter. If it was hostile or malevolent, why did it go silent when you were gone instead of just picking the next guy who plugged in? Seems to me that, for whatever reason, it wanted to talk to you, specifically. In a way it put its trust in you, didn't it?"

"I guess so."

"You're the only one here who has been able to directly talk to that thing. I know it's been hard on you, I know it's affecting your mind, but you're not crazy. The fact that you're cognizant enough to ask for advice tells me it hasn't brainwashed you."

"So . . . I should trust it?"

"You need to trust your *gut*, Cassandra. That's how I do my job and it's the only thing you can do now. Listen to what your instincts are telling you. What *feels* like the right thing to do?"

"I . . . I think we should set it free."

"Are you sure?"

She was quiet for a few seconds. "As sure as I can be."

"Alright, then. Do what you need to do."

"Thank you, Easy. Don't tell Dagny about this, not yet. Just tell her that I love her."

The communication ended before I could answer. The screen turned blue again, with white text that read SESSION ENDED. I took the headset off and, with shaking hands, set it aside. Standing up, I walked over to the observation window and watched as the technicians removed Cassandra and the professor from the interface station. Cassandra was unconscious and they gently loaded her onto a gurney.

The professor, on the other hand, was shaky, but managed to stand up on his own. One of the technicians guided him out into the observation room. At the same time, a couple of his COF attendants came in and steadied the old man. I was supposed to ride with him back to the elevator to get out of the pit. "Are you okay, Professor?" I asked.

He was leaning heavily on his assistants now, his coverall soaked with sweat. He looked at me, wide-eyed, and put a hand on my shoulder. "My eyes have been opened, Mr. Novak," he said, weakly. "Come with us. There is much to do."

CHAPTER 19

Several days went by without a word from Professor Farseer, Cassandra, or anyone else. Dagny and I were locked back in our dormitory and left to our own devices. Per Cassandra's wish, I didn't tell Dagny about what had transpired down in the pit. I didn't like keeping it a secret from her, but as much as the Seraph had frightened her, as dangerous as she thought it was, I couldn't be certain that she wouldn't try to warn somebody.

Instead of talking about the session, I relayed Cassandra's message to Dagny, that she loved her sister. Dagny, for her part, was distant. She spent most of the time in her room and barely spoke to me.

For my part, I hoped like hell I'd done the right thing. Sure, my logic sounded good, but that was *human* logic. The Seraph wasn't even remotely human. Who could say how it thought or what its priorities were? I wondered if I was wrong, and if I'd signed the death warrant of the whole planet.

The fourth day was the same as the others had

been—cold, gray, and blustery outside. Our meals were served at the normal intervals and we heard nothing from anyone. I was beginning to think that whatever plan Cassandra had come up with hadn't worked. Around midday, I sat in a chair in the living room, trying to read a book on a tablet, but the stress and boredom had been wearing on me. I set the tablet aside, reclined the chair, and drifted off to sleep.

My eyes snapped open when I felt a deep rumble. The building shook, slightly at first, then more noticeably.

"Easy!" Dagny had appeared from her room. "What's going on?"

"That's a good question. Quake, maybe?"

"You don't think the volcano is erupting, do you?"

"Let's go outside and take a look," I suggested.

Stepping out onto the balcony it was obvious that we weren't the only ones who had that idea. Workers from all over Site 471 had stepped outside to look at the volcano. Mount Gilead was smoking, but no more so than it had been before. I began to think maybe it *had* been a quake; that part of Hyperborea is seismically active, after all. The rumbling quit just as suddenly as it began, and everyone kind of shrugged and got on with their day.

"Well, that was anticlimactic," I said. Dagny and I went back inside and found that the screen had powered on. It displayed the words PLEASE STAND BY on it and nothing else.

"What's going on?" Dagny asked. We got our answer a moment later when the screen changed. "Is that Professor Farseer?"

"Sure as hell is," I said.

"Greetings!" the professor said. His voice was cheery but he was looking ragged. His hair was messier than usual, his eyes were bloodshot, and he looked less like the eccentric wizard and more like a vagrant. "Brothers and sisters of the Cosmic Ontological Foundation, it is I, Zephram Farseer, Distinguished Scholar and highest ranking representative of the Foundation on site. I bring you joyous news today, joyous news indeed!"

"Oh, hell," I said quietly.

"What's happening?" Dagny asked. "Easy?"

I ignored her and listened to the broadcast. "As you may have heard," the professor said, "I had the incredible honor of personally communing with the Seraph. Through a neural link I was directly connected to its vast intellect, and I have been enlightened. While bestowing me with its wisdom, the Seraph showed me a shocking and unsettling truth: it has been here for eons, bound by the Spears, alone, unable to move, unable to live, unable to die! That is, until we found it!"

"Easy what's happening?" Dagny repeated. She was scared. Hell, I was nervous myself.

The professor continued his rant. "I have learned from the Seraph itself that we have been complicit in its suffering. Through its chosen Avatar it beseeched us to remove the second Spear, to finally set it free . . . and we refused. Xavier Taranis, in his greed, his lust for power, *denied* the will of the Seraph! The task of righting this wrong fell to us, my fellow seekers of knowledge, and I am overjoyed to tell you that we have done what was asked of us. The Spear has been removed! Soon, very soon, we shall bear witness to the resurrection!" He raised his hands over his head like a congregant at a religious revival. "Gather, my friends, gather and rejoice! *Deus ex stellaris!*" The transmission was cut short and the PLEASE STAND BY screen resumed.

Dagny grabbed my arm. "Easy! They pulled the Spear out!"

"Seems that way."

"You don't look surprised. Did you . . . did you know about this?"

I took a deep breath and looked down into her eyes. "Yes. Your sister told me she had a plan when I saw her the other day. I just wasn't sure if it was going to work."

"You knew? You knew and you didn't tell me? How *could* you? I *trusted* you!"

"Cassandra trusted me, too, and she told me not to tell you!" Dagny's mouth was open like she was going to say something, but no words came out. I could see the hurt on her face, the sense of betrayal. She lowered her head.

"I'm sorry," I said. "I really am. It was just . . . you were really rattled by what the Seraph showed you. Cassandra was worried that . . . well . . ."

"She was worried I'd rat her out to Taranis," Dagny said, bitterly. "Is that what you think of me, too? That I'd betray my own sister?"

"I think if you really believed that all ninety million people on this planet were in danger, yeah, you'd put that above family loyalty. Your sister probably thought the same thing. Were we wrong?"

"*Yes!* I mean . . . no! I don't know, goddamn it, okay? I don't *know!*"

"I don't know, either!" I said, raising my voice to her

for the first time. I took a breath and took a calmer tone. "Look, I'm just a detective. I'm not cut out to decide whether or not to trust an ancient alien so advanced we don't understand it, but I trust it more than I trust Xavier Taranis."

Dagny was quiet for a second. "Well . . . what do we do now?"

"Get your jacket. We need to get the hell out of here."

"The doors are still locked!"

"I know, but sooner or later somebody's going to come for us and we need to be ready."

I was right about them coming for us, and we didn't even have to wait long. As I returned to the living room with my coat and hat on, the door was unlocked and slammed open. Four men in full tactical gear, pointing weapons at us, stormed into the room. We were ordered to turn around and put our hands on top of our heads. They pushed us to our knees, forced our hands behind our backs, and handcuffed us. Dagny and I were marched out of the residential building and through the attached lab complex, restrained and at gunpoint. Bewildered Ascension employees stopped to gawk at us as we led out into the parking lot.

There were two company security patrol vehicles there, armored 4x4 trucks, but no corporate security in site. Leonard Steinbeck was waiting for us instead, scowling from behind sunglasses. He was wearing the same suit he'd had on at the dinner with Taranis, with a long black overcoat on top of it.

"Where are you taking us?" Dagny demanded.

Steinbeck shook his head. "I gave you two a way out of

this situation that would have been beneficial to everyone. I tried, I really did. I even warned you what would happen if you pulled something like this."

"Something like *what*?" I said. "What the hell did *we* do? The COFfers are the ones who pulled the damned Spear out!"

He raised a gloved hand and stuck a finger in my face. "Don't play dumb with me, Novak. Your job was to keep Cassandra Carmichael happy for just a while longer and you fucked it up. I don't know how she was able to coordinate all this, but you're going to tell me everything you know."

"Why don't you ask Professor Farseer?" Dagny said. "Didn't you see the video? He's the one behind this! We've been stuck here the whole time!"

"Oh, don't you worry, we're bringing him along, too." Steinbeck looked up when a long string of automatic weapons fire echoed across the site. "What the fuck was that?"

"Somebody's shooting, sir," one of his men said.

"I know that!" he snapped. "Load these two up and let's go. We need to get the hell out of here."

We were roughly shoved into the back of one of the two security trucks and locked in. Steinbeck and one of his men got into the front seat, while the others piled into the second vehicle.

"Where are you taking us, Steinbeck?"

"We're leaving, and you're coming with us." There was a ring-shaped road that ran around the interior of Site 471, following roughly the same path as the tram system. Our two-vehicle convoy went about a quarter of the way around the site and took a left turn, toward the very middle of the installation. I realized then that we were headed to the landing pad.

The man driving the truck had a radio in a pouch on his vest. It crackled to life as we entered the landing pad area. "Specter-Six, this is Alpha Team, do you copy?"

"What is it now?" Steinbeck grumbled, grabbing the radio out of the pouch. "This is Specter-Six Actual, go ahead."

"Sir," the voice on the radio said, "we've got Farseer but we're encountering heavy resistance!"

"Resistance? Resistance from *who*?" the SIS man demanded.

"From Ascension! We're still in the east administrative office and fifteen to twenty armed personnel have surrounded the building."

The SIS man was losing his cool. "What? What the fuck is going on?"

"It's Farseer!" the subordinate said. "They won't let us take him! Please advise!"

"Goddamn it!" Steinbeck snarled. "Fucking COFfers!" He spoke into the radio again. "Alpha Team, maintain a defensive position and stand by. Bravo Team will be en route momentarily. I'm authorizing weapons free, you're cleared to fire at will. Do you copy?"

"Uh, understood, Specter-Six. Alpha Team out."

"Seems like you got a lot on your plate right now, Steinbeck," I said.

"Laugh it up, Novak," he growled. Our vehicles pulled to a stop behind a parked VTOL jet. It was painted black and had no exterior markings. "You won't be laughing when you're under enhanced interrogation." The doors were yanked open and Dagny and I were pulled out of the truck. During the short ride from the dormitory to the landing pad, Site 471 had exploded into chaos. Alarms blared in the distance. Sporadic gunfire had erupted across the installation and several columns of smoke were now rising into the air.

"What's happening?" Dagny asked. She had to shout to make herself heard. The jump-jet's engines were idling hot, and it was uncomfortably loud. The rear ramp was down and more SIS guys in combat gear were pulling security around the aircraft.

"I think the COFfers are trying to take over," I shouted.

Before I could say anything else, one of Steinbeck's men shoved us forward. "Get on the aircraft," he said, his voice distorted by the modulator in his helmet. "Move!"

As Dagny and I were pushed toward the rear ramp of the VTOL, Leonard Steinbeck approached one of his men who was standing near the ramp. He was a hard-looking man with a bald head and a goatee. He was armed with a rifle and had a sidearm on his leg. "Jacobs, what's our status?" Steinbeck said.

"It's a real shit show out there, sir. You're the only team that made it back so far."

"What?" Steinbeck said. "Where's Charlie Team?"

"We lost contact with them after they went down into the pit," the security man said. "Sir, we need to think about cutting our losses and getting the hell out of here. The facility AI is commanding the COFfers to keep everyone away from the Seraph."

"What do you mean, *the AI is commanding them*? It's a fucking computer! Who told it to do that?"

"The orders claim to be coming from the Seraph!"

"What? That doesn't make any sense!"

"I'm just telling you what we know, sir. Either way, hundreds of COFfers answered the call and armed themselves, including two-thirds of the security force. We are seriously outnumbered and they have heavy weapons at their disposal."

"We can't leave without Cassandra Carmichael and Dr. Sarkar!"

Before either man could say anything else, another tremor, this one more powerful, erupted from deep under the ground. The VTOL swayed on its landing gear. "And what the actual fuck is *that*?" Steinbeck demanded.

"I don't know, sir," the subordinate said, "but we need to— Oh, shit!" I turned to see what he was looking at. There were no fewer than three heavy combat robots, like the one that had been guarding the elevator to Taranis's mansion, approaching the SIS VTOL. With them were several trucks full of people.

Steinbeck just shook his head. "You have *got* to be fucking *kidding* me!" he shouted. "What is going—" He was cut short when the combat robots opened fire, spraying two armored trucks we'd rode in with machine gun fire. "We're leaving! Everybody on board, now!"

I saw an opportunity. They were distracted and we had a chance to escape. "Dagny, let's go!" Hands still cuffed behind our backs, we ran away from the idling jump-jet, trying to get out of the crossfire. I was relieved when the SIS guys didn't give chase, instead running to their aircraft. The VTOL lifted off and flew away, the robots firing at it as it went. It was out of sight before they could damage it.

We were in a bad spot, though, caught out in the open with nothing between us and the approaching force. The group of trucks, a mixture of the armored security vehicles and standard utility models, pulled up to our position and came to a stop, leaving us with nowhere to run. People in Ascension employee uniforms unloaded out and approached us. They were armed, but weren't pointing their weapons at us. They all had red cloths tied around their arms and most of them had COF pendants around their necks.

A short, stout woman in a charcoal gray security uniform stepped forward while the others held back. Her armband looked to be made from a ripped-up T-shirt and she was carrying a rifle in her hands. "You must be Ezekiel Novak," she said.

"Sure am," I said. "Thanks for chasing off those SIS guys. What, uh, can I do for you?"

"I'm so happy we found you!" she said.

"Who's 'we,' exactly?" I asked. "Look, I'm not sure what's going on here. You folks are COF, right?"

"*Deus ex stellaris!*" the woman declared. "We are! We have been sent to find you both and ensure you have safe passage off-site."

"Sent by who?" Dagny asked.

"By the Seraph, of course!" the COFfer said. "Its Avatar has told us its will. It has taken control of most of the site systems. We are in the process of securing the rest of the site for its resurrection. You are to take one of these trucks. The gates will be open and you can go in peace."

"Where's my sister?" Dagny cried. "She told you to do this?"

"She's communing with the Seraph," the COF lady said. "That is her honor."

"Listen, before we get too carried away here, would you mind uncuffing us? I'm starting to get a cramp." I turned around, showing the woman that my hands were still bound behind my back.

"Oh! Certainly!" she said. In a few seconds she had removed the cuffs from Dagny and me both. "One more thing. I was instructed to return these items to you. Grady?"

Another fellow in a security uniform walked up to me with a box in his hands. "What's this?" I asked as I took it.

"Your personal effects," Grady said.

"Really?" Sure enough, inside the box was my wallet, handheld, and most of the stuff I had on me when we were captured. Dagny's belongings were there, too. Most importantly, though, my trusty Sam Houston Mark IV was there, still in its shoulder holster, along with my spare ammunition. I set the box down, took my jacket off, and put the holster on. I drew the revolver, locked a full cylinder into it, and re-holstered it. "I can't tell you how happy I am to have this back," I told the man. "Thank you."

"The Avatar insisted," he said.

"Yeah, about that. I appreciate you people taking care of us like this, but we need to see the, uh, Avatar before we go."

"She's my sister!" Dagny said. "I'm not leaving without her!"

Yet another tremor, this one even more powerful than the last two, shook the site. In the distance, rocks dislodged and tumbled down the cinder cone of Mount Gilead. "What is causing that?" I asked.

"The Seraph stirs!" the COF woman said. "It is even now being reborn. It will rise soon."

Dagny and I looked at each other. I turned back to the lady. "I need you to take us down into the pit right now."

"I don't understand. We were given instructions to—"

I cut her off. "What don't you understand? When that thing blasts its way out of the ground, everything in the pit, including the Avatar, is going to be buried under a million tons of rock!"

She seemed confused by that. "I was told that this matter was taken care of. I will have to call in and request guidance."

Bunch of damned lunatics, I thought, shaking my head. The COF woman got on a radio and called somebody. What she got in response was a panicked plea for help and the sounds of gunfire.

"What's happening?" Dagny asked. "Is Cassie okay?"

"Th-the Lambda Facility is under attack!" she said, wide-eyed.

"Under attack by who?"

"I don't know," she said. "We need to get down there!"

"We're going with you," I said. "You'll need all the help you can get."

The COFfer nodded at me. "Let's go! There's no time to waste!"

We piled into their trucks and, together, left the landing pad and headed for the Canopy. As another tremor shook the site I noticed, with some dismay, how the massive structure swayed and wobbled. The Ascension mutineers assured me that it was designed to withstand moderate volcanic and seismic activity, but I wasn't as confident as they were.

Instead of getting out of the truck, going through the personnel entrance, and taking the elevator down to the floor of the pit, this time we drove. The Canopy's large vehicle door was open and our small caravan drove right in, nearly colliding with a trio of black, armored trucks going the opposite direction. There was no telling who was fleeing, so we pressed on, down into the pit.

The ramp zigzagged back and forth, one switchback after another, and it took us a few minutes to make the descent. At the bottom, we followed the length of the Seraph's gigantic body toward the head, passing the huge winch that had dislodged and removed the second Spear. That Spear, made of shimmering black metal of some kind, was now lying on the ground. Huge cracks, some hundreds of feet long, spread across the volcanic rock that made up the floor of the pit, radiating away from the Seraph. Fissures had appeared in the rocky walls of the excavation site.

We stopped short of the laboratory complex, where at least eight other vehicles were parked. Dead bodies littered the ground and there wasn't a single person left standing. The COFfers located a couple of their own, wounded but still conscious, sitting on the ground behind one of the bullet-riddled trucks. For my part I found it hard to pay attention to something as mundane as all that at the moment. Instead, I could scarcely take my eyes off the Seraph.

"Oh my God," Dagny said, squeezing my hand. "It's really happening."

All I could say was "Yeah," as I stared up at the thing with my mouth hanging open. The silver-white matter it was made of appeared brighter, smoother, *newer*. The three wings protruding into the air had a faint glow to them. It was warmer down there than it was on the surface, and you could feel the energy crackling in the air. The hairs on my arms stood up again. It *was* really happening. The Seraph was going to rise again, after sixty-eight million years.

"Mr. Novak!" It was the COF woman, jogging up to me after questioning her wounded comrades.

"What did you learn?"

"The group down here was attacked three times. The first time it was Ascension security, non-Foundation, I mean. The second time it was the men from the Security Intelligence Service. They held off both of those attacks, but then Xavier Taranis's personal security team came down here and broke through the remaining defense. They went inside the laboratory complex."

"How many of them were there?"

"He wasn't sure, maybe a dozen. Taranis's team took some casualties, but they had full combat gear, armor, and heavy weapons—our people didn't stand a chance."

"They're in there now?"

"Some might be, but he said that when the last tremor happened most of them got into their vehicles and fled. That must be who we passed on the way in."

"Alright, we should head inside," I said. "We need to find Cassandra."

"There's one more thing," the COF lady said. "Xavier Taranis was with them."

Dagny cocked her head. "What? That crazy old bastard came down here himself?"

"Maybe he thinks this is his last shot at immortality," I said. "Come on, let's go inside."

I followed the impromptu militia as they entered the laboratory. The security people had body armor, for one thing, and most of them had automatic weapons. I had my revolver drawn and Dagny was armed with a pistol she'd gotten off one of the wounded COFfers. It seemed prudent to let the COFfers go first. We didn't encounter any resistance, but the route to the test chamber was lined with half a dozen bodies. Two had been Taranis's security men, the rest, regular Ascension employees. We didn't find anyone alive until we reached the test chamber itself.

"Cassie!" Dagny cried. Cassandra was in the test chamber, lying in her chair at the monitoring station. Her neural link was connected but the visor of her VR headset was flipped up. Xavier Taranis was in there with her, a shriveled, ancient man being kept alive by a robotic chassis. Extended in his hand was an elaborately engraved pistol with gold inlays. Dr. Sarkar was on the floor, next to Cassie, in a pool of blood. There was a bullet hole right through his visor.

We tried the door, but the test chamber had been sealed from the inside. Dagny was going to try shooting the ballistic glass, but the Ascension workers told her it wouldn't work. We were so close to our goal, only to find ourselves powerless.

Taranis saw us approach but ignored us. He focused on Cassandra, whom he was holding at gunpoint. The intercom between the test and observation chambers was active and we could hear him talk. "I built all this!" he shouted. "All of it! I spent billions of dollars and I will see a return on that investment! I will, damn you!"

"It can't give you what you want!" Cassandra shouted back. "That's not how it works! It's not God and it can't make you immortal!"

"You lie!" the only man wheezed, sending himself into another coughing fit. "There must be a way, there must! How else could it possibly be alive after so long? Tell it that if it gives me what I want, I'll let you go free. If it denies me what I'm due, I'll kill you right here, do you understand?"

"I keep trying to explain to you—"

"Tell it!" he screamed, spittle flying out of his mouth.

"It knows already!" Cassandra said. "It can see and hear everything we're doing!"

"Then it clearly doesn't think I'm serious," Taranis said. "Allow me to apply some pressure." He pointed his pistol at Cassandra's chest and fired.

"Cassie!" Dagny screamed, pounding helplessly on the glass. "You bastard! I'll kill you!"

The old man ignored us. "Did you see *that*?" he shouted, waving the gun around like a madman. "You're not the only one with power!" Cassandra was still alive, but her shirt was soaked through with blood. "She has minutes to live. I know you care for this woman! All I ask is that you grant me more life! If you save my life, I'll save hers!"

A deep, deep rumble resonated from the grown below us. Another tremor shook the excavation pit. The Seraph's carapace at the back of the room shimmered even brightly now. The black substance, the stuff between the hard plates of its exoskeleton, ebbed and flowed as if it were alive. The lights flickered and dimmed. Clouds of dust were shaken loose as the Seraph stirred.

Taranis had really, *really* pissed it off.

Unfazed, he continued his diatribe and threatened to kill Cassandra on the spot if the Seraph didn't answer him. "How dare you ignore me like some insect! If not for me, you would have been buried here forever!" He finally took notice of the black mass behind the carapace as it bubbled and seethed. Lowering the gun, he cautiously approached. As he drew near, the inky substance took shape. It formed a long tendril, reaching out toward the old man.

Dropping his gun, he reached a hand out to the glossy black mass extending itself toward him. It touched his fingers, delicately at first, then began wrapping its way up his arm like a snake climbing a tree. "Yes, yes!" he cried. He closed his eyes. "At last. Thank you, thank you!"

The viscous tendril reached his shoulder and stopped. Solidifying, it began to contract. Taranis screamed in agony as it crushed his arm, exosuit and all. Then, in an instant, it slammed him back into the door of the test chamber. He hit it so hard his exoframe was smashed, sending bits of broken metal flying. The heavy security door was blasted out of its fixture and clattered to the floor of the observation room. It happened so fast he didn't even have time to scream. The Seraph released the old man's pulverized corpse and left it on the floor. The tendril disappeared back into the inky mass that had spawned it.

"*Deus ex stellaris!*" one of the COFfers said, and they all echoed her. Then they all turned and fled, leaving the three of us alone.

"Cassie!" Dagny cried. She ran into the test chamber, stepping on Taranis's body as she clambered over his crushed exoframe to get to her sister. I was right behind her. She pulled the VR headset off her sister and dropped it to the floor. "Cassie? Cassie! Cassie, no," she sobbed, holding her sister to her breast. "Please, God, no."

"Hey, Sis," Cassandra said, weakly.

Dagny's eyes went wide. "Cassie!"

"You hold on," I told the wounded woman. "We're going to get a first-aid kit and get you patched up." I was as confident as I sounded. The wound was bad and she'd lost a lot of blood.

Cassandra slowly shook her head and smiled. "It's too late for that. I'm dying. I can feel it. The Seraph can, too." The VR headset was on the floor, but her neural link was still connected. "It's not just the bullet. I have . . . I have pretty severe neurological damage. Too much time connected, too much . . . too much . . ."

Dagny was having trouble standing. She held her sister's hand and wept. "I'm so sorry I doubted you, I'm so sorry."

"There is one thing you can do for me," Cassandra said. "The Seraph told me it might not work, but we can try."

"Try? Try what?" I asked.

"Help me up," Cassandra said, unplugging her neural link. "I need you to move me." Dagny and I carefully hoisted the wounded woman to her feet. She groaned in pain but told us to keep going. "Now, I need you . . . I need you to take me over there, to the black stuff."

"Are you sure about this?" I asked.

"It's the only way," she said.

We did as she asked and carried her across the room, to the back wall that was the exposed exterior of the Seraph itself. "Now what?" I asked.

"Now this," Cassandra said. Four new tendrils emerged from the unknown substance and began to wrap around her. We let go as they gently lifted her body up, keeping her upright and supporting her head. They began to retract, drawing Cassandra ever closer to the inky blackness.

"What's happening? Cassie?"

Cassandra smiled again and spoke softly. "You know, it's funny . . . Taranis wasn't entirely wrong. Turns out the Seraph *can* extend a human life, but there's a catch. It can't make us immortal, but it does have the ability to keep us alive almost indefinitely."

"I don't understand," I said.

"This is goodbye, Dagny," Cassandra said. She was still smiling, but tears rolled down her face. Another ribbon of the Seraph's black goop wrapped around her and covered the wound in her chest. "Don't be sad. I'm not dying. I just have to leave for a while."

"My God," I said. "It's absorbing you!"

"Not like that, Easy. I'll still be me. It just needs to cocoon my body for a while, until it figures out how to fix me."

"This . . . this doesn't make any sense," Dagny said. "Cassie, you can't go with some alien! You can't!"

"Not your decision, big sister. It's the only way. Please don't be sad. Don't you see? This is the greatest adventure of all!"

"But where are you going?"

"I don't know yet. I'm going to see the universe, it tells me. I'll see things no human has ever seen before. Isn't that exciting?" Another powerful tremor caused the lights to flicker. "You need to go now, both of you. It won't leave the Spears here for us to tinker with. It's going to destroy them, destroy this whole place. Get as far away from here as you can. Everyone topside is fleeing. The site AI is telling everyone to evacuate, but there are still vehicles left."

Dagny held her sister's hand as Cassandra was pulled further back into the strange goop. "Please don't leave me like this," she pleaded.

"Sorry, Sis, I have to. I'll come back someday, I promise."

"I love you!" Dagny said.

"I love you, too," Cassandra replied.

Dagny let her sister's hand go, and Cassandra disappeared into the strange, viscous substance. She was crying, in shock, but we couldn't linger. "We need to go," I told her, and led her out of the test chamber.

The excavation pit was rumbling and shaking as we fled the Lambda Facility. An Ascension security truck was still operational, its armor having protected it from the gun battle, so we climbed in. The COFfers we'd ridden down with were nowhere to be seen.

"Buckle up," I told Dagny, and stepped on the accelerator. We raced back down the length of the Seraph, hitting bone-jarring bumps where the cracks had turned to fissures, but I wasn't about to stop. Up the switchback ramps we went, back and forth, taking the hairpin turns as fast as I dared. The Canopy itself was starting to give way now; pieces of it broke away as we climbed, falling the nearly six hundred feet to the bottom of the pit. The Seraph's wings were glowing brightly now, bathing the chasm in brilliant white light.

I had never been so relieved to see daylight as I was when we reached the surface. Another violent tremor was shaking the site now, and the Canopy began to collapse just as we exited it.

"I think we're the last ones here," I said aloud, turning onto the ring road that would take us to the main gate of the installation.

"Easy, the whole pit is collapsing!" Dagny said, looking in the side-view mirror. I didn't take the time to look myself, I just kept driving. We followed the road around to the far side of the site. The main gate was open and had been abandoned. There was nothing before us now but a single open road, winding a path through the rocky wasteland, away from Site 471. I could see other vehicles speeding away in the distance, but they were far ahead of us.

A couple miles later, I slowed to a stop. Dagny asked me what was wrong, but I didn't bother to answer. I parked the armored truck, opened the door, and stepped out onto the pavement. Dagny joined me a moment later, staring back at Site 471 with me. I put an arm around her and held her close as we watched, in awe, the scene unfolding before us.

A great cloud of dust rose from where the excavation site was, so thick that it dimmed the afternoon sun. Through it, though, we could see something massive rising out of that hole. First there were tons of rock, debris, and remnants of the Canopy. That fell away as the great mass continued to rise and finally, after so much, we got to see the resurrected Seraph in all its glory.

It levitated upward silently, its limbs relaxed at its sides, its long, segmented tail hanging below it. The ten holes in the head were now glowing bright blue, and the silver-white carapace gleamed and refracted sunlight into prisms of color. The six structures on the Seraph's back radiated with energy, pure white, the glare from them extending far beyond their physical length.

"Wings of light," Dagny said, quietly. "It's rising on wings of light."

"Some kind of antigravity?" I could only guess. We continued to watch, mesmerized, as it rose higher and higher into the sky. Several thousand feet up, it was just about to pierce the lowest layer of clouds when it stopped. The Seraph paused and seemed to look down, as if considering the place in which it had been entombed for so long. It slowly brought its forelimbs together, pointing them down at Site 471.

"What's it doing?" Dagny asked.

"Get back in the truck," I said. "Get back in the truck!" Just as we pulled the doors closed, the sky was seared with light. Dagny screamed and I threw my arms around her. Moments later, the shock wave hit us, slamming the truck so hard it was like being in an accident on the highway. The heavy vehicle was spun around more than ninety degrees. The armored windows cracked but held.

From our new angle, we could see the gigantic fireball rising from Site 471. We watched it in silence for a few moments, until ash, dust, and grit began to rain down from the sky, covering the windows and leaving us in the dark.

We huddled in the truck for fifteen or twenty minutes, until everything was quiet. "You think it's over?" Dagny asked.

"I don't know." I pushed the truck's start button but nothing happened. "The motor's dead."

"It was running fine before," Dagny said. "What kills an electric engine like that?"

"That blast hit us pretty hard," I said.

"Maybe it was an electromagnetic pulse," she suggested.

"That's as good a theory as any. I'm going to get out and take a look. I need some fresh air."

"I'm coming with you," she said. We pushed the heavy, armored doors open and stepped out into the daylight.

"Jesus Christ," Dagny said, looking back at the ruins of Site 471. The scene was apocalyptic. A gigantic mushroom cloud of dust and smoke rose thousands of feet into the air. Lava was flowing from the volcano, pouring into the smoldering crater where the excavation site had been. "What do we do now?"

"We start walking," I said. "An explosion that big will trigger a response. Somebody will find us. Come on."

EPILOGUE

So that's my story. I know it's hard to believe, but every word of it is true, and a lot of it has been independently corroborated by now. Satellite footage of the Seraph rising into the upper atmosphere before vanishing has been all over the infostreams. The blast from its weapon kicked up enough dust that it disrupted the normal weather patterns of southwestern Hyperborea. The seismic effects of the blast were recorded for hundreds of miles.

If the government was ever inclined to cover it up, they never had the opportunity.

There's more to the story, of course, but that's the end of the interesting parts. A few miles up the highway we were picked up by a Commonwealth Defense Force aircraft and brought in for debriefing. Deitrik tracked me down after a few days, overjoyed to learn that I was alive, and dying to know what had happened to me. I was happy to see him, too. The Baron chuckled when I told him about Leonard Steinbeck's claim that he'd been captured.

As for the Security Intelligence Service, holy hell did

this incident make a splash. When the government of Nova Columbia learned that the SIS had sanctioned experimentation on alien technology without so much as notifying them, it became the biggest political scandal in the history of the colony. Nova Columbia expelled the SIS from the planet and even threatened to withdraw from the Terran Confederation if the matter wasn't investigated thoroughly. That investigation is still ongoing, but so far Leonard Steinbeck hasn't been found.

They never found Professor Zephram Farseer, either, and they think he probably died in the destruction of Site 471. Hundreds of people remain unaccounted for from that incident, though many more escaped. Blanche Delacroix turned state's witness and testified in exchange for a reduced sentence. Ascension Planetary Holdings Group was bankrupted by all the fines and lawsuits, and their assets were auctioned off. *Good riddance*, I say. That damned company had too much of a hold on Nova Columbia even when they weren't conducting illegal research.

For my part, I was offered a pretty substantial sum of money from the Commonwealth government if I agreed keep the details of the whole thing to myself for a set period of time. In twenty-five years or so they'll declassify the details and I'll be free to publish my memoirs. In the meantime, I'm keeping the agency open. I like what I do, and like to think I'm pretty good at it. Besides, it isn't just my legacy, it's Victor's. Had he not talked me into coming to work for him all those years ago, none of this would have been exposed, and God only knows what would have happened with the Seraph. All the money I had coming in allowed me to not only give Lily a well-deserved pay raise, but to hire Dante on as a consultant as well. Those two make a good team.

There was one thing I decided to do, though, something that I hadn't done in years. I took a long and badly needed vacation.

Six weeks or so after the incident, I was in a luxury hotel suite fixing two drinks. I'd booked two weeks at an oceanside resort a few hundred miles south of Epsilon City, on the coast of the Equatorial Ocean. Despite being the dead of winter, the weather was warm, the beaches were spectacular, and palm trees were swaying in the evening breeze.

The company was pretty easy on the eyes, too.

"Hey, beautiful," I said, stepping out onto the balcony. "Come here often?" Dagny smiled at me and gave me a quick kiss. I handed her the cosmopolitan I'd fixed for her and kept a small glass of Darwin Ducote for myself. She was a knockout in the short, turquoise, floral-pattern dress she wore, standing on a pair of white stilettos. We'd been there for a week already and she'd gotten herself a nice tan. Night was falling and, as she often did, she was out on the balcony gazing up at the stars. "Thinking about Cassandra?"

"Yeah," she admitted. "I wonder where she is, what she's experiencing now. I look out at all these stars and wonder if she's visiting one of them right now."

"It's a lot to process," I said. "You've been through a lot even without the business with the Seraph."

She rested her head on my shoulder. "It's not all bad. I found you."

"I consider myself to be pretty lucky, too," I said, and put an arm around her.

"You think we'll ever see Cassie again?"

"I don't know. She said she'd come back someday."

"Wouldn't that be something? An ancient alien returns with a human ambassador."

"I'd say stranger things have happened, but honestly, I don't think that's true. That might be the strangest thing to ever happen in human history."

"Here's to Cassie," Dagny said, raising her glass.

"Cheers," I said. We clinked our glasses together and drank the booze. "Now . . . how about we head downstairs and find some dinner?"

THE FAMILY BUSINESS
TPB: 978-1-9821-2502-8 • $16.00 US/$22.00 CAN

After a devastating war for humankind, the Visitors'
willing human collaborators were left behind. Now,
federal recovery agent Nathan Foster and his 14-year-
old nephew Ben must hunt them down and bring
them to justice.

"Kupari is a skilled tradesman, deftly creating charac-
ters that are easy to get invested in and easy to care for.
You will cheer at their successes and commiserate with
them in their failures. . . ."   —Warped Factor

Trouble Walked In
TPB: 978-1-9821-9203-7 • $16.00 US/$22.00
PB: 978-1-9821-9281-5 • $9.99 US/$12.99

Cassandra Blake, an employee for the Ascension
Planetary Holdings Group has gone missing. When
questions need answering on Nova Columbia,
Detective Ezekiel "Easy" Novak is the man folks turn to.
He gets results—one way or another.

Michael Mersault

THE DEEP MAN

TPB: 978-1-9821-2584-4 • $16.00 US/$22.00 CAN

A relic of humanity's violent past, this ancient weapon stands ready for the Emperor to wield. The Galactic Imperium of the Myriad Worlds slumps into centuries of decadent peace enabled by a flood of advanced technology from the mysterious nonhuman "Shapers." Among the great families, only the once-mighty clan of Sinclair-Maru remembers the maxims of the warrior emperor, Yung I, ready to defend the Imperium from any threat. With spies and assassins on every side, trusting only in his considerable skill and the bizarre competence of his companion Inga, Saef Sinclair-Maru must complete his Imperial mission, restore the greatness of his family, and uncover the chilling plot meant to extinguish humanity's light from the galaxy.

And watch for *The Silent Hand*, an original trade paperback, in September 2023.